KILL THE CLOCK

Sunny Kreis Collins

iUniverse, Inc.
New York Bloomington

Kill the Clock

Copyright © 2010 Sunny Kreis Collins

All rights reserved. No part of this book may be used or reproduced by any means, graphic, electronic, or mechanical, including photocopying, recording, taping or by any information storage retrieval system without the written permission of the publisher except in the case of brief quotations embodied in critical articles and reviews.

This is a work of fiction. All of the characters, names, incidents, organizations, and dialogue in this novel are either the products of the author's imagination or are used fictitiously.

iUniverse books may be ordered through booksellers or by contacting:

iUniverse
1663 Liberty Drive
Bloomington, IN 47403
www.iuniverse.com
1-800-Authors (1-800-288-4677)

Because of the dynamic nature of the Internet, any Web addresses or links contained in this book may have changed since publication and may no longer be valid. The views expressed in this work are solely those of the author and do not necessarily reflect the views of the publisher, and the publisher hereby disclaims any responsibility for them.

ISBN: 978-1-4502-3071-1 (pbk)
ISBN: 978-1-4502-3070-4 (ebk)

Printed in the United States of America

iUniverse rev. date: 5/18/2010

For my Mother, Frances Geraldine Kreis
and
my French grandfather
Emil Kreis

ONE YEAR AGO

IT WAS AN ANOMALISTIC DAY all around. The warm, moist air was typical for New Orleans in July. The almost eighty-mile-an-hour winds were not. Reports in from Lafayette were that Hurricane Lily had been downgraded to a Category One and that The Big Easy had dodged a bullet. Hermione Toussaint had closed most of the tall French windows of her home on St. Charles Street in concession to the tornado threat and left one open in concession to her characteristic contrariness. The house, like its mistress, was a relic—a redbrick colonial house boasting gothic columns.

The mistress was now walking slowly around the first floor of the house, pointing here and there at the figurine lamps, a wing chair covered in parrot-green silk, a Louis XV table, and a pair of caned Regency armchairs. Her granddaughter, who most people called Freddy and whom she called Frédérique, responded with a listless *yes* or *no* as each item was indicated. There was a sudden crash of thunder and the older woman suggested they go upstairs as if the outside noise signaled act two of the selection process. Together they went into the foyer and executed the spiral staircase very slowly, the grandmother by proclivity of her eighty-two years and her tall, blonde granddaughter by current inclination to inertia. In the guest bedroom, Freddy said *yes* to a mahogany sleigh bed, *no* to a white wrought iron chandelier, *yes* to an Italian gilt wood mirror and a 19th century Louis XVI loveseat and *no* to a small vanity table, its mirror edged in shells.

"When your mother was alive, she just adored that little table."

"Then I want it, Gram. I'll take it."

Mrs. Toussaint made an entry on the notepad she was carrying around, listing the things Frédérique wanted shipped to California.

"What's your condo look like exactly, darlin'?" the older woman asked.

"Haven't seen it. Laid back and mellow undoubtedly."

Grandma T. frowned.

"You haven't seen it?"

"Buck picked it out. He's handled all my transition details, a man among men."

The older woman snorted.

"How you went from being born in Paris to moving to some hovel in that ridiculous state is beyond me."

"Being born in Paris doesn't make me someone special, Gram."

The grandmother shook her head.

"My darling girl, I was born in Paris as was your dear mother before you and, *mais oui*, it does make us special as does growing up here and on Park Avenue in New York does and you should…"

Freddy interrupted.

"I'm sure Buck's selection is no mere hovel."

"Sugar, why in blazes are you moving to that desert anyway?"

"Gram, I just got tired of the New York scene and all the reminders of my marriage. And I knew Buck had moved there so it's not as though I don't know a living soul in California."

"Well, it's bad enough the only friend you have there is some former police officer, and didn't you say his roots were Cajun?"

The older woman inhaled deeply, then exhaled, as if collecting herself.

"Well, so much for all that. However, letting him also select your living quarters is beyond the pale, Frédérique."

"It's more like beyond the call of duty, Gram. He also found a tenant for my Brooklyn place. He's been my rock since my divorce."

"Oh shush about the divorce. I actually liked that ex-husband of yours for a period of time."

"For a period of time I did too. Sometimes I think I still…."

Freddy left the thought, and instead contemplated a small vase she'd been carrying, acquired along the route of the present acquisition tour. She listened to the whisper of rainfall coming from the back lawn and hoped Gram would also dismiss the subject of Sonny.

"Tell me who *is* this Buck person anyway?"

"Buck Lemoyne. I told you about him. He used to be a New York police officer. He'd moonlight as a security guard at big fashion shows and parties in New York. That's how we met."

"And now he's some sort of private eye in Los Angeles?"

"He's some sort of very successful private investigator. And it's Santa Monica, to be precise. Not L.A."

"*Les américains sont étranges.*"

"No stranger than the French, Gram."

"Well fine. I mean who exactly are his people?"

Freddy had to smile at this. For all her opinions and verbosity, Gram was not judgmental at heart. But conversely, she picked up a hint of haughtiness from her son, Freddy's dad. She'd been a housewife and her husband a saloonkeeper in the Quarter when her son had been born. Together they'd launched him and watched their boy navigate college, law school and beyond. But Judge Toussaint ultimately forgot he was not to the manor born, that rather his human existence had set sail in the back room of Jean Claude's Tavern.

"I've never met his people, Gram. But I'm sure they're lovely. Going way back, the Lemoynes were an important New York family."

Buck's family consisted of a long line of fire fighters and cops that hailed from Brooklyn, but Freddy stretched the truth, indulging a momentary aversion to her grandmother's snobbery.

"Nonsense. You said he went to elementary school right here in New Orleans just like you."

"He did. The New York origins were long ago," she continued. "When his folks lived here, they were somewhere near the Garden District I believe. When Buck and I met in New York, New Orleans was the great bond between us. You remember me telling you about that."

"Well, at least that speaks well of him."

Freddy surveyed the room.

"I'm about cleaning you out, Gram."

"Oh pish tosh. I've more stuff here than a reasonable person needs and you know it."

"Then that should do it, Gram".

"We're not done" her grandmother insisted. "What's that kitchen in your Santa Monica place like? Never mind, let's just go to mine and see what we can see."

In the kitchen, Freddy paused to look out a window at the weeping willow trees, rain-soaked and bent by the wind.

"I've plenty of extra pots and pans. Just take all the copper ones; they're cheerful."

"Thanks, Gram. To hold stuff I'll take that thing over there off your hands if you can spare it."

"You're welcome to it, sugar. And that 'thing' as you call it is a seventeenth-century French cabinet designed for rising bread."

"Oh well then I couldn't…"

"Indeed you could, Miss Sourpuss. It's yours."

Freddy hugged the older woman. "You're a treasure, Gram. Let me make us some tea."

"Tea schmee. It's after five, my dear girl, make me a scotch and soda."

The granddaughter laughed.

"You rock, Gram. You're the living end."

Freddy went about gathering the scotch, club soda, ice, glasses. And thought of that word *end*. Today represented many endings. Her modeling career, as far as New York was concerned, had ended. Her marriage had ended. Her brief to-make-ends-meet jobs in corporate America had ended. Living in New York was ending. Another thunderclap. A signal, she thought, from God, to end the self-pity.

Aloud she said, "It's an end of an era, Gram." Brave smile. "And a new beginning."

"Damn right, a new beginning," Mrs. Toussaint said.

The two women clinked glasses. Tree branches pressed against the window and the rain came down hard.

"You never should have married Arthur Robert What's-His-Name in the first place."

"Sonny Bob Bonnaire. And maybe you're right."

"Of course I'm right. And I never understood why he called himself Sonny Bob."

"More suited to his profession than Arthur Robert."

"Exactly my point. You should have never married a country Western singer in the first place! Actually, darlin', your brother should have never introduced the two of you in the first place. What Henri was doing consorting with a no-account singer is beyond me."

"Sonny Bob was Hank's client, Gram. And they were friends."

"Your brother, Bernard-Henri Toussaint, works for one of the most prestigious law firms in New Orleans. It's housed on that marvelous street, I forget the name. Even hurricane Katrina couldn't make a dent in that firm's building. And as for Henri, well, he should concentrate on shipping magnates for clients, not hillbillies."

"Oh Sonny Bob's no hillbilly by a long shot. He's actually pretty smart when he wants to be."

"Well, if he were all that smart he would of hung on to you and not spent all your money."

"When you're right, you're right, Gram," Freddy said and reached for the scotch bottle.

Hermione Toussaint straightened her spine, cocked her head and frowned.

"He's a vile worm...not clean enough to spit upon!"

"You said it, Gram."

"Actually Shakespeare did," the older woman mumbled, and held out her glass, nodding for a refill.

ONE MONTH AGO

In another city, a mild rain was coming down. It was dark out and unseasonably cold, especially for California. Outside a small bar in Venice, tropical trees took a battering by the wind. Even the Pacific Ocean, normally calmer than the Atlantic due to its different currents, was restless and frothing at the shoreline.

Inside the shabby, barely lit bar a figure sat alone at a small table for two. A Corona beer and an empty glass rested on the chipped Formica table, the bottle untouched. A yellow, lined pad on the table received singular attention as a ballpoint pen swiftly etched long slashes upon it, paused, scribbled some writing, returned to broader strokes, then paused again.

"That beer okay?"

A portly man with heavily tattooed arms called from behind the bar. He wore a red tee shirt, a white apron tied at the base of his gut and a gray baseball cap.

"Noticed you haven't touched it. Get you another brand?"

The patron looked up, irritated, and nodded in the negative. The beer was then poured into the glass and a sip taken as if to comply and be a good guest.

Encouraged, the bartender spoke again.

"Have I seen you around here before? Even the regulars don't come out on a night like this, and you don't look like one of 'em."

Again, the nod. Several quick chugs of the beer. More scribbling, head bowed over the pad. A white surfboard with the word Budweiser gleamed from the wall directly above the writer. Fake parrots hung from different points of the bar's ceiling, suspended on black link chains. Neon emblems of other beer brands dotted the walls. A replay of last night's basketball game reverberated from one of the bar's three television sets.

"Didn't mean to disturb you none," the bartender offered. "Thought maybe you could use the company, but I can see you're busy."

The patron looked up, smiled briefly, nodded affirmatively.

Then why are you hassling me, jerk?

It was just a thought, not spoken.

The rain outside increased, in both velocity and sound. A column of cold air punctuated the stale, musty air of the bar as a couple in their twenties swept through the door shivering and laughing. Both the man and the woman wore shorts and sneakers. The woman wore a lavender tank top. She'd covered her head with a gray sweatshirt, which she clutched at her throat in lieu of an umbrella. The man had light hair, cut short, now wet and plastered to his head. He wore a black jersey under a blue-checked short-sleeved shirt, also soaked.

Stupid tourists. Did they really believe that song that says it never rains in California?

"Hi," the man smiled at the bartender. "Can we get something strong? Maybe a scotch and soda?"

He turned to the shivering girl.

"Honey, you want a scotch?"

She nodded in the affirmative, smiled at the bartender and shrugged.

What does that shrug mean? The little bitch is apologizing for being wet and a mess? Well, maybe she should. There were gray clouds all day today, and rain was predicted. Didn't she know that? And if she did, why didn't she dress for it? Didn't she know it got cold at night in California? Did she think the way she was dressed would keep her warm once the sun went down and keep her dry when the predicted rain fell? People don't think. They don't think of the consequences of their actions.

The patron alone at the small table drank a little more beer, focused again upon the pad of paper and thought more specifically of certain people who did not consider the consequences of their actions. The first sheet of paper was carefully folded back and around the bottom of the pad; scribbling commenced on a second sheet.

"Wind sure is fierce out there," the young man said.

"Yep," the bartender replied. "Tomorrow there'll be dead brown palm leaves all over them sidewalks. My wife's got a lotta those outdoor potted plants and trees. They all get knocked down whenever this happens. Damn things spill out all over the place. She just goes out and buys more."

I know something about destruction, the solo customer thought. I know something about one person destroying another's life, several lives really. I know such destruction and I know it must be avenged.

The young couple took seats at a table for four, one table over from the lone patron at the table for two. Then the man got up, went to the bar, picked a stack of napkins from a holder and began patting his wet hair with them. He laughed at himself and looked over at the customer alone at the small table.

"Not what they're for, but they'll do the trick," he smiled. "You look dry. You musta had the good sense to bring an umbrella along."

I had the good sense to plan, you idiot. I plan. I plan what I'm going to do. I'm planning now. If you'll just shut up, I'll continue planning. This will work if I plan. If I plan it just right.

The bartender handed two glasses of scotch to the man as he stood by the bar. The prospect of the warming liquor provided distraction from the fact that his social chitchat had gone ignored by the other customer.

A thin man, who appeared to be around sixty, pulled open the door and stood at the entrance gazing inside, a loopy grin on his face. A fake fichus tree leaned against the wall near the door, its leaves fluttering from the onslaught of wind. The bartender, wiping out a glass, turned to look at him. He wore a dirty raincoat over gray pants that looked muddy, a ragged wool scarf wrapped around his neck. Cold air spun inside as he continued to stand and stare. He leaned against the doorframe, then straightened, then repeated the process.

"In or out, bud," the bartender said.

The disheveled man spun around, with almost balletic grace, and went back outside.

Another homeless man, this area is lousy with them. In or out is right.

People can't commit these days. They say they'll do one thing, and they do another. Can't be trusted. Another example of not appreciating the consequences of their acts. And there are consequences. A price to be paid. A price they must pay.

"You want something to eat, Hon?"

The young tourist looked at his girlfriend as he walked back to the table with the drinks. The bartender brought menus to them and returned to the bar. They examined the menus and conferred quietly.

That's better. Keep quiet. That bozo had to ask if I had an umbrella. Can't people just live their lives and mind their own business? Don't they have a life?

The single customer sipped more beer, the ballpoint pen now resting on the pad, and thought of other people who did not mind their own business. Who savaged other people's lives.

The young man rose from his chair, clutching the two menus and spoke loudly as he walked toward the bar.

"We'll each have burger, Mac. Mine well done, hers medium rare. With fries and coleslaw."

He looked back at the young woman.

"But no onions," he laughed.

As if that was funny. Where was this idiot from? Did the tourist think everyone wanted to know his business? Why can't some people just live their lives and not incessantly bother others? Not interfere in their lives.

The writing began again. Slower now, more thoughtfully. The basic plan was hatched. Only the details remained.

The young couple ate heartily. They laughed and chatted between bites. The man called over at one point to the bartender and said, "My compliments to the chef."

They were ecstatic to be inside, to be warm, to be filling their bellies, to be together.

They're happy. Will they now be quiet? Better still, leave. I need to think. I need to think a little more. They're laughing again. Having the time of their pathetic lives.

The scribbling had stopped, but the pad of paper was being examined. The solo customer thought about life. Not life in general, a specific life.

A life that will soon run out of time. Because I have time to plan. A plan to kill. And time to kill.

CHAPTER 1

Sidney Matthew Avarson was an arrogant, sadistic bastard of the corporate persuasion. Now this morning's *Los Angeles Times* was—on page one yet—advising its readership that someone had taken a gun and aimed it square at the estimable Mr. Avarson. And missed. Unfortunately. The other ill-fated aspect of this incident, the *Times* reported, was that the bullet had hit one of his employees. Said employee was in critical condition, and the name would be released, pending notification of next of kin. The actual article merely related the shooting of the employee poolside at Avarson's home. The speculation that the bullet was intended for Sid is my personal reportage.

I was reading this account of tragically poor marksmanship in the unlikeliest of places in which to become informed of recent events in America's world of finance—an assisted living home for the elderly. I was at the Morningside Villages on a Sunday doing my regular volunteer stint when I came upon the Avarson article because the near demise of Sid was the hot topic of conversation that day among the patients and staff alike. Two copies of the front-page section were being passed through the small hospital and by ten a.m. one copy had been scissored out and thumb tacked to the lobby's bulletin board. The board copy was the one I spied when I stopped at the front desk and waited while the receptionist briefly checked the mangos and pink tea roses I was carrying for one of the patients who'd become a good friend, Mr.

Nazitto. As I waited, Hannah, Nazitto's favorite nurse, joined me. We exchanged greetings, and she offered me some coffee from a pot nearby for the employees.

"Thanks, Hannah, I could use some. Tell me, how did this Avarson shooting incident make it to the bulletin board?"

Hannah raised one delicate dark hand to smooth back wiry gray hair and sighed.

"Oh, his company works for us, you could say. Has a consultant come in here most days for about three weeks now. Guess the boss thought we could use advice on how to run things better. That man almost got hisself killed. What's his name? Avarson? He's donated money to us people tell me. So folks kinda look up to him here, you know what I'm sayin'?"

"Noble."

"You could say."

Hannah favored me with another sigh and headed down the hall, intent on other duties.

I should explain that I label Sid Avarson a mean-spirited, unreasonable S.O.B. from personal knowledge. When my modeling career in New York was going through a lean period, I clutched the financial straw of temp secretarial work and drew a gig at the Manhattan consulting firm of Potter, Wood & Penn. PW&P was once the management-consulting arm of one of the Big Five accounting firms but spun off into a separate concern largely due to SEC regulations and related stock investment restrictions. This was the practice of similar divisions of other Big Five members.

My secretarial agency had given me a temp assignment as one of three secretaries to Sid. For a too-long period of eight months. Now I had begun a new life in California and apparently so too had Monsieur Avarson. Before I left PW&P, there'd been rumors of the company transferring Sid to the Los Angeles branch and, as bad luck would have it, rumor had morphed into fact. So it was on that Sunday morning in October that I stood in front of the bulletin board reading a name I'd long since delegated to past events best forgotten.

My mango/roses offerings passed muster with the receptionist, and I tucked both under one arm so I could carry my coffee to Nazitto's room.

Eric Nazitto and I hit it off immediately three months ago when I began visiting Morningside. This probably had something to do with our similar backgrounds: both of us had lived in New York and we both spoke French. Nazitto's linguistic skill was gleaned from living in Paris for fifty of his eight-three years and mine derived from having a French nanny for nine of my thirty-one years. Nazitto was frail but tall and with skin as pale as his full head of white hair. With the luxuriant hair and a goatee—both always immaculately trimmed—he looked as aristocratic as he sounded.

"So, Frédérique, you've brought me some designer coffee today? Make a Starbucks stop first?" was Nazitto's greeting.

"No, but I'll share this" I answered. "Can I pour some in that mug on the night table?"

"Please do, gorgeous girl. And I'll take whatever's in that bag."

When you're eighty-three, everyone under sixty is a "girl". Thus flattered, I surrendered the mangos and half my caffeine.

The *Times* front-page section was spread across Mr. N's lap, so I knew our topic of conversation for the day was covered. Actually, I was relieved, as I couldn't dispel the Avarson shooting from my consciousness.

I sipped my share of the java.

"Are you going to ask me about Sid Avarson, Mr. N?"

"Why should I ask you, my dear? I'm not yet so senile I can't read the article for myself."

"Of course not. I should explain I once worked for the man."

Nazitto sat up a little straighter and pulled the collars of his maroon robe forward in a gesture meant to be one of authority.

"He's a Wall Street legend, executive in some kind of accounting firm. I know you once lived in New York, but I understood you to be an elegant fashion model. How could you have worked for this Monsieur Avarson? Oh, my dear, don't tell me you were one of those models that provided an…um…escort service on the side?"

I grinned.

"Sorry to deny you some titillation, but I was simply an assistant to the great man."

The heavy flowered drapes were nearly closed in Nazitto's room, only a sliver of sunshine visible. Light was provided by two end table lamps and a floor lamp next to his lounge chair.

"Well, this brings up queries more disturbing than titillating,

Frédérique. You seem well fixed financially. You dress well and always bring such beautiful flowers. You've said you own a brownstone in Brooklyn..."

"Park Slope in Brooklyn, to be precise," I injected.

"Hmmm, have I heard of Park Slope?"

"It's in the western section of Brooklyn. Lots of historic buildings there, great restaurants and it's near Prospect Park, Brooklyn Academy of Music, Brooklyn's Botanical Gardens and..."

"Yes, yes, so much for that, my dear. And you said you have a condo here. So what were you doing toiling away as a secretary? Or have you been pulling an old man's leg for the sheer deviltry of it?"

"I would never visit devilment on you, Mr. N, sheer or otherwise. I do own those two places, but they're all I managed to hang on to. The rest of the filthy lucre I'd squandered away and my bookings dwindled for a period, hence the office job."

I determined not to depress Nazitto with scenarios of my divorce's impact on my career or my ex-husband gambling away much of my earnings.

Hannah came in with tea and toast for our friend, briefly interrupting partial confession time. As Hannah set her tray down on a tiny occasional table, she nodded toward the newspaper.

"Just heard on the radio some more news about that shooting."

"Which was?" Mr. Nazitto said.

"The employee that got herself shot is in critical condition. Mighta found her next of kin."

"*Her*?" I said.

"It was Avarson's assistant they said. A Doris somebody or other."

Several mangos rolled across the floor as the bag I'd been holding fell from my hands.

CHAPTER 2

"How long had you known Doris what's-her-name?" Buck said.

I'd invited him to come over for dinner at my place and we'd ordered in from a small restaurant on the Third Street Promenade. I guess the California transplantation has not quite taken when you're ordering food from a place called Johnny Eats New York. The reason for my invitation was to ask Buck to investigate the shooting at the Avarson estate. My beloved Doris was wounded and I didn't trust the police to care about an assault on a secretary. Sid was not that big a name in financial circles that he could use clout to encourage the police even if he were so inclined, which I seriously doubted.

I'd told Buck over the phone that I wanted to work for him, and gave as the reason that I needed a job. He knew since I'd come to California my modeling gigs were mostly print jobs and that, so far, they were few and far between. He'd offered to loan me money and I'd refused, so I felt the offer of being his assistant would have appeal. I'd told him about the tragedy that had befallen my friend Doris but had not connected this to my job request. We were sitting at my kitchen table, having a nice Zinfandel with our garlic pasta.

"Doris Hernandez," I answered. "I only knew her during the period I worked for Avarson but it was long enough to fall in love with her. She was a hard worker, was helping to raise two grandchildren in addition to her job. She was just a sweet lady. Smart and funny too."

Buck took a quick gulp of his wine.

"What the hell is that three foot monstrosity over there? Now you've got one with little crystal balls hanging from it?"

Buck was referring to my latest addition to my extensive collection of Eiffel Towers.

"I picked it up at a flea sale in L.A. Please, let's get back to the subject at hand."

"According to you, *we'll* be working together. I'm smart and funny. Any chance you'll fall in love with me, *cher*?"

I laughed, because of course Buck was joking. And the *cher* appellation was a Cajun term for affection, not necessarily indicating a romantic interest. Buck has always been my friend. Platonic friend. We met when I was still married to Sonny Bob and I didn't think of him in a different role even since my divorce and my move to California. Actually, such thoughts have misted through my consciousness and other parts at times, but hopefully we'll be working together now and such a possibility is decidedly unprofessional. Buck was dating a nurse for a while. They broke up over something, he didn't say, and he seems to be playing the field of late. I haven't been playing with the field or much of anything else in the seven or so months since Sonny Bob and I parted and my grandmother back in New Orleans is always nudging me to get out more.

To be specific, I should explain that the Buck in question is the one, the only Joseph Buckley Lemoyne, top dog at Lemoyne Investigations, a crack private investigator organization Buck started here in Santa Monica, California after retiring from the New York police force. We met when I was a model in Manhattan and he was doing security on the side.

"The paper played it as if the bullet was intended for Doris and implied the police are investigating on that basis."

Pierre, my red, longhaired Persian, entered the room, sat down and prepared to glare at my guest. Buck, who hates cats, glared back. Pierre decided this exchange was beneath him, got up and slowly walked out. No harm, no foul.

"And you think different?" Buck asked.

"Well, of course. Sid Avarson is a bastard of the first water. Doris is the only assistant who's stayed with him longer than a year. Most of the other partners can't stand him. I will say he's an equal opportunity employer. He's just as nasty to his peers as he is toward those beneath him."

"The *Times* said the shooting took place alongside Avarson's pool in back of his Beverly Hills home; this Doris usually go there?"

"Doris and various other staffers. Like most consultants with PW&P, Sid travels a lot. When he's in town, he works out of a home office," I said.

"Cushy life," Buck said.

"Can't fault him for that. All that traveling is draining. I'd work from home too," I said.

Pierre wandered back in and lapped from his water dish, deciding to drink just to be sociable.

Buck poured some more wine into my glass.

"So no one would have just cause to want to whack the lovely Doris?"

"Of course not. Well, it's hard to imagine. As for killing Sid, the line forms to the right."

"I know corporate politics can get down and dirty; but, excepting Mafia involvement, isn't attempted murder a little over the line?"

"I know, I know. You think I'm being melodramatic. Well, maybe the Mafia *is* involved. At any rate, a shooting did take place and Sid's the more logical target. I just wish there were some way we could be involved."

"Who's the *we* Tonto?"

"You know what I mean." I squeezed Buck's arm affectionately. "If I'm going to help in the office, I need to know all about your cases and clients. Heck, maybe I'll decide to get a license and then my name goes on the door and we shall be a *we*."

"Absolutely, babe."

"Absolutely is right."

"Speaking of the Mafia," Buck grinned, "They have a term for your job of working for me. It's called sinecure."

Buck's vocabulary and knowledge astound me at times. They argue against one's stereotype of a former NYC cop/private eye.

"I'll bite. What does *sinecure* mean?"

"A position requiring little or no work, especially if it pays well. Term used for jobs Mafia insisted be created for their pals."

"Ha!" I said. "Just watch how hard this *pal* of yours will work."

It doesn't take much alcohol to give me a warm, pleasant buzz and delusions of grandeur. I could tell by the outrageous thrill Buck's casual agreement had given me that the buzzing had commenced. I sipped some more wine and regarded my new boss. I didn't really entertain the idea of making a career of private detecting, but it sounded good as part of the verbal job application I was presenting. I had no idea what Buck would pay me. Fortunately, I'd made enough money from some recent print jobs and one department store runway gig to tide me over for a while in any case.

Pleased that this meeting was going well, I sat back, sipped some of my second glass of wine and regarded my friend across the table. At five foot eight, Buck was about two inches shorter than me but built like a bodybuilder. At forty-two, he was eleven years older and, according to him, light years wiser. When it came to street smarts, I had to agree.

Pierre was now in the living room and peered toward the kitchen to see if the enemy was still within. Satisfied Buck's visit appeared interminable, he hopped on the couch to wait the intruder out.

"Actually, babe, in a round about way, Lemoyne Investigations is somewhat involved with your Sid Avarson."

"What are you talking about?"

"Well, you know that rap artist who's suing Potter, Wood for allegedly mishandling his dough?"

"Sounds like something you learned from the Business section of the *Times* which you know I avoid."

"That's where I first heard of it, but it became relevant when *Mrs.* Rap artist hired me."

I was shocked. Buck and I were frequently on the phone, got together regularly for a drink or dinner, sometimes Sunday brunch, and he always kept me posted on his current cases. Even Pierre looked astounded.

"When did this happen? We had breakfast Friday together, and you said you were just working on a cheating husband and a couple of insurance fraud cases."

"She called me at home over the weekend. Sounded somewhat more frantic than most wives scorned."

"But you have an unlisted number."

"Fred, celebrities have a way of getting around just about everything. Her hubby Alex King—his rap moniker is High Top De King—has millions. Records, produces, has a clothing line—the whole ball of wax. He's got his people- - the usual hangers on who come with all that. Hell, his people probably have people. And the missus has access to all that staff, one of whom learned of my excellent rep and tracked down my number."

"Let me guess. Madame King thinks High Top may have a cheating heart and wants Lemoyne Investigations to do the usual surveillance."

Buck picked up our plates and took them into the kitchen.

"That's the ticket, kid."

I followed him with our glasses.

"So do I start tomorrow?"

Pierre joined us, in search of leftovers. Buck placed my plate on the floor, which still contained a teaspoon of pasta and one small shrimp.

"This is too high profile for unlicensed help, Fred. Gonna do the deed myself."

Pierre sniffed at the small offering on the plate and turned on his heel, apparently feeling insulted. For different reasons, I joined him in that sentiment.

CHAPTER 3

Buck had entrusted a key to me, and I arrived at his office extra early the next morning, a gesture meant to testify as to the sincerity of my intentions to one Joseph Buckley Lemoyne. In truth, I was both lucky and grateful that Buck deemed me worthy to serve temporarily as his assistant, as my general business, or even office, experience was sketchy and generally lacking. The two positions I'd held in the business world during a dry spell in my modeling career just after my divorce had been as a temp for Sid Avarson's firm for less than a year and a three-month gig at the office of a fashion magazine. The latter consisted primarily of fetching coffee and picking up dry cleaning.

I put my purse down on the desk in the front office and dutifully started the coffee before heading into Buck's domain. Lemoyne Investigations is quartered in the downstairs right-hand side of a white frame house on Ocean Avenue in Santa Monica. It was a residence until a new landlord converted the rooms to offices that he rents to Buck, an interior decorator and a chiropractor. The decorator was awarded the largest space—appropriate because he seemed to possess the greatest number of clients. I love the place because it boasts a view of the mountains and veritable carpets of bougainvillea on the front lawn. Buck loves it because a parking area in back is large enough for his Dodge truck, his Ford Explorer and his Honda Civic. Nothing like going whole hog for the California car mentality.

When the coffee was brewed, I filled two mugs and took them into Buck's office.

"Good morning wise investigative one."

"Mornin', world's tallest assistant."

"So that's what's distinctive about me?"

Buck grinned.

"One of but numerous assets, *cher*. Additionally I bet you make lousy coffee."

The phone on the corner of Buck's desk rang and I picked it up.

"Lemoyne Investigations. This is Frédérique Bonnaire."

I felt I was being presumptuous in adding my own name, but doing so might annoy Buck just a little and something about him begged for annoyance today.

"It's Amanda," I said, and handed the receiver to Buck.

I knew his client Amanda Roberts to be a high maintenance movie star, always in dire need of major handholding. I sat in one of the client chairs and sipped my coffee as Buck blathered the usual pleasantries.

He continued the small talk, pausing to place his hand over the mouthpiece at one point and lip synch "foreplay" to me.

Buck put Amanda on speakerphone, reached into his left-hand desk drawer that I knew to contain his prized Cohibas, snipped the end of a cigar, lit it, and began scribbling on a legal pad. I wondered how long this was going to take. I also wondered, not for the first time, if Amanda had the hots for Buck.

I regarded his crew cut, pale blue eyes, slight tan and appealing square jaw. And his wardrobe. Buck wore Hawaiian shirts every day. It wasn't an L.A. affectation; he'd worn Tommy Bahama Hawaiian shirts in his off duty hours even as a New York cop. Just something he loved—like cigars, cars and bugging models down on their luck. Looking at his broad shoulders, I could see that such a persona would have appeal after Amanda's two pretty boy actor husbands.

The small talk had ceased and Buck's end of the conversation was limited to constant *uh huh's* and *okay's*, as he continued to write.

Finally, he said, "Goodbye, take care, see you soon."

Buck puffed on the cigar, looking both pleased and smug.

"Why am I one happy Cajun?"

I put my coffee mug on the desk.

"You took the question right out of my lil' ole mouth."

"Madame Roberts has a gig for me."
"I gathered as much."
"Miss Roberts has a gig for me in Mexico."
"Nice locale for a gig."
"Amanda baby has a gig for me in Puerto Vallarta, Mexico for a full two weeks."
"Nice length of time for a Puerto Vallarta gig."
"Damn straight."
"Damn shame," I said.
"How's that?"
"You won't be here to do surveillance for Mrs. High Top de King."

CHAPTER 4

Some P.I's eschew domestic work because of its sleaze factor but in L.A. it's hard to avoid if, like Buck, many of your clients are *in the industry* as they say and you want to have a lucrative practice.

I'd convinced Buck that filling in for him on this assignment constituted part of the solve-the-Doris-shooting quest. If I'm going to help, I need to get my feet wet, as it were.

The address in Thousand Oaks where the Kings resided was in a broad expanse of upper middle-class homes nestled between mountains. The area was attractive but didn't fully qualify as the usual Hollywood celebrity hovel. But then I'd learned from Buck that the King's main residence was a Connecticut home, and they had two additional abodes in West Palm Beach and Aspen, so I guess even the very wealthy must scale down here and there.

I'd dressed for this stakeout in a gray Black Dog sweatshirt—Martha's Vineyard circa 1998, black turtleneck, black jeans, white sneakers and had tucked my hair into a Lakers baseball cap. I'd become a passionate fan of the basketball team since my West Coast arrival. Kobe Bryant and Derek Fisher were my gods. Since I had no car of my own, I'd borrowed Buck's Ford Explorer.

I hate to admit it but I felt very excited, as I took a swig of my bottled water and headed east on the number ten freeway. Then north to the 405, north on 101, where I took the number twenty-three off ramp to Westlake Boulevard. A right on Westlake Boulevard took me to Lang Ranch Parkway. After about half a mile, I could see the house Buck had described. It had the best spot in the entire development, high on a hill with an astonishing view of the mountains.

I parked at the bottom of the hill and shut off the engine. It was 5:00 a.m. and cold. Holly King had advised Buck that High Top left for his office slash studio at different times of the day, so I wasn't taking any chances. I belatedly realized that a thermos of coffee would have been more appropriate than my bottle of Evian.

And I call myself a private eye?

The King home was a two-story edifice done in pale gray brick with a shingled roof in a darker gray. Tall trees rose on either side and full, healthy shrubs lined the edge of the house but there was no evidence of flowers anywhere. On the left side of the house you could barely discern a narrow path heavily shaded by the thick shrubs and short trees. When I drove toward the house and up the hill I'd detected a bright aqua pool through silvers of gaps in the foliage. The windows boasted black shutters but the front door was a shiny forest green. I would have painted it black to match.

A teenage boy strolled down the hill with a wirehaired terrier on a leash. Buck had allowed me to do surveillance on two other philandering spouse cases since he'd hired me. I'd come on board initially as a strictly typing-and-filing assistant but fate, and my persistent begging, had garnered me more exotic duties. In the other two cases, Buck had done the groundwork and I was simply dispatched, with a camera to the motel that had been identified as the love nest of choice. Spying in a refined, quiet neighborhood where families, dogs and children abounded felt...well...sleazy.

Another dog walker appeared. This time on one end of the leash was a fortyish red haired man, on the other end a golden retriever. Red fancied dog walking a more aerobic enterprise than the earlier teenager and was heading down the hill at breakneck speed. He continued toward the side of the road where I was parked and looked right at me. My face felt pinched in an expression both worried and furtive. I promptly switched to a relaxed smile, more appropriate for the role of young suburban mom who just happens to be sitting in her car at five o'clock in the morning. I kept auditioning a little smile for Red and hoped he'd give me the part. Red came so close to the car I was sure he was going to tap on the window so I tipped my head with what I hoped looked like a typical suburban-good-morning-neighbor nod but not so friendly it would encourage a chat. Red gave me a similar nod and added a thumbs up with the hand not holding the leash. Still bending down to my eye level, Red gave a couple of quick taps to his head with his index finger. I then caught on—he was indicating my cap and the thumbs up meant he, too, was a Laker fan.

I drank some more water and watched Red and dog go back and forth over the same one block area, seemingly more focused on exercise more than achieving distance. It occurred to me I had not brought any food and that my rapper friend might not be inclined to head out to the studio until noon, at which point I might well be comatose from hunger. I took off my hat, relaxed and closed my eyes.

Wouldn't hurt to rest for just a few minutes.

CHAPTER 5

Two hours later I opened my eyes and my view had changed. I was now staring at the glove compartment and the floor beneath it. I was also horizontal. I retrieved my cap from the floor, plopped it on my head and sat up, ramrod straight. My watch said seven forty-five. Rats. If I missed High Top, Buck would never let me forget it. I drank water again, wishing it were hot coffee.

Well I can't just leave because I fell asleep I said to myself. My self cheerfully added that I just might not have missed the stalkee. I fished in the glove compartment for Buck's binoculars should action kick up. Sure enough ten minutes later a well-built black man around age thirty exited the house wearing black jeans, a blue denim jacket, a very large silver watch and a white knit cap. He didn't seem to resemble the man in the fuzzy Polaroid Holly King had supplied but then I didn't get that good a look at his face. He got into the driver's seat of a bronze-colored Bentley G500 parked in the driveway. Six months ago I would not have been able to tell the difference between a Volkswagen and a Ferrari but Buck's obsession with cars and his habit of identifying different makes to me as we drove together had made me an expert.

I hit the ignition and turned on the heat. Now that we were ready to roll might as well be comfortable. Minutes passed and the Bentley didn't budge. I shut off the ignition and put my sweatshirt back on. Why the delay?

When a second black man came out the front door, I checked my watch and noted another fifteen minutes had passed. This gentleman was also muscular, also around thirty and also sporting a knit cap—in red. He wore a black velour windbreaker, open, collar turned up, a spanking white v-necked undershirt beneath it. Around his neck was some kind of silver necklace and narrow sunglasses tinted royal blue rested on his nose. He wore blue jeans but got in front passenger seat of the car before I noticed his shoes. Wiser now, I decided I would not start my car till I saw these cats move. These *cats*? Hey, I was already talking rapper lingo—how cool am I?

My knit-capped friends remained in place for what seemed thirty minutes, but was probably ten. The front door once again opened and a tall, slim, light-skinned black man appeared. Wearing a baggy black leather jacket over a crew-necked white tee, black sweat pants and orange and yellow running shoes, he headed for the Bentley while talking on a cell phone and climbed into the back seat of the car.

I was in an upscale neighborhood, and yet these guys looked like gang members. Ex-New Yorkers like me are supposed to be used to things like that, what with our famous muggings and drive by shootings and the like. I'd lived in Brooklyn during my three years of marriage to Sonny Bob, but in the Park Slope area in a chic, three-story brownstone. Before that I'd had a loft in SoHo and before that in my parents' Park Avenue apartment. All in all I'd led a sheltered lifestyle. The tough, gritty side of New York was unknown to me. I'm not bragging and certainly not complaining, but these dudes were scaring me already and I'd only observed them climbing into a car. I retrieved my water bottle from the car floor. Only two drops left. Once in a while on a runway I'd get cottonmouth from nerves and a major case had now arrived. I swallowed hard and tried to summon some saliva.

Still feeling cynical regarding takeoff probabilities, Buck's Ford Explorer and I made no movement. Open door time again and a small black woman in a knee-length, pink silk robe came running out. A short white nightgown appeared to be under the robe and pink high-heeled satin bedroom slippers completed the ensemble. Her hair looked wild and natural and her facial expression appeared distraught. The tall, slim man got out of the car. He and the woman kissed and embraced. Tall-Slim began speaking to her and her features appeared to soften. She was light skinned like the tall man and looked slim and sinewy.

Another kiss and Miss Pink ran back in the house. My shrewd powers of observation deduced this lovely couple was none other than High Top and our client, the missus.

At last the Bentley rolled down the driveway and turned right. I waited a couple of minutes before following—something I should have done the first time had I not been so anxious to get heat in the Ford. We were the only cars on the street. I hoped that if any of the Bentley's tenants glanced backward I looked very suburban-mom-going-to-pick-up-milk. Then I realized I'd shed my Laker cap and my long hair was in full bloom. I'm a natural blonde in the shade some people call dirty blonde or ash blonde if the shade callers are of more tactful ilk. I get regular highlighting done to add zest to my drab color, the last treatment administered just yesterday. I always feel overly bleached the first two days until blonde and even-lighter-blonde appear to blend into a tasteful co-existence so I now felt that I must look like a large yellow happy face from a distance. At the first red light I found a rubber band in the glove compartment, used it for a pony tail and popped my cap back on, clever disguise in place.

I was confident our destination was the West Hollywood address Buck had given me of the studio High Top used. My cell phone rang. Buck's voice. He appeared to be directing conversation to someone about a credit card. I waited.

"Hi kid. How's the hottest make-believe private eye in the West?"

"I don't know, but *I'm* fine. How goes life in P.V. so far?"

"So far? It sucks. I'm checking into the third hotel in as many hours. Amanda thought the last hotel was too beige. I forget what was wrong with the first one."

"So how can I reach you? On the remote chance that I'll need to."

"I just now left the address and phone number on your home answering machine. It's some place in the Hotel Zone. Amanda will have her own private villa, private pool, private terrace so she's a happy camper."

"I always say if Amanda's happy, I'm happy."

"I say that too, Fred. Rarely mean it. How goes surveilling?"

"Going well. Heading down Sunset, as we speak, toward studio."

A red Volkswagen came out of a side street and busted in front of me but didn't obstruct my view of the Bentley. Then a gray BMW did what BMWs always do: cut in front of me, no turn signal. The road veered left and the Bentley was nowhere in sight.

"Freddy?"

"Yes?"

"You're doing what I told you? Don't follow and don't point your car at High Top's. Get in front of him and use your rear view mirror."

"That's exactly what I'm doing, Buck."

I wondered if I could catch up to a decent length behind High Top *and also if my nose just reached Pinocchio length.*

CHAPTER 6

IT WAS THE BEGINNING OF day four of executing surveillance of our rapper friend, Mr. High Top de King. I was sitting in Buck's car, discreetly parked on a side street across from the recording studio parking lot. The morning sky was a tent of vivid blue and luminous sun, as only a California day can produce. If this were summer, I'd be aching to be at the beach and deeply resentful of my current assignment, virtually self-appointed though it happened to be. As it was, I was merely marginally resentful of this gig.

So far High Top's routine was leave home in the morning, drive with his two bodyguards to the recording studio in West Hollywood and work there for what amounted to several hours but always felt like a day and a half to me. As surveillances go, it was boring. My prior assignments amounted to quick, snappy sightings of the cheating spouse and his or her lover dashing into a motel room or hotel, waiting while they made the world rock for two or so hours and, lastly, my camera work during their furtive exits.

I had changed my own modus operandi somewhat, quick study P.I. that I am. I no longer dressed in all black as if the project were that of cat burglar but wore blue jeans, one of my many white turtlenecks and white Reeboks. Today I'd felt daring and had donned olive green baggy nylon sweat pants, gray tank top, gray knee-length sweater and

Frye boots—California shlubby. Each day I also accessorized with a thermos of coffee, brown bag lunch and several bottles of Evian.

For the first three days High Top and his fellow musicians had lunch delivered. Today he left the studio around twelve thirty with his two bodyguards, three other black men and a short, heavyset young black woman carrying a briefcase. Thru binoculars I watched them walk across the studio parking lot. High Top was taller than his bodyguards and they seemed to be struggling to match his stride. At the moment High was doing all the talking. The other three burst into laughter, seemingly at something he said. The small chubby woman looked up at High Top as she giggled with an expression that seemed worshipful. High grinned and patted her on the head.

They headed for lunch at a small Italian restaurant directly across the street from the studio. I was very familiar with this bistro myself, as I'd been using their ladies room every day. The luncheon appeared to be a two-hour, uneventful affair, after which the entourage strolled back to the studio for four more hours of whatever rappers do in studios.

It was one forty five, and I had yet to work up at appetite for my brown bag meal that, having run out of ham at home, was now mayo and peanut butter. I was contemplating how many calories I'd save if I just forgot the idea entirely when Buck buzzed my cell phone.

"Frédérique, my little sleuth, what's exciting?"

"Not a thing. Our High Top's a man of honor. All work and no play. No sightings of a bare breasted hussy bird."

"Give it time. Lemoyne and associates always get their philanderer… or philanderess. Is there a new unisex term for that? What's politically correct?"

"What would be correct is if we could retire this particular mission and go on to bigger and better things."

"Ah, do I detect disillusion with the detecting life?"

Ohmigod. I sounded so petulant and unprofessional.

"Not at all. Just a momentary lapse in my otherwise steely dedication."

"I thought as much. Well, let me tell you about my day in glorious Puerto Vallarta, *cher*. It's raining more on than off and twice the lovely Ms. Roberts almost got hit by a bus. I understand that's a common occurrence in these here parts but Amanda blames me. I guess if I were sufficiently imposing as a bodyguard—and we all know no one's more imposing than I—no self respecting bus would dare trespass in milady's path."

"Experiencing movie star temperament are we?"

"In spades. Anyway, stay on High Top's heels. I assume you're doing some night duty too. There's the going home after work to mama and then sneaking out for yonder mistress scenario as well as the working-late-at-the-office ploy."

"Got both covered."

Now did not seem like the time to tell Buck I was taking tomorrow off.

CHAPTER 7

Yesterday while driving to High Top's home, I heard two disturbing news items on my car radio. One I already knew via Buck's inquiries, which was that police lacked a key piece of evidence in the shooting at the Avarson home: the bullet. It was still lodged in Doris, who remained in a coma. Physicians could not go in for the bullet because the patient was not stable. Thus far, the police had failed to recover any shell casings on the scene. Further complicating matters, a heavy rain commenced minutes after Doris was shot, and in the intervening period Avarson staff, family members, and neighbors had trampled over the surrounding area, which made finding significant footprints and forensic evidence nearly impossible.

The other piece of news, that I was not aware of, was that the shock of the apparent attempt on her daughter's life had caused Edna Torres, her mother, to suffer a fatal heart attack. Damn, damn, damn! Tears welled up in my eyes as I thought of the increasingly tragic plight of the Hernandez family.

The next day I began to recall one day in the city when Doris Hernandez and I took our lunch hour together. We were walking down the north side of St. Patrick's going toward Fifth Avenue when a voice called out to us.

"Hey, got a quarter?"

This was hardly an unfamiliar request in midtown Manhattan. The speaker in this case was a blonde girl around seventeen. I often gave to panhandlers but usually just those who were elderly or missing a limb. This kid looked like a tennis player—tan and able bodied enough to hustle some kind of honest work. The girl was sitting in the shade on the steps of the church. Doris, who at fifty-three, was pleasingly plump with the beginnings of arthritis, slowly made her way over to our little beggar friend.

"You *do* look hungry," Doris said.

"That's not all I am," the blonde replied, delivering the line with a snarl.

Doris and I were already in late-to-termination status regarding our ETA back from lunch, and Avarson had been calling in from London on an almost hourly basis all week with one imagined crisis or another. She turned away from the girl and motioned me to go on without her. I took a couple of steps toward them and made no-let's-go motions only to be waved off. Since I was a temp and Doris had tenure of four years with Avarson, I decided my job security was the more precarious and left.

It took me five minutes to get back to Potter, Wood & Penn, but Doris was not to return until almost five. Shortly thereafter Avarson called in from his suite at the Brown Hotel and read her the riot act over the speakerphone for a full fifteen minutes. Sid didn't fire her, and Doris never offered an explanation. She never told him she'd taken the girl for a soda and hot dog and wormed out of her the main dilemma, which was that she was pregnant and the father had taken off for parts unknown. Thereupon Doris hailed a cab and took her to a friend's home in Queens. She knew her friend had recently taken a niece to a home for unwed mothers upstate and could be prevailed upon to transport the blonde to the same safe haven.

One interesting aspect of this incident was that the blonde was white and while her current condition was soiled and surly, her clothes and general bearing suggested upper middle-class origins. Doris was Hispanic and someone very much like her probably did laundry and scrubbed floors at blondie's Long Island parental home. A cynical guess, but possible.

It was this incident and other more minor, but just as telling, testimonies to Doris' goodness that I was recalling as I stood under an umbrella at her mother's gravesite and half listened to a Father Antonio speak. It was another shimmering bright day and I'd arrived too late for a spot in the shady section of the assemblage. A petite elderly lady had brought an umbrella to ward off the sun's fierce rays, and decided the tall blonde stranger needed similar protection. I could smell the freshly dug soil piled nearby next to a lone palm tree. I don't think the older woman spoke English but she looked up at me from time to time as the Priest spoke, a wan smile on her face, sharing our grief. After the service, I helped her down the hill to a car where some Hernandez relatives were waiting and drove back to my place in Buck's Honda.

When I got home, the message light on my machine was flashing. I fed Pierre, kicked off my heels and hit the play button. It was grandma Toussaint with a weather report. It seems tropical storm Isadore had moved onshore, causing a lot of flooding in New Orleans and elsewhere. Gram added that the paper said there were sixty-five mile per hour winds.

"But, sugar, I know it's more like a hundred and they're just not admitting it."

I immediately dialed gram's number to make sure she was okay. A recorded message came on, giving today's date and saying she had left for cocktails at the Villalon's. Not exactly a recommendation for federal disaster aid.

Thus satisfied that Isadore had not cramped Hermione Toussaint's style, I sat on the couch and pressed the remote to get the TV news. Channel 4 was occupied with matters meteorological also, advising this was the driest year on record and went on regarding the status of the fires in the Angeles National Forest. They added that distant areas, which included my own Santa Monica, were experiencing dust and soot. I doubted dust and soot trumped Gram's one hundred mph winds, so I didn't call to share this.

Instead, I headed toward the kitchen cabinets and refrigerator to see what they'd yield as a dinner resource. There were plenty of soups and canned spaghetti and vegetables in the cabinets and even a new package of ham in the fridge but I was not inspired. Both my mother and Gram had taught me much about cooking, but knowing is not necessarily liking—and I didn't. Like to cook, that is.

I don't normally admit this. I usually find a scapegoat for my culinary lethargy. The excuse *du jour* happened to be valid. I was dispirited because in light of the Doris tragedy the High Top possible-cheating-husband surveillance seemed—as Gram would say—piddly. If I was going to private-investigate anything, finding Sid Avarson's would-be assailant seemed far more imperative. But I wasn't a cop. Hells bells, as Gram would also say, I wasn't even a private investigator. In view of all these circumstances, there was but one thing to do. Go out for a drink.

CHAPTER 8

"UH-OH, REALLY BAD DAY?"

I'd just ordered a scotch instead of my usual white wine spritzer and Nick, the bartender, knew what this suggested.

"You could say that," I said, "How are you?"

Charming wide smile from Nick.

"Never been better."

I smiled, not so widely.

"Glad to hear it."

I was sitting at the bar of Emile's Cafe, a French bistro that was more bar than restaurant but still boasted a respectable menu. It was within walking distance of my condo and was owned by Nick Bernstein and his brother, Matt, two nice Jewish boys originally from Philadelphia. A year before opening Emile's, Nick had vacationed in Paris and had been inspired by the Curio Bar in the Latin Quarter. I'd learned this three months ago when I first discovered the place and had dined alone at the bar. Nick and I had struck up a conversation that evening when I overheard him mentioning the Curio to another customer.

"I'm a perfectionist," he told me then. "We have a lot of special drinks and it's been a lot for the staff to learn. But, so far, they've all been very gung ho. I wanted this place to be something like a speakeasy, like a bar resurrected from a hundred years ago."

I'd entertained a slight crush on Nick ever since my first encounter with Emile's. Maybe it was the suave manner in which he greeted all customers, his masterful but gracious command of his staff, his way with a crab cake appetizer. *Or maybe I was just lonely.*

Emile's was a charming combination of French refinement and American convenience. Dark and intimate, the walls were brick from the floor to a halfway point. The remaining wall was white plaster as was the ceiling. Every five feet or so the walls were adorned with brass lamps and sepia prints of Parisian landmarks. The prints were surrounded by wide white matting and narrow black frames. The floors were hardwood and there was nary a hanging green plant—the norm for most California eateries—in sight. The bar was a dark rustic wood fronted by black wrought iron stools with black imitation leather cushions. There were booths opposite the bar upholstered in the same black leather.

The individual tables throughout were marble and in the center of each stood a small white pitcher, bearing their logo in black—the name *Emile's* over a silhouette of Napoleon. I never figured out the choice of Napoleon, but you don't argue with a committed Francophile. Black wrought-iron chairs with peach and black striped cloth cushions surrounded the tables. Sometimes restless customers complained about the mobility of these loose cushions, but Nick wouldn't cave on this decorating point. A surprising discretion coming from a guy who was all man's-man, whose life seemed to revolve solely around working out at Gold's Gym, football and basketball games and his golf score. Somewhere there must have been a woman's influence. I must ask him some time.

On a television in the far right corner, Bill O'Reilly was sounding forth on foreign affairs. I took two healthy swallows of the Chivas Regal.

"Whoa. We're not ourselves tonight are we?"

Nick usually teased me about my how little I actually consumed alcohol-wise during my bar sit-downs. I didn't have a snappy comeback tonight. I took a more ladylike sip.

"Nick, did you catch much of the local news? Any new developments about the lady who was nearly killed at Sid Avarson's home.

"Oh I heard about that. The CEO dude."

Dude? The acculturation from Philly was complete.

"That's the one," I said.

"He was in the news but it didn't have anything to do with the woman who got shot."

"What did it have to do with?"

"Some consultant who works for his company is reported missing. Police think it may be related though."

"Did they give the consultant's name?"

I remembered only a handful of consultants by name that had worked in the New York office. If it was a Los Angeles employee, I'd be clueless but if it was someone who had transferred west with Sid I might know him or her.

"If they did, I don't remember it. But I recognized where he worked."

"Where he worked? Well that would be the Potter, Wood office downtown."

"No, they said he was working on a client's office."

Well that made sense. Their consultants mostly work on site.

"You say you recognized the name?"

"Yeah. Place near here. That nursing home. Morningside."

CHAPTER 9

ONCE AGAIN I HAD FALLEN asleep in the Ford Explorer near High Top's Thousand Oaks home. This time for a more noble reason. I felt so guilty about the time I took off for the Edna Torres funeral that immediately after dinner at Emile's I bee lined to my post outside the studio. Waited the remaining evening and then followed High Top and friends back to his home. The plan was an all-night stakeout so for midnight-snack-and-breakfast purposes I'd purchased food at the Italian restaurant, sat briefly at a table and then asked the waiter to doggie bag the whole thing before taking it to the car for consumption. I seemed always to draw an older waiter named Mario as my server. He'd say repeatedly, "'scuza…you no want to sit down?" Between that scenario and my restroom stops, I'm sure they deemed me their strangest customer in years. My modus operandi allowed me to have dinner in the car, stay the night in case High Top did a late-night hussy run and ultimately fall asleep until eight the next morning.

During last night's stakeout I sat in the car's back seat, erect but with legs stretched out comfortably. I was pampering myself on the unlikely chance I would again doze off during my vigil as opposed to my goal of going twenty-four hours without a wink of sleep. Plus I was still wearing funeral attire—black Chanel knitted jacket, black jersey dress and my favorite Manolo Blahnik black satin heels. Years of modeling left me somewhat of a clotheshorse, and I wanted to preserve these designer duds in as pristine a condition as possible.

I was nibbling on Romano cheese when the usual morning drill went down: bodyguards came out, then High Top exits, first kissing wife goodbye. Holly King never repeated her first morning's needy sprint to the Bentley but these days garnered her smooch at the front door. As their car pulled away, I briefly ruminated on how devoted a husband High Top appeared to be and how many months was I going to have to stalk him to prove this to the satisfaction of Buck and Mrs. King.

Our two-car caravan rolled on toward Hollywood. The Bentley pulled into its usual reserved spot. I pulled into my usual street spot. All's well with the world. I'd added a portable CD player to my stakeout survival tools and popped in a Zachary Richards tape to keep me entertained and in a sufficiently bright-eyed, bushy-tailed state.

Around noon High Top exited the studio by himself, *sans* bodyguards. He was carrying a hard cover copy of a book, but I couldn't make out the title. High was wearing a black turtleneck, slightly baggy jeans, white Reebok sneakers. He was wearing his customary sunglasses and walking faster than usual. His destination was once again the Italian restaurant where he stayed for about forty-five minutes and then left, still walking rapidly, still carrying the book.

I swigged water and told myself I was not at all bored. Sidewalk traffic was minimal as it is in most of Los Angeles and its environs. Made me very nostalgic for New York. I like life out where you can see it.

Ma Louisianne, Buck's favorite Zachery Richards tune was playing when the man himself called.

"I miss you, boss," I said.

"Ha! Cold day in hell. Someone else you're not missing—I hope—is the object of Mr. King's affections."

"That would be Mrs. King."

"Not according to her. Don't tell me you're coming up empty?"

"You must have experienced this, Buck. Aren't suspicious spouses sometimes wrong?"

"Rarely. Holly King's reasons were quite credible. She's a sweetheart. I'll let you meet her when I get back. Did you...."

"Buck you're breaking up. What did you say?"

"I'm in a damn restaurant," Buck said, "Can you hear me now?"

"Yes."

"Every freaking one of these restaurants has a jungle motif. Between that and the rain..."

"You're breaking up again."

"Can you hear me now?"

"Yes."

"Okay. Did you...."

"More static, Buck. Can you go outside or something?"

I heard some classic Lemoyne cursing, then someone speaking to him, then nothing.

I felt it would probably be fruitless to try to call him back and turned up the volume on the CD again. Richards was singing a song about being in Hollywood and somebody stealing his monkey.

Well, Zach, that makes about as much sense as my current Hollywood experience.

I couldn't fathom what the remainder of Buck's "Did you" sentence could be. What further duties could a mind-numbing round-the-clock stakeout possibly entail? I guess just asking that question clearly meant I was losing my professional edge. High, bodyguards and *la petite femme* with the briefcase—the latter I'd decided was his lawyer—had earlier done the Italian restaurant bit. I decided I'd do the same. Bowing to my current feeling of petulance, I decided this time I'd sit down at a table and stay.

CHAPTER 10

Pierre and I were having our morning coffee. Well, Pierre's was mostly cream in a small dish. but we were so cozily compatible it felt like sharing the same experience. After three laps, Pierre sat up in all his orange hairy glory and looked at me as if he could read my thoughts and as if his response was "combatible-schmatible where the hell have you been these days?"

I looked him straight in the eye and said, "I have to work, Pierre."

He looked downward at the cream as if to say, "Oh puh-leeze", turned on his paws and slowly walked out of the room.

It was seven a.m. By now I'd observed that High Top never left his house before nine so there was no reason to rush. I took my coffee into the living room to catch the local news on the telly, check out Fox's *America's Newsroom* and see how Megan Kelly's hair looked today. Never say I don't stay *au courant*. I've never bothered to have the *Los Angeles Times* delivered to me as there's a bubble machine on the street just outside of my condo containing the paper. But any day I didn't have the requisite correct coins I went news-less until I found time to turn on the tube.

The annoying commercial for the rug company was running, then a weatherman came on to report that in Los Angeles there was smokiness around Mt. Wilson from the fires. I left to warm up my coffee and when

I returned Bill Hemmer was talking about the Potter, Wood & Penn consultant disappearance. This time I caught the name: *Scott Kelly.*

CHAPTER 11

I WAS ONCE AGAIN ON A stakeout. Just the wrong stakeout.

I'd encountered Scott Kelly about a dozen times during my temp stint as Sid Avarson's assistant-third-class in New York. When I heard Scott's name on the tube I guessed he either was here from the East Coast on a business trip or had been, like Sid, transferred. A search of the phone book proved the latter to be the case. There were several Scott Kellys but only one with the middle initial of Q and the operator supplied the address.

So here I was once again covertly parked in an upscale neighborhood. I'd met Scott's wife, Nan, at a country club party Sid had thrown for the staff during the Christmas season and on one occasion when she'd stopped in the office. Was that sufficient familiarity to warrant my prancing up to her door, inviting myself in and grilling her on Scott's disappearance? Absolutely not. If Lemoyne Investigations were legitimately handling this case, this type of interrogation would be Buck's domain. Quite apart from that, Nan was the wife of a Potter, Wood partner. I'd been less than a mere assistant. I'd been a mere temp assistant. Hardly grounds for social intercourse. To presume otherwise would be rude and overbearing.

I moved the knocker up and down expecting to see a maid, but Nan herself opened the door.

"Mrs. Kelly?"

"Who...? I think I know...did you used to work for Sid? Yes, you did, didn't you? I'm so sorry. I can't recall your name. But come in."

Nan delivered this rush of questions and answers in a startled but pleasant tone ending with a smile. I hadn't anticipated such a cheerful reception. And I didn't remember her accent. Was it possible she was from New Orleans, we'd once discussed this and that was the reason for the warm welcome?

"My name is Frédérique Bonnaire...Freddy...I'm from New Orleans."

My God, I sounded like a six year old.

Nan gave no sign she'd noticed my sophomoric blabbering. She stood holding a glass of what looked like tea and continued to regard me with a pleasant expression.

"Right. I remember. You and I were the only females at that party with southern accents. I'm from Alabama, but I probably mentioned that. I was just out on the patio, going over mail and having iced tea. Can I get you some?"

"That would be lovely."

"Follow me."

I followed Nan Kelly down a long narrow hallway strewn with small oriental rugs. The wall to our right was covered with framed paintings in various sizes and to our left were stained glass windows. Just before the hall ended at the kitchen I glimpsed a living room to the right. It had large overstuffed couches and chairs in a textured forest green material and the far windows were covered with closed plaid drapes. A rather dark effect for a beach house, but attractive. We entered the kitchen and Nan pointed to the right.

"Go thru that door to the patio and make yourself comfortable. I'll be out in a minute."

I took a quick survey of the kitchen. It had stark white walls and appliances but there were ceramic pots and pans and bowls and vases all around in different colors together with hanging baskets here and there.

On the patio there was the usual round glass-topped table with an umbrella rising from the middle and two white wrought-iron chairs with blue and white striped seat cushions. An array of mail and magazines and a yellow legal pad and pencils was on the table in front of one of the chairs. I sat down in the opposite chair and waited for Nan.

The view of the beach and the ocean was dazzling. *Buck and I should move our office down here some day.* Later I would wonder why in the world a business office occurred to me instead of a house for Pierre and me.

Nan came out bearing two glasses of iced tea, each containing a sprig of mint. She obviously really yearned for mint juleps. For one hopeful moment I thought that's what they might be but a quick sip betrayed no alcoholic content.

Nan sat down and we smiled at each other. I began to speak by calling her Mrs. Kelly. She interrupted and asked me to call her Nan.

I was still flabbergasted by all this immediate hospitality. Coming from a fellow southern belle I guess I should not have been surprised, but husband Scott had always impressed me as being what Buck would call a real hard ass. He had a cordial but somber personality and was always groomed to perfection. Normally I admire a person with self-control and some sense of style, but Scott Kelly had those qualities to a degree most of us lesser mortals find annoying. His blonde hair was only a little flecked with gray and cut short military style. He had the flattest stomach on the planet; one could hate him for that attribute alone.

Nan spoke before I could continue. She seemed to have also been mulling over the subject of appearances.

"Who's that blonde actress? What's her name? Is it Molly? No, no, that was the name of that movie. No, it wasn't Molly, it was Mary. That's it...something about...or do you know Mary. Gosh, I just can't remember. Oh, you know, she's tall like you...she was in that movie... you know, it was a comedy...with that short guy...last name starts with a "D" I believe...oh, what *is* her name?"

I couldn't stand it much longer.

"Cameron Diaz?" I supplied.

"Why, yes, have you been told that before?"

"A couple of times. We're both tall and blonde but lately I..."

"Well, of *course* you have. I always thought you looked exactly like her."

Exactly?

"I'm flattered."

"I think it was the glasses that threw me or I would have identified you immediately."

"I got lazy about wearing contact lenses after I moved to L.A."

Also got lazy about dieting. Wonder if that had thrown her.

CHAPTER 12

NAN KELLY AND I CONTINUED with several more minutes of chitchat about the transition from New York to California, the locales of the best grocers, hairdressers and health clubs and how we missed the 59th Street Bloomingdales. She was attractive without the aggravating perfection of her spouse. Nan had dark brown hair pulled back in a ponytail; she was slim without looking as if she worked out frantically with a personal trainer. She looked well put together but relaxed in a white golf shirt and navy shorts. Nan looked to be a size four. I used to be a size four but was now an eight. I liked her anyway.

I was just about to bluntly veer us away from all this girl talk when it began to rain. Nan gathered up all her mail, I took our iced tea glasses and we headed for the green and plaid living room.

I sat down in a corner of the large forest green couch and placed our iced teas on a long, distressed wood coffee table.

Nan had walked over to the drapes, opened them and stood contemplating the rain for a few minutes. Apparently Nan had the drapes closed to keep the sunlight out but a gray, wet view was acceptable.

As if she could read my mind, she turned toward me with a tiny smile and said, "This more fits my mood."

I was about to say *why* but realized the stupidity of such a query. Her husband had disappeared. Not a good day in anyone's black rock.

Outside the rain was coming down heavily, a couple of small fichus trees were whipping furiously in the wind and the horizon beyond was a charcoal blur. The rain somehow made me feel more relaxed. It reminded me of when I was a child and had experienced some of my most secure and content feelings while riding in a car in the rain. When my family lived in New York we went to stay with my aunt and uncle in Manhasset, Long Island for a month-long visit. For some reason, we always had some rainy July days and I spent part of such days in the large gray Buick, surrounded by my mother, cousin and aunt as Uncle Kenneth steered the car safely thru rain, hail and dark of night.

Nan left the window, walked over and stood before me.

"You know Scott is away."

Her voice was soft and serious, the brittle cheerfulness gone.

"That's what I came to discuss" I said.

Nan sat down on a straight-backed chair with a green velvet seat cushion and took a sip of tea.

"I can't imagine how this would concern you, Freddy. Are you working for Sid Avarson out here? I personally have not heard from Avarson except for one phone call when Scott didn't show up for work for two days. Did he send you?"

"I have no affiliation whatsoever with Avarson these days, Nan. I have a personal interest in the shooting that took place at his home as the victim is a friend of mine. But the question is how can I help *you*? I assume you've filed a missing person report. Have any leads come of that?"

"I didn't file a report. I considering it, but the one time I spoke to Sid over the phone he was against it. He didn't explain why, but I agreed. The police might think Scott being mysteriously absent could be related to the shooting at Sid's home, when the truth of the matter is Scott's done this before. It's occurred to me that the shooting could have been an attempt on Sid's life, rather than on the life of that poor unfortunate woman who's in a coma. If that occurred to me, it could occur to the police. That woman, you say she's your friend? Isn't Hernandez her name? I never saw her at any firm parties but I believe I met her in the office once."

"Well, as the police always say in these matters, they have to pursue all avenues," I said. "You say Scott's disappeared before?"

Nan pursed her lips, looked away and contemplated the gray seascape outside her window.

"Oh I know it's logical that the police could consider Scott because of what looks like a suspicious disappearance. And a timely one. I wouldn't fault them for that."

She was changing the subject, avoiding my question. I knew I was prying here. None of this was really my business, and Nan wasn't being overly forthcoming.

"If I may ask…when Scott went A.O.L. the other time, what was the reason?"

"Other *times.* There have been three or more such occasions. They have to do with our marriage, Freddy. Simple as that."

"As I mentioned, Nan, Doris Hernandez is a very dear friend. I knew her for a relatively brief period of time, but I greatly admired her. If the bullet was actually intended for her, I'd like to know that. It could mean other members of her family are in danger."

Nan suddenly stood up.

"I quite understand and I wish I could help. As for Scott, he'll show up in the next day or two and all of this will blow over."

"I don't know if it will blow over that quickly for the Hernandez and Avarson families."

Nan's head bobbed backward briefly, either stunned by the reality of the dilemma if one were a Hernandez or an Avarson or my impertinence in pointing this out, I wasn't sure which.

"Let me get an umbrella and walk you to your car."

I stood up, finally taking the hint that the time for cozy sharing was over. From a brass container at the end of the long hallway Nan retrieved what looked like a large golf umbrella, and we ran for the Explorer.

I'd wanted to ask Nan why she was positive Scott's latest M.I.A. was for reasons marital. I wanted to ask what she knew of his relationship with Sid Avarson. I wanted to ask just where she got that perfect manicure. All these pertinent queries were to go unsatisfied.

We did the thank-you-for-coming and thank-you-for-seeing me routine and I headed home, anxious to relate the whole experience to Pierre and see what he thought.

CHAPTER 13

"When the cat's in Puerta Vallarta, the mouse will play."

I was speaking to Pierre. I thought he'd be particularly appreciative of a maxim involving a mouse but he burrowed his face down between his paws, tuning me out.

We were curled up on my couch together as I gave him his regular grooming. I'd assembled on the coffee table all the tools necessary for this routine—a wide toothed comb, toothbrush, wire brush and talcum powder. I'd sprinkled his coat with Johnson's baby powder to help ease the brush thru his longhaired fur. Pierre purred in his aristocratic restrained way, and I brushed and talked. I think I was trying to have with Pierre an extension of the productive conversation I had hoped to have with Nan Kelly.

I went on to confess to Pierre how inconsistent I'd been in executing the assignment Buck gave me of following High Top de King night and day and how unsuccessful I'd been in uncovering his more prurient interests and his exact partner or partners in said enterprises. I explained why attending the funeral for the mother of Doris Hernandez was so important to me.

Pierre yawned. Undeterred, I continued. I explained why I took the time to visit the Kelly home, elaborating that there could be real danger for the Hernandez family and this mattered to me. I was less alarmed in regard to Sid Avarson. But, I assured Pierre, that however difficult, controlling and manipulative he may be I didn't wish him dead. I further admitted to a grim curiosity as to who Sid's would-be assassin might be were he, in fact, that actual intended target.

Pierre stretched and purred as I used the toothbrush to groom his facial hair. I outlined Sid Avarson's general management style and backed this up with several anecdotes and comments about him from fellow partners and described some particularly intense confrontations. Were these sufficient to provoke murder? I didn't know and Pierre had no comment.

I hated to admit it but murder was somewhat rare in the tony area of Beverly Hills where Sid lived. And I had another tidbit. At the funeral I'd overheard two of the teenage boys in the Hernandez family alluding to what sounded like gang problems. Drive by shootings were equally uncommon in the Avarson neighborhood but if Doris were the intended target could this be an explanation? I took Pierre's silence for agreement. Something to note.

Doris, I advised Pierre, was still in a coma at Cedar Sinai—not her neighborhood hospital but rather Sid Avarson's choice I began waxing nostalgic over Doris again and Pierre suddenly raised up and walked out of the room. I was really getting tired of having humans and animals stand up and walk away just as I was about to launch meaningful dialogue. Would no one talk to me? Like the proverbial answer to a prayer, my cell rang. I picked it up from the coffee table. It was Buck.

"Your man in Puerto Vallerta. How goes it?"

"Fine, just fine. How goes it with you?"

"Predictable bodyguard trails after big movie star stuff. Surveillance going okay?"

"Perfect."

"No little chippy on the side yet?"

"Completely chippy-less."

"Okay, hang in there. Anything else you need to tell me?"

"Not a thing."

I put down the phone and headed to the kitchen. I was being evasive with Buck, not to mention irresponsible. He was my friend; but he was also currently my boss, so to speak. And I was taking advantage of the former to play hooky. I needed to get clarification on just how long I was to stalk High Top before Mrs. High would be confident of his fidelity. I needed to share with my friend my unauthorized snooping over at the Kelly home and let him set me straight. Who do I think I am? I'm just some undefined kind of assistant to Buck, but he's entrusted a vital part of his business to me and all my amateur tramping around is proving unproductive.

I decided to call Buck back, but later, when he'd put Amanda to bed, figuratively speaking, and finished his duties for the day. By the time I'd had some dinner, some wine and a nice long bubble bath Buck's workday would be over and I'd be composed and articulate.

I was in the bubble bath phase of my evening's plans, enjoying the sensuous pleasure of hot scented water around my body and warm wine in it. I'd uncorked a nice Chardonnay and had my glass perched on the rim of the tub. My cell rang. Rats! It was still on the coffee table. I got out of the tub, grabbed a large bath towel and ran for the living room.

Buck's voice, always a nice low baritone, was deeper than usual, serious. There was a new development. He needed me to do something. I listened. Went into the kitchen for a pad and pencil, took notes. Listened some more. Assured him I'd keep him updated. We said goodbye.

To say I was shocked by Buck's revelation is an understatement. The wine bottle was on the kitchen counter and I took a little swig. Pierre wandered in the kitchen and began lapping at his milk dish.

"That was Buck. High Top de King's been called in for questioning in the shooting of Doris Hernandez."

Pierre raised his head and looked at me.

"Oh yeah?" I said, "*Now* I have your attention."

CHAPTER 14

I had a breakfast of cold leftover spaghetti together with instant coffee enhanced with Hazelnut non-dairy creamer. Do I know how to live graciously or what?

While enjoying my gourmet coffee, I went over my mail. It consisted of one bill I could barely pay (American Express), two I had to pay (phone and electricity) and a postcard from my friend Jeanette. The postcard was not from where she lived (the Bronx) but from where she worked (Manhattan) and featured the Twin Towers when they were still in existence, which made it a card to treasure. Actually any card from Jeanette was one to treasure—she was a tall, red-haired model I'd come to know when we were both doing runway gigs and a wonderful friend. When we met, she had the elegant cheekbones of Nefertiti, the slender frame of Audrey Hepburn and a mouth that could sound like a long shore man. She'd since morphed into a model of plus-size proportions, but the New York attitude remained intact. Her note said she was coming to visit me but didn't say when.

I hadn't checked my answering machine for messages the night before so I put down my coffee mug and went back to the bedroom. There was a cryptic message from Buck advising a major storm threatened to hit Puerto Vallarta, and Madame Amanda refused to fly out until satisfied all danger had passed. Couldn't blame her. There was a message that was a far-from-cryptic dissertation from Gram regarding current conditions in New Orleans. A lot of conversation about roads turning into rivers...spawning tornados...how the city's expensive system of pumps and drains was supposed to provide protection from this very type of natural disaster, etcetera, etcetera, etcetera. A final message was from Kraig, my hairdresser, in response to a call from me inquiring if the recent L.A. fires had harmed his home. He chatted about other things, finally said the fire had not hurt their townhouse and added that fighting the fires had cost L.A. eight point seven million to date. All my callers assured me of their safety and that of their loved ones so that was satisfying, but you know your social life is in the dumper when all your voicemails are weather reports.

My morning rituals accomplished, it was time to get dressed for the day. I put on a black pants suit I hadn't worn since my other life in New York. A professional appearance seemed to be in order when one is meeting with a homicide detective.

"Thank God it still fits," I said aloud.

Pierre was lying on the middle of my double bed, lightly dozing. He raised his head at the sound of my voice, his copper eyes wide.

I fastened the last button on the new, never worn, white blouse that had been hanging in my closet for weeks, pulled on some black suede high-heeled ankle boots, spread my arms and said, "What do you think?"

Pierre was too well bred to point out that the pants zipper just barely made it and the jacket had to be left open because it wouldn't close without buckling. I expected no less from one of his pedigree.

I'd been keeping Buck's Ford Explorer in my condo garage, a perk of his absence, and it would be just a twenty-minute drive to the Beverly Hills Police Station. I waited for a light to change at Wilshire and fourth and contemplated my mission. Apparently Holly King had frantically called Buck in Puerto Vallarta and shifted the focus of her concern from High Top's alleged infidelity to High Top's alleged involvement in the shooting at the Avarson place. She was alarmed by the fact that the police would actually question her husband and wanted Buck to, for all intents and purposes, investigate the police. Buck assured Holly he would find out the level of police interest in High but, no, he couldn't take care of it personally at the moment so he would send an associate. I had to confess I liked the sound of that. *An associate.*

Buck had even allowed that his necessary unavailability for this project and my resultant substitution might be propitious. He said his long-time pal and contact Homicide Detective Bob Quest had retired and a new man who'd just transferred down from Santa Fe, New Mexico was on the case, and that I might well have better luck with him than he, Buck, would. That is, he averred I was the right man for the job because I was cunning, artful and slick. Okay, he actually said I was foxy, but I knew what he meant.

He'd given me the name of the new detective but had not contacted the station in advance. I'd suggested doing so might smooth the way for my interview but Buck insisted, absent Bob Quest, he felt he no longer possessed a certain cachet. Quest himself had been pretty much a loner, had mostly been a drinking buddy of Buck's and they didn't go to the usual cop hangouts for their imbibing.

The morning smog had dissipated earlier than usual, revealing a horizon freshened by the recent rains. The temperature was in the seventies, typical for October. A perfect day for a bumbling office clerk to put the screws to an undoubtedly sharp and sophisticated homicide detective. No sweat.

CHAPTER 15

IF YOU ADOPTED A HOLLYWOOD mindset when envisioning the Beverly Hills Police Station, it would meet your expectations and then some. It was an attractive example of architecture with a clean, minimalist interior, and everyone who worked there was good looking.

I'd parked the Explorer on a block next to nearby City Hall, which represented the closest available spot and walked over. You access the station itself by walking up a winding path bordered by palm trees and other green flora to the second floor of a cement building that looks more like a museum from the outside and whose exterior is punctuated by balconies encircled by blue wrought iron.

I entered the reception area...*I doubt they call it that...* where to my left was a glass enclosed pit with a desk and a handsome young black officer acting as the receptionist *I'm certain he doesn't call it that.* Behind the officer was a large, glass enclosed framed photo of a police chief, two men in civilian suits and another officer. One of the suits looked exactly like Edward G. Robinson but probably not. That far Hollywood even the BHPD would surely not go. To the right of the glass pit was a door with glass paneling at the top and an adjacent sign advising *Administrative Offices* were within. Peeking inside, I saw several green cushioned chairs and an elaborate award board of some kind, almost five feet long with green and brass accoutrements.

To the right was a long hallway, its walls decorated first with photos of police chiefs followed by seven, floor-to-ceiling, glass-enclosed frames containing emblems from various California precincts. There were conference room doors in the middle of this emblem assemblage and the "In Use" sign was up. At the end of the hall was an open door next to a black sign with white lettering proclaiming *Crime Prevention* on one line, *Community Relations* beneath it.

The black officer said "hello" with a friendly smile. I said "hello" with a friendly smile, handed him one of Buck's business cards and said I wished to see Detective Whitehorse. He was then approached by a white guy of medium height in a gray dress shirt of some highly polished material with a tie of a slighter darker hue of gray and pants a slightly darker shade of gray than the tie. The young officer showed my card to the man, then nodded to me and said, "This is Detective Ryan." I nodded back and repeated "I'm here to see Detective Whitehorse" just on the possibility this was some kind of cagey cop scam to pass me off to an inexperienced underling.

He maintained his friendly smile, got on the phone for a minute, hung up and relayed that Detective Whitehorse was expecting me. I resumed my friendly smile and thanked him.

He further advised Detective Whitehorse was on the next floor and indicated my options of the elevator or the stairs. I took the latter and at the landing saw a sign that read *Third Floor* with an arrow with subsequent lines listing *Police Records, Traffic Division and Detective Division*. The walls on floors second and third were a tasteful pale gray and the wall-to-wall carpeting a tasteful gray-blue. Thus it was not surprising that the walls of the waiting room preceding the Detective Division boasted three tasteful downright pastoral landscapes. What was surprising was the choice of magazines on the square coffee table, which consisted of mostly stacks of *Cooking Light*. Other tomes were the equally benign: *Traveler* and *Westway.*

I was about to sit down in one of the gray upholstered chairs when I decided to take advantage of the glass wall and do more peeking. There were small, neat cubicles lined up on the right side facing a row of cream-colored filing cabinets. A pretty black girl in a brown skirt and a white ruffled blouse with her hair in a pony tail took my nosiness for impatience, stuck her head out the door and with what I'd come to recognize as the customary friendly smile advised Detective Whitehorse was expecting me and would be out in a minute.

A scant five or six minutes later, a pleasant looking man somewhere in his fifties walked through the door and greeted me. He had a trim salt and pepper moustache and beard, was about five feet ten, nice medium build and like his gray-clad brother downstairs could have just stepped out of *Esquire* magazine. He wore a white dress shirt with navy stripes, a tie with some kind of navy on navy design, dark blue pants, polished black shoes. He smiled and said "This way" and I handed him one of Buck's business cards. Maybe I would have good luck with this Detective Whitehorse simply because I was female and about twenty years his junior. I've noticed men react favorably to both attributes.

We walked past the vertical row of cubicles and stopped to our right where there were two similar open cubicle-style arrangements but with longer desk and cabinet units facing each other, fronted by swivel chairs. He pointed to a younger man with his back to me and said, "My partner's on the phone" and sat down. I guessed that Detective Whitehorse deemed he needed support for an encounter with me; hence we must wait till his partner finished his phone call. I've heard of police backup, but this was ridiculous. There were no client chairs as such around and it didn't feel seemly to sit down in an official swivel chair so I cooled my heels and remained standing.

My heels were barely room temperature two minutes later when the guy on the phone hung up, stood up and turned toward me.

"Hi. I'm Detective Whitehorse."

CHAPTER 16

THE VISION BEFORE ME WAS around six foot three. I guessed this because my dad is that height, and Detective Whitehorse loomed over me in the same degree of loom as Dad. There, of course, the resemblance ended. Where Dad has silver hair and a matching goatee, the stunning example of law enforcement before me had black hair cropped short and was clean-shaven. Where Dad was slope shouldered with a bit of a paunch, the detective was broad shouldered with abs The Rock would envy. He had high prominent cheekbones and a mouth that women would call sensuous and men would call stern. They'd both be right if you can imagine the combination. I was naturally favored with the standard BHPD smile, but the Whitehorse version featured especially white teeth and more laugh lines in the corners.

I had the presence of mind to extend my hand and mumble, "It's nice to meet you, Detective."

It didn't occur to me to offer my name but the gaff was covered as Detective Whitehorse shook my hand while simultaneously studying the card in his hand. While I was distracted by my own drooling he apparently had picked up or been handed Buck's business card.

"Lemoyne Investigations," he read aloud. "And you would be J. B. Lemoyne of course. What's the J. B. stand for?"

I was mute as if this were a tough question but this *faux pas* also seemingly went unnoticed as he smiled again and offered, "I'm Guy by the way."

All right, Frédérique, for once think on your feet. You want to impress this man. You want information from him. You want information he might normally not share with a non-professional.

All these professional wants were co-mingling with some non-related prurient wants so I struggled to become centered, I focused on the teachings of my childhood. As outrageous an Auntie Mame character as Gram could be, her core was staunchly ethical and honesty is always the best policy was one of her many bromides.

"Josephine," I answered.

"Pretty name. And the 'M' stands for? Or do you just answer to Josephine?"

Clearly my need to impress trumped any moral code handed down by Gram.

"Actually, everyone calls me Josie."

Somehow shortening my so-called name made it seem less of a lie. Logic becomes convoluted when paired with sexual tension.

"Okay, Josie, we've got a room around the corner where we can talk. Right this way."

I followed him a short distance to a door with a sign stating *Conference Room* and *Not In Use.* He held the door open for me as I entered a small room that barely held a six-foot-long table and several chairs.

As I sat down Guy remained standing, said he was going to get some coffee and asked if I'd like some. I answered in the affirmative and he left. While I waited I thought of the name *Guy*, savoring it. I'd never known anyone by that name. But then I did not know by any name many men way taller than myself and no Native Americans that I could recall. Now I knew an embodiment of all of these traits in one glorious package.

"Guy."

Egad, I just realized I said it aloud. Now I was talking to myself. This was definitely not going well.

Guy returned. He'd managed to grasp the handles of two coffee mugs in one hand and open the door with the other even though it contained little packages of sugar and powdered cream. He placed one mug in front of me and spread the cream and sugar bounty between us. He sat down.

"Didn't know if you took cream and sugar, Josephine. Hope that's enough."

All right. Now we're cooking. He'd forgotten I'd told him I go by Josie. Now I could hate his guts and get to work.

"Just cream, thanks."

"So you're here about the Hernandez case. How can I help?"

I sipped my coffee for fortification. It was still too hot.

"I'm actually here on behalf of our…my…client High Top de King. That is, Alex King's wife Holly is my…our…client and I understand he's been questioned as a suspect."

"That's true." A man of few words.

"So?"

Two can play at the few words game.

"We're investigating the possibility that someone wanted Doris Hernandez dead. We're also looking into the alternative that the bullet was intended for Sid Avarson. As you probably know, Avarson's firm is the subject of a fraud and negligence suit brought by King's attorneys. He feels the firm mismanaged his investments and lost him millions. Maybe he doesn't have much faith in the justice system or a successful outcome of his suit and thought he'd seek his own kind of revenge."

I put more cream in my coffee, stalling for a cooler temperature. Guy gulped his. Tough Beverly Hills detectives can obviously drink their java scalding hot.

"I can't claim to know King intimately, Detective Whitehorse, but what I know of him doesn't lead me to think he's the killer type."

What a crock. Spying on King from a distance doesn't constitute knowing him at all. I wondered if my deception was transparent. I wondered if he'd noticed I'd called him Detective Whitehorse, not Guy.

"You may be right. But naturally we have to pursue all avenues. And—whatever the character of King himself—sometimes a pretty rough crowd surrounds rapper types…violence of whatever degree, money laundering, drug trafficking. Sometimes all those things are part of the mix."

I finally took a healthy swallow of coffee, proud of myself.

"I can understand all that."

How big of me.

"Are there other people you've questioned?"

"We're working several different angles."

"But you are interrogating other people in addition to High Top?" I asked.

Clever girl detective asks same question twice.

"It's probably more accurate to say some were interviewed, rather than interrogated."

"I guess what I'm really asking, detective, is just what is the level of your interest in King?"

"As I say, we're working several angles," he said.

"Got that. But why King at all?"

Guy sipped his coffee, then just looked at me for a couple of beats.

"He has no alibi for the time of the shooting."

CHAPTER 17

Pierre was stomping in and out of my kitchen on his little cat feet, his tail twitching with anger and confusion. He could tell by the aromas that something edible was going on but his mistress was not sharing any of it with her feline friend. I was adding some roux to a heavy pan on the stove in which onions, bell peppers, garlic, dried shrimp, celery, red and black peppers and garlic were simmering in water the shrimp had soaked in earlier when Pierre returned for one of his visits. His little orange upturned face looked so sad that I relented and cut of a small piece of shrimp and gave it to him.

"Look, this gumbo is for Buck so that's all for you, my friend."

Pierre looked unimpressed.

"Tonight is when I confess to those times I neglected my surveillance duties so we need to butter him up, don't we?"

Pierre remained unconvinced.

"Not only that but I'm not so sure how he'll take to my unauthorized visit to Nan Kelly," I explained.

Pierre gave me a look that clearly said, "Not my problem toots. Give us some more shrimp."

Cold-hearted cat owner that I am I ignored this request and commenced stirring. I planned to put Tchaikovsky on the stereo just before Buck was due to arrive to create a soothing mood. I'd gotten a nice Pinot Grigio to go with the gumbo. Buck usually brings the wine for our dinners *a deux* but didn't mention it this time—probably due to being in shock when he learned we weren't ordering in.

For the next forty-five minutes or so I continued occasional stirring and fat skimming. To help the time pass I watched a basketball game on a small television set on my kitchen counter. The Lakers were playing an Eastern Conference team who were leading ninety-four to eighty-seven.

When it was just about time for Buck to arrive I went to the living room, put on the on the selected CD and returned to the kitchen to add the green onions and catfish. I turned the television volume lower but kept it on so Kobe Bryant, Lamar Odom and Josh Powell could continue while the New York Philharmonic played.

During a timeout I added a little more salt and did some more fat skimming as Kobe was talking to his teammates. They appeared buoyed by whatever words he was using. By the time my doorbell rang the Lakers had taken control of the game. Confident a Luke Walton slam-dunk combined with Kobe's various talents and maybe a Derek Fisher three-pointer would save the day I switched the telly off and went to open the door.

Buck had foresworn a Hawaiian shirt for a black v-necked sweater with a white crew-necked tee underneath. He was sockless and wearing black loafers, pressed jeans and a happy grin.

"Good to have you back," I said, giving him a light kiss on the cheek. "And good to see the master of Lemoyne Investigations in such fine spirits."

"The master?" Buck said. "Well now does that make you my mistress?"

I laughed.

"You wish, cowboy."

"Could be."

He almost looked serious.

Pierre had followed me to the door and arched his back slightly when he saw our guest. Buck returned the sentiment by aiming a thumb and forefinger mock gun at my cat.

"Come join me in the kitchen," I said.

Buck and Pierre, despite the mortal enemy status of their relationship, followed me into the kitchen together. I poured two glasses of wine and handed one to Buck. Pierre stood on his hind legs leaning his front paws on the kitchen cabinet next to the stove signaling a more aggressive pursuit of additional shrimp.

"What's on the menu?" Buck asked.

"Your favorite gumbo."

"My reaction is *wow* and my question is *why*?"

"And my answer is *just because*," I replied, delaying the inevitable.

"Doesn't matter," Buck said. "I'm in rare form due to the fat fee for babysitting Amanda baby in P.V."

"Glad to hear it," I said.

I picked out a small shrimp and gave it to Pierre before spooning rice into two large bowls and ladling the gumbo over the rice. I'd created two place settings in the dining room in advance complete with a large candle shaped like a Buddha head in the center of the table. Buck carried the gumbo bowls from the kitchen; I brought the wine glasses and then went back for the bottle.

Buck raved about the gumbo. Well, he said, "This is good." That's downright gushing in Buckspeak.

As we ate and sipped wine, I explained about the gap in my High Top surveillance due to the Torres funeral. Buck listened politely, expressed sympathy for the loss of the Hernandez and Torres families and assured me that constituted just cause for missing a few hours of surveillance.

"There's more," I said.

"A nice after dinner liqueur?" Buck asked.

Rats. Another omission in my menu planning.

"No. Another gap in my stalking duties."

I described my visit to Nan Kelly's home and my reasons for same. I interspersed my recitation with descriptions of the home's general layout, living room décor, the delightful patio and the wonderful ocean view to add a light touch to my transgression. Didn't have the desired effect. Buck went ever so slightly ballistic.

"Damn it, Freddy. I don't know enough about the Hernandez case to know whether it's a good idea to approach Scott Kelly," he said.

"Well actually I talked to Nan Kelly. Scott's still missing, making him rather unapproachable."

"Cute. You know what I mean. May I remind you you're not licensed so don't go taking such damn independent actions. And why the hell didn't you mention this when I called from P.V.?"

“Well I guess I was afraid you’d get mad. Thank goodness I was wrong.”

CHAPTER 18

My perturbed guest and I finished our meal in silence. Buck helped himself to a second helping of gumbo, then a third. I nursed my one glass of wine. A limitation that was uncharacteristic of me of late. Buck had a fresh glass with each gumbo refill. He helped me clear the table and stack the dishwasher. Without a word, Buck picked up our glasses in one hand, the wine bottle in another and headed for the couch. I followed and we both sat down on opposite ends. He placed the glasses and bottle on the coffee table, refilled my glass and his own.

My silent companion then reached in his hip pocket and pulled out a cigar. He unwrapped it, sniffed the cut end. Since I didn't smoke, Buck never indulged his love of stogies when visiting me. I'd never asked him not to; he'd just assumed. Tonight this was to be his gesture of protest, my punishment as it were. He lit up and took a drag. I was thinking how sophomoric he was being when the aroma hit me—sort of spicy and flavorful like a light cappuccino with a hint of cinnamon. I had to admit I rather liked it so I relaxed and sipped my wine.

Buck's face was puckered into what passed for a scowl. Tchaikovsky was still playing but he'd seemingly only managed to sooth Pierre who, his hunger appeased by two extra shrimp—one from me and one from his nemesis, was dozing contentedly nearby in one of Gram's velvet chairs.

Buck went into the kitchen and brought back a saucer to serve as an ashtray. He finally spoke as he walked toward the couch.

"Okay kid, what did you learn from Scott Kelly's wife?"

He tamped out the cigar, settled in on his end of the couch and gave me a small smile.

I sighed.

"Only that Scott's disappearance is not the first time. And that such leavings are part and parcel of their marriage. She was quite sanguine about the whole thing."

Buck grinned.

"Sanguine, huh?"

"I always use fifty cent words when I've failed as a private eye. Restores my feeling of being smart," I said.

"A common device of us private eyes," he said. "I lose my usual sangfroid on occasion myself."

Pierre raised his head to look at us, then lowered it, closing his eyes as if to say *gimme a break.*

"What should I have found out?" I asked.

"Actually I don't know. Maybe more about their marriage, especially how it's been since his last hiatus. Probed some to determine if the current leave of absence really was because of marital grief—fighting on their part, or one fight, or money problems, in-law problems, kid problems. Like that. Hell, you're both women; ask about their sex life."

"What if she asks about mine?" I asked.

"Asks about your what?"

"My sex life," I said.

"Damn, see what you mean. That'll end the conversation right there."

"What I wouldn't give for a baseball bat right now," I threatened.

Buck chuckled soundlessly.

"Okay, let's get serious," he said. "Here's the deal. Holly King is eager for us to continue working for her" He punctuated the air with his cigar. "And, doll, I'm eager to do so because that gal seems to have connections."

"She does? More so than Amanda Roberts?" I asked.

"Well I don't know about the *more so* part but in a different venue. Amanda runs strictly with the actor crowd with a director or two thrown in for good measure. She speaks well of me to that clique judging by the business we get from her referrals. But Holly mingles with the rappers and the rock and rollers. She drops names with every other sentence. How much of that is show and how much is substance who knows, but it's worth considering."

"So we're going to do what? You're going to take over tailing High Top?" I asked.

"Nope. Holly may question hubby's fidelity but she's certain he didn't attempt to whack Avarson. She doesn't trust the cops to prove this. In Holly's mind, the cops are eager to pin it on High Top, a black guy. She doesn't trust them to pursue other suspects. Wants me to find the sonovabitch that shot Hernandez and put lover boy in the clear," he said.

"So no more stalking High Top to catch him in a love nest?" I asked.

"Oh she wants us to keep trailing her husband and also find the killer."

"No job too big for Joseph Buckley Lemoyne, ace detective," I said.

"It would be if I had to do both. No, you my friend are going to continue stalking Mr. King while I do the heavy lifting would-be-killer-wise," Buck said.

"Starting when?" I asked.

"Starting tomorrow."

"Oh…well….it's just…," I began.

"Oh…well…it's just…what?"

"A friend of mine, Tulabelle, is having an art exhibit in Santa Fe tomorrow. I promised I'd fly out for it. It's her first real break and they want all the bodies they can get in attendance," I said.

"What the hell kind of name is Tulabelle?"

"She's from London but with more of a Liverpool accent. I think her last name is Noel."

"She's such a good friend you're flying to New Mexico for her but you don't know her last name?"

"Actually I don't know her that well. But she's my friend Kraig's girlfriend."

"And Kraig would be?"

"My hair dresser."

Buck's features folded into a tormented pucker again.

I knew I should have served dessert.

CHAPTER 19

I'D TAKEN A SOUTHWEST FLIGHT to Albuquerque, as there were no direct flights from Los Angeles into Santa Fe. Now I was chugging along in a shuttle bus I'd picked up at the Albuquerque International Sunport airport for the final leg to Santa Fe.

It was a bright sunny day. The ride was straight highway surrounded by desert, mountains and cactus. I was told the drive would take a little over an hour so I had plenty of time to stare out the widow at jagged mountains and cacti and ruminate on my solo stint as a private eye vis-à-vis the Avarson case. Doris Hernandez was still in a coma. I'd called her home number, her sister Rosa had answered. After inquiries as to Doris' latest medical status and how the family was holding up, I'd attempted some delicate questioning in regard to possible suspects and motives.

I knew Doris had been widowed years ago so there was no disenchanted spouse with murderous intentions. Rosa had begun quietly crying while assuring me that Doris was loved by one and all. A common assertion when a loved one is killed or almost killed but in the instance of Doris Hernandez it was not hard to believe. I asked how the young people in the family were coping with the tragedy as a way of approaching the subject of the two teenage boys I'd heard murmuring at the funeral. Rosa's sobs increased as she commenced a litany of names and emotional reactions. Maria had been too distraught to go to school or resume her high school cheerleading duties since the incident. Anthony was going to school but then not coming home until very late; she suspected he was out drinking with his buddies. Theresa appeared to be handling it very well but then she always kept her feelings to herself. Pedro, she said, was like Maria—he would not leave the house, but he was telling his homies that he had the flu.

Rosa continued her descriptions punctuated by sniffles and "Jesus Mary and Joseph, why this happen?" and similar exclamations. The remaining names were predominantly female so I'd stopped making notes and waited for her fervor to subside. Rosa ended her dissertation with a plea to St. Anthony to find the shooter and then made the same request of me.

"It is so senseless, Frédérique. I remember Doris telling me you're a model and now you're a private detective? So can you work for us? Can you find the person who did this? We'll pay your fee whatever it is," she said.

"I'm still a model, Rosa," I'd said, "and I'm not a *licensed* investigator, but I work for one and we'll do whatever we can to bring this person to justice."

Bring this person to justice? My delusions of grandeur knew no bounds. That and I'd been watching too much Law & Order. But it felt like the right thing to say to Rosa.

"Thank you, Frédérique. Thank you so much. Doris always say as a person you very, very good," she said.

But as a private eye not very, very smart.

"Thank you, Rosa. I promise to keep in touch and call you the minute I learn anything," I said.

I'm not a private eye but I play one on T.V.

"I know you will, Frédérique. Go with God," Rosa said.

Earlier at one point in the middle of Rosa's discourse, I'd managed to interrupt and pinpoint the male names she was providing.

"Rosa, I wonder if I could talk to some of the young men in your family sometime. Maybe Pedro and Anthony? I have no sisters but I grew up with one brother. We've always been very close so I relate to young boys very well," I said.

As I thought of those good looking, twenty-something Hernandez boys, the Art Garfunkle song that mentions Mrs. Robinson slid through my thoughts but I hoped not Rosa's.

"That is, perhaps I could say something that would help them cope and in questioning your family it would be a place to start," I added.

If a more lascivious motivation occurred to Rosa, she gave no sign.

"Of course, Frédérique. You call when you get back from your trip and we will make a plan. The boys, they love for to meet a tall, pretty blonde," she said.

Maybe she read my mind after all.

I hadn't wanted to alarm Rosa by mentioning that at the funeral I'd overheard what sounded like gang-related conversation emanating from two of the teenaged boys present so I thanked her, apologized for interrupting and urged her to continue. The succeeding list of girls' names was punctuated by those of a couple of males but the stories attached to them indicated they were under the age of eight or ten so they were not in the running as candidates for information.

Something else nagged at my consciousness as the bus rolled along amidst the juxtaposition of desert plain and mountains. I'd changed the message on my answering machine to announce my out-of-town absence for two days. When I checked my messages remotely from LAX just before departing, there was a cryptic call from Nan Kelly.

"Freddy...Freddy, please call me when you get back... something strange is going on."

CHAPTER 20

I'd checked into the Hotel Santa Fe, unpacked a few things and taken a long shower as a restorative after the rigors of travel. Kraig had recommended the hotel as he and Tulabelle were staying there. I called their room, they were out so I left a voicemail.

A couple of hours of daylight remained so I decided to go for a run before dinner. With the exception of a guest visit now and then to Buck's health club and occasional swims in a nearby YMCA, the obsession I'd had for exercise when modeling full time in New York had become a thing of the past. But guilt or just a desire to be outdoors overtook me from time to time. Today I was experiencing equal parts of both, so I donned black sweat pants, a red tee and my white Reeboks and fastened my fanny pack around my waist to hold my room card, cell phone and money.

I walked thru the lobby, a tribute to Native American culture with its large white Kiva fireplace and colorful couches and pillows, and headed for the front desk. There I asked about a good running area. A tall lanky young man with a head full of tight brown curls recommended the route he uses.

Thus directed I headed out toward Paseo de Teralla. Through a canopy of willow and oak trees purple splotches of evening shadow invaded the last tendrils of hazy sunshine. I passed several old Victorian homes. One of the yards must have contained freshly dug earth as I detected the aroma I'd noticed at Edna Torres' funeral. As the streets narrowed I slowed my run to a walk to admire the old adobe homes, some surrounded by high walls but visible through wrought-iron gates. If I ever foreswore the more confined existences in my Brooklyn Heights brownstone and Santa Monica condo and became the owner of a real house, I mused that I would have high walls like these. Strong, impenetrable, keeping the outside world at a distance. If any such refuge really exists. A bullet had invaded the sanctuary of wealth and privilege of Sid Avarson's Beverly Hills house. It had penetrated the homes of the Hernandez and Torres families as surely as if it were imbedded in the stucco walls of their small East Los Angeles homes. And if Nan Kelly's brief phone message foreshadowed the intrigue it suggested, then the intrusive bullet had washed up on the shores of Malibu as well.

I tousled my hair with my fingers as I often do when its gotten too flat but on this occasion as a gesture to dispel gloomy thoughts from my brain. I was here to have a good time. To lend Kraig support, mingle with the other gallery guests tomorrow, compliment Tula belle's art to them and probably drink complimentary champagne. I'd try calling Kraig's room again when I got back and perhaps the three of us, alone or together with any of their other friends in residence, could have a pre-exhibit celebratory dinner.

It felt good to jog along at a gentle clip. The neighborhood was peaceful and quiet. There were no other pedestrians and the only sign of life I encountered was a gray cat perched on the roof of a parked car. It made me think of Pierre. And inexplicably I next thought of basketball. I didn't know the televised schedule by heart, but I believed I'd missed a game last night. I worried about Derek's arthritic toe and Kobe's illness from a bad hamburger. There was nothing I could do about either. It's not easy being a Laker fan, so much responsibility.

A slight wind had dusted up and the sky was dimming to a silver blue so I turned around and retraced my steps to the hotel. As I entered the lobby I spied a gift shop off to the right. My little white Reeboks headed straight for it despite my stern protestations. You can take the girl out of New York but not Fifth-Avenue-shopping inclinations.

Browsing around the tiny shop there was fortunately very little jewelry to tempt me but there was an array of Native American pottery and blankets that called out to my American Express card with equally compelling urgency. I was the sole customer and there was but one employee in the store, a short balding man with a kind face. He smiled. I smiled. Two happy occupants of the world of commerce.

I was examining an orange, black and turquoise colored ceramic jar as a possible addition for my mantelpiece when I heard a voice behind me.

"Josie Lemoyne?"

I turned and saw the source. Detective Guy Whitehorse.

CHAPTER 21

HE WAS BEAMING DOWN AT me with the same engaging grin I'd enjoyed at the police station. I stood perfectly still looking up at him, temporarily mute like a smitten schoolgirl. I was suddenly aware that I'd worked up a bit of a sweat, that most of my lipstick was probably gone, that my hair was probably matted to my head unattractively and that I wasn't speaking. Well I could at least correct the last part.

"Well, hello there, Detective," I smiled. "Fancy seeing y'all here."

I lapse into Gram's southern colloquiums when un-nerved.

"Come to this hotel all the time. I've never seen you here," he said.

"It's my first time. Visiting here, that is. I've never been here before."

"How do you like it?" he asked.

"It's great. It's so…so uh…"

"So Indian," he said. The grin again.

"That too," I said. "It is really lovely here. I just went for a run and the area is just charming."

"I'll bet the area thought the same of the runner."

"Why, sir, you do make me blush."

All right, Frédérique, now you're carrying the southern shtick too far.

"What brings you here?" he asked.

"A friend is showing her art in a gallery here tomorrow night. It's a big opportunity for her, really the first exhibit of any note she's ever had. I'm just here to lend moral support," I said.

"Very nice of you," he said.

Out of the corner of my eye I could see the little bald man looking at us. His countenance remained pleasant and he showed no impatience.

"And you're here because…?"

"Just taking some vacation time. I like the area and friends of mine have an interest in this hotel. I'm just going to relax, hang out with them. And it doesn't hurt that they give me special rates," he said.

"Relaxed down time in this beautiful place where you can save money to boot. Doesn't get any better than that," I smiled.

"Oh it could get better."

"It could?"

"It could if you have dinner with me tonight. The hotel has a nice restaurant. Can I meet you in the lobby about an hour from now, or whatever time works best for you, and take you there?"

I thought about Kraig and Tulabelle. I was their guest in a sense. I thought of my plan to call them for dinner, at least give them the first option on my time.

"An hour would be fine," I said.

"Great. I'll see you then."

Guy turned and left, strolling toward the lobby door with a long stride, headed for the outside. He'd been standing so close to me in the gift shop I'd only noticed the gray tee shirt he was wearing and his muscular arms. Now I saw that he was wearing navy sweat pants and sneakers, probably going for a short run.

I put the jar I'd been clutching on the counter with a nod that I hoped looked apologetic. The little bald man just smiled and said, "Have a lovely evening."

I headed for the elevator and thought about how nice it would have been if we'd run together.

Then I thought about how I'd abandoned an understood commitment with Kraig and Tulabelle to have dinner with Guy.

Then I thought about the sweet little old man in the gift shop.

Overcome with one guilty thought too many, I went back to the shop and purchased the damn jar.

CHAPTER 22

A MUSICIAN PLAYING A FLUTE WAS weaving his way around and between the guests' tables in the Corn Dance Café. I didn't recognize the tune he was playing, but it was mellifluous and soothing.

I was examining the wine list. As I did so Detective Guy Whitehorse seemed to be examining me. At least, he was staring and ignoring his own menu. Tonight I was unapologetically clad in my New York style. It's what my wardrobe primarily consists of and what I know best. A slim, gray skirt, gray print chiffon blouse and my favorite Christian Louboutin red ankle boots. I was carrying a brown Chanel bag my mother gave me years ago.

"Do you like champagne?" Guy asked.

"Yes."

"Then let's have some," he said, beckoning the waiter.

The waiter came over, Guy ordered a bottle of Perrier and a bottle of Louis Roederer Vintage Brut.

"Is it some special occasion?" I asked.

"You mean because of the champagne?"

"Yes."

"It is if you say it is," he grinned broadly, "Josie."

"Ah," I said and looked away momentarily.

"And what does *ah* mean?"

I looked back at Guy, unconsciously stiffening my back.

"*Ah* as in the-night-is-still-young special occasion?" I said.

"Miss Josie," Guy said, "you're a sharp detective but in this instance your deductive reasoning is flawed."

"That so?"

"Yep. In this instance the meaning is this: it's a special occasion simply because I'm having dinner here with you," he said.

"You know what? I believe you."

"Highly intuitive of you," he said.

The waiter arrived with the champagne and Perrier.

"You're not joining me?" I asked.

"Never touch the stuff," he smiled.

"Never touch the stuff now or have quit touching the stuff?"

"Never got in habit. I'm not a recovering champagne drinker if that's what you mean," he said.

"I'm sorry. That was a rude question on my part."

"No offense taken. Us detectives are always probing. Comes with the territory," he smiled.

I sipped my wine and Guy continued to study me.

"Do you like your wine?" he said. "I'm not a connoisseur, but I know that brand of champagne is preferred by the chef here."

"It's perfect and, don't worry, you can't go wrong. Champagne is the most quality controlled wine there is."

"Then drink up, little lady. Just don't get a headache."

"That's an old wives' tale, Guy. Champagne is actually one of the gentler wines. You shouldn't get a headache from it unless you really over-imbibe. It's low in histamines and calories but full of healthy minerals."

"Watch out, you'll convert me."

"No, I wouldn't try to do that. I should cut down on booze myself."

"You've got a problem?"

"Oh no. At least not yet. I mostly stick with wine, avoid the hard stuff. (*Ha*!) And at some long dinner party, I'll drink the young wine first, then the old."

"The chef here seems to prefer the older wines."

"That idea goes back as far as the New Testament. At the marriage of Cana, the best wines were served first, before the guests got too drunk out of their minds to appreciate them. That's why it was surprising to them when the wine Jesus made from water was served later in the meal and proved to be the better wine."

Guy nodded with interest, but I decided to change the subject.

Maybe my Park Avenue roots were becoming too apparent. I was already operating under a false name with this good man and now I sounded pretentious.

We chatted about the basics regarding our backgrounds in general.

"So you were born in France, Josie. Always thought there was something special about French women, do you agree?"

"Well, I left Paris when I was six and grew up mostly in New Orleans, moving to New York when I was eighteen, but I know what you mean. You see women in Paris who may not look like classic beauties, but they carry themselves in such a way that makes them seem profoundly beautiful," I said. "Even if they have odd features or are somewhat overweight or whatever, there's an air of confidence about them. The French call it *bien dans la peau*, when you're fully at ease with yourself."

"Go back there much?" Guy asked.

"When I was a child, we went there regularly on holiday but, no, not recently. I have dual citizenship, and I do long to go back."

"Never been to Europe," Guy confessed. "But have a yen to. For now, coming here every few months is very satisfying."

We talked more about Santa Fe, about how I liked life in New York generally and how he liked life in New Mexico generally. We both had rave reviews for the towns we'd abandoned for California. Guy didn't make small talk. His commentary was substantive and to the point.

I sipped my wine and looked at Guy as he rhapsodized about going horseback riding near a reservation located between Albuquerque and Santa Fe. He was wearing a well-tailored black and white tweed jacket, black turtleneck sweater, pressed jeans and cowboy boots.

The waiter left the dinner menus with us. Guy offered his recommendations. I listened and offered my caloric concerns and weight loss goals.

"I'm not going to say you're a perfect size the way you are because I have a hunch you know that," he said.

"Well a girl likes to hear that but I used to weigh around one hundred and five."

A lot of guys would see that as a bid for more flattery but Detective Whitehorse wasn't taking the bait.

He looked up from the menu.

"You haven't said what you think of my size."

"I think you're perfect," I said.

"Well a guy likes to hear that."

Turning back to the menu, he said, "I'm having the bison tenderloin. Comes with my favorite garlic mashed potatoes."

"I'm going to go with the duck breast with blackberry sauce. Something called griddled grits comes with that. How would you describe griddled grits?" I asked.

"I'll use it in a sentence," he replied. "That dashing Guy Whitehorse really griddles my grits."

"Oh my. Just when I'd decided you were of a humble, unassuming breed."

"We Navajo are exactly that. Peaceable and not aggressive," he said.

"Navajo. Is that your tribe?"

"What's your tribe, Josie?" he smiled.

I laughed.

"Mostly French with a couple of Cajuns we don't talk about."

"Mine's mostly Navajo with a few Hopi we don't admit to," he said.

"And your friends who have an interest in this hotel? They're Navajo?"

"No the tribe that owns this hotel is the Picuris," he said.

He pronounced it *pick-a-reese.*

As our dinners arrived, we began to eat, mostly in silence. The flutist had left. We were seated near the fireplace and at one point we realized we were both gazing at the fire at the same time, turned to each other and just smiled, wordlessly acknowledging our mutual appreciation.

As I sipped my wine, I suddenly saw Kraig and Tulabelle walking toward us, their expressions vibrant and happy. They greeted me with an effusive "There you are!" and kisses on the cheek. Last week Tula's hair had been chestnut with purple-ish overtones; today it was jet black and gelled into small spikes all over her tiny head. I'd loved this girl since I first met her in Kraig's shop. She had big almond eyes that fairly popped out of her little heart-shaped face, was warm with an eccentricity aided by being British.

Guy stood as I made introductions all around. Kraig and Tulabelle had eaten dinner elsewhere, returned to the hotel and stopped by the Café on a last minute whim for some dessert. There were no tables available so they'd decided to call it a night when they spied us.

There was brief chitchat about Guy's being here on vacation and Tulabelle's gallery exhibition. Guy asked about the type of painting Tulabelle did and Tula insisted Guy join us tomorrow night.

"You can escort this lady," Kraig suggested, nodding toward me. "That way the lonely little tart won't be trailing us around."

"Thanks, pal," I murmured.

"The tart will be safe in my care," Guy said.

"You'd better take good care of our lovely friend, ducks," Tulabelle grinned.

She was wearing a loose pink jersey with black tights that fit like a second skin. At five feet tall, Tula always favored stiletto heels and today's version was gold pumps. Guy definitely seemed to notice the pink creation and the tights. I felt a jealous twinge, but decided if he'd noticed only the shoes I'd really be in trouble.

Tula waggled one stubby, unpolished fingernail at Guy. "Is that a promise?"

"Not at all," Guy smiled.

Before leaving, Kraig gave Guy directions to the gallery and an invitation for a nightcap later in their suite.

As Kraig and Tula departed, I breathed a sigh of relief. *Thank goodness they never called me Freddy.*

The waiter brought the check at Guy's signal.

"Do you feel like a nightcap either here or elsewhere?" he asked.

"No thanks. Between all the travel and my run I'm done in."

"I'll walk you to your room" he said.

"You Navajo are so gallant."

"Gotta take care of the little tart."

He relished quoting Kraig just a little too much.

We reached my room. I opened the door, then turned to Guy and did the thank-you-for-a-wonderful-evening thing.

Leaning against the door with his left arm, he bent down slightly and gave me a kiss that was tender and gentle but long lasting.

"Good night *Frédérique*."

CHAPTER 23

"I'D LIKE TO BUY YOU breakfast" I said.

I had just rung up Guy's room and he'd answered.

"Is it some special occasion?" he asked.

"You mean because I'm treating you to breakfast?"

"Yes."

"It is if you say it is, Detective Whitehorse."

"Ah," he said.

"And what does *ah* mean?"

"*Ah* as in I'm-sorry-I-gave-you-a-false-name-Detective-Whitehorse?" he said.

"What?" was my clever retort.

"You lied." Guy said it lightly.

"Only verbally."

It was Guy's turn to say *what*?

"Nothing," I said. "Just a line I remember from a Broadway play."

"Oh."

"Do you want a free breakfast or not?" I said.

"Shall I meet you in the Cafe?"

"Give me thirty minutes."

"See you then," Guy said.

I smiled to myself and stretched. I was still in bed, barely awake with visions of sugarplums, champagne and one long kiss in my head.

I had called Guy the minute I woke up, just in case he was an early riser and would go for a morning run or something and I'd miss him. After my call, I got up, went over to the coffeemaker, did the coffee filter drill and pushed Brew.

I took off my Victoria Secret long red jersey nightgown and headed toward the shower. My cell phone rang. It was Buck.

"Hey big time hotshot detective," he said.

"You've got the wrong room."

"No, no. That must be you. Can't be me. Cause I'm sitting here in the Honda doing small time P.I. stuff, enjoying another tedious day of tailing one High Top de King," he said.

"And he's clean as a whistle, right?"

"Pure as the driven snow. Not a ho in sight," he said.

"What's the word on Doris?"

"Still in a coma I'm sorry to say," he said.

"Have you talked to her sister?"

"That's who updates me on her condition. You asked me to keep in touch with the family."

"Thanks so much. You're a sweetheart."

"From your mouth to Angelina Jolie's ear," he said.

"I thought your true love was Sharon Stone."

"Decisions, decisions."

Changing the subject, he said, "More bad news kid. The game with Portland? Score was Portland 102, Lakers 90."

"Rats. This is what happens when I don't watch the game wearing my lucky number 24 tee shirt."

"What can I say? You suck as a fan, Fred. But here's some good news," he said.

"Lay it on me."

"My ole buddy Bob Quest spoke to the new guy in Beverly Hills…" he began.

"Detective Whitehorse?"

"That's the one. Guy Whitehorse. Got a good rep from what I hear. And Quest laid it out for Whitehorse—how far he and I go back, what a good dude I am, etcetera. Suggested he cooperate with me on the Hernandez case. Turns out they're both alums of the University of Arizona. That probably helped too," he said.

"Well that *is* good news. Tell me, did Whitehorse mention my visit to the station?"

"Matter of fact he did. Whitehorse is supposed to be a sharp hombre but he was confused on that score," he said.

"How's that?" I asked.

"Had to set him straight. Kept referring to you as Josie somebody."

CHAPTER 24

THERE WERE MORE IMPORTANT QUESTIONS spinning in my brain. Why was Doris still in a coma? Was someone after the Hernandez and Torres families? Why did Nan Kelly think something strange was going on? Why were Buck and I spending our days tailing a famous rap artist for infidelity when no hanky-panky whatsoever was occurring? Could Alex High Top de King, seemingly devoted spouse and successful businessman, also be a killer?

I couldn't solve those puzzles at the moment, but I could ask myself what I'd wear for breakfast with a certain police detective to knock his socks off and hopefully worm some answers from him.

After a quick shower and washing and blow-drying my hair, it was wardrobe time. I settled on my favorite black cargo pants, rolled up a few inches below my knee and right-on Manolo Blahnik ankle-high, stiletto heel boots. The shoes were a pale gold color and laced up the front, which I hoped gave them a sort of frontier flavor. I topped this off with a white tank top and added round turquoise dangling earrings for more Western flair. The earrings had been a costume jewelry purchase from Bloomingdales so the turquoise wasn't real. I doubted Guy would divine the fake jewelry aspect of this getup. He'd just be blown away by the fashionably Santa Fe look of it all.

As I approached the Café, I saw Guy already seated at one of the center tables. His chair was pulled to the side and his long legs stretched out in front of him crossed at the ankles. He was wearing jeans a darker shade of blue than yesterday's, a red flannel shirt with a v-necked white tee underneath and tan cowboy boots. Guy was holding a menu, talking, and laughing with one of the waitresses. She was pretty, looked to be around twenty-two or so, with waist-length black hair. She was also very well endowed in the chest region, a claim I can't make.

Another waiter joined them. The waitress leaned down and whispered something in Guy's ear. He roared with the laughter and she rubbed his shoulder affectionately. The other waiter chuckled and went on his way.

As I neared the table, Guy stood. The waitress remained at his side, holding a stack of menus.

"Good morning," I said.

"Good morning," Guy said and leaned over and kissed me on the cheek.

Take that Miss Mammary Glands.

"Freddy this is Sophie Lonetalker. Sophie, Frédérique Bonnaire," Guy said.

We each said *hi* and shook hands. Sophie handed me a menu, asked if I wanted coffee and departed.

Guy selected a multi-ingredient omelet that sounded good so I said I'd have the same. Sophie returned with two beige mugs of steaming coffee, then left after Guy gave our orders.

"This place must be very relaxing for you. You have friends here and the whole area is so peaceful. You can really clear your head and leave police work behind," I said.

"It's exactly like that," he said. "I hope it's the same for you."

"It is," I smiled.

We sipped our coffee. There had just been three young couples occupying the tables when I'd entered the restaurant. Now a group of middle-aged men arrived informally dressed but more in the style of business casual. No one wore jeans or boots, just golf shirts and slacks. It reminded me of Sid Avarson, and I wondered how life after the shooting was treating him and whether he'd hired a bodyguard or called a moratorium on travel or had a nervous breakdown. Although he was more often an inflictor of the last circumstance.

"Do you have a strong hunch the bullet was really intended for Sid Avarson?" I asked.

"Ah," Guy said, "Only one of us is leaving police work behind."

"I'm so sorry. I just..."

"As we told the press, the shooter remains at large and we have no information on motive," he said.

"I bet I'm as aggravating as the reporters."

"But a lot better looking," he smiled.

Sophie brought our omelets just as I was saying, "No more shop talk," and I could swear she cracked a small smile.

Over dinner last night we'd mostly talked about Santa Fe and other cities where we'd lived so I asked him about his life prior to becoming a cop and he answered in anecdotal style, briefly touching on funny tidbits of college life in Arizona, being a cop in Colorado, making detective in Santa Fe.

I hopefully amused him with comical incidents during my modeling days in New York and my life in general there, including a much-abbreviated synopsis of the Sonny Bob marriage and parting. I left out my brief period of doing secretarial temp work as this had involved Avarson.

Also hoped he wouldn't ask whether I was a licensed private detective.

"Must have been great fun to be a New York model," Guy said.

"It certainly has its perks," I said. "I loved a lot of it, but I never felt grounded. You don't have a set schedule. I was always running around, not knowing where I'd be next."

"But you're still pursuing it?" Guy said.

"I am. It's all I really know at this point. I'm hoping for more commercial gigs. With that kind of work, your weight can fluctuate a bit. You don't have to be super skinny, not every little inch counts."

"How'd you get started?"

"My mother sent some pictures of me to a couple of top agencies. She was sure I'd succeed, and I caught her fever. But I was independent. Moved out of my parents' apartment and into a cramped, four-bedroom number with three other models. It was an old building, but we didn't get a break on the rent—charged us each eight hundred a month. I walked around New York for three or four years before booking any major gigs."

"I imagine New York can be a tough town," Guy said.

"It can, but it wasn't just New York. I pounded the pavement in

London, Paris, Milan and Miami. Back in New York I eventually got a booker—a great guy named Marc Caress—and I was on my way."

"The travel part must have been great," Guy said.

He was letting his coffee get cold, so intrigued was he with my real profession.

"Yes, loved going back to my native France of course. As for Italy, I hate Milan. It has some sleazy people. It can be full of temptations for models, but I managed to avoid them. In Europe, and even New York, I generally avoided the party scene. Was a hermit, compared to some of the girls."

Sophie arrived for our empty plates and to refresh our coffee. I gave her my room number to cover the bill.

"By the way, Lemoyne told me you're working for him temporarily. You've given up modeling?"

"Oh, no. It's just going kind of slow for me here..."

Not to mention I'm not twenty-two anymore.

"...but I'm optimistic. Cindy Crawford has crafted a career with real longevity. I plan to do the same."

Saying it out loud like that made me believe, for the first time, that I could do it.

"Speaking of plans, what are yours for today?" Guy asked.

"Just kill a few hours sightseeing or shopping till it's time to get ready for Tulabelle's exhibit."

"How's going horseback riding with me strike you?" he said.

"Strikes me just fine."

"Great. I know a place near here. It's about an hour's drive but the scenery's worth it," he said.

"Okay," I said. "I don't really need any more coffee. But you finish yours and I'll go up and change."

"Good idea," Guy grinned. "Lose that L.A. look."

CHAPTER 25

Guy had borrowed a friend's car, a mint-condition red 1975 Corvette convertible with tan upholstery. The ride to Broken Saddle Riding Company passed pleasantly and felt a lot less than an hour. It was cool and sunny with a sharp wind whipping around the Cerrillos Hills.

At the stables, Guy and I were given horses that the owner said were Tennessee Walkers. We mounted the western saddles. I'd only ridden English saddles, but Guy assured me I'd be fine.

"We even have tee shirts, honey," the owner said, "that say no English spoken here."

Swell.

We started off single file in a group that included two other couples. After a few minutes, Guy moved off to one side and paused so I could catch up to him.

"Are you doing okay?" he asked.

"I'm fine," I said. "All these horses look pretty tame. Actually downright shaggy."

"Oh shaggy they may look but Roy Rogers' Trigger was a Tennessee Walker. Anyway they're easy going. That's why I knew you'd do fine."

"He *is* comfortable. Sort of rocks with me," I said.

"Exactly. Story is the Tennessee Walker was developed by southerners who wanted to ride in comfort over their vast plantations."

"So an ole New Orleans girl like me should feel right at home," I said.

"You got it."

The trail cut along the sides of hills, going gradually higher and higher amid sporadic piñon and juniper. The views were spectacular. Just by shifting in our saddles, we could see what Guy identified to me as the wide purple slopes of Sangre de Cristos, the Sandios, the Jemez and the Ortiz ranges.

As the trail widened, we all rode faster, cantering around bounders and large chamisas and between ridged and fan shaped sandy walls.

Guy rode a horse as if he seemed to do everything, with calm self-possession. I rode with what I hoped was the kind of possession that keeps the rider in possession of the horse and saddle.

The afternoon sun melted into streams of shadows and the mountains became a distant horizon, gray and amber tinted. The other riders rode in silence and at an appreciable distance from each other, respectful of our mutual commune with Mother Earth and Sky.

With the quietude and the peaceful landscape, it was certainly a prime opportunity for reflection and I found my thoughts drifting.

I watched Guy riding up ahead of me. With his erect posture, broad shoulders and long legs he seemed to meld as one with the large, forceful animal beneath him. Would he be the one to erase my pain over Sonny Bob?

Gram said to me once, "Everyone's looking for love sugar,
and all they find is someone else looking for love."

Gram and I had many heart to heart talks during my stay with her in New Orleans and by phone since, and Gram had a parcel of wisdom to impart each time. When the subject was Sonny Bob or the fallout from Sonny Bob, she'd say, "Let go of the myth of the perfect man. If you think you can fix a man, think again. Let go of the myth of the perfect man. It's a myth after all, Frédérique."

I'd invariably respond that I felt like half a pair of scissors without Sonny or a similar whine of self-pity.

"Oh, pish tosh, you're Frédérique Toussaint and you always will be, darlin'. Focus on your own powers…and you've got 'em whether you realize it or not. Never apologize for who you truly are. You got inner strength in spades, sugar. Remember that."

"I'm told I have poise, Gram, but…"

"*But* nothin'. Practice that poise by what you don't give away about yourself. Have real relationships with every livin' soul you know and if a relationship isn't workin', move on..."

"I've certainly done that, haven't I? But..."

"Stop buttin' me, Frédérique. And stop feelin' so everlastingly sorry for yourself. Your real enemy is not a cold, cruel world. Your real enemy is your completely unnecessary anxiety about that world!"

At this point, Gram would terminate the call to go pour herself a glass of Sherry and I would sit up straighter and take deep breaths, resolute in my goal to go forth and conquer any demons, from within or without.

As Gram's various bromides swirled in my consciousness, I noticed the stables a short distance ahead. The time had passed pleasantly and had felt like a marvelous solitary experience, despite the presence of Guy and the other riders.

One by one we arrived at the Stable's hitching post. Guy and I dismounted and headed for the Toyota for the ride back to the hotel. Guy got a blanket out of the trunk and suggested I get in the back seat and take a little nap.

"You'll be sore for a while so get some rest," he said.

I gratefully climbed in, pulling the blanket around me.

Back at the hotel, two men seated on a couch called out a greeting to Guy. He waved back and raised his forefinger to indicate one minute. Guy walked me to the elevator and excused himself to join his couch friends.

I got another cheek kiss and a "See you later."

I didn't exactly know what *later* would mean. We hadn't discussed a time to meet to go to Tula's exhibit, if we'd have a drink beforehand or if we'd ride over with Kraig.

Perhaps it was the desert heat or the peaceful ride or the comfort of Gram's voice in my head, but right now such details didn't matter.

CHAPTER 26

THE CROWD AT TULABELLE'S EXHIBIT more resembled a group at one of Manhattan's galleries than the cozy gathering of Kraig's friends I'd anticipated. There were, to quote a phrase I think I saw in W magazine once, a veritable sea of who's who. There were even two of Buck's top clients. One an aging male actor, the other a young up and coming actress who was a friend of Amanda Roberts and used Buck's services as a bodyguard for premieres and similar events from time to time as a buttress against what she hoped would be a groundswell of eager fans and salivating paparazzo, but which rarely was the case.

The gallery itself was more spacious than I imagined. It was housed in an adobe-style building with a red rough-hewn wooden front door with wrought iron knockers that led to a large white-walled room with an arched door that led to another equally large white room and then to another until I believe I counted four rooms in all.

Kraig appeared from around the corner of the first arch and greeted us effusively. He looked trim and polished from his short-cropped blonde hair, full black leather jacket over a white dress shirt and jeans to his lizard cowboy boots.

Did everyone get the cowboy boots memo but me?

He also looked radiant and proud and escorted us over to the bar and hors d'oeuvres table. After we gave the bartender our orders, a club soda for Guy, a scotch and water, light on the scotch, for me, Kraig told us that Tulabelle was sharing the exhibit space with one other artist, an older gentlemen named Ward and he nodded toward a nearby painting of Ward's, a wild looking desert landscape done in purples and reds. We got our drinks as Kraig took my arm and guided us to the next room that contained Tula's work.

As we walked, I eyeballed the said sea of notables. I spied one more Buck client—a studio head honcho whose teenage daughter was always running away from home. Buck would bail her out or sober her up or just provide a listening ear as he drove her back to the homestead. There was a British rock star with his significant other, a sixty-ish actor with his wife of some thirty years, and what appeared to be the entire cast of a very popular television sitcom I never watch.

I whispered to Kraig.

"Don't get me wrong, I'm thrilled to be here. But I didn't know you'd have such a huge and stellar bunch of guests. I came because I thought Tulabelle needed all the bodies in attendance she could get."

"Your body, Freddy, is welcome anywhere any time," Kraig said.

"Wow! Who says all hairdressers are gay?" I teased.

"You could make any one of 'em go straight, Bonnaire."

"I heard that," Guy leaned down and whispered. "Stop hitting on my date."

"Then you take over the escort duties," Kraig said, taking my arm and wrapping it around Guy's.

Thus intertwined we slowly strolled around for some serious art appreciation. The subjects of Tulabelle's work were men or women or in some cases a group of people and her style was very reminiscent of Picasso. Some would say downright derivative but if Braun could do it, why not Tulabelle?

We were standing in front of a rendering of two men done predominantly in purple when the bartender arrived with a silver tray containing a fresh scotch for me and a new club soda for Guy. We thanked him and looked at each other in astonishment. Such service! We were still sharing grinning wonderment when the young-actress/ Buck-client approached us, hand in hand with a portly gray-haired gentlemen.

"I don't remember your name but I know you work for Buck Lemoyne. This is Frank and he really needs Buck's services."

She said all this with the kind of excited cheerfulness with which a woman usually announces her engagement and that indeed may have been one of her other intentions for all I knew.

I'd remembered to pack my contact lenses for this event together with the black lace blouse, black jersey skirt and long black suede boots I was wearing but forgot a suitable evening purse. Therefore I was lugging my big leather all-purpose bag and the fortunate thing was it contained Buck's business cards, so I fished one out for prospective client Frank and handed it to him.

Frank took the card, mumbled *thanks*, added "nice meeting you both" and led young-actress away.

"What a productive night," Guy said. "Culture and networking combined."

"I'm sorry I didn't introduce you. She didn't remember my name but I don't remember hers either," I said.

"No problem. Even Frank didn't have a last name."

I sipped my scotch and then I saw someone whose name I *did* remember.

Sid Avarson.

CHAPTER 27

SID WAS STANDING IN FRONT of one of Tulabelle's paintings that looked a lot like Picasso's blue period. The L.A. Sid looked exactly like the New York Sid. Still rather short at barely five foot four, dark hair with a slight curl and a slim, compact build. He wore a gray dress shirt, lightly starched, black slacks and black oxfords that gleamed.

Sid was talking to, of all people, the aging actor who was one of Buck's clients. I found myself pausing to stare at them because I could not recall the actor's name any more than the young actress's. Their conversation appeared intense, something above and beyond cocktail party chitchat in any event. I knew the actor to be a man of considerable wealth—owned quite a bit of real estate, had an extensive art collection and about twenty vintage automobiles—so it was conceivable that he might use the financial consulting services of Sid's firm. All of a sudden, aging-actor threw back his head and laughed. The toothy grin did the trick and I remembered his name: Jack Osborne. That was one name easy for me to recall, as Osborne was the spitting image of the actor, Jack Nicholson. I met him at a cocktail party I attended with Buck a few weeks ago, after Buck had broken up with his nurse friend and needed a date.

as Jack's laughter subsided, he turned his head to the right, which put me directly in his line of sight. That I was probably still in stare mode undoubtedly also brought me to his attention. He shook his index finger at me as if he were about to scold me, called out "Freddy!" and waved me over. I turned to Guy who was talking to Tulabelle, touched his arm briefly and whispered "excuse me a minute." Guy nodded and turned back to Tula.

I had to say "excuse me" several times to navigate the very thick crowd. Convergent brands of expensive perfumes filled my nostrils and I didn't know if the slight nausea I was beginning to feel was due to the pungent aromas or the prospect of an encounter with Sid Avarson.

I reached them, put a smile on my face and said, "Jack, it's a pleasant surprise to see you here and I…"

I was about to say to Sid that it was also nice to run into him when Jack interrupted.

"No more pleasant than for me, my tall beauty," Jack said. "Freddy this is Sid Avarson. Sid's a financial genius, sets me straight on offshore shelters, tax losses on capital outlays, restructuring and a lot of other gobbledygook I don't understand…"

I enjoyed a small moment of delight in Jack's reference to Sid's field of expertise as gobbledygook. Having toiled in the acronym-laden and arrogance-invested firm of Potter, Wood & Penn, Jack's irreverence was refreshing.

"…and this is Freddy…I'm sorry your last name escapes me at the mo…"

"Bonnaire," I fairly whispered the word.

"…anyway, I was impressed with Freddy after just knowing her twenty minutes. I could tell she's one of the nicest and kindest women in L.A.," he continued.

Jack laughed and hugged my shoulder.

"And you know I know 'bout every damn broad in the state of California." He laughed some more.

Sid extended his hand and I shook it. "Great to meet you," he said.

His expression was pleasant although he wasn't exactly smiling. But then I'd never seen him smile.

"Buck has done a lot of personal stuff for me I won't bore you with but there was one funny incident that was priceless."

Jack didn't bother to clarify for Sid how I was connected to Buck.

"Freddy," Jack said, "do you remember the time when…"

Jack launched into a monologue regarding an actress he was dating last year who he suspected was cheating on him. He'd had Buck perform the usual surveillance to affirm the dastardly deed only to discover her supposed paramour was her biological mother who she kept a secret to conceal her less than aristocratic origins.

As Jack talked, I listened and looked at him with sporadic glances at Sid. When Sid had been introduced to me, there was no smile on his face but something else was lacking that was far more interesting: there was no hint of recognition. I mused on this and realized it was not entirely improbable. First of all, I had worked for Sid when he was based in New York and now here we were three thousand miles away in a different state. I had worked for him for a total of about eight months, not exactly a memorable tenure. Also, I looked different. When I was assigned to Potter, Wood I weighed about twelve—*okay, fifteen*—pounds less than I do now, I wore glasses and my hair was very short. Sid was rarely in the office since he was usually traveling or working from home, and when he would make an appearance he conferred primarily with Doris. There was no reason in the world why I should have made a lasting impression on him. I'd quit Potter, Wood & Penn very abruptly, without the usual two weeks' notice, but all that had been handled by their human resources department; I doubt my breach of corporate protocol had registered more than a momentary blip in the life of Herr Avarson.

During his protracted monologue, Jack eventually mentioned I was a friend of Buck's and that I was a model. Still no spark of recognition from Mr. Sid. I felt a great rush of joy over my disguised state. It was incongruous to think I had Sid's-former-assistant written across my forehead, but that was precisely the feeling I'd entertained. Between running into Guy and fooling Sid Avarson, this art exhibit trip was turning out to be far more fun than I'd anticipated.

Jack completed his story with what he considered to be the punch line and even Sid cracked a polite smile. I chuckled appreciatively because Jack really did manage to give it a humorous twist.

"If you'll excuse me," I said. "I'm with a friend who doesn't know anyone here, and I don't want to leave him stranded for too long."

I headed back to the spot where I'd left Guy but he'd gone missing. So I went on to the adjoining room where several people were grouped around a small rendering of two coyotes by the other artist, Ward. In the background, the cacti were beige, the sand orange and the sky a lime green. The coyotes themselves were a bright turquoise. *Go figure.*

"Coyotes are not solitary and form long term pair bonds," Ward was lecturing. "They can live for twenty-two years in captivity and about four years in the wild."

Sonny Bob Bonnaire and I paired for four years also which I wouldn't characterize as long term, so I was less than impressed with the relationship records of these mammals.

Guy was not one of the coyote worshipers so I moved on to the next room where the collection was Tula's. Kraig was holding forth on some topic with an audience of about five women who looked like Santa Fe matrons, all adorned with turquoise jewelry, suede skirts or jackets and, of course, cowboy boots. Still no Guy.

I retraced my steps through Ward's collection and back to the first room of Tula's. I realized I'd barely touched the second glass of scotch I'd been carrying and stopped to remedy that omission and survey the room.

As I did so, I was hit by the second surprising sight of the evening: Sid Avarson was again deep in conversation and this time his companion was Guy.

CHAPTER 28

Some vagrant impulse prevented me from intruding upon Sid and Guy and reminding Sid I'd once worked for him. I'd like to think my decision was clever, not whimsical, but the reason for my choice was not fully formed in my mind though it later proved to be prudent.

I ducked back thru the arched doorways to join Kraig and try to blend in with the Western ladies despite my complete lack of turquoise and boots.

Guy eventually came looking for me, found me and we decided it was time to leave. We searched out Tulabelle and Kraig to say our goodbyes.

Tulabelle hugged me hard, saying, "Pop by our suite later if you'd fancy that, luvs."

Kraig and Guy shook hands. We headed out, and hopped in the Corvette.

During the drive back to the hotel—this time with the top up—I asked Guy how he knew Sid Avarson. He answered that he interviewed him at his home recently in conjunction with the Hernandez shooting.

Duh, of course.

He avoided informing me of the questions and answers produced by the interview, choosing instead to make lightweight comments on Sid's general manner ("obstinate"), the appearance of his home ("ostentatious"), his wife ("opinionated") and his nine-year-old daughter ("obnoxious").

"Sue Grafton could have used you when she finished with 'N'," I told him.

Guy appeared unfamiliar with the famed mystery author, but managed a faint smirk. As he walked me to my room, I invited him in for a nightcap.

"If a club soda can accurately be called a nightcap," I added and grinned.

"It's night and we want to cap off a pleasant evening together so I don't think we need to worry about accuracy," Guy said, returning my smile.

We went inside and Guy called room service for our drinks. What followed was what could be termed nightcap nightmare. Or at least it was not the variety of nightcap experience Guy and I exactly had in mind.

Guy took me in his arms, and there was a knock on the door.

It was a waiter with our drinks. Guy tipped him, he left.

I encircled Guy in my arms, raising my face to his, and there was a knock at the door.

It was Kraig and Tulabelle bearing a bottle of Chivas Regal.

"We've got three well-heeled and currently well oiled housewives in our suite right now, together with one studio mogul and a ninety-year-old guy no one introduced," said Kraig. "And none of them will leave. We thought if we snuck out they'd eventually miss us and vamoose."

"Thought we'd hide out with you blokes," Tulabelle giggled.

"Be my guest," I said. "There's extra glasses in the bathroom."

"Tula headed for the glasses and, again, there was a knock at the door.

A very inebriated Jack Osborne stood before us.

"That damn hussy," he said.

It came out as *hushy*.

"She led me on all night and then announces she's got a husband."

Of course it came out as *announce-shays* and *hushband*.

He was waving a bottle of Warsteiner beer in one hand and a cigar in the other.

As he entered, the aroma of the latter reminded me of Buck's Montecristos.

Right on cue the phone rang and it was the great man himself.

"Are you down there missing us California yokels?" he asked.

"Trust me, all the California yokels happened to have turned up right here in Santa Fe," I said.

Buck didn't express any interest in what I meant by that comment and instead gave me report on his daily tailing of High Top.

"Ah ha," I said. "And again it doesn't sound like any illicit stuff the Missus was hoping for has turned up. Told you."

"Nope, Fred. Nary a love nest in sight. There was one sight that was a bit of an *ah-ha* moment though."

"And that was?" I asked.

"High Top de King outside his studio having big confab with two teenage boys name of Hernandez."

CHAPTER 29

BUCK IS THE ONLY PERSON I know who drinks bourbon. He was sitting at the bar in Nick's restaurant, Emile's, waiting for me and drinking a concoction Nick had made for him called a Bourbon Daisy, some parts of bourbon, Southern Comfort, lemon juice, grenadine and club soda. It was Buck's favorite drink and Nick had perfected it.

When I arrived, I saw a threesome laughing and talking. Nick, Buck and a friend of Buck's, Luke Jefferson. Luke is a truck driver and another frequent patron of Emile's. On the bar TV the Lakers were playing the Clippers.

Before joining them, I ducked down the hallway to the immediate right of the door, to the Ladies Room. I had to pee and, more importantly, I wanted to check my hair and lipstick so I could look my best while Nick ignored me. After taking care of Mother Nature and washing my hands, I stood in front of the full-length mirror to pull myself together. I was wearing my gold Manolo Blahnik boots, beige cargo pants hitched up mid calf, a very hip sleeveless beige top, and a long white ribbed coat sweater that reached my knees. Guy Whitehorse would say it was so L.A. but hey that's where I live. Or rather Santa Monica. Close enough.

Buck had called and said, "Meet me at Nick's at seven."

The invitation was for me to join him for dinner before our meeting with High Top de King's wife, Holly. Tomorrow I would take over the tail to convict hubby of infidelity while Buck addressed the more imperative matter of finding out who shot Doris Hernandez in order to dispel the suspicion the bullet had actually been intended for Sid Avarson and fired quite possibly by our famous rapper. Buck advised Madame Holly had wanted to check me out since the inception of our employment to make sure I had the stuff of a good erring-spouse sleuth.

As I headed toward the bar I could see friends Nick, Buck and Luke were still talking and laughing even more uproariously. Luke was chug-a-lugging his beer, Buck was now doing the talking and Nick was listening, seemingly spellbound. He was at this moment dancing more attention on Buck than he had toward me in all my visits over the last three months.

Buck and Nick could have been body doubles, both muscular and compact. Nick was a little taller and Buck a little grayer, but physique-wise they were mirror images. Most women would say Buck was the better looking of the two, but in my book they were both studs.

Luke didn't match them. He was tall, probably six-four, and a little on the chubby side. His head was shaved, his skin the color of coffee and cream. He wore stylish narrow glasses and had a smile that could light up Rockefeller Center's Christmas tree. Tonight Buck was sporting his customary Hawaiian shirt. Nick wore one of his many golf shirts, this one in pale yellow.

Luke was wearing a gray quilted ski jacket together with his standard uniform of black jeans, white tee shirt and spanking white Nike running shoes. Obviously a distant relative of Calvin Klein, although Klein was white and Luke, African American. Also a stud in my book, excess poundage notwithstanding.

"Hey, my fine soul sister," Luke greeted me with a big grin. He moved over one stool so I could sit between him and Buck.

"You got it going on, girl."

"Careful with the flattery, Lucas," Buck said. "Thought you didn't like white women."

"Boy, inside and at heart she just like me," Luke countered.

"Hear that? I've got a black heart," I said.

"Always knew it," Buck said.

"White wine spritzer?" Nick asked.

I nodded and Nick moved away to fix my drink. He returned,

wordlessly placed the wine in front of me, then headed toward the other end of the bar.

Man's crazy about me.

"Shall we take our drinks to a table?" Buck said.

I nodded and said, "Join us?" to Luke.

"Don't mind. Unless I'd be intruding. Buck, you plan to talk business?" Luke said.

"Nope. Meeting client at my place after dinner."

"We are?" I said.

"Yep. Need for privacy, no publicity, all that good stuff," Buck said.

"I wouldn't have thought she'd attract that much attention," I said.

"Probably not. But you know how all the chicks stare at me and then, after the fact, they'd notice her." Buck said.

"Of course," I said. "I hadn't thought of that."

"No one would," Luke grinned.

CHAPTER 30

Buck's home is located in Venice, the funky town bordering Santa Monica and the Pacific Ocean. Its prime tourist—as well as local—attraction was Venice Beach. The beach's boardwalk is famous for its circus-like collection of humanity in the form of fortunetellers, artists, poets, bodybuilders and vendors selling incense and all sorts of strange herbs. Add to this the usual tourist shops with cheap luggage, cheap beach attire, and cheap souvenirs with a few quality restaurants thrown in the mix, a resident population largely left over from the sixties and parking lots that cost twelve dollars a day.

In the early 1900's, millionaire Abbot Kinney dug miles of canals to drain the marshes near his residential area, and Buck's modernistic split-level house stood on the border of one of these small canals.

"It was built in the late 1930s," Buck had told me once. "I added the redwood siding on the outside."

The house is bordered by two other homes with equally eccentric architecture. Clearly a residential street but so Venice in that they are down the road from a tattoo parlor and various marijuana supply shops.

It boasts two bedrooms, one tiny bathroom, a kitchen and a dining room that was not much more than a hallway. I especially liked the living room. It makes no pretensions of being anything other than a comfort zone. In one corner to the right of the fireplace was a fifty-seven-inch television. Two loveseat-sized couches, both covered in cocoa-brown cotton slipcovers, sit cattycornered to the fireplace so that they faced the TV, as did two upholstered chairs also covered in cotton slipcovers—in their case, navy and white stripes. In front of one couch are two red Chinese lacquered chests, pushed together to serve as a coffee table upon which rested a huge glass ashtray, a stack of *Sports Illustrated* magazines, and several days' worth of newspapers.

The floor is hardwood, its effect softened by two colorful Indian rugs I'd had shipped to Buck from Santa Fe. There are three floor lamps scattered about and some very healthy philodendron plants on the top shelf of an entertainment center that cover the wall facing the fireplace. To the left is an arched door to the small kitchen, which is all white and strictly utilitarian in appearance.

Buck turned the TV on to the Lakers game and went to fetch beers.

It was the third quarter and the Lakers led the Clippers, seventy-four to sixty one. We were just three games into the season. Coach Phil Jackson was clean-shaven which was the good news. Pau Gasol was out, recuperating from toe surgery, and Kobe Bryant was playing on an ankle he'd twisted in a previous game.

Buck brought out two bottles of Samuel Adams and placed them on the coffee table. The doorbell rang and he went to answer it.

The ringer was Holly King. Buck invited her inside, she entered and stood very still, solemnly surveying her surroundings. Mrs. King wore earrings that hung down in long columns of diamonds. Numerous slender diamond bracelets graced her left arm. There was no wedding band but on her right hand sparkled an enormous pink diamond. In addition to all the gem excess, she wore a black knit cap, off-the-shoulder peasant blouse in an animal print of fuchsia and gold, black pants that ended just below her knees and…gold, laced Manolo Blahnik boots exactly like the pair I was wearing.

Buck made the proper introductions. I smiled at Holly and extended my hand. She clasped it very lightly and offered only a dim suggestion of a smile. We'd been taking each other's measure while this was going on. I didn't know whether to comment on our matching footwear or not. Some women would think it was funny and others were devastated when their fashion choices were duplicated. I belonged to the former persuasion, but something told me Madame King might well belong to the latter breed.

Buck asked Holly what she would like to drink. She said she'd have whatever we were having. *Ah, a woman of the people after all.* I relaxed somewhat and invited her to have a seat which she did on a leather chair by the fireplace.

Over dinner Buck had explained that this evening's appointment had been made because Holly knew High Top to be a passionate basketball fan and would be home watching the Laker game at this time of day. Thus she could leave the house, free of the fear that he'd take off for parts and women unknown.

Up close she looked much like she did the morning I saw her floating around her driveway in the pink nightgown and robe—petite, around five foot three and fit. Her hair was tamed this time, pulled tightly back from her face in a small knot in the back. Earlier Buck had described her as resembling the actress Jada Pickett Smith, but Jada's much prettier in my book.

Holly placed her cap on the ottoman beside her chair, reached into her purse for a menthol cigarette. As she lit it, I carried the amber ashtray over to her, placing it on the small round table beside her chair. Buck brought her beer, which he'd poured into a Pilsner glass as a concession to her guest/client status. She coughed a little, placed her cigarette on the ashtray and sipped her beer.

Buck and I sat down and sipped our beers. Holly considered the contents of her glass as if it contained tealeaves that were revealing something important. Buck was uncharacteristically quiet and appeared to be patiently waiting for her to speak, as if he knew this to be the drill. Thankfully, he hadn't turned off the game but merely muted the TV. Holly appeared not to notice.

I noticed Luke Walton had just made a successful free throw and waited less patiently for this meeting to commence.

Holly finally spoke.

"It's nice to meet you, Frédérique. Buck tells me you're very good at what you do."

She said this with the same serious manner in which she studied her beer, then glanced down at my shoes and began nervously bouncing her crossed leg.

It always mildly annoys me when people do this. Are they nervous? Do they want to leave? Are they exercising and will switch legs at any moment for a balanced workout?

"Well, Buck's a great teacher in all things investigative," I said. "I learn from him every day."

She bowed her head and contemplated her beer again for several beats. I felt edgy. Kobe Bryant executed a slam-dunk and the score was eighty, sixty-nine, Lakers. I felt better immediately.

"I want you to feel free to tell me everything you find out, Frédérique," Holly said.

"Please call me Freddy. And I definitely will report to you immediately if I find anything wrong during my surveillance. But as I'm sure Buck has told you, so far your husband just goes to work at his studio."

I smiled, happy to convey good news.

Holly frowned and Derek Fisher made a three-point shot.

Holly savored the frown for a few more minutes, coughed, then turned to Buck and said, "She could be anyone. His lawyer. His lawyer's secretary. A fan. One of the guys' girlfriends. I just want you to find her."

I understood "her" to be the suspected paramour. Holly had directed her remark to Buck as the only other rationale person in the room who did indeed know a "her" existed as opposed to my Pollyanna assumptions.

Mrs. King's demeanor and long silences were beginning to creep me out. Steve Novak of the Clippers missed a free throw. She was creeping him out too.

Buck made some reassuring conversation about how diligently I had followed and would continue to follow High Top. He described the hours I'd put in and would continue to put in and threw in the times I'd parked outside their home all night for good measure.

I excused myself to use Buck's bathroom. I actually just needed a change of scenery. It was a small room but had two sinks on opposite walls. Above one sink was a framed Andy Warhol poster. There were two narrow cherry cabinets on either side of the second sink with a mirror framed in cherry wood above it. Tiny green fern plants topped the cabinets and their open shelves held white towels and various male toiletries. The flooring was a hexagonal tile, giving it a vintage look.

I dabbed my neck with a washcloth I'd soaked in cold water and used Buck's hairbrush to fluff more body into my locks. Thus revived, I returned. It was the fourth quarter and Lamar Odom landed a free throw, making the score 104-91, Lakers.

Holly was speaking.

"He can't go to jail. Even overnight or something. He's not from the streets."

She had apparently been addressing the subject of High Top as shooting suspect as opposed to High Top, the philanderer suspect. As I entered the room, she looked over in my direction for a couple of beats and switched subjects, elaborating on the it-could-be-anybody paramour theme, not providing any helpful specifics but adamant in her cheating-husband convictions.

I'd sat back down on the couch and had finally shamelessly directed my full attention to the game, which previously I'd watched via peripheral vision.

Minutes later I glanced back at my companions. They'd both risen from their chairs, were walking toward the door and Holly was obviously taking her leave. I stood up and followed them.

"Don't worry, Holly, we're going to find her," I said.

I was feeling charitable: the Lakers had just won, 108-93.

CHAPTER 31

Buck was driving me to Nan Kelly's house in the Ford Explorer. We had no access to his other rides as he'd loaned his truck to a friend, and the Honda would be in a shop for a couple of days getting new brakes. Buck would drop me off and then commence tailing High Top. He agreed to handle one more day of surveillance to allow me to meet with Nan Kelly, as she was a source in the Hernandez shooting, and I was the one who had a relationship with her. Luke had graciously offered to provide transportation at the conclusion of my interview. He was in town for a few days until his next run and killing time tooling around on his Harley.

We turned down the California Incline and headed north on Pacific Coast Highway. The sun was up, the air cool. To our right were cliffs topping off to the grassy, palm tree oasis of Palisades Park. To our left were a series of private homes punctuated by the occasional roller blade and bike rental shops and hamburger concessions, backed by the sand and the Pacific Ocean, today calm and a blend of blue and green.

"So tell me more about the message the wife left when you were out of town," Buck said.

"There's no more to tell. She left one line, 'something strange is going on'. That's it," I said.

"And you think you know what that something strange is or pithy phrases just get your juices going?" he asked.

"I think it's a sure bet it has to do with hubby's absence and that she's not so convinced it's just one of his vacations from marriage."

"You don't think it could be she's being threatened, stalked, blackmailed or her country club blackballed her, stuff like that?"

"Could be any or all of the above but my keen investigative instincts tell me it's Scott's disappearance," I said.

"Because when you initially talked to her she actually seemed doubtful then," he said.

"No, she seemed absolutely confident marital trouble was the explanation."

"Then you're using some clue you didn't tell me about," he said.

"I'm using some clue you don't have access to."

"Freddy, honey, baby, sweetie, there's not a source in this town I don't have access to, in all modesty," Buck said.

"Buck, honey, baby, sweetie, there's one you don't."

"Which would be?"

"Female intuition."

"That's where you're wrong, toots," he said.

"Oh?"

"I have *you*."

CHAPTER 32

We arrived at Nan's house. It was teal blue clapboard with a gray roof and somewhat resembled a Tudor farmhouse. I climbed out of the Explorer, and Buck took off.

One quick knock produced an open door. Nan Kelly stood before me wrapped in a maroon bathrobe that seemed to overpower her, a white satin nightgown underneath and high-heeled white satin mules.

I know I'm not the only woman in America who wears socks to bed but why don't I ever catch anyone else in the act?

Her dark hair was caught up in its usual ponytail, this time pulled back more severely, and her face appeared blotchy and dry.

"Come on in, Freddy. It's good to see you."

"It's good to see you. Tell me what's wrong?"

Nan had turned her back and headed down the hallway before I finished speaking, her mules clapping against her heels. I followed her to the kitchen where she offered me some coffee. I accepted and added lots of cream to the mug she handed me.

"Have you had breakfast? Can I get you something to eat?"

"I'm good, thanks," I said.

"Let's go in here," Nan said, leading me out of the kitchen.

This was obviously a serious go-right-to-the-green-living-room day. No patio time for us even though the sun was bright as ice and the ocean and mountains in crystal-clear fettle.

I sat down on the couch. Nan turned on a lamp on an end table next to the couch as the plaid drapes were closed and the room fairly dark. She pulled over a straight chair and sat down, clutching her coffee mug with both hands. She took a sip, stared off in the distance to some point behind me and remained silent.

I guess I should be grateful Nan Kelly was not the hysterical type but her constant reticence was beginning to gall. I had distractions of my own involving the condition of Doris Hernandez, the safety of her family—particularly the two teenage boys, High Top's alleged involvement, even Sid Avarson's well being. Not to mention the question of why a certain Detective Whitehorse had not called me since our return from Santa Fe.

I sipped more coffee.

"Nan, can you tell me..."

"I'm sorry," she interrupted, "I'm in my own little world these days."

"Understandable," I said.

Despite her apology, she appeared to be zoning out again.

"You said something was strange," I offered.

"Yes, yes. And this is why it's strange. This time Scott has been gone longer than ever before."

Her words came in a rush.

"Oh, I know that fact alone is not a big deal. Maybe he has business to attend to wherever he is. But there are other things that are different. Or at least one other thing. The other times he'd send me pink roses after he'd been gone one or two days. There would be no card, no message. It was just his way of saying...oh I don't know...of just saying I still love you...I just have to do this...I'll be back soon. At least that's the way I always interpreted it."

"And this time no roses, pink or otherwise?" I said.

"That's right."

She wrinkled her face and the tears began. I reached for some tissue from my purse, but she used the sleeve of the big maroon robe on her nose and eyes.

"Look what I've done," she said, examining the sleeve. "This is Scott's robe. He'll have a fit."

I was sure he would. Scott Kelly seemed precisely the kind of man who would be more disturbed over a blemished robe sleeve than the anguish he caused his wife.

Nan excused herself to get some Kleenex so I was left to wait some more with only the missing-pink-roses clue to ruminate upon. Didn't seem like a whole lot. Maybe Buck would have deduced more from this revelation, but I came up empty.

Nan's clapping slippers had drifted beyond hearing and the house was silent. I noticed for the first time the absence of any children or pets. I saw some framed photographs atop a miniature organ across the room and went over to inspect them. There was one of Scott with a Senator, Scott with a well-known director and a small shot of Scott and Nan on a tennis court. Finally, there was a close up of Scott and two children, one on either side of him. The boy appeared around fourteen, the girl ten, maybe twelve. They were on the beach, all smiling broadly.

Nan returned and I asked her about the children.

"Kevin, he's fifteen. Julie, she's thirteen. They're both in boarding school,"

Of course.

I stood where I was and folded my arms across my chest, too edgy to sit down again.

"Nan, if you don't think Scott left for his usual reasons, why do you think he left? Do you suspect foul play? Does he have any enemies you know of? Could he be ill? Do you think it's time to bring in the cops on this? And, if not, why not?" I said.

For God's sake, talk woman!

"Freddy, I don't..." she began. A phone rang, probably from the kitchen. "...excuse me."

I went back to the couch to resume the waiting game. My coffee had cooled, but I didn't want to go to the kitchen to warm it up and intrude upon Nan's call.

More minutes ticked by and the tension I felt was part and parcel of this house once again overtook me. I decided to treat myself to a tour of the house. Isn't that what cops and private investigator types do anyway? Ballsy things like that? Detective Elliott Stabler of *Law & Order* would not have waited around for an engraved invitation.

There was a small den off the living room. It contained a bright red velvet loveseat, two wingback chairs covered with a tiny print and a medium-sized television on a round table. Well-stocked bookshelves began midway on the wall behind the loveseat. The wood in the room, like that in the living room, was mahogany—an unusually dark choice for a beach house. The whole house looked more Cape Cod traditional than Malibu hip. Maybe this indicated its mistress would like to be someplace else. Certainly its master did.

Earlier I'd noticed a staircase off the far end of the main hallway, and I headed in that direction. I also admitted to myself that I was not simply entertaining myself with interior design; I had a specific goal in mind.

CHAPTER 33

WHEN I WORKED FOR POTTER, Wood & Penn, most of the consultants in New York, and around the country, worked from their homes whenever they were in town. The nature of their work did not necessitate their being physically in their headquarter offices, save for the occasional partner meeting. Therefore it was highly probable that somewhere in the Kelly abode was a home office specifically for Scott, or at the very least a desk somewhere.

I moved down the upstairs hallway, passing first what were clearly the master bedroom, a bathroom, then two closed doors. Finally, bingo, a room that was all business, its contents a desk, swivel chair, two file cabinets and a low-slung chest of drawers. It was much like Scott himself—spare, neat. No frivolities like plants or artwork were visible. The only wall hangings were a maps and some sort of organizational flow chart.

Scott's laptop was in the room, which was strange. Normally Potter, Wood consultants are joined at the hip with their laptops, taking them along wherever they travel whether on business or pleasure. This practice obviously did not extend to Scott's A.W.O.L. excursions. The problem was I didn't know how to gain access to his programs. In the movies, the good guys always seem to know exactly how to get around passwords and other such obstacles, but I was totally clueless.

There was however an array of file folders on the desk next to a neat stack of loose papers. The folders turned out to be client files, each one representing a different company. Their contents contained the usual geek babble I'd been exposed to when working for Sid. Didn't understand it then. Couldn't understand it now.

The stack of papers proved somewhat more promising. They were printed emails—the main currency of communication in the consultant world. The subject matter was primarily administrative. On top were several independence alerts—general memos to all partners and staff advising of the acquisition of a new client company and the attendant requirement that all employees divest themselves of any stock in said company.

There were memos from individual staff members advising of progress with particular clients, followed by a message from the U.S. senior partner—again aimed at all staff—informing of a recent settlement with the Internal Revenue Service for an alleged violation. It spoke of a "settlement" paid to the IRS, adding "we did not admit to any wrongdoing."

Yeah, right.

There was an epistle covering opportunities in the marketplace and touting the firm's various new client projects or "wins" and listing the companies involved. The next email was from Sid Avarson's immediate superior, Charles Penn. It looked interesting so I set it aside.

It was followed by several copies of the same email memo entitled *Secrets of Success.* It lauded the value of networking, sharing knowledge and skills and spending quality time together. It devoted an entire paragraph to the subject of trust among colleagues, invoking the highly original concept that it must be earned. It ended with regards from the author and a replica of his handwritten signature. Below that was a drawing of a pyramid, its base divided into three columns labeled Professionalism, Teamwork and Trust, just in case any of the yahoos failed to grasp the verbiage above.

The rah-rah success tabloid completed the stack, so I turned my attention to the email from Chuck Penn to Sid. The first line had been what caught my eye. It simply said *This is a very serious matter.* The next paragraph went on to describe in generalities Sid's work in the global market, the support he'd received from other partners and managers, the need to drive business at key clients.

The final paragraph spoke of the acquisition of fresh perspectives, a different outlook and that he knew Sid would understand *this eventual necessity.* It sounded suspiciously like *we need new blood.* Did this portend Sid's firing or merely the loss of a leadership role? Knowing Sid, the loss of a leadership position would have no *merely* attached to it in his mind.

I contemplated my first impulse, which was to fold the Penn memo and stuff it in my jeans pocket. I further contemplated that perhaps such an act was akin to tampering with the U.S. mails. I could be comfortable with garden-variety petty theft, but if it amounted to a tampering violation I felt a little less adventurous. Rather than hanging around for further meditation, I decided my most prudent course of action would be to get the hell out of there and downstairs where I belonged. As long as I didn't hear Nan's voice calling my name I assumed she was still absorbed in her phone call. But I could be wrong. She could have searched only the downstairs and outside for me and simply assumed I'd left.

What did I suppose would happen if she'd come upon me roaming around the upstairs and rifling through papers no less? What was I thinking?

As I descended the stairs I realized Nan was absorbed in a phone call, but not her own.

CHAPTER 34

"You took Campbell soup to that place?...and it's a Starbucks product...York is a thriving place...lotta warehouses there...centrally located between Baltimore, Philadelphia and New York...you go home and get some rest...you can get a price on it...it's $3,000 or $6,000...he might grade yours in...labor and Freon is free...if that's all that bothers you about that trailer, swap it out."

Luke was standing in the hallway just inside the front door of Nan Kelly's house, talking on his cell phone. Nan Kelly was watching him, mesmerized. He had undoubtedly already introduced himself and declared his mission to be to give me a ride home, but that did not seem to diminish Nan's wonderment at a tall black man standing in her home while he made cell phone conversation she could not even remotely translate. Luke probably looked to Nan like the kind of callers who delivered dry cleaning or pizza or came to fix leaky faucets. And they undoubtedly didn't presume to use her hallway to conduct business on a cell phone, leaving her as a mute onlooker. But maybe she was more egalitarian than I gave her credit for, and I'd misread her facial expression.

Nan suddenly noticed me, arched her eyebrows and smiled.

"This gentleman is for you I believe Freddy."

If she thought it strange I was coming down the stairs, she gave no indication of this. Maybe the only bathrooms were upstairs although it seemed unlikely in a house like this. Or maybe the life force of Luke's height and personality had knocked any other considerations from her consciousness. Whatever the explanation, I was grateful she didn't chose to interrogate me.

"Sorry."

Luke stuffed his cell phone in his jacket pocket, favoring us with one of his blindingly white-tooth smiles.

"Had to take that call. Ready to go?"

"Thank you so much for coming over Freddy," Nan said.

"No problem. We should probably talk more," I said.

"Yes we should, Freddy. Before I was interrupted, I was going to ask you something."

"Yes?"

Nan glanced quickly at Luke and pressed her lips together.

"I can wait outside," Luke said.

"No need," Nan said. "Freddy, I simply want to hire you to find Scott."

"You don't want to report him as a missing person to the police?" I said.

"No, no, no. Let's not talk about it now, if you don't mind, let's discuss the particulars tomorrow."

"Okay. I'll have to discuss this with Buck."

"Of course," she said.

We all said goodbye, Luke and I left. He'd parked his Harley on the Kelly's brick walkway rather than the adjacent lot. Luke handed me an extra helmet and put his on.

"Wanna buy me lunch for this limo service?"

"My pleasure," I said.

We took off and didn't talk again until we were parked and inside Nick's restaurant. I'm actually afraid of motorcycles and just hung on for dear life.

The lunch crowd had descended upon Emile's. The view was clusters of older men in white business shirts in all different shapes, women here and there mostly in pants suits, younger men in golf shirts and khaki or jeans. Nick's waiters briskly glided around and between the tables, carrying trays. Matt, Nick's cousin, had drawn *maître d'* duty. He greeted us at the door, led us to a tiny table in a corner that had somehow been overlooked in the noon rush and gave us menus.

"What can I get you lovely people to drink?" Matt asked.

"Freddy?" Luke said.

"I'll have the Cabernet Blanc."

"Same for me," Luke said.

Luke took his cell out of the black corduroy jacket he was wearing, announcing he was calling his broker. I studied the menu. Matt said he'd be right back. Luke, always considerate in restaurants, spoke softly and briefly and hung up.

"I'm having the crab cake appetizer," I said, and turned my attention to people watching. Luke was ignoring the menu and doing the same.

Matt returned and said, "How's it look?"

"Like you're doing a bang up business with the luncheon crowd," I said.

"Yesterday it was more bang up, an actual line formed outside the door. Today, not so much."

"Well, hope tomorrow's like yesterday. Miss Bonnaire will have the crab cake appetizer and I'll have a cheeseburger, heavy on the onions," Luke said.

Matt wrote down the orders, took the menus and left.

"Onions huh? Your love life must be like mine," I said.

"Oh I don't know. I hear tell of you dating a certain Indian detective."

"Buck has a big mouth," I said, "I can't imagine what else he told you since there's nothing to tell."

"Just said you had a couple of dates down Santa Fe way. Didn't elaborate."

Odd. I'd mentioned only casually and briefly the time I'd spent with Guy Whitehorse when I reported on my Santa Fe trip. Buck had given no indication he'd noticed that part of my dissertation.

"What did you think of Nan Kelly?" I asked.

"Change of subject. Okay. Don't want you nosing around my love life either. Seems like nice enough lady. Did I hear her hire you as an honest-to-God-real-life detective?"

"Well I guess so. Buck doesn't exactly advertise that I'm not licensed," I said.

"A dude what wears Hawaiian shirts every damn place ain't exactly a slave to convention. You gonna get licensed someday?" Luke said.

"Not at all. I've got some modeling years left in me. Plus the state of

California says I would have to do P.I. work with Buck for three years before I can even take the exam," I said.

"Picky, picky," Luke said. "You qualify in Nan Kelly's book."

"Yeah and that's flattering, especially since her knowledge of me is as a secretary to Sid. I'll have to run the idea of my looking for Scott Kelly by Buck for approval. It would be his gig anyway. I'm barely qualified to sit and flush out cheating spouses."

"Speaking of which, hear you're tailing my man High Top de King," Luke said.

"You know High Top?"

"'Course not. But he's a brother. Buck says you coming up empty," Luke said.

"Our unconventional friend doesn't exactly adhere to client confidentiality, does he?"

"Oh, Buck know I don't repeat nothing. I seen other guys here—and some women—pump him for juicy tidbits. He don't give them the time of day."

"I know. Buck's a righteous man," I said.

"So's High Top from what I hear."

"I really wouldn't know. I've never even heard his music."

"He's known for clean rap. Versatile cat too. Done a couple of movies. Does charity gigs. His parents not poor but he worked his way. Was a model before he started rapping," Luke said.

"No kidding. I've got to talk to this man sometime."

"He the real deal. Worked in a hardware store when he in high school and years later when High made it big and the store hit hard times he gave owner enough bread so's he wouldn't have to shut down the business."

"That's nice. He remembers his roots."

"Well, wouldn't say that. Not like Watts or any place in L.A. his roots. He a Massachusetts boy," Luke said.

"I guess the name High Top comes from wearing high top shoes?"

"That's the word. Mostly he wore them when he younger, when he living in Boston and writing poetry," Luke said.

"He writes poetry?"

"Yeah. Went from that to rap. Could say it be a natural progression."

"Haven't heard of that happening but it makes sense. I think of rappers as so tough and hard-core. It's interesting that he once wrote poetry," I said.

"More interesting where he wrote it."

"Which was?" I said.

Luke's cell rang; he picked it up, cupped his hand over the mouthpiece, and whispered, "Harvard."

CHAPTER 35

BUCK HAD BUZZED MY CELL while we were having lunch and announced he was calling a powwow. He'd actually used the word *powwow,* which I took as an affront to my recent romantic venture. The meeting was to take place at Buck's house and Luke, who'd done various odd job assignments for a fee for Buck in the past, was invited. Lemoyne Investigations was lousy with unlicensed employees.

"Are you available?" I'd asked Luke.

"Yep. Have a run to sticker patch, but not for two days."

Luke often used the Citizen Band lingo favored by truckers. I knew the "sticker patch" was Arizona.

I'd argued for a change of venue to my apartment instead. I hadn't been home much lately and knew Pierre was pining away for his mother. No dice.

This big confab would take place around eight and it was only one now. Buck had asked us to pick up the Honda from the shop. It wouldn't be ready until four so Luke and I had some time to kill. The waiter cleared away our lunch dishes and we ordered some coffee.

"You know what I have a really deep desire to do right now...?" I said.

"I can guess," Luke interrupted, "But Buck discourages fraternization between employees."

"Rats," I grinned. "A loser at love again. Well, apart from the fact that you're irresistible and I of course was referring to an urge to jump your bones, the other project I'm thinking of is visiting the Hernandez family, particularly two of their teenage boys."

"Ah, I get it. Rejected by sophisticated hunk like myself, you turn to gullible younger generation."

"Am I that transparent? Well let's say secondary to my lascivious interests I also want to find out what they can tell me about who would want to harm Doris," I said.

"And you got it in your head that the kids are the family members who'd know?"

"Well, at the funeral for Edna Torres I overheard some conversation that sounded suspiciously like gang talk. And where's there's gang talk there could be violence. Wouldn't you agree?"

"Have to agree. You being the expert that you are on gang talk and all," Luke smiled.

"Oh come on. Anybody who rides New York subways picks up some street smarts."

"To a degree," Luke said. "Okay, I'll bite. What you hear?"

"Oh just bits and pieces. One said, 'He oughta tell her to chill out...'and..."

"That translate to murder in the first to any fool," Luke said.

"I know, I know. But it somehow sounded like they were referring to Doris. I overheard the tall one say, 'I not tell her but I wanna say don't be bringing that shit around here. That's serious shit'."

"Hell, Freddy, he could be talking about his old lady," Luke said.

"Anything's possible. But what do you talk about at a funeral? You talk about the deceased. Or when a recent traumatic event has occurred, meaning the attempt on the life of a relative of the deceased, that's what you talk about."

"Sounds logical. 'Cept when it come to teenagers. They could be at a funeral and be talking about video games."

"I don't disagree. But I think it's worth pursuing," I said.

"Okay. Let's go. I'll drop you off, do some errands, then pick you up and we'll go get the Honda."

"I'd really appreciate it if you'd stay with me while I talk to these kids."

"Cause you want minority help with another minority?" Luke grinned.

"Nope. Cause I'm gonna be bringing around some serious shit."

CHAPTER 36

I FISHED MY CELL PHONE FROM my purse and called Rosa Torres to see if this was a convenient time to visit. She was confused at first, thinking I must be coming to see Doris and reiterated that Doris still lay in a coma. I told her I knew this and merely had a few questions for her that might shed light on the shooting incident. She was gracious enough to take this reason at face value and said she'd be glad to see me. I was sure I had the address in my appointment book, but Rosa repeated it for me and I wrote it down on an extra napkin. I didn't mention the boys.

"It's in Montebello," I said, handing the napkin to Luke.

Luke shook his head slowly, sighed, then described the travel time and distance from Santa Monica to Montebello.

"Sure you can stand the hog that long?"

I thought about this for a moment. Could I keep Buck convinced I should help on this case even though I get all girly about the relatively benign act of riding around on a perfectly good motorcycle?

Luke saved me from the certain humiliation of my certain answer in the negative.

"Look, I got a solution. One of the guys I bunk with when I'm here in town has an extra ride. If we're lucky, he'll loan it to us."

"I'll never complain about Angelinos and all their cars again," I said.

"Yeah, you will, but let's roll."

Luke's friend Darren lived in one-half of a small white duplex on Fourth Street. He shared his digs, I learned, with Luke and two other truckers. Luke buzzed open the door to an adjoining garage. We drove in, parked the motorcycle close to a door leading to the house and entered. Luke called out Darren's name. No answer. He yelled "Mike" and then "Brian." The house was apparently empty. Despite this kitchen shout out, I decided to go into the living room in search of human life and found some in the form of a short black guy snoring on an L-shaped leather couch, a saxophone resting on the floor next to him. Luke followed me in, yelled "Darren" once again and the sleeping guy stirred.

"Hey, bro," Luke said, "Time to rise and shine."

Darren slowly sat up.

"You can go…"

He suddenly noticed me and stopped in mid-sentence.

"Man, I'll rise and shine you," he continued, "I worked till 3 a.m. last night."

"Sorry," Luke said. "Need to borrow some wheels."

Darren smiled and quickly stood up.

"Yo, you must be Freddy. I'm Darren Styles. Play sax at Harvelle's here. Accountant by day, cool sax player by night. I hope to…"

"Give us your autobiography 'nother day, dude," Luke said.

"My one cars in the shop," Darren said, addressing me and extending his hand. "Girlfriend's got the other one. Take Brian's Chevy, keys are on the kitchen counter."

I shook his hand.

"Thank you so much, Darren. I'm sorry we can't stay and visit but…"

"Let's roll," Luke said. With his fist he gave a quick jab to Darren's shoulder. "Thanks, bro."

Brian's Chevy was a medium gray with a slight dent on one fender, upholstery in a sort of tweedy gray that had seen better days and a back seat that contained more magazines, loose papers, empty Pepsi cans and used fast food wrappers than I'd ever seen in one place. Compared to the terror of the Harley, it was a beautiful sight.

We got in. Luke put the key in the ignition, looked over at me and grinned.

"I'd apologize for this class of transportation but you so damned happy to be in it I know there's no need."

"Rats. I'm transparent in both my sexual and vehicular proclivities. You just know me too well," I said.

I spied a two-day-old newspaper in the back seat and read while Luke drove. We took the number ten, then headed south when we reached Monterey Park.

"I'm sorry this is so out of our way, Luke."

"No problem. I do hauls to Montebello all the time; they got mucho bakeries, beer and meat companies, the whole enchilada. Know the place like the back of my hand."

"You do? I've never heard of it."

"Not likely you would, you being new to California and all. It's mostly Mexican-Americans. Some white, some Asian. Lotta Armenians too. They got *mucho grande* Armenian church there."

"Come to think of it, Father Howard mentioned that at Mass one Sunday. Only Armenian cathedral in the west."

"Could be. Maybe we'll swing by on our way back. Twenty minutes we'll be at the Torres place."

Luke concentrated on his driving, and I read the paper. We drove the rest of the way in comfortable silence.

Rosa Torres lived in a small house the size of Darren's duplex but with clapboard painted a pale yellow and an A-frame roof. To the right a narrow driveway led to a small garage. A large weeping willow sheltered the left side of the house. Rosa had avoided the shade of the willow and was sitting at the edge of the brick path on a metal yard chair. A bottle of Corona was in her right hand, and she'd raised her face skyward to catch the diminishing fall sunlight. Luke parked the Chevy at the end of the driveway and we got out.

Rosa stood up as we approached. She was wearing a flowered tee shirt, pale blue jeans and red flip-flops. I hugged her and introduced her to Luke. Rosa switched her Corona to her left hand, extended her right to Luke and they shook.

"Come on inside. Let me get you some beers. It's getting hot out here anyway," she said.

The three of us entered a tiny living room. As Rosa headed for the kitchen, I seated myself on the larger of two wine-colored couches. Luke sat on the matching loveseat size version and picked up a magazine called *Hola* lying on the coffee table. Rosa came out with a fresh bottle of Corona in one hand and a bowl of nachos in the other. She handed the beer to me and placed the nachos on the coffee table as Luke rose.

"Let me help you."

He followed Rosa back to the kitchen, and they returned a minute later with their beers. Rosa sat on a worn beige chair that sported a similar floral motif as the wine upholstery but obviously had been purchased years earlier. The small coffee table was only in arms reach of Luke so he would have to be the official nacho consumer. He munched away, unperturbed by this advantage.

"Did you want to talk about Doris' condition?" Rose asked. "I only know what the doctors tell me and I don't understand half of what they say."

"I wouldn't be able to understand them either. Especially when it concerns someone so close to you. They're talking away, and you're feeling so emotionally charged."

I sounded patronizing even to my own ears.

Rosa took a sip of her beer. Her expression was pleasant and expectant.

Luke, a man not usually uncomfortable with silences, said, "Lovely weather we're having, isn't it?"

I took a healthy chug of beer and dove in.

"Rosa, I'd like to talk to two of the young boys who were at Edna's funeral."

"Oh yes. You wanted to talk to Michael and Anthony," she said.

"I don't know their names. They were standing very near me during the service. They looked to be about fourteen and sixteen. One was about your height, the other almost as tall as me."

Rosa frowned, sipped her beer and frowned some more.

Outside a woman was yelling for her dog as the dog, a Chihuahua or similar breed judging by its high-pitched bark, ran back and forth.

"I don't know," she said. "There were several teenage boys there. I remember the Fitzgerald boys were there..."

Rosa paused as if she had more to say but then simply turned her gaze toward a statue of St. Francis sitting on a table near the front door.

Luke chugged his beer more enthusiastically. Outside the sound of the dog's yapping grew closer. I heard the woman's voice say, "Yuri, you little shit come here."

I waited in case some pertinent data was forthcoming but Rosa had nothing to add. I looked over at St. Francis but he was fresh out of revelations also. The yapping now seemed right beneath the living room window and the female voice repeated, "Yuri, you little shit."

"These boys were Latino," I said. "They were just a couple of feet away from me and I was standing under an umbrella with an elderly lady."

"Oh," Rosa's features became more animated and she waved her beer bottle toward the ceiling in some kind of gesture of triumph. "That was Aunt Tiana! So the boys were probably Carlos and Pedro. They drove her to the funeral."

"Great. Are they home now? Can I see them?"

"Oh, they don't live here," Rosa said. "They live in Venice with their uncle. I can get you the address. Just a minute."

Rosa disappeared down the hallway to the right of the living room.

I glared at Luke.

"Say one word and I'll bean you with this bottle."

"What I gonna say, Sherlock? That we coulda called first since we already right next door to Venice? Who knew? You being an unlicensed detective and all."

Rosa returned, looking a little perplexed at our laughter, and handed me a sheet of notebook paper bearing the Venice address.

I took the paper, Luke and I stood simultaneously and also in unison thanked Rosa for her hospitality.

Outside the sunlight had dimmed and the air was beginning to cool. A woman of about thirty stood on the sidewalk talking to a heavy-set woman around fifty. The latter woman held a leash and on its end was a toy poodle I presumed was the dog formerly known as *Yuri-you-little-shit.*

Rosa walked us out to the Chevy.

"Oh, one thing Freddy."

"Yes?" I said.

"Don't call them Carlos and Pedro. They go by Charlie and Pete."

It turned out the boys had bastardized Carlos and Pedro to more colorful extremes than Charlie and Pete but we didn't know that yet.

CHAPTER 37

"What up, bro?"

A black kid in a Texas Longhorns jersey appeared to be yelling the question at Luke as we parked the Chevy next to a lamppost on Navy Street in Venice. He was short but he had the look of an eighteen year old, and the jersey had the look of attire meant for someone a foot taller. There were new Air Jordans on his feet and an angry expression on his face when he seemed to deduce that Luke was not the bro he had in mind.

"Know him?" I asked.

"Can't say I do" Luke said. "But there do seem to be more my peeps here than our Hispanic brethren."

There were several black males clustered around the porch and front yard of the address Rosa had provided. A couple were just arriving themselves as we approached. They greeted the others with some kind of rhythmical hand gestures ending with leaning one shoulder into the greetee.

There was a lot of loud laughing, talking and cursing. I resisted the urge to take Luke's hand.

Don't show fear.

The house was white, had shutters in a teal blue with a front porch that looked surprisingly inviting despite the current somewhat menacing inhabitants. We proceeded down the path toward the porch stairs. Behind us was the sound of more new arrivals and the decibel level increased. The house was half a block off the boardwalk and a glimpse to my left revealed a good view of the beach and then the sea. The clouds high in the horizon were pink blurs, those closer to the sea almost golden. There were very few people around, but I could see the silhouette of a man playing a saxophone at the boardwalk's edge.

The corduroy jeans, heavy socks and white Reeboks I was wearing provided some warmth but the sea breeze was penetrating my thin white jersey. I felt the familiar sharpness of a hunger headache. I almost longed for our former and comparatively more peaceful milieu where the only sound was that of a toy French poodle and its owner.

Oh, get a grip Freddy. It's not like someone here is going to stab you.

"They always trash talking. Those muthafuckers are nothing but street niggas."

The speaker was a muscle-bound male wearing several piercings on his nose and ears and a black Nike jogging suit, the sleeves rolled up to reveal tattoos of eagles and snakes on each forearm.

On second thought, maybe stabbing is a distinct possibility.

The front door was open but the screen door was closed. Monsieur Eagle/Snake Tattoo was leaning against it, making doorbell ringing appear a pointless exercise.

Not similarly terrified, Luke strolled up to Eagle/Snake.

"Hey, bro. We be looking for two cats. Charlie and Pete. Latin types. Know 'em?"

Eagle/Snake turned to a tall light-skinned kid who looked like he might be twenty. He wore a Houston Astros cap, black turtleneck jersey and dark blue jeans.

"Who these dudes?" Eagle/Snake asked.

Thinking he meant Luke and me, I started to make introductions. Astros cap beat me to the punch.

"Charlie and Pete? He mean Lil' Ice and Dangerous J," Astros cap said.

"Dudes live here, right?" said Luke.

"Come on," Astros cap said and reached behind Eagle/Snake for the knob to the screen door. Once inside Astros closed the screen door and the wooden door behind it, muting the ruckus outside. I felt inordinately grateful.

Astros walked past us as we stood just inside the door, turned and grinned. There was intelligence in his brown eyes, and the smile seemed to acknowledge the depth and breadth of the initiation we'd just experienced.

He nodded toward me but held out his hand to Luke.

"I'm Tony Pitts."

"Call me Luke." He put an arm around my shoulders. "This here's Miss Bonnaire."

I extended my hand and Tony took it. His handshake was warm, but not overbearing.

"Call me Freddy."

"Freddy and Luke, your Charlie and Pete are upstairs. This way."

We followed Tony up a dark stairway. The sun was going down, but no one had bothered to turn on lights in this house so I could barely make out the steps let alone the various framed artwork on the wall to our left. The pictures were hung neatly in a graduated pattern and the wallpaper behind them appeared to be a small flowered print. So far, the atmosphere seemed to grow increasingly gentile. The rooms on the second level substantiated this impression. The doors to two bedrooms were only slightly ajar but a brief glance produced a feeling of cleanliness and order. Voices and music came from a large room at the end of the hall. We entered and I saw my two friends from the funeral who I now knew to be Lil' Ice and Dangerous J.

Some kind of music was emanating from a portable stereo in a corner. Or ghetto blaster as even I knew they were called. Dangerous J was mouthing some vocals as he beat on a small bongo drum held between his knees. He'd pause between phrases, and Lil' Ice seemed to be writing down what he said. They sat on straight back chairs facing each other.

Tony walked up to Dangerous J, bent over to be seen at his seated level and made a time out hand signal. Pete stopped talking and drumming and looked up. Charlie was still scribbling furiously.

"People here to see you, man. *Está bien*?" Tony said, nodding his head in our direction.

Pete turned toward us. He rose slowly, looking hesitant, but not hostile.

Thank heaven.

"I'm Freddy Bonnaire. I'm a friend of Doris. At the funeral for Edna Torres, I was standing near you with your Aunt Tiana," I said.

Pete remained standing where he'd risen. He also remained mute.

"Cómo está usted," Luke said, walking toward Pete, one hand extended. "I'm just a friend of Freddy's. Not into rapping, man. Just into trucking. Drive a rig to pay the rent."

Pete shook Luke's hand, grinned, appeared to relax. That gave one wuss of a wanna-be private eye courage, so I likewise approached Pete and extended my hand, which he likewise shook.

"Yeah, man, I remember you. You had on this black dress."

As did just about every female there.

"Hey, Charlie, this here's that lady with Aunt T. Wore that black dress."

Apparently amidst civilians one need not strive to be super cool and Lil' Ice had become Charlie again.

"Oh yeah," Charlie said and rose to shake hands with both Luke and myself.

"Is there somewhere we can talk?" I asked.

The two chairs the boys had occupied were the only ones in the room. The rest of the décor consisted of guitars resting against the walls, a serious set of drums, with speakers and keyboards scattered here and there. The one other piece of furniture was a rectangular table by the front window with stacks of paper piled on every square inch.

Charlie and Pete looked at each other like this was a tough question.

"Well, there's downstairs," Charlie said.

A great deal of noise had begun emanating from downstairs suggesting that the guests previously on the porch had come inside so that didn't seem like a viable option. Luke strolled over to the window table, said "May I?" and, without really waiting for an answer, began to stack the papers on the floor. Tony walked over and pulled the two straight back chairs into a position facing the table, then helped Luke remove the papers. Men of action.

Luke patted the surface of the now uncluttered table top and said, "Climb aboard gentlemen."

The boys did as instructed. Luke clasped the top of one chair and looked expectantly in my direction, like a maitre 'd about to seat a guest. Luke and I sat down. Tony said "Catch you later", thoughtfully turned off the boom box and closed the door behind him.

"I work for a private detective who's looking into the shooting that almost took the life of your Aunt Doris," I said. "We're trying to find out who would want to shoot her. Do you have any ideas on that?"

The boys looked at each other.

"We askin' ourselves same thing. Everybody love Aunt Doris. Don't make no sense," Pete said.

"We read cops think shot mighta been meant for that cat with her," Charlie said. "Guy she work for."

"That's another possibility. But we have to look into all angles."

"What about you guys?" Luke asked.

The boys looked shocked. "You think we tried to whack Aunt Doris? Now just a..."

"I think Luke means would someone want to harm Doris because of you."

"Oh I get it" Pete said. "You see too many movies lady..."

"Hey J," Charlie interrupted, laying a hand gently on Pete's forearm. "Lady..."

"Her names Miss Bonnaire," Luke injected.

"Call me Freddy."

"Freddy," Charlie continued, "We ain't a part of no gang. What? You think this some kinda gang crib? You talking trash. Ain't like that."

There was some loud knocking on the door, followed by the door immediately opening, the knocking obviously a perfunctory courtesy. Three young black men entered. They appeared to be in their late teens or early twenties. All three wore black leather jackets and snug-fitting knit caps, two in white and the third in red. They looked at Luke and me with expressions that did not invite cordial introductions.

"We're splitting, man, less you got better ideas," Red Cap said.

Messrs. White Caps seemed to be glaring at me, but perhaps I'd grown paranoid. The door was now ajar and the voices and laughter from downstairs filled the room.

"No, that's cool man," Pete said. Charlie nodded.

They left, leaving the door open.

"We gotta check out too, man."

Pete directed this statement to Luke. They slid down from the table in unison and collected jackets and caps from a pile of clothes in a corner.

"Here's my card if you think of anything," I said.

Pete took it without comment, shoved it in a pocket.

As they headed for the door, Luke said, "We'll see ourselves out gentlemen."

"Yeah, cool," Pete said. "Nice seeing you, Miss."

Luke rose and stretched. "Ah, the lack of etiquette in gangland."

"You heard them, this isn't gangland."

"Coulda fooled me," Luke said.

"They're musicians, doesn't have to be the same thing."

"No. But often is."

We headed down the stairs. The voices were muted now, the crowd seemed to have adjourned to the kitchen. Outside it was dark, the ocean breeze cold and penetrating. Luke got in the driver's side of the Chevy and leaned across to open the passenger door for me, which was partially stuck.

"You sure found those dudes intimidating, right?, he said, as I eased into the seat.

"Showed, huh?"

"Not like you," Luke said.

Truthfully, it was *exactly* like me but that he would think otherwise was high praise indeed. Luke Hall was one of my favorite people. He was always gracious, gallant and seemed to have his own code of honor. His posture was always erect, and he moved gracefully despite his height and bulk. He spoke in a deep, modulated voice at a measured pace and usually paused before answering a question.

Buck had struck up a conversation with him at Emile's bar almost a year ago, and a warm friendship and mutual respect ensued. Despite this generally high regard, Buck harbored a suspicion that Luke trafficked in marijuana in addition to his legitimate hauls. I never asked Buck why he thought this—I didn't want to know. It was a mystery best left for another day.

CHAPTER 38

"I'M GOING TO RETURN DARREN'S car, hang with him awhile, maybe have a beer or two, and make some calls to my broker. Then swing back for you and we'll head for Buck's."

Luke had just dropped me off in front of my condo. The breeze from the sea had gained new strength during our short ride from Venice, and I felt chilled to the bone. In the darkness I could see a few palm fronds on the sidewalk, already felled by the wind.

"Sounds good," I said. "See you then."

I made a beeline for the front door and the warmth of the lobby. As I waited for the elevator, I thought of the simple delights of home. I'd cuddle Pierre, to the extent the feisty little feline would allow, and then fix myself some nice hot tomato soup. We'd probably order in pizza once at Buck's so I'd keep lunch light. Probably just add some crackers and chamomile tea. Then a nice long, hot shower.

The elevator arrived and thankfully was empty as I wasn't up to neighborly chitchat. I turned the key in my door and reached to my left to flip the switch connected to my sole end table lamp. Nothing, no light. Rats, bulbs don't last two weeks these days. There was a strong smell of something familiar. Clorox. How did Pierre manage to knock over a Clorox bottle? I'd left the drapes drawn so no light sifted in from the street; I'd have to feel my way to the floor lamp across the room. I took two steps and my left foot hit something metal. The metal and my foot slid on the hardwood surface and I went flying downward and backward. As I hit the floor sideways, my arms and legs seemed to hit more metal. I rose up on my right elbow. The floor was wet, reeking of the Clorox odor. An immediate sharp pain cruised through my right arm, so I pressed my left fist to the floor to achieve a sitting position. I caught my breath and began to feel the area around me. What I thought had been metal was instead ceramic. A dish. In fact, several dishes. I felt some more. Several cracked dishes, and cups.

What in the world? Had Pierre gone berserk from loneliness?

"Pierre. Pierre."

I was whispering for some reason. Still, he should be able to hear me in this quiet. No pitter-patter of little feet, no movement, no answering meow. I was aware of a pungent smell, also familiar. It was very much like my perfume, only it permeated the air to an unnatural degree. I struggled to my feet, even more anxious to get to the floor lamp. Another crunch beneath my feet. I bent down, this time broken glass.

Okay I've been burglarized, but why all this destruction?

I zigzagged my right foot in front of me in order to displace further debris and make a clean path. Three steps, then a sound from somewhere.

I was not alone.

It seemed to come from the bedroom. I moved as swiftly as I could in that direction, this time not caring where I stepped. I was filled with rage. All my years in famously crime-ridden New York and I'd never been vandalized, now this. I approached the bedroom door. A figure was struggling with the window. In his effort, the curtains had parted just enough so I saw his back. He appeared to be all in black. Hardly original, but appropriate attire for a cat burglar.

Need something heavy as a weapon. Wrought iron camel on my large chest of drawers that serves as a candleholder. The candle is thick and white; I should bed able to locate it quickly.

As I turned toward the dresser, he grabbed my leg from behind and I went flying downward, face forward. My arms instinctively broke my fall somewhat so my face did not hit the floor. But, once again, I hit the hardwood surface and not a carpeted area.

"You sonovabitch! Get out of my house!"

The intruder made no reply but I could hear him panting. His grip on my ankle felt strong and powerful.

Silly to fight back.

My cell phone was in my purse, which I'd set down on the floor as soon as I'd determined I had to make my way to find a light.

Phone in kitchen. Get to it.

I rose up from the floor yet again. There was lots of material on the floor.

My clothes.

A sharp pain in my right arm yet again. I got to my knees, heard an outcry behind me like agh-h-h-h, then a sharp object hit my rectum.

Ohmigod. A knife? No, not that sharp. The toe of his shoe.

I yelped in pain but managed to hunker back down and crawl to what I hoped would be beyond reach, at least long enough for me to get upright. Made it. I'm standing. I ran, or at least moved with some haste, toward the kitchen.

Just a few more steps and I'm home free. He doesn't seem to be following. Maybe gone out the window.

I made it to the kitchen door but something was in the way. My butcher-block table, normally in the center of the kitchen, barred the entrance.

Easy enough to push aside.

I grabbed each side. *Ye-ooooow*! A slippery substance covered the block, a hot slippery substance.

Good Lord, what is happening here?

I rubbed my hands on my pants. Then heard footsteps.

I pushed at the butcher block with one hip.

Knives in drawer. Get to a knife, then the phone.

The table moved. I took two steps but not quickly enough. He was right behind me, bending in toward me. I briefly felt his breath. I turned to face and strike him. He was faster. He ducked his head down, grabbed my wrist and shoved me backward. The hot substance was also on the floor and I slipped and fell. He was backing away but I could see his leg. I reached for it but grasped his foot instead. Something sharp tore at my hands as I grabbed. I screamed in pain.

Just get to phone, don't fight. Get up. Move, move now!

I heard another agh-h-h-h-h. Everything went purple. Then nothing.

CHAPTER 39

There was a tight feeling around my neck and right shoulder. My hands felt leaden and achy, a description that also fit the condition of my head come to think of it. I felt a little too cool but suddenly there was a large warm hand on my forearm. I opened my eyes. He gave me a little smile.

"You're in St. John's," he said.

"I figured."

I never could understand why in old movies the patient awakens and so frequently says, "Where am I?" Where the hell do they think they are? They must have some semblance of memory regarding the injury they sustained; and when they see they're in a single bed in a sparsely decorated room, antiseptic and pedestrian in appearance, where could they be but a hospital? As for me, I must confess I possessed a very fuzzy memory myself regarding what put me in a bed in Santa Monica's St. John's Hospital. And the memories I had regarding the tall, handsome stranger at my side had diminished to a bit of a blur.

I turned my head in his direction even though it hurt to do so.

"Are you gonna say 'I came as soon as I heard'?"

A wider smile.

"It would be the truth. I was out of town at the time."

Waxing indignant promised to be as difficult as head turning what with my mouth feeling stiff and dry, but I thought I'd give it a shot.

"What about other recent times?" I licked my lips. "Where yah been?"

He straightened up a little and rubbed my arm gently.

"Had some R&R time and needed to get out of town for a while. Didn't mean to be elusive. Time got away from me for a while there."

"I'd say so. Where'd yah go? What'd yah do? If I'm not being too personal," I said.

"Went back to see some friends on the reservation. Relaxed, took some time at a sweat lodge. Sort of a ritual of healing, renewal. A thing we redskins do."

Then the famous all-out Guy Whitehorse grin.

I slid my eyes away from Guy. The drapes were almost closed. Through the five inch or so parting I could see a dismal gray sky punctuated by charcoal clouds. I surveyed the room.

"That large bunch near the chair with the Tiger Lilies is from Buck. I was here when he brought it in. I don't know who sent the others. Just a few of your many admirers no doubt. The yellow roses are from me," Guy said.

Yellow roses. Signifying friendship. So that's where we are.

"Thank you very much. They're lovely."

"How do you feel exactly? Can I get you anything?"

"Kinda in pain. I wonder if they gave me Excedrin."

"I'm sure they gave you some painkillers. Don't know how long ago."

"Yeah, but nothing works like Excedrin. Don't have any on yah, do you?"

"No, but there's a pharmacy downstairs. I'll go get some. Be right back," Guy said.

Guy stood and headed for the door. He was wearing dark blue jeans, pale blue denim shirt and what looked like Nike sneakers. He'd taken off a brown leather jacket at some point before I awoke and it rested on the back of the chair drawn to the right side of my bed. I should have also asked for a Pepsi or something. There was a water pitcher and a glass on the small table to the left of my bed, but it felt like too much trouble to access them. I studied my floral displays. Buck's was the largest in the room. It contained a variety of flowers in addition to the Tiger Lilies, pink rosebuds, Baby's Breath, blue Iris, red and pink Mums, lots of green fern. There was a small round bowl containing a similar variety, absent the Tiger Lilies, a tall vase of white Lilies and a shorter one of a dozen red roses next to the yellow two dozen from Guy. Whatever happened to me, word had obviously gotten around.

I held up my left hand for inspection. My palm was swathed in bandages, as was each finger. My right hand felt tremulous when I attempted to raise it but I could see it had received identical attention. Outside something sounded like a thunder clap. My head jerked at the sudden noise. Post-traumatic burglary stress.

Guy returned with the Excedrin, a cold can of Coca Cola and a straw. I grinned and suddenly it didn't hurt quite as much to move my mouth.

"Bless you my child," I said.

I made fists with my hands to push myself up to a sitting position and the pain was excruciating. I heard myself give out a yell appropriate to the occasion.

"Let me lift you," Guy said.

And he did. I looked at my bandaged hands as Guy popped the soda can, inserted the straw and set it down. He got two Excedrin pills out and put the can down.

"Open," he said. I opened my mouth; he popped one pill in and moved the Coke and straw to my mouth. I took several swallows and we repeated the procedure with the second Excedrin.

"Your hands are badly torn up and you have a hairline fracture in your shoulder," Guy said. "And, to top it off, you've suffered a nasty concussion."

"Well that describes me. How would you describe my apartment?"

My memory was returning.

"Haven't seen it. Pretty badly messed up I'm told. Vandalized big time. Furniture slashed. Someone wanted something you've got and wanted it big time. Cordoned off as a crime scene of course. When you're better you can take a look and tell what's missing," Guy said.

"Could be Gram's antiques, the small pieces. Wouldn't have to slash furniture for that."

Ohmigod, Gram's antiques. Slashed furniture. Her chairs.

I started to cry.

"I'm so sorry, Freddy. They'll catch the bastard. Do you have insurance?"

"I have insurance. But that's not the point. Gram's things are priceless."

I used the sheet to dry my eyes. Not classy, but served the purpose.

Guy rose, got a box of tissues from the dresser and pulled one out for me. I took it, dabbed my eyes and blew my nose for good measure. The latter exercise hurt my head. I sipped the Coke. My lips seemed to have loosened up but still felt abnormal. If my breath was as bad as my mouth tasted, I was really winning company.

"Gotta get back to work. I left one of my cards by the pitcher there. Wrote my home phone and cell on it. Call the minute you need anything at all."

Guy had remained standing and was shrugging on the leather jacket.

"Will Noble from Robbery will be by to question you. I've heard from my buddies with the Santa Monica force he's a piece of work. In cases like this, he immediately suspects insurance fraud."

"Like I gave myself a concussion, cracked my shoulder, ran my hands over broken glass."

"Some so-called victims have an accomplice in such cases, strange as it may sound. You'll set him straight. Just be prepared for a lot of grilling and more Texas corn than you'd care to hear. Noble was born and bred there, thinks of himself as one tough hombre."

Everyone in California is from somewhere else. Are there no natives here?

"Bring him on," I said.

"Thatta girl."

Guy leaned down, deposited two kisses on my right cheek, a gentle one on my mouth and left.

I couldn't help it, the tears started up again. *Gram's beautiful things.*

CHAPTER 40

"*PIERRE!*"

I woke from slumber once again and the most important victim of my apartment's destruction struck my consciousness like lightening.

Someone had completely drawn open the hospital room's window drapes. I could see a heavy rain slanting down, the tree branches bending in obsolescence to the force of nature.

After Guy left, an orderly had brought a lunch tray for me. I'd consumed about half of the usual soft food and green Jell-O fare, then dissolved into a nap. From now on, I won't be so critical of unconscious patients and their where-am-I opening statements. My own memory was definitely incremental in that I'd had an entire conversation with Guy about the incident and only focused on the material damage. Not one thought for my little feline buddy.

Have to sit up. Have to call someone to get Pierre.

I lay there for several seconds contemplating the pain ahead in achieving a sitting position when an answer to a prayer walked in. Actually two answers to a prayer in the forms of Buck and Luke.

"Hey babe, you're looking much better," Buck said.

The problem was too extreme for civilities, I cut to the chase.

"Buck," I said, "Pierre. We've got to find him!"

Luke looked at Buck. "Pierre?"

"The cat," Buck clarified.

Reading my mind, Buck walked over and cranked up the bed to an upright slant so that I was sitting up.

Luke laughed.

"Oh yeah, Freddy's cat. Forgot that's his name," he said. "I thought we were talking about the perp or something."

The 'perp'? Give a trucker a little detective work and he starts talking like a cop.

"Pierre's a perp alright. Hey, I think I'll start calling him that—Pierre the perp," Buck said.

"Not funny. We've got to find him."

"Pierre, that cat's living the life of luxury. I should have it so good," Luke said.

"What?"

"Fred, we found Pierre. I've got him at my place," Buck said.

"Oh thank God. Where was he?"

"Gone I thought at first. Luke called me and I arrived minutes after Robbery. Didn't see him prancing around with his usual arrogance, so I got in the car and drove around looking for him. First, I'd knocked on your neighbors' doors to see if they'd rescued him from the hall or something. Drove around some more, got out from time to time and called his damn name. Never felt so silly in my life. Then I drove back to your place because one neighbor on your floor had not been home. Thought I'd try again."

"When Buck got to your place," Luke injected, "The door was open, and a female cop was holding Pierre and cooing to him. Seems he all of a sudden came strollin' outta a closet."

"Always wondered when that cat was gonna come out of the closet," Buck laughed. "Always seemed a little swishy to me."

"You're both such comedians. Is he okay? Was he harmed?"

"No cats were harmed in the commission of this crime, mam. Not a red hair on his head, or elsewhere. While your home was being demolished and your body brutalized, your friend went into hiding and kept safe," Buck said.

I would have protested this disparagement of Pierre's character and courage but suddenly we had company. He was short, about five six, but looked sturdy and compact. At least what I could see of his build, camouflaged as it was under a khaki-colored raincoat. He had thick brown hair, flecked with a fair amount of gray and a moustache to match. Under the coat he wore a blue and white checked cotton shirt over a gray turtleneck, black wide-cord pants and beige suede shoes that looked rain spotted.

"Detective Will Noble, Santa Monica PD, Robbery," he said, extending a hand that looked large for such a short guy. His clasp was strong and brief accompanied by a smile that was automatic and brief. He was chewing gum with a vengeance.

"I'm Freddy Bonnaire," I said, and introduced Buck and Luke.

"We need to talk about who mighta have done this. From the looks of things, someone had an agenda to just plain wreck your place as well as steal property. CSI guys went over the place, no fingerprints. Someone wore gloves and wiped the place as they went along. Plus the furniture, floor, the whole place was soaked with bleach. Pretty much obliterates a whole heap of evidence." Noble said. "Also," he arched an eyebrow, "There's no sign of forced entry anywhere."

I licked my lips and tried to concentrate. "I can't think of who would do this."

"In addition to yourself, who has keys to your apartment?"

"No one," I answered.

Arched eyebrow again and some more furious gum chewing.

You're sure?" Noble asked.

"Positive."

"Well, you probably don't feel up to talkin' right now. Here's my card. Call me tomorrow or the next day. And we have to look over your place with you, determine what was taken."

"I'm ready to leave now," I said. "The place will have to be cleaned up after you're through with it, so the sooner the better."

"Hold on, missy," Buck said. "They're not releasing you until tomorrow morning. And for a while you're staying right where Pierre's staying."

"That would be on the floor in front of the TV," Luke laughed.

"Little better than that. I've got a second bedroom."

Buck addressed this comment to Detective Noble as if my living arrangements were police business. Or perhaps he sought to categorize our relationship correctly to Noble.

Luke's cell phone rang, and he moved to a far corner of the room to answer although his deep voice filled the room. Buck and Noble started chatting about a good time to meet at my apartment for the inspection. Noble pulled out a pad and wrote as Buck supplied his own phone numbers and my cell. There was a thunderclap, and I looked out the window again at the incessant rain. I felt like the trees—whipped and buffeted around by some greater force.

Buck and Noble were shaking hands and saying goodbye. Luke had finished his call and joined them.

"With no fingerprints and nobody busted a door down or nothin', there's not much in the way of clues is there?"

Luke, the crime expert.

Noble sort of grimaced at this remark and headed for the door.

"Oh, I might be able to figure something out, Luke. Even a blind pig will find an acorn once in a while."

CHAPTER 41

"I'll wait outside while you change," Luke said.

He had set down a large brown Macy's shopping bag on the floor and left my hospital room to wait in the hall. I looked in the bag. It contained a white lace push-up bra and black bikini-style underpants. *Embarrassing.* It also contained my orange nylon sweat pants, a jersey turtleneck, a sleeveless black nylon quilted ski vest and a pair of old black Converse basketball sneakers I hadn't fished out of my closet in years. Clearly Luke wasn't outfitting me for a chi-chi lunch at Ivy at the Shore. But just as clearly his choices were not a huge departure from the way I usually dressed since I'd arrived in California so how could I blame him? He hadn't thought to bring any makeup so let's hope no *National Enquirer* photogs are lurking in the parking lot. I gingerly removed the arm sling the hospital had provided in order to dress, but I still possessed insufficient mobility to pull on the turtleneck so I settled for zipping up the ski vest. I opened the door to call Luke in from the hall and then sat back down on the bed, exhausted.

Channel seven's weatherman on the morning news had predicted another all-day soaker. He'd commented that he loved using the term all-day soaker, so rare was the opportunity to do so in our sunny state. The downpour outside my window bore testimony to his accuracy.

"Don't like my taste in shirts?" Luke asked.

"Taste fine," I was actually gasping for breath. "For awhile I'll have to wear things that button down the front."

"Damn. Didn't think of that. Sorry."

"That's okay. Help me put this contraption back on and we can leave."

Luke restored my arm sling just as a nurse appeared on cue with the requisite departure wheelchair. By pre-arrangement, a young orderly I'd befriended arrived with a box in which to haul home my flower arrangements. He followed us. Luke pushed me to the elevator, then out to the lobby. We took care of the release papers, and he told me to wait by the door while he brought Buck's Honda around. As Luke pulled up, I executed the four or five steps from the outdoor awning to the car with as much haste as I could manage. Umbrellas and raincoats were apparently as expendable as lipstick and blush in the Luke patient-pickup preparedness agenda.

"Damn, Freddy," Luke said, as I slipped into the passenger side, "Didn't think of an umbrella."

"Well damn again, Lucas, you sure as heck didn't."

"Haven't been in a relationship with a woman for about four months now. Must be losing touch with my feminine side," Luke grinned.

"Feminine side my eye. These omissions border on misogyny, my friend."

"Just chill, young lady. Will make it up to you. Buck waitin' for us at your place."

The parking was underground at my condo so I didn't have to do the rain dash bit again, but we did have to wait for our private eye friend who'd been doing High Top surveillance duty. Buck had had the lock changed, and only he possessed the new keys. Luke and I and my box of flowers stood outside my apartment in the hall, chilling for what felt like an eternity till the man himself arrived.

"Sorry I'm late guys," Buck said. "But King's doing a video shoot in Malibu or it would have taken longer. Even with everything's that going on, the missus won't tolerate any let up in the cheating hubby mission."

"No problem," Luke said. "The good Detective Noble ain't showed either."

"He'll probably be here in about five minutes. I gave him a later time than I gave you so we'd all be present and accounted for when he arrived. Hear he gets especially testy when civilians make him wait."

Buck was wearing a black London Fog raincoat, a navy and cream Hawaiian shirt, khaki pants and Adidas sneakers. He took a cigar out of his pocket and lit up, taking advantage of the I'm-not-actually-in-Freddy's-apartment-so-I-can-smoke circumstances. He paused to survey my attire.

"Good God, Freddy, you're half naked and you're wet."

"Talk to your friend here."

"*Mea culpa*," Luke said, "Blame the black dude…and this time you be right. Makes me wanna to turn in my detecting badge."

Will had stepped out of the elevator and was approaching. "What's that? Gonna give up detective work, Luke?"

"No sir. Give up my private detective license? Never," Luke deadpanned. "Protect and serve, that's my motto."

"No, that's *my* motto," Noble said. "Let's have a look."

Buck got out my key and opened the door. The temperature in the apartment was freezing.

"Okay," said Noble, "Let's start from square one. Miss Bonnaire, let's walk slowly through the living room first. Tell me what you see missing."

"Job one is Miss Bonnaire needs some hot coffee in her," said Luke.

He picked me up and carried me into the kitchen, stepping between the broken pieces of glass and ceramic.

"I'll make it," Luke offered.

Buck and Noble remained at the entrance.

"Come on guys," I called out, "Join us for coffee and then I'll tour the living room from this end." They obeyed.

I am woman, hear me roar.

Buck helped Luke find the Folgers and mugs and the coffee began happily perking away. The kitchen window had been left open, and the sill and nearby counter were wet. I wiped these off and looked for some cookies, a fruitless expedition since I never keep cookies in the house. A model's diet habits.

It occurred to me that a nice fluffy towel could get me into more of a dry state right about now.

"Excuse me, gentlemen. I'm going to look around the bathroom for stuff, maybe the bedroom."

"We shouldn't be wandering around the crime scene to this extent. I'd prefer you and I check out each room together. Miss Bonnaire, wandering around like a pony with the bridle off don't get you to the end of the trail."

"This pony just needs to pee and get a dry towel, Detective," I said.

"Oh, okay. Go ahead."

I returned with a bath towel draped over my shoulders. We all had our coffee flavored with dollops from my jar of French vanilla creamer, save for Noble who took his black. Must be a habit gleaned from all those years riding the Texas outback where such niceties were scarce.

In a few minutes, Noble and I began our living room surveillance. It would be hard to determine what dishes or wine glasses were missing as everything was in pieces, although those are undoubtedly not high priority items for career cat burglars in any event. I'd recognized the remains of several of Gram's antique bottles on the kitchen floor and sink. They'd been on the dining room side table so I figured he'd carried them in the kitchen, the better to smash them against the porcelain. I settled for counting the copper pots and pans lying around, accounting for all of them. The backs of the couch and chairs suffered deep slashes. The coffee table and other wood pieces were scarred and missing legs. Gram's green wing chair was slashed in several places on the seat cushion as was the 19th century Louis XVI loveseat. A straight back chair upholstered in black velvet I'd picked up at a Hollywood flea market was left untouched. A burglar evidently with zero discernment. Gram's Italian gilt mirror had been smashed, and the legs broken from two caned regency armchairs.

"Unfortunately," Buck grinned, "The dude's no Francophile like you, Fred," Buck said.

"Yeah, yeah, wise guy. He didn't pinch a single Eiffel Tower. Although that small copper one in the corner looks bent at the base."

Buck walked over, picked it up. "I'll take it home and fix it."

Joseph Buckley never ceased to amaze me.

We progressed to the bedroom where there were knife slashes on the backboard of my sleigh bed and more destroyed clothes lying on the bed and the floor. No wonder Luke came up with the outfit he did;

he had very limited choices. I opened drawers, most of their contents were undisturbed. I may now lack designer duds, but I'd retained a full compliment of lingerie, gym wear and jerseys.

Scattered among the other debris on the floor were various pieces of my clothes. Re-laundering, hanging and folding all of them was going to be a chore in itself. I could identify some better pieces such as a mink cap, a Marc Jacobs jacket trimmed in gold, a chinchilla vest and a Ralph Lauren blazer even in their bunched up states, perplexed that they were not taken. Definitely this thief lacked taste.

I stooped to pick up the Ralph Lauren blazer. It would provide some much-needed warmth right now. One sleeve had been cut off entirely. Ralph would have been shocked; I certainly was. I moved around, picking up other pieces. They were in similar condition. A dress had been severed at the waist, jackets and sweaters were missing sleeves, the mink cap and chinchilla vest bore slashes here and there and a red silk robe my ex-husband Sonny Bob had given me was cut in half at the back. He'd paid for it with my money, but still it had some sentimental value.

A few items in the closet were untouched. My favorite Christian Louboutin heels and a Jimmy Choo pink pair, which had been kept in their original boxes and stored on the closet shelf, were spared as well, but a lot of my other shoes from the hanging shoe bag had their heels yanked off. Then I noticed the worst part: the small vanity table my mother loved had been scratched with some sharp instrument repeatedly and most of the shells trimming the mirror were missing. I stifled the urge to cry.

Noble had been following me around with a pad and pencil, posed to record all stolen bounty but I had nothing to offer.

"What's missing, Miss Bonnaire?"

Gee, how did I know you were going to ask that?

"I don't see anything. Everything's wrecked but everything's here."

"What about jewelry?" Noble asked.

"The few good pieces I have are in a safe, in New Orleans as a matter of fact. The stuff I have here—costume jewelry—it's all here."

I led my little scouting party of one back to the kitchen. "I need a drink."

Buck and Luke were still standing in the kitchen, on their second cups of coffee. I greeted them with a repeat of my announcement, "I need a drink."

"Lotsa luck, Fred. We looked. I know you never keep much booze around, and this time you're full out," Buck said.

"No, I remember I had a bottle of cabernet sauvignon right here on the counter."

"Unless it in one of the other rooms, it be gone," Luke said.

Noble looked irritated.

"Are you telling me the one item missing from this unholy mess is a bottle of red wine?"

I raised his irritation with two exasperations.

"That's what I'm telling you," I said.

Noble seemed to note my aggravation, tamped down his own and stopped chewing gum for a whole three seconds.

"That may have been what he hit you with," he said softly.

"And then took the bottle with him? Sentimental bastard," Buck said.

I moved to pour myself some hot coffee and my eye glanced upon a sweater lying on my small kitchen desk. It appeared to have, yes, one, then two sleeves. I picked it up. The sweater had covered my answering machine. I could now see the message light was blinking.

"I have messages," I said dully, as if this constituted a miraculous sign of life amidst all the destruction.

"Play 'em," Noble commanded.

I hesitated a minute.

Could they contain an embarrassingly mushy message from Guy? No, not likely, but then again…

I looked at the three men in my kitchen, moving my head to allow my gaze to rest on each one.

"They could be personal," I said.

Noble grunted and said, "No problem."

Buck and Luke nodded. All three departed for the living room.

I hit the button.

"*Die, you hypocritical bitch*!"

CHAPTER 42

"She positively glared at me," I said.

"Babe, with everything's that going down, that's the least of your problems," Buck said.

Buck was right. I was practicing a form of denial. I'd been alluding to our brief visit with Holly King and her reaction to me, supposedly based on my wearing the same high-fashion boots she was sporting. It was easier to stress out over trivia than focus on more compelling questions such as was someone trying to kill Sid Avarson…and who, or was someone trying to kill Doris Hernandez…and, again, who, and did Scott Kelly's disappearance make him a prime suspect…and, more recently, who under the sun thought of me as a hypocritical bitch—enough to trash my apartment and threaten my life? *Little things like that.*

Now it was three days after the mysterious break-in. Luke and I were having dinner at Buck's. The master of the house came out of the kitchen clutching three bottles of Samuel Adams beers and set them on the red chest in front of the sofa. Coasters were considered nonessential equipment in this household. We'd thrown most of my unmolested clothes in a suitcase yesterday and hauled it and my flower box to Buck's house. I'd taken a long, hot, soapy shower and later shared a pizza with Buck and Luke. Buck had stocked up on cat food, and Pierre joined our repast from his dish in the kitchen. Then Pierre and I had repaired to the guest bedroom and spent the night in our new temporary residence. Pierre slept like a baby while I remained wakeful, but then he didn't have to deal with an endless recording in his brain of a low, gravely voice saying, "Die, you hypocritical bitch."

This morning I wanted to be out and about, even if it meant tailing High Top de King in our endless quest for his phantom love nest, but Buck was having none of that. At least, not yet. So Pierre and I had spent the day enjoying each other's company while I read and he dozed or I watched television and he dozed. If you're at all worried and require distraction, daytime television is not the answer. In my opinion. And now that something worth watching was going to be on the telly—notably the Los Angeles Lakers playing the Memphis Grizzlies at the Pyramid Coliseum in Memphis, Tennessee, Buck had chosen to call to reinstate our postponed meeting. Or, as he chose to call it—for the second time—our powwow.

Luke and I were sitting at opposite ends of one couch. Buck dragged an ottoman over and sat down facing us.

"The Lakers are on," I said softly.

"Oh okay," Buck frowned. He got up, turned on channel nine and kept the sound low.

"First of all, Fred, you're staying here until this gig is resolved," Buck said.

"This gig being?" Luke injected.

"Who shot the Hernandez woman or who tried to shoot Avarson. When that's been answered, we'll have cleared Alex King."

We all sipped our beer, great investigative minds pondering the case before us. Pierre wandered in, looked at us as if to say, "Why wasn't I notified of this meeting?"

Devout subscriber to anthropopathy that I am.

Having failed to obtain our attention or a credible explanation, he wandered toward the kitchen. Outside, Venice and adjacent environs were enjoying their third straight day of precipitation.

On the tube Luke Walton had just been knocked down but the Lakers were up 17-11.

"So, boss, as this case crawls to solution, am I grounded? No, don't answer because the answer is no," I said.

"I hate to bring up a mundane subject," Luke said, "But I thought this be a dinner meeting. Can I order us a pizza? Tell me what y'all want, my treat."

"Damn," Buck fairly yelled. "I almost forgot. Gotta put the pot on. Just a minute." He got up and headed toward the kitchen.

"Pot?," Luke and I said in near unison.

"*Gumbo de pule et gombo fēvi,*" Buck shouted from the kitchen. "Or to you non-gourmands, chicken and okra gumbo. Couldn't sleep last night so I got up and cooked. Just have to heat this brilliant creation up."

I wasn't entirely surprised. I knew in difficult times Buck de-stresses by cooking. For me to be inspired to cook, my world must be spinning in perfect harmony, all stars in alignment and the tides just right.

"Damn bro, you rich, good looking and can cook too? If that nurse don't marry you, I will," Luke yelled.

"The nurse and I are *fini.*"

Luke raised his eyebrows at me as if this announcement were meaningful news. I pointed to the TV.

What I found meaningful was that Derek Fisher just landed a three pointer and we were up 24-18.

Buck returned just in time to hear me cheer Derek's shot. He sat down sideways now on the ottoman, watched the game for several seconds, then turned back to face Luke and me.

"Here's the plan," Buck began. "Freddy, you can resume surveillance of High Top. Holly King insists upon this continue. She also insists I do it myself, but what she doesn't know won't hurt her. I'll provide her the usual daily reports; it's not necessary she knows who does the actual tail."

Luke chugged the last of his beer and rose to get another.

"We dismissing Freddy's burglar? We not figuring anyone out to get her?"

Buck raised his voice so Luke could hear his reply from the kitchen.

"I'm getting to that. You're going with her every day. You're her bodyguard, bro."

"Sound good to me. Who we figure is the break-in dude, by the way?"

"By the way," Buck said, "I'm getting to that too. What do you think, Fred? We can assume it's related to your questioning the Hernandez boys..."

"They looked none too happy the day we saw 'em," Luke interrupted.

"...or we can figure someone learned of your visits to Nan Kelly and is afraid you're on the right trail."

"I don't think Nan would...," I began.

"Hold it," Buck said. "There's another option we got to think about. What about jealous boyfriends?"

I sighed.

"What boyfriend and jealous of who? Who have you known me to date since I've been in California?"

"Well, boyfriends from your past who've carried a grudge. What about your ex?"

"Sonny Bob? We haven't talked in ages, but we parted on good terms. I paid a heap of his bills when we split. He has no call for a grudge."

Kobe Bryant missed a free throw but at the end of the first quarter we were still up 28-20.

Luke stood up. "I gotta let my broker know I'm outta commission for a few days."

He pulled out his cell and strolled to the kitchen.

"How about when you were modeling in New York, Fred," Buck said. "Make any enemies among the other girls? What about when you worked for Avarson's firm? Make any enemies among your co-workers? Did you and Doris Hernandez have a common enemy of any kind?"

Memphis was edging up on us. The score was Lakers 30, Memphis 29. Kobe got poked in the eye after Memphis missed a slam-dunk.

"Buck, that seems like a lifetime ago. Well, okay, a little over a year. But my relationships were good—as far as I know—both with the Manhattan agency and at Sid's firm. As for Doris, she didn't have an enemy in the world, let alone one in common with me or anyone else."

"Hey, I think this pot's done boiled," Luke called from the kitchen.

Buck got up.

"Okay. But think about it. Maybe something will come to you

when you least expect it. Think about anyone you might have known who was a little off, a little crazy."

"Okay."

On the telly the Memphis cheerleaders, in red and white outfits, bounced around with great glee. No one had left any of them a die-you-hypocritical-bitch recording I was willing to bet. And what, I kept asking myself, was I hypocritical about?

Luke returned carrying a beer and a bowl of gumbo, both of which he placed in front of me on the coffee table. Buck came in with two bowls of gumbo, went back for another beer and plunked down on the couch across from me and Luke. We ate in silence and watched the game. Pierre returned and watched us, lured by gumbo aroma. No one offered to share, so he padded over to the leather chair, hopped up on its cushion and prepared to sulk. Once in a while he deigned to look at the game because Pierre, like me, was a passionate Laker fan.

Buck brought the pot to the living room to spoon out second helpings for everyone. He took the pot back to the kitchen, returned and sat back down on the couch.

"I'm going to interview Nan Kelly tomorrow, Fred. You can come with me. I've already talked to her; we scheduled it for eight in the morning. She wasn't too thrilled with that timeslot, but she agreed," Buck said.

"I'm game," I said.

"Damn. Almost forgot the corn bread. It'll just take a minute to warm it up," Buck said.

He returned with two fresh beers for himself and Luke, and then asked for the details regarding our Venice visit with the Hernandez boys. Luke filled him in. Pierre had dozed off, and I went to the kitchen to monitor the corn bread. It was dark now and there were droplets on Buck's kitchen window, the rain having downgraded to a light shower. I pulled the corn bread out of the oven, sliced off several squares and arranged them around the edge of a serving platter, placing a square of butter in the center. I picked up three butter knives and brought everything out to the coffee table. We ate and watched the game in silence again, save for my grunts, moans and whoops as Memphis was gaining on us.

I noticed my injured copper Eiffel Tower lay sideways on the floor in a far corner, still bent at its base, seemingly ignored. Well, Buck had plenty of other things to do rather than repair a knick-knack he hated. I turned my attention back to the game.

The score was 98 even. We were going into overtime.

"Tomorrow I'll want to talk to Nan Kelly about any enemies Sid Avarson may have, Freddy, so be thinking about that too," Buck said. "Think about what corporate politics existed when you worked there. Who hated who. Who was sleeping with whom. Who didn't get a promotion. Who didn't get credit they thought they deserved. Like that, *cher*."

Lamar Odom made a shot and we were up 102-100.

"Okay," I said.

"And I'm thinking about those papers you saw at the Kelly's when you were snooping around. If necessary, I want you to help me convince Nan Kelly to turn that stuff over to me."

Kobe made two free throws and the score was Lakers, 108; Memphis, 101.

"Okay," I said.

"Freddy was snooping? Hey, proud of you, babe!" Luke said.

Things were looking good. We were up 111-106.

"Okay," I said.

"Do we have this young lady's full attention?," Luke asked.

"Doubt it," said Buck.

We won! 112-106!

"Hey, how come we're not tailing brother High Top right now?" Luke asked.

"Don't have to," Buck answered, "when Mrs. K knows he'll be home. She said he'd be in watching this game."

"High Top's a Laker fan?" I said. "How bad can he be?"

With a rare period of California rain beating outside, the warmth of good friends around me, the coziness of Buck's living room, the time seemed propitious to come clean about my *die you hypocritical bitch* phone call. I hadn't reported the unsettling message to the police nor to Detective Noble who was in my apartment, but out of earshot, at the time I discovered it. Already traumatized by the break-in, I was not ready for yet another threatening situation.

But more than that, I was not at all certain the two were related. Several weeks ago, I'd landed a major watch campaign, a gig I learned a certain other model, more known for commercial work than I, had coveted. Rumor had it she was seething and was making derogatory remarks about me on the L.A. club circuit. The party scene held no allure for me in New York and California was no different. I was a hermit by the standards of many models, so it was easy for me to ignore this.

If I mentioned the call to Buck, would he shrug it off as probable crank call or insist I report it to the police? In his current mood, the latter seemed more likely. Either way, he'd have some questions. Therein lay the problem. Two days after the discovery of the message on my machine, I'd received my phone bill in the mail. I was astounded at the information it yielded, and now I would be was faced with trying to explain to Buck what I could not understand myself.

The threatening phone call had come from my own home number.

CHAPTER 43

THE RADIO ALARM IN BUCK'S guest bedroom went off at 7:00 a.m. A female voice was singing, "Once I had a little, now I've got a lot..." I sat up. "I'm still, I'm still Jenny from the block," she sang. It was Jennifer Lopez. I rolled over. The Lakers would be singing no tunes this morning. After the Memphis win, they'd lost to the Utah Jazz, 93-85. I thought of my own losses—or rather what I'd left behind and was at this moment sorely missing—my brownstone in New York, the parties, the clothes, weekends in Southampton. I thought of my remaining New York wardrobe, now mostly destroyed, and, most of all, Gram's treasured antiques.

"It's just the opposite with me, Jen," I said aloud. "Once I had a lot. Now..."

Pierre bobbed his head up from his resting place at the end of the bed and looked at me as if he understood. I think Jennifer would have too.

I stood up and put on my robe.

"Enough of this pity party, Pierre. Things to do, people to see."

Pierre stretched and hopped off the bed, once again agreeing with me, ready to start our day. I went to the bathroom to answer nature's call and brush my teeth. Then I stepped on the scale. I'd lost five pounds. Home invasion robbery and assault will do that I guess. I went back to the bedroom long enough to call Guy's office. His voicemail came on and I left him a message advising of my temporary address and adding my cell number, just in case he'd forgotten it.

Who's insecure?

I padded out to the kitchen, where Buck was making coffee. Pierre followed.

"I'll take a shower first, Fred," he said.

"We have to take turns?" I teased.

"I'm your bodyguard right now." Buck fairly scowled. "I don't want us both in some vulnerable situation at the same time. While I'm in the shower, stick your cell phone in your pocket so you at least have that."

By the time both Buck and I were showered and dressed, he declared there wasn't time to stop to make breakfast. Buck made my day by wearing one of my favorite shirts of his, a number with a black background and orange and red flowers. He was also wearing a holster with a gun. Meant to *save* the day. He put a black blazer over it. After putting out food and fresh water for Pierre, we took off in the Honda. The rain had ceased but the sky was still gray. At this hour it was too early to tell whether from smog or more rain clouds.

Nan Kelly greeted us at the door dressed as if she were heading for a ladies lunch in Manhattan. Black wool suit with a nipped in waist, large white pearls at her throat and ears, sheer black hose and high-heeled black suede pumps. It almost provoked another bout of nostalgia for my former life, but I caught myself.

"Are we interrupting some plans, Nan?" I asked.

She looked down at her suit with a slight giggle.

"Oh no, I'm just going to a brunch at the club. But that's not for a while yet. I just thought I'd get dressed and get that out of the way. Follow me."

We followed Nan down the hall. Buck turned to me, flapped his hand at the wrist and lip-synced "I'm just going to a brunch at the club."

"You," I pointed at him and lip-synced. "Jealous." He grinned.

We entered the green and plaid living room. The drapes were drawn again and several lamps were lit. Nan's perfume filled the air.

"Can I get you some coffee or tea?" Nan asked.

"Coffee would be great," Buck said. "Black."

"Just a little milk in mine," I added.

Nan was back quickly with two white, gold-rimmed mugs; she

wasn't partaking herself. We sat side by side on the green velvet couch, Nan in a chair facing us. Buck thanked her for the coffee and got right to the point.

"Where does your husband go when he takes these brief vacations Mrs. Kelly?"

"Please call me Nan." She turned from us, gazed at the drapes for several beats as if they were open and provided a view. "I've never known," she added. "He's never said and I've never asked."

"But he always contacts you shortly after he leaves?"

"As Freddy may have told you, he sends flowers. He doesn't call or send mail. Just flowers."

"Well, if you had to guess where he might be, what would be your guess?"

"I don't know. I always assumed he went to some vacation spot. That always seemed to be the reason for his…uh…absences. To get away from the pressure of work." She looked down at her lap. "And… and I guess to get away from me."

I could tell Buck was struggling to mask his irritation, that he felt questioning Nan was like pulling teeth. I had to agree. He took a quick gulp of coffee.

"Okay, what vacation spots does he favor?"

"Oh I don't know. We've never taken many vacations. Scott hates to leave work. We went to Acapulco on our honeymoon and to San Francisco once, but that was on business."

Nan smoothed her hair. It had been pinned back in a sleek bun.

"The police asked these same questions. I got the feeling when I told them about Scott's habit of taking…er…little trips from time to time and about the flowers he sent and all that they just wrote this off as a marital problem situation. That's why I'm hiring you."

"I understand. Has he ever talked about places he'd like to go? Places he's daydreamed about even, things like that?"

Buck adopted some restraint and sipped his coffee. I knew about now he was wishing it were bourbon.

"No…no…not really," Nan said. "Scott's just all business."

We were getting that.

"Does he have relatives nearby or in another state? Any particular friends he might stay with?" Buck asked.

"He has a brother in New Jersey. But he's married and they have six children at home. I can't imagine Scott using their place as a refuge."

"Friends?" I chimed in.

Nan got up without answering, crossed the room and pulled open the thick plaid drapes. It was still gray out, still no rain. She gazed out the window for several seconds. I was beginning to decide the open-drapes-gaze-wistfully-outward was a dramatic affectation. I was beginning to yearn to join Scott Kelly, wherever he may be.

"What about Scott's business associates, Nan?" I said. "What about his relationship with Sid? Were they buddies? Were they competitive? Wasn't Scott in some sort of leadership position himself? Did anyone under him have issues with him? Could someone be out to get both he and Sid?" I caught my breath long enough to take a quick sip of coffee. "And his office upstairs, we'll need any business papers you've got there."

Nan turned, looking more than slightly startled at my barrage of questions. Buck just looked at me, pursing his lips as he stifled a grin.

Well, rats, I was getting tired of her reticence. Plus I was getting damn hungry.

Nan walked back, sat down and addressed Buck.

"All Scott's friends were people from the firm. I didn't know any of them intimately; we saw them at special functions mostly. As for the papers…yes, there's an office upstairs." She turned to glance at me at this point. "…but I don't know what papers it contains and I don't know if Scott would want to divulge them. Or that Sid would want him to, as far as that goes."

Buck reached for a cigar in his pocket, then thought better of it.

"They don't have to know about it, Mrs. Kelly," Buck said. "My specialty isn't business espionage. I won't share any data I'm privy to with competitors. You want me to find your husband, and I need all the help and information I can get."

"Well, of course. I'm sure I can trust you. Well, I have to, don't I? If you'll come with me, I'll show you his office."

Nan led us back down the hallway. Her heels clicked on the tile in the places where there were no scatter rugs, her perfume wafting behind her. She reached the stairway, went up two steps, then paused and turned to us.

"There is one new development," she said.

"What's that?" Buck asked.

"Scott called yesterday."

CHAPTER 44

"I'LL HAVE THE EGGS BENEDICT with the creamed spinach on the side, not on the biscuits," I said. "And I'll have it with the fruit, not hash browns."

"Just scrambled eggs and sausage for me," Buck said. "And hash browns. And a large O.J."

The waitress was somewhat overweight, had a light brown ponytail. Her nametag said "Deana." Her manner was solemn, with a dash of arrogance. She took the menu and left. She'd already brought us coffee. We were sitting at a table near the window at Pier View restaurant on Pacific Coast Highway in Malibu, about to comfort ourselves with a hot breakfast after the draining meeting with Nan Kelly.

"Do you suppose that waitress was offended that I insisted on the spinach on the side?" I asked Buck.

"Getting paranoid over nothing, babe. More interesting things afoot for you to be stressed over."

"That's true."

At the last moment Nan had revealed to us that her husband, Scott Kelly, had called her straight from his whereabouts-unknown locale. All he'd said, according to Nan, was "Don't worry about me. I'm all right." She had tried to find out where he was but Scott had greeted her queries with silence. This aggravated her and she'd told him that she was having Buck hunt him down. Except in her momentary pique, what she'd actually said was, "I've told Frédérique Bonnaire about this latest trick of yours, and she's on your tail."

In her emotional state, my name had sprung more readily to mind than Buck's. *Thanks a lot, Nan.* She'd been sitting on this piece of information until she could speak to me, or Buck, in person. Apparently the drama of the announcement would be wasted on a mere phone call. *Who says everyone in California doesn't want to be a star?* Her memory was even fuzzy as to the exact day he called. She thought at first it was yesterday, then amended her recollection to "about three days ago" which would make it pre-date the break-in at my apartment.

In all fairness to Nan, since she did not have the presence of mind to hit star six nine to determine the source of the call and since Scott did not provide any really compelling data, one could see how only the emotional portent of the call seemed relevant.

Perhaps only highly intuitive investigators like me would have sprung into immediate action.

"By the way," Buck said. "I'm having Vesta clean your place today. Pack up stuff that you told me could be repaired. Trash the rest."

Vesta was the lady who cleaned Buck's house once a week.

"That's very sweet of you. You remember what I said I could salvage?"

"Yeah, wrote it down on the scene," he said.

"Very smart."

"Making all kind of notes a habit from my cop days," Buck said.

"Of course."

We sipped our coffee. Outside the sea was gray and calm, as was the sky. Clustered on the sand, just beyond the shoreline, was a convention of seagulls and pigeons.

"Notice how efficiently those seagulls are made," I said. "They're elegant and graceful and can fly and yet they have nice long legs, good for walking. Unlike the pigeons."

Buck looked at me intently for several beats.

"You're elegant and graceful with nice long legs, Fred. Are you going to fly?"

His expression was serious, not playful.

"What does that mean?"

"I mean are you planning to fly back to New York? Give up on

L.A., when all this craziness is over?" Buck asked. His eyes appeared extremely sad.

My right arm was still in a sling so I crossed my left over to his hand that was not holding a coffee cup.

"No, of course not." I smiled. "We tough private eyes don't run at the first sign of trouble."

"Wouldn't blame you," he said.

"*I'd* blame me," I said. "I'm fully committed to finding out who shot Doris. And I haven't given up on forging a really good modeling career here. It's just taking time. Modeling gave me a good life in New York and it will again. But I have to say, in the modeling world did I use my brain? No. Working with you feels like doing something substantial."

"These days must also feel like doing something dangerous."

"Enough. I'm not thinking about that. You're protecting me. Luke's going to hang with us for a while. I'll be fine."

"Well...," Buck began.

The waitress appeared with our orders before he could continue. She glanced down at my hand still resting on Buck's with what appeared to be disdain. It did look somewhat romantic and he is currently my boss in a sense, but she didn't know all that. I decided there'd been ample evidence thus far that disdain was her usual expression.

Apart from a brief discussion wherein Buck quizzed me for the umpteenth time about whether or not I recognized the caller's voice on my "Bitch" answering machine message and I assured him I did not, we ate in silence and watched the gulls and the sea.

"I'm going to call Luke," Buck said, pulling out his cell. "See where he's located in the High Top tail so I can drop you off there."

"Sounds good."

Buck dialed. "Hey bro. Where you at? Yeah...yeah...okay... check you later."

"So where we going?" I asked.

"You're going to my place missy. Luke says H.T. is on a Rodeo Drive shopping spree; he's following on foot, got it covered. Says on foot the two of you would stand out as an inter-racial couple."

"I guess people still gawk at that. So who's protecting me, Mr. Former Cop, while I'll at your place?"

"There's a neighbor friend of mine, an actor who lives across the street. He's currently unemployed and mostly without funds right now so he hangs at home all day. I'll alert him."

"Okay."

"I'm also going to alert Nick," Buck said.

"Nick? Nick of Emile's Cafe?"

"Yeah, Nick Bernstein. Is there another Nick?" Buck asked. "His place is just minutes away. Can't be too careful."

"Won't he consider that an imposition?"

"Nah. No problem. He likes you."

Interesting.

"And there's a project you can take care of at home," Buck said.

Nan Kelly had handed over all the papers and files contained in Scott's home office, plus some floppy discs lying about the desk and the firm's directory of names and addresses. Buck wanted me to go over these again, highlight pertinent information and make notes.

"This actor friend," I said. "Is he cute?"

"Drink your coffee."

Buck summoned Disdainful Deana over, making check signing motions in the air. She brought the bill, Buck handed over his credit card; she returned with the tab and the card and placed them on the table with a "thanks" but no smile.

We returned to Buck's house, parked and crossed the street. He introduced me to Ben Fry, actor. Ben was built enough like Arnold Schwarzenegger to inspire my utmost confidence. We smiled and shook hands, then waited while Ben went inside his house to get something bearing his phone numbers. The plan was for me to call Ben immediately in case of an appearance by my mystery caller. He came out with an eight by ten glossy, saying sheepishly that was all he had. My aforementioned confidence dropped just a notch.

Buck let me into his house, said his housekeeper Vesta would be over as soon as she finished with my place and left. In all honesty my head and right arm still ached somewhat, and I was grateful for a day of relative calm. I heated up some coffee, squatted on the living room floor and spread Scott's papers out in rows. Nan had given us the password so I retrieved Scott's laptop and a yellow magic marker from Buck's very small and cluttered desk in a corner of the living room and brought these to my improvised floor work area also.

On top of the first stack were random blurbs simply entitled "Talk

Notes" for a speech Scott had given or was going to give. "Technology is always the vanguard of a bull market," blah, blah, blah, "cash will beat the overall market for the next ten years," blah, blah blah, "could be a bear market for years like it was in the 90's and 80's," blah, blah, blah, "almost every economic wipeout has occurred because of an international event. The '98 plunge was caused by Russian debt," blah, blah, blah.

I read on. And on. There didn't seem to be anything here that leapt off the page as an attempted murder clue. Pierre had jumped down from one sofa and was sniffing around some papers, his fluffy orange tail scanning others. He seemed to share my opinion. I read the notes to the end anyway.

I was about to turn on the laptop and see what could be culled from Scott's email library when the phone rang in Buck's kitchen. I got up to answer; it was Vesta.

"Miss Freddy. The doorbell rang, I opened it and this strange creature just stomped into your apartment and sat down on your best chair. I don't know what to do!"

CHAPTER 45

I SAW THEM THE MINUTE I opened the door. Vesta and the strange interloper were standing in my living room conducting a stare contest, complete with intimidating glares and insouciant postures. Vesta was about five foot one and weighed about sixty pounds less than the stranger, so clearly she was overmatched. Vesta's background, as far as I knew it, was one of an insular, large, loving family on a farm in Arkansas. Roots, which were also no contest for the stranger's, which were firmly embedded, in working-class New York soil, the Bronx to be exact. Both of them were chewing gum furiously.

"Jeannettesky!" I made a dash to hug the intruder.

She hugged me back.

"Shit, girlfriend, this lady was about to call the cops on me. And where's all your furniture? Some fucking welcome this is."

Jeannette Sullivan—I call her Jay for short—and I met over two years ago when we both lived temporarily at Manhattan's Melrose Hotel. I had just separated from Sonny and needed temporary digs. Jeannette had decided she'd outgrown sharing a Bronx apartment with two cousins, and we both sought refuge there—actually based on misinformation. My mom and her aunt advised us there was a hotel on 63rd Street that was strictly for females. Actually, this multi-story hotel, which was erected in 1927 as a combination of Italian Renaissance and neo-Gothic architecture, was once called The Barbizon Hotel for

Women and had been precisely that. They began admitting the male of the species in 1981. In 2002, it underwent a forty million dollar renovation and the transition was complete with a change of name to Melrose. One evening found us both going for a swim in their large indoor pool. We met, and hit it off famously.

Jay was now twenty-nine. She'd fallen into a modeling career when she was fourteen but in a couple of years the powers that be in the business told her to lose almost a third of her total body weight. She became anorexic, had a health crisis, dropped out, eventually going to college for three years. Got restless about college life and headed back to modeling, this time her weight was acceptable. She was twenty-three when she got a big break via a fashion layout for *Seventeen* magazine and was once again established in the business. The genes from Irish ancestors had bestowed upon her huge blue-green eyes, creamy skin with a nose that was anything but pert, and a curly halo of red hair. Jeannette was what the French would call *jolie laide*—a woman who is not a classic beauty, but attractive nonetheless. An Irish brogue had not been passed down to Jeannette, instead she spoke with a deep, throaty New York accent. She was a plus-size model, and her generous five-foot-ten frame was supported on long legs, courtesy of her mother's genes. The potty mouth was mostly her own invention. Jeannette is definitely a character but, again, she is, as we French say, *bein dans sa peau*—comfortable in her skin.

"It's so good to see you," I said. "Why didn't you tell me you were coming?"

Jeannette was still collecting herself. She attempted to smooth a tangle of curls above her forehead and examined the vivid pink polish on her nails. She was wearing a knit mink vest over a white sweater, black leather pants and Jimmy Choo red and black leopard heels. Gold loop earrings the size of handcuffs were in her ears.

"Hello? I left you a phone message a couple of weeks ago. And then two days ago I left you one with my flight and arrival time. Where the hell were you?"

"Ohmigod," I said. "Your message may have been on my machine or erased by mistake. I received one message that called me a bitch and virtually threatened my life. That sorta stopped me in my tracks."

"Say what? I told you there's nothin' but nuts out here. I'm gonna get me some fashion show gigs in this God forsaken town and you should too."

"You're going to work here in L.A.?" I asked.

"I'm here, ain't I? If you can fucking find work in la-la land, so can I. Shit, I'm not getting any younger and the Big Apple don't take kindly to us mature broads."

Jet lag exacerbates Jeannette's expletive vocabulary.

"I'm sorry," I said. "I'm forgetting my manners. Vesta, this is Jeannette Sullivan. She was my best friend in New York. Jeannette, this is Vesta Washington. I had a sort of burglary-like incident recently. Vesta's helping me put things back together. And this is Ben Fry, Buck's neighbor. He's sort of guarding me today."

"Well, while you're sort of getting by with a little help from your friends, all my shit's sitting down in the lobby. Anyone care to help me lug my luggage?" Jeannette said. "And what's a *sort of* burglary?"

"Let's go. I'll be happy to help with your bags," Ben said.

"I'll explain about the burglary later, Jay," I said.

Ben and I helped Jeannette bring her luggage to my apartment. I told her to select one suitcase and make it an overnight bag because she may well have to stay at Buck's with me. After some vehement histrionics objecting to such an arrangement on Jeannette's part—the jet lag again—she agreed to leave with us. After we arrived at Buck's, I persuaded Ben Fry to drive Vesta to her home in Culver City so she wouldn't have to take the bus. I assured him I'd be safe here with Jeannette keeping me company. I think by now Ben was convinced Jeannette could hold her own with anyone; in any event, he agreed. Vesta's objections to this transportation option were less profane than Jeannette's earlier protestations but ultimately she too caved and accepted the ride.

Ben and Vesta left. Jeannette plopped down on Buck's couch and rested her feet on one of the red chests. Pierre seemed to remember her and crawled onto her lap. As Pierre began to purr, Jeannette ceased her chatter. I took a deep breath. Peace at last. I put some Thelonious Monk on the stereo, then went into the kitchen and fixed two ham and cheese sandwiches and brought them with two glasses of Merlot to the living room. Jeannette took a healthy swig of the wine. I watched her then carefully separate the ham and cheese from the bread and break off and nibble small pieces of ham.

Ridiculous the lengths even plus-size models will go to cut calories.

Jeannette switched to nibbling small pieces of cheese. "I'm just tired of the New York scene, you know what I'm sayin'. It's a lotta hard work and it ain't gonna last forever anyway. Now acting, that's a different story."

Ah ha," I said. "I should have guessed. Lil' ole Jeannette Sullivan's out here to be a big movie star."

"Okay, go ahead and laugh at me. But I'm practical. I'm gonna get some menial job first, then take acting lessons at night. Take it gradual, you know what I'm saying."

"I'm not laughing at you, Jay," I said. "I think that's a perfectly good plan. What kind of menial job?"

"One like those print jobs you been gettin'."

"Thanks loads."

"No, no. You know what I mean. You got ambition and all yourself. The jobs you got here so far, they're just stepping stones, right? Well, that's what I'm gonna do, you know what I'm saying. Do something like that until...," she had the decency to grin..."the movie star thing takes off."

"Go for it, girlfriend," I said, "It's not like I've cut a huge swath in the modeling world here so far."

"Hell, Freddy, you had three *Vogue* covers for God's sake. It'll happen for you. Think positive."

I sipped my Merlot and thought. I separated the bread from my ham and cheese, broke off a piece of cheese and ate it. And thought some more.

Things were looking up. Jeannette was here and last night the Lakers, from 30 points behind, and by scoring 44 points in the fourth quarter, defeated the Dallas Mavericks, 105-103.

"Actually, Jay, I think I know just the job for you."

CHAPTER 46

After lunch, Jeannette repaired to the guest bedroom to take a nap. She slept for over three hours while I resumed pouring over Scott Kelly's various papers and emails. The subject matter had bored me when I worked at Sid's firm and it bored me now. There was a voluminous article on China. It claimed "China did not report true unemployment figures, blah, blah, blah, that the U.S. owns about 15,000 corporations in China, blah, blah, blah, that the four biggest banks in China are run by the government and that eighty percent of all of China's exports are now over supplied but the U.S. president wants to keep China as an ally."

All rather interesting but I didn't think Sid Avarson's would-be assassin was an accountant named Lee so nothing was relevant. There were several emails dealing with individual layoffs and the reactions of those fired. One consultant in San Jose had attacked a partner with his fists upon receiving the news. A subsequent memo dealt with hiring a private investigator firm to be present at future layoff interviews. I highlighted in yellow the names of those laid off and of the private investigator firm—our competitor. I also highlighted the names of the male and female partners or managers involved in the layoffs.

Buck called in the early evening. He took my advice about Jeannette's presence and that she'd by our new roommate in stride, said he was impressed with my work as I'd described it and suggested we all go out to dinner at Nick's. He'd called Luke's cell and couldn't reach him but said he'd keep trying and Luke could join us at Emile's. Jeannette eventually awoke from her nap and revived herself with a shower, a change of clothes and copious amounts of mineral water

Good for a model's skin, as we all know.

She was now excited about meeting Buck—"a real life detective"—and about going out to dinner and—after I provided a description of Luke—she was especially intrigued.

Our waiter was new to Emile's, a short, stocky guy with curly blonde hair almost to his shoulders and an Australian accent. Like the rest of the staff, he wore the usual thin, black suspenders over a starched, button-down shirt. The whiteness of the shirt contrasted nicely with his deep tan. Surfer dude turned waiter, undoubtedly. Mr. Aussie greeted us, took our order and thanked us, his expression unchanging.

Jeannette and I ordered the poached salmon with sour cream and assorted vegetables. Buck ordered something called Lobster A L'Americaine and explained that Nick's chef flamed it in cognac, then simmered it in vermouth. Lucky lobster. Buck was chugging down a Budweiser. Jeannette and I had each ordered a Black Velvet, which is equal amounts of champagne and Guinness Stout, and one of us was making swift work of it. I'd also ordered a bottle of mineral water.

We made mostly small talk about the various benefits of living in California versus New York. We also reminisced a lot about some of the New York parties where Jeannette and I had been attendees and Buck had provided security.

I was saving my announcement as to where Jeannette could obtain employment for when everyone had plenty of food and drink in their systems and would be most inclined to be receptive to my stellar idea. While I switched my imbibing to mineral water, Buck ordered another beer, and Jeannette ordered a second Black Velvet.

Good—ramps up the receptivity quotient.

The young Aussie brought our food and we dug in. I glanced over at the bar to see if Nick was looking this way. He wasn't. Had he not heard about the criminal assault visited upon me? I wasn't wearing glasses tonight, thought maybe he'd notice. At work, Doris used to say the partners wouldn't notice the assistants even if they were stark naked with their hair on fire.

Something to try.

Meanwhile Jeannette started drinking my mineral water as I contemplated whether being ignored by Guy or being ignored by Nick was more upsetting. Or just maybe getting attacked and receiving a threatening phone call topped both.

"I have an idea," I said.

Drowning one's sorrows in work was the best remedy.

"I have an idea that will get Jay a place to work and help in our investigation."

"I'll take over stalking High Top de King," Jeannette said.

I'd filled her in on our current caseload after her nap.

"He sounds like a cool dude. Maybe he can introduce me to some musicians."

"No, that's not it." I took the last couple of swallows of my Velvet. "Jeannette can go undercover for us. Work as one of Sid's assistants."

Buck gave me a dubious look. The waiter had returned with a bottle of mineral water Jeannette had ordered, and he gave me a look but it wasn't dubious.

"I don't know, Fred. How do we know he needs one and, even so, what are the odds he'd hire Jeannette," Buck said.

"Excuse me," Jeannette said. "I'll have you know I got all A's in typing in high school and I used my New York boyfriend's computer all the time. Not to mention I'd probably be the best looking candidate they ever saw."

"You see there," I said. "Her office skills are exceeded only by her modesty."

"I repeat…" Buck began.

"First of all, when I spoke to Rosa yesterday to check on Doris' condition—she's still in a coma—she mentioned that they have a temp at the office working in her place. Sid hates temps. Even if they're good. We'll present Jeannette as someone looking for a permanent job or at least as someone amenable to a temp-to-perm position."

"Fine, but…, Buck started to protest.

"Whoever the temp is," I interrupted, "Sid undoubtedly is dissatisfied with her by now and ready for a change and…"

Buck picked up my bottle of mineral water and gently pressed it to my lips.

"Let's say he does want someone new. Jeannette just moved here. California agencies are always suspicious of new residents. They think they're here on a lark, will bolt and go back home any minute. So, again, the odds aren't good that they'll pick her."

"Ah, I've got that covered too," I said. "I called Darva Pinover, the owner of the New York agency that placed me with Sid when his office was on 57th Street. She's good friends with a woman who owns Topflite Temps out here, Anna Darwin. Darva can guarantee Anna will slide Jay in."

"Well…," Buck began.

"I'll give Jeannette my list of highlighted names. She can also go over our Scott Kelly papers beforehand. And Jay gets people to talk. She's an ideal mole."

"You make a compelling argument, babe. There's just one…" Buck's cell phone rang. "Damn. Excuse me."

"Yo," Buck said. "No! How bad? Where? I mean the location. Okay. Okay. I'm coming over. Tell him…okay."

"Tell Nick to put the bill on my tab," Buck said.

He stood, picked up his jacket from the back of the chair and shot a quick glance at me as he began to head for the door.

"Luke's been shot."

CHAPTER 47

THERE'S SOMETHING DEPRESSING AND UNSETTLING about the general ambiance of not all, but most, hospitals. Apart from the drab décor, so much about the physical atmosphere—the walls, the equipment, chairs, desks—all of it looks all too shabby, shopworn, not quite clean. Seedy even. On the other hand, maybe I was getting hypercritical due to the fact that this evening represented my third trip to such halls of healing in little less than a month.

Jeannette and I had insisted on accompanying Buck to St. John's. When we arrived, Luke was still in the Emergency area. The damage had been merely a flesh wound. His left thigh had just been grazed; there was no bullet to excise. Luke was sitting upright on a gurney, waiting to be released.

Nearby my good friend and quasi-romantic love interest, Detective Guy Whitehorse, was in deep conversation with a young intern, who looked nervous. Guy was wearing a dark olive raincoat and underneath appeared to be a tux, complete with white ruffled shirt and black bow tie. *Hmmm.*

I remember my late mother, who was exquisite, brilliant and wise, was appalled at *les mœurs* in the U.S. When I became old enough to date, she was puzzled and annoyed at the inclination of American youth to date sometimes two or three different people at the same time.

"In France," she said, "Such a practice would not work, chérie.

When a man and woman go out, it very quickly...er, soon...becomes sexual. Therefore, even if it is not considered a serious relationship, it is exclusive. *Pourquoi pas?*"

Why not, indeed.

I turned my thoughts away from Guy and to the most important man of the moment, giving Luke a hug and then introducing him to Jeannette, who was moved to hug him also. Buck joined Guy and the doctor and the three talked in low voices. After three or four minutes I saw the young intern give a sort of shaky salute to his interrogators and walk off. Guy and Buck talked, just the two of them, for a few minutes, then joined us at the gurney.

"Hey bro, what happened?"

Buck patted Luke's right shoulder with his fist. Male affection. Guy introduced himself.

"Got too ambitious I guess," Luke said. "Followed that cat home and noticed they parked the car and went around to the back instead of going in the front door. Nothing big about that but when they be walking a Chevy pulls up with some young guys who get out and go tearing after them when they see High Top and troops going back down the path..."

"What did the young guys look like?" Guy asked.

"Latino."

"Any further description you can provide?" Guy said.

"One tall...one kinda short seemed like."

Ohmigod, sounds like the Hernandez boys.

"Go ahead," Guy said. "Then what?"

"I don't know what I expected. Violence maybe...gang meeting? I got out and went down the same path. Seemed to be... the thing to do. Was wearing my Nikes...being real quiet. Sun wasn't all down... but was real shady in that area...especially the farther back you got. Crouched behind some bushes, close enough...to check it out. Well... look like everybody cool, smilin' and talkin', so...I decide to split. Head back just as quiet. All a sudden I hear a shot and my leg feel like somebody knifed it. I take off...limping to...car. Had my gym bag in the car, had...towel in the gym bag. Put towel over wound, tied my belt around it and drove like bat outta hell to Darren's house; it's his car. Almost black out once I get inside...Darren hauls me over here."

Buck bowed his head and rubbed his forehead.

"Shit. I'm getting people nearly killed here."

"It's not you," I said. "You gave Luke and me simple things to do. Somebody out there's evil. Don't blame yourself."

"How many shots did you hear?" Guy asked.

"Seems like…I'd say three," Luke said.

"What can you tell me about the direction of the shots?" Guy asked.

"Coulda come from the sky for all…all I cared once I felt it," Luke spoke haltingly. They'd given him pain medication.

"Actually hadda come from the back of the house…that's where H.T. and his…goons were."

"Goons?" I said.

"Well…I call 'em that. They could be record producers…or movie stars…for all I know. But they're the dudes…they're the ones always with him. Bodyguards…probably."

"Anybody follow you there?" Guy asked.

"Who'd that be? I was the dude who…I was the…follower."

Buck turned to Guy, his posture stiff, his manner defensive.

"As I told you, High Top's wife hired me to tail him," Buck explained. "Simple cheating hubby surveillance."

"Got it," Guy frowned. "And Luke here was doing that for you."

Huge sigh from Buck.

"Right," Buck said. "Freddy had tailed him some days. Me too. I doubt he made any of us. This looks like one of his boys thought Luke was a burglar, don't it?"

A home invasion. Violence. A burglar who isn't really a burglar. Lot of that going around.

Guy had turned away from Buck and looked at me as Buck spoke.

"Did you recognize the kids you saw, Luke?" Guy asked, his eyes still on me.

"Kids," Luke said listlessly.

"The Latino kids who joined High Top in the back of the house," Guy said.

Luke slid his eyes toward me, then back to Guy.

"Nope. No, I can't say…can't say as how I did. Wouldn't say that… no."

"Listen, I can see they've got you good and doped up, Luke,"

Guy said. "I'll have some more questions, but they can hold till tomorrow."

As Guy turned to leave, Buck motioned for him to stay, then went to Luke's side and whispered in his ear. Luke nodded affirmatively.

"Detective, I don't wish to press charges," Luke said.

Guy didn't look all that surprised. "You're sure?"

"No doubt at all."

"Okay," Guy sighed, heading for the door. Looking back at Luke, he added, "Change your mind, let me know."

"That Mrs. King, poor woman," Luke said to us after Guy left. "I scared the shit outta her."

"I'd done the same thing," Buck said. "But not your fault she's high strung."

A nurse arrived with a wheelchair and I pushed him out to the Honda, then Buck and Jeannette helped him onto the front seat.

"We'll get you crutches in the morning. Meanwhile you'll stay at my place tonight," Buck said.

Luke protested but Buck said he felt responsible and wanted to keep an eye on Luke at least for a day or two.

Our purposeful little commune headed back to Buck's house. We got Luke settled on a couch with blankets and extra cushions under his butt to give some lift to the injured thigh. Buck dialed for pizza delivery, and we called out our orders to him. Once sated with food and bottles of Sam Adams, Buck interrogated Luke some; but the day spent tailing High Top's shopping spree was unremarkable and the shooting incident was just as he'd described it in the hospital with no revelatory clues or comments to be added.

Neither had any revelatory clues or comments been forthcoming during the hospital scenario regarding a certain tuxedo.

CHAPTER 48

THIS MORNING BUCK ANNOUNCED HE wanted to confer with Holly *vis-à-vis* the shooting before the cops arrived. High Top would also have to be questioned in regard to Luke's shooting; thus, our cover would be blown in regard to the surveillance. But before undertaking this project, he'd had gone out to pick up a box of Crispy Crème donuts for everyone. Buck broke a Crispy Crème in half, nibbled a little and admitted he didn't relish an early a.m. confab with the redoubtable Mrs. King.

"She'll probably fry my ass for not coming up with a little blonde paramour by now," was how he put it. "I've also got to meet with Nan Kelly again, Fred. You might as well go with me when I do that. The sooner, the better."

He poured coffee into a thermos, grabbed his car keys, stuck a donut in his mouth and flew out the front door, leaving his houseguests and about twenty remaining Crispy Crèmes in his wake.

Last night we learned that the two upholstered chairs in Buck's living room open up into single beds. Luke was now comfortably ensconced on one, garbed in some red plaid pajamas Buck had fished from the bottom or a drawer and, he'd inferred, another lifetime. One box of donuts rested on Luke's lap. Jeannette had just brought him a fresh cup of coffee. The pleas I'd anticipated to be taken to Darren's place were not forthcoming. Crutches supplied by the hospital were leaning against a nearby couch. Luke had the television turned to the *Today* show, seemingly mesmerized by Meredith Vieira's interview with actor Kevin Bacon.

I found the number of the employment agency in New York and put in a call to Darva Pinover. I'd lost the paper containing the information Darva had supplied as to the name of the Los Angeles agency and last name of the agency's owner. Anna somebody. Proof positive that I was not good at details and thus not suited to be an assistant, but rather a full-fledged detective, if anything. My rationale anyway.

After leaving word twice and being on hold for what seemed like twenty minutes, I got thru to Darva. Another anticipation blown: she wasn't at all irritated at having to supply the data all over again. Darva had been a counselor, as well as the owner, when we'd met in New York. We'd bonded when she revealed she was a former model. We'd giggled together when I admitted some folks claimed to mistake me for Cameron Diaz, and she shared that her friends insisted she now resembled Julia Child. She'd laughed a year ago when I'd advised I'd moved to California, accusing me of lusting for some Cameron-like fame, and laughed again this morning upon learning I'd misplaced the agency data, mentioning something about losing brain cells once on the Left Coast.

Being a transplanted model in the land of Hollywood is an endless source of amusement it would seem.

"You know, Freddy," Darva said. "It's best I call Anna myself anyway. Sorta grease the way for you. She can be a bit of a bitch, but I can convince her to get your friend installed at Sid's. Give me a half hour or so. I'll call you back."

Pierre had wandered in the kitchen to lap at his water dish while I was talking to Darva.

"She's going to call us back, Pierre," I said. "Project corporate spy is about to roll."

Pierre gave me a dubious look. Surprising. I really thought he'd appreciate the cleverness of the plan.

By now Jeannette had joined Luke's *Today* show viewing, curled up on the nearby couch. I plopped down on the other couch to pass the time until Darva called back. Meredith was now interviewing a chef behind a low table of various casserole dishes. The whole thing didn't look all that interesting, but Luke and Jeannette giggled every time Meredith did. I made a comment that the salad looked rather soggy. No one replied or seemed to notice. After the cooking segment blessedly ended, some commercials and a bit of news from Matt Lauer, the phone rang.

"Freddy, here's the deal," Darva said. "Anna will get Jeannette the gig but only if I supply another assistant. She needs someone to replace the temp who replaced Doris and also Sid's second assistant who's turned in her resignation and will just be around for a few more days. If I can deliver two girls to her right away, she'll go for it. If not, she's got other people she wants to use."

"And the second assistant would be…" I began.

"You, Cameron baby," Darva laughed.

It could work. Sid had not recognized me in Santa Fe as his former temp and even if my identity eventually dawned on him I'd be working in the same capacity so that enhanced the believability of the ruse.

"You've got a deal," I said.

"Great. Anna wants to see you both at her office at two today. Don't worry, it's just a formality. But make a note, some days she's warm and friendly, other days she's snippy. On all days she loves to talk so just humor her and you won't have a problem."

"I'll hang on her every word," I said.

"Good. Let me know if there's any problems. And let me know when you're coming East again. There's this great Italian place I discovered in SoHo, near that bar we used to go to."

"The Ear Inn," I said.

"Yeah, that bar. Gotta run, kid."

I heard someone talking to Darva in the background. The phone clicked before I could say goodbye.

Jeannette was delighted when I told her we'd be working *a deux* at Sid's. She reminded me her good clothes were still stashed at my place, so I grabbed the keys to Buck's truck and we made a quick trip over and back to pick up her luggage and whatever outfit in my closet that was both uncut and appropriate. Once back we took mugs of fresh coffee into the guest bedroom and executed a dual wardrobe search for the perfect interview outfits. I picked a black Bill Blass suit and black Jimmy Choo's. I took off my arm sling and the band aids on my cut fingers, not the best accessories for a typist's job. My arm still felt tremulous when I even picked up a hairbrush but I could fake it. Jay selected a beige Bill Blass suit and her only shoes that seemed to match—brown satin Manolos. Not your typical secretarial garb, but it was all either of us had. Hopefully the high-end duds would not alienate Madame Anna. I hauled out an ironing board, and we pressed the suits into employment-ready crispness.

As I searched my jewelry box for the right watch and some tiny pearl earrings, Jeannette stood in front of the bureau mirror arranging her wild curls into a business-like bun. She nodded toward my hospital flowers still languishing on the dresser in front of her.

"You know I been watering those babies for you."

"Thanks. Luke brought them in here. I guess I just ignored them," I said.

"Who are the roses from?"

"Oh, from Guy Whitehorse. Yellow roses mean friendship, right? Really knows how to sweep a girl off her feet."

I found tiny diamond earrings.

"I know, I read the card from Guy. I mean the *red* roses," Jay said.

"You know, I didn't notice. Look at the card."

"They're the only ones that didn't have a card," she said.

CHAPTER 49

IF ANYONE THOUGHT THE SIGHT of two tall women in designer suits driving a pickup truck into the high-end corporate and commercial environs of Century City posed an intriguing sight, you could not have proved it by us. No one gaped, honked or whistled. Rather disappointing.

On the way over, Jay and I had a friendly argument over the mysterious red roses. Her contention was their sender was my would-be burglar and attacker. My rebuttal was that the gesture of sending a dozen roses was not an act provoked by the same emotion that rendered me kicked and cut and hit over the head, even considering tough love, and the card had probably just been lost between the hospital and Buck's house.

Topflite Temps was located in the southernmost building of the twin towers on Century Park East. We parked the truck in the bowels of the appropriate tower and took a crowded elevator to the twenty-second floor. At Topflite, a receptionist gave us applications to complete. Two other women in their twenties sat in nearby chairs addressing the same project only without the constant conferring and giggling Jay and I brought to the effort. Our entries were mostly fictitious; theirs must have lacked our creative flair. The reception area boasted gray carpeting, narrow gray upholstered client chairs, a glass coffee table whose surface contained a stack of thin *Working World* magazines and a gray ceramic bud vase, absent any buds. The twenty-something's regarded us with curiosity. The receptionist, a slightly pudgy lady in her early sixties with dyed black hair teased to the max and serious false eyelashes, favored us with a glare. In a few minutes, the receptionist rose from her desk, advised the two other applicants they could go in for their tests, indicating a small hallway jutting off the right side of the waiting area. Then she approached us.

"Are you through?"

She gave us a sweet, benign smile that didn't match the sour tone to her voice.

"Are we ever," Jeannette said as we handed over our papers in unison.

Miss Black Hair returned to her desk, accidentally knocked over a glass jar full of pencils and spewed forth a stream of expletives just as a smiling woman of about forty appeared from the hallway. The new arrival wore a cream crew-necked jersey and black pants with brown faux alligator loafers.

"I'm Anna Darwin," she said, extending her hand. "Did Carla get you some coffee?"

Carla, the charmer formerly known as Miss Black Hair, favored us with one of the scowls she'd bestowed during the application procedure.

I said, "No, we're good."

"Right this way to my office," Anna said.

We followed her down the narrow hall to a tiny room, surprisingly more cheerful with guest chairs, a desk and an étagère all in blonde wood. We must have caught Anna on one of the good days Darva described, as she was warm and friendly. She said she'd wave the usual tests based on the stellar recommendations we'd both received from Darva Pinover. She asked a lot of personal questions, where we lived, what we thought of Los Angeles, did we go to the beach often. She schmoozed on and on, and I almost dozed off when she began to hold forth on the merits of various dry cleaners in the area. Still, it was a hell of a lot better than typing and computer tests so even though the interview stretched to a little over an hour I left with warm and fuzzy feelings for Anna Darwin, and a great sense of relief.

Once back at Buck's, Jeannette got a beer and joined Luke in front of the television for some *Oprah* watching. I got a diet Pepsi and hauled

Scott Kelly's laptop and Buck's printer, which blessedly was compatible, back to the dining room table. I used the password Nan had provided to get into his email library for some serious research. There wasn't much of interest in the memos directly to and from Scott. Just the usual accounting firm jargon and the ubiquitous acronyms. Every memo contained statements along the lines of *The CRM's will have a meeting with the LIM's regarding SACSE and the RAD problem.* I was reminded of exactly why I'd suddenly risen from my desk at Potter, Wood & Penn and walked out for the last time at a quarter to five on a Wednesday, scratching the nervous rash I'd developed on my hands all the way down in the elevator.

The emails on which Scott Kelly was copied proved to be a bit more titillating. The subject matter of these memos was ostensibly client issues, administrative concerns and new business procurement. But woven into a great many of them were comments on Sid Avarson. He was variously described as over reaching, a control freak, excessively intense. He was the leader of an important division, but obviously not a popular one. It was no news to me that the support staff members and middle managers hated his guts. That his peers used much the same descriptive invective as many of the secretaries employed was a bit more of a revelation. And a gratifying one.

"He thinks he motivates people to rise to their highest competence," one partner wrote, "but he doesn't, he pisses them off." A regional manager wrote about his "confrontational style" and another partner said Sid "won't survive in this company as a top gun. Top dogs get picked by their peers who are fans and this guy's got no fan club out there."

But then there was one reply to these attacks by none other than Scott. Scott wrote that although "some folks think he's a first class jerk" that he, Scott, and others he inferred, deemed Sid to be "extremely smart, a great deal maker and a visionary." Scott did allow that Sid could be a "grade A sphincter at times." Which means—if you look up 'sphincter', and I did—that Sid was a prize asshole.

I hit 'print' and produced the whole lot in paper form, then began applying the yellow highlighter to all this verbiage, including Scott's 'visionary', etcetera comments.

While Luke and Jay were enjoying a second round of beers and television's Nancy Grace was pontificating on some criminal case,

Buck arrived home with pizzas. I was grateful for Buck's protection and hospitality, but the steady diet of donuts and pizza was beginning to wear thin.

I cleared away all the Potter, Wood & Penn debris and set the dining room table. The four of us attacked the pizzas—this time green pepper and sausage—and Buck reported on his meeting with Holly King.

Actually, "Nothing much to report," was what he announced.

"I got there before the BHPD," he said, "but High Top and his cronies were elsewhere. Whitehorse was due there in fifteen minutes and Master King would return in time to meet him Holly said but they'd gone off somewhere in his Bentley."

"So just who shot Luke?" Jeannette asked.

"Holly did. Thought he was a prowler. Simple as that. She said she saw Luke through the windows—or 'a shadowy figure' as she described it. Said there'd been a lot of burglaries in the area of late and she thought this was the perp. Grabbed a Colt Pocket Nine 9mm she knew High kept in a desk and just started firing through the window."

"Damn," Luke said, "She ever hear of dialing 911?"

"She's a pretty high strung chick," Buck said. "Plus she's still wired over the shooting at Avarson's. She's sure someone's out to frame her husband for it. She's sure someone's out to get High Top period. She's still chewing on this other-woman theory, feels there's some broad out there also eager to screw him, one way or another."

"Has she no faith at all in your surveillance reports?" I asked. "Plus you told her you'd do everything possible to find who actually shot and hit Doris or tried to shoot Sid."

Buck shrugged and sipped his beer.

"Maybe she trusts me at the end of the day. She was pretty hysterical when we talked, probably in anticipation of having to meet with the cops in a few minutes."

"Well," I said, "I've got the Scott Kelly stuff all ready for you. And Jeannette starts working at Collins, Penn & Wood tomorrow. I don't start until Thursday because that's when the other assistant gets back from vacation and can train me."

"That works for me because I need you to trek over to Nan Kelly's with me again."

“What more can we get out of that woman that we didn’t get and you didn’t get the other day?” I asked.

“She was so uncooperative I never got into half the stuff I need. When she didn’t talk much even with you there, I figured she’s one of those I gotta soften up first. But I need a lot of names and places from her—any family doctors, psychiatrists or therapists they might go to, financial records, names of places like their country club, vet, personal trainer, barber, dry cleaners and so forth. Plus I want to talk to the household help when Nan baby isn’t around.”

“How do we find out when she won’t be around? Stage a stakeout and just watch the door?”

“Easier than that. My appointment with her yesterday? She wasn’t home. Never called to cancel. I called her later and the maid answered. Maid’s name is Angelina Rios. She was about to leave for the day when I called so we’ll buzz over there tomorrow and see what we can get out of her.”

“I repeat,” I said. “How do we know Nan won’t be there when we want to interrogate this Angelina?”

“Because Angelina said Nan Kelly left a note and hasn’t been home for the last three days.”

CHAPTER 50

SOMETIMES LIFE SUCKS. DORIS HERNANDEZ remained in a coma. One of our clients, Nan Kelly, had inexplicably gone missing. The other, Holly King, was dogging on Buck constantly. Jeannette and I had just been sentenced to an open-ended stint at corporate hell, and because of that I'd turned down a modeling gig at Fashion's Night Out, a big extravaganza featuring L.A. designer Trina Turk. *Vogue* was involved and many other designers would be there. Just not *moi*. No one by the name of Guy Whitehorse had given me so much as a recent nod and, worst of all, the Lakers had just lost to the Minnesota Timberwolves, 80-96. Even Kobe and Lamar were in a slump, the team's general performance as unpredictable as Nan Kelly of late.

Speaking of which, Buck had checked with his answering service early this morning to hear a message left by Nan: "Don't bother looking for Scott. It's all hopeless."

That was right up there in the rational department with "Die, you hypocritical bitch."

Come to think of it, maybe the purveyors of both cryptic gems were one and the same person. That can't be. I'm getting paranoid.

"Almost sounds like a suicide message, doesn't it?" I asked Buck.

He was standing beside me in his kitchen, opening two Crispy Crème boxes as I poured fresh coffee into four non-matching mugs. Jeannette was primping in the guest bedroom, garbed in a white blouse, black skirt, and black opaque hose. Such conservative dress was against her religion of style, but she was game. Luke was perched on a stool, Pierre parked at its base, both eager for donuts. Luke, at last, was also eager to go home and had changed into his newly laundered day-of-shooting attire of black jeans and turtleneck after days of lounging around in clothes borrowed from Buck.

"Not necessarily," Buck said in reply to my suicide theory.

He carried his coffee and one Crispy Crème box out of the kitchen and sat down to peruse Scott Kelly's papers, which had been spread out on the dining room table. Luke and Pierre followed the donut trail.

"Girlfriend, we gotta get a move on," Jeannette came flying out of the bedroom, a large black tote bag in one hand, a hairbrush in the other.

"You're right."

I took one more bite from an untouched donut, retrieved my purse from the bedroom and joined the others in the dining room. Buck was absorbed in paper sifting, Pierre had jumped on top of the table and was being fed donut crumbs by Luke. Jeannette was taking deep breaths.

"Buck, if you don't get your ass outta that chair, I'm not doing this gig," Jeannette said.

She was right. We had a full day ahead of us. First we had to drop Jay off. She was headed for Century City again but this time for her first day at Potter, Wood on Avenue of the Stars. Needless to say, she loved the street name. Then we were taking Luke back to Darren's, after which Buck had promised to take me furniture shopping so I could move back into a habitable apartment. And after that we were slated to interview Nan Kelly's maid. I was grateful for the full schedule; it would take my mind off Detective Whitehorse, Derek Fisher's missed three pointers and Luke Walton's listless performance.

"Get your ass outta that chair, Buck," Luke mimicked in his best falsetto.

"Okay," Buck grinned. "If you three girls will just be patient, I gotta get my gun."

Gun? The three of us stared at each other, amateur sleuths all. It wasn't news to me, of course, that Buck occasionally carried, but he was always very low key about it.

"I didn't sign on for no gig that involves guns." Jay began brushing her hair furiously.

Buck returned from his bedroom, adjusting his holster.

"Relax, I just want to be prepared for any foul play over at the Kelly's. I don't expect any, it's just good to be prepared."

Our little party trooped to the garage and climbed into Buck's Honda. He headed for Main Street and then over to Montana Avenue in Santa Monica as he had to drop off something to a client there.

On Seventh there'd been two priests talking to some school kids next to the cream-colored walls of St. Monica's. On Fourth two little girls of around six or seven, dressed in school uniforms of gray and navy, exited a corner apartment building and walked swiftly along the sidewalk bordered by tall palms. They were each clutching the hands of two adult women—either their moms or nannies, obviously needing an escort to the school a mere three blocks away. I remembered when I was a pre-schooler in Paris and my mother sent me off on a field trip to London. All of the French children in our nursery school piled on the bus *sans* mom or dad, but the American children in our class were either absent from this adventure or accompanied by their mothers.

"Kids don't rule in France, like they do in the U.S.," my mother advised me one day shortly after my hasty Las Vegas nuptials with Sonny Bob. I think she believed our marriage portended pending parenthood and thus some child-raising commentary was in order.

She then cast a skeptical eye at me and declared, almost defensively, that my own childhood was *pas mal.*

"No, it wasn't bad at all," I'd replied.

Indeed when my mother and father sent my brother and I off to my paternal grandmother's in Saint-Remy-de-Provence in southwestern France for the entire summer, we were overjoyed and not in the least resentful that my parents were now together in Paris to enjoy that city's delights...and each other, without the kiddies.

I could hear my mother's voice so clearly saying, "In France the children must adapt to adults, not vice versa as here."

She'd elaborated on the subject at some length, then lit a cigarette—her only vice—and gave me a sad smile. Regret for the independent life she'd led or a yearning for my long-lost childhood, I knew not which. But I did know she'd been a spectacular mother. Cancer had claimed her six years ago and I'd missed her every day since.

If I didn't cease this reminiscing I'd cry so to shake off the nostalgia, I rolled down a window to get some air and peer at the gray sky. It was unseasonably warm for December, and the low clouds were keeping the heat in. In the back seat, Jeannette continued fussing with her hair, and Luke lit up a cigar he'd pinched from Buck's coffers.

By the time we reached Century City and the Potter, Wood building, the sun had come out. We pulled up and Jeannette got out.

"Are you nervous?" I asked.

"Hell, yes. Girl, I don't know what I'm doing. I don't know what we're doing. I can barely type, you don't know from filing, I can't..."

"We both use our home computers big time," I said. "Sid's big deal is travel, and we've both done a lot of that. I'll do fine. You'll do even better."

"Thanks," Jeannette said softly.

Rather than flippant, she sounded sincerely grateful for the vote of confidence, flashed an absent-minded smile, turned and walked swiftly toward the lobby door, furiously smoothing a few tangled curls that threatened to escape from her bun. If her height and red hair didn't make an impression on PW&P, the bright pink Christian Louboutin heels surely would.

We backtracked, headed to Marina del Rey where Luke parked his rig on Washington Boulevard near the duck pond. Buck had also lit up a cigar, and I hung my head out the window. There was a slight breeze and the sight of all the docked boats gently rocking on the calm waters was soothing. Luke needed to get things from his truck first so we pulled up to the opposite curb and waited. He had graduated from the crutches to a cane, and he crossed the street and returned with a knapsack with relative grace. We dropped him off at Darren's, then headed for the California Incline to Pacific Coast Highway and Malibu. A stream of cars was heading into the parking lot of the peach-colored Jonathan Beach Club. Must be hosting a brunch for the members' wives. As we passed, I saw two anorexic blondes in white tennis shorts exiting their car as an attendant greeted them. The next lot boasted a sight prettier than the blondes: a nearby wall of lush red Bougainvillea. On the boardwalk two tanned, dark haired young men bicycled by, prettier than both the blondes and the Bougainvillea.

We pulled into the lot near Nan's house, parked and headed for her teal blue front door. Buck gave two heavy raps with the large brass knocker. We waited a couple of minutes. I pushed the doorbell and heard the chimes from within. We looked at each other, waited, then tried the knocker again. No response. Buck moved as close as he could get to a nearby window to peer in. Thick foliage of different varieties was planted around the immediate edge of the house, making it hard to see inside any of the windows. I leaned on the bell.

Buck returned to the door, gave the knocker three heavy-handed raps, then retrieved from a zippered pocket on his windbreaker a thick metal wedge and slid it vertical to the hasp. The house was not particularly new and the door was slightly warped. It gave immediately.

As we stepped inside, Buck shook his hand, returned the wedge to his pocket and momentarily sucked on one finger.

"Damn, that hurt. Where the hell is Angelina? Is this the freaking house of disappearing females?"

He was loud when he spoke, but I thought I heard muffled voices from somewhere.

"Buck, listen."

"What?"

"I think I heard people," I whispered.

I went to the window to see if it came from outside. The sun had gone behind the clouds, and I could tell some wind was kicking up but there was no one in sight.

Buck headed down the hallway and called out, "Angelina!" No answer. We traipsed into and around the living room, back out to the hall and into the kitchen. Buck went out the back door to the patio as I stood and watched from the door. In the process of our tour, he'd yelled out "Angelina!" four more times, to no avail.

"Maybe she's out running errands," I said.

"Why are you whispering?" Buck asked.

"I don't know," I whispered.

"Well, let's go check the upstairs, Sherlock," Buck whispered.

We headed back down the hall toward the stairs. As we reached the entryway, a pretty Hispanic woman was slowly coming down the stairs. She was very slim, barely five feet two or so and wore a loose white peasant blouse over white jeans. On her feet were yellow sandals.

"Angelina?" Buck said.

"I'm Angelina Rios, yes," she said to me even though it was Buck who had spoken. "Call me Angie."

She seemed shy, almost nervous. She didn't extend her hand, so Buck made introductions.

"I'm Buck Lemoyne, a private investigator. This is my associate, Freddy Bonnaire."

I merely smiled and nodded. She looked too ill at ease to handle a handshake.

"Miss Angie, were you sleeping?" Buck said pleasantly. "I must have yelled your name a dozen times just now."

"I'm very sorry," Angie said. "Right this way."

We followed her back down the long hallway and into the living room.

"Please sit. What can I get you to drink?"

"I take it Mrs. Kelly is still among the missing," Buck said.

"I don't…I don't know," Angie replied. "Today is her monthly spa day. She's always away all day on this day so maybe…maybe she'll be back tonight. I just don't know."

Clearly talking to private eye types was not Angie's favorite thing. Buck grinned to put her at ease.

"Sure, we'll have something to drink. Anything that's easy."

"I made some iced tea," Angie said.

Almost in unison Buck and I chorused, "Iced tea will be fine." We sat down together on the green couch.

"Well, I mean I was about to make some iced tea. It will take a minute."

"No problem," I said.

Buck let out a heavy sigh, and I gave him a *be-nice* frown.

Buck picked up an issue of *Town & Country* from the coffee table and began thumbing through it. I sat back and gazed out the window. In Nan's absence, Angie apparently kept the heavy plaid drapes open. I'd kind of miss Nan's little part-drapes-gaze-wistfully-at-sea drama. The sun had gone missing also, and the sky remained a washed-out gray.

After what seemed a painfully long wait, Angie returned with a silver tray bearing two tall glasses of tea, in which there were a lot of ice cubes, two slices of lemon each and a large mint leaf. Presentation is everything. She placed the tray on the coffee table and retrieved coasters from a nearby end table.

Angie sat on the straight chair where Nan had always sat during my previous visits. She folded her arms across her chest and rubbed them as if she were cold. With the sun behind clouds, the room was dreary even with the drapes open so I made myself at home, got up and turned on a couple of lamps. This was a house, it would seem, given to darkness.

Buck took a quick gulp of tea and set the glass down.

"Angie, as you may know, Mrs. Kelly has hired me to find her husband. She recently left me a phone message to the contrary, but I have to assume she's in an emotional state right now so I'm operating on the assumption that I'm still employed."

He brought out a pen and a folded piece of white paper from an inside pocket.

"I've jotted down a few pieces of information I need about Mr. Kelly. Places he goes to, services he uses. Well, you take a look at it."

He handed the paper to Angie. She took it and slowly unfolded it.

From a pocket Buck drew out a pen for Angie, but she appeared absorbed in his notes.

"If you'll just write down the information in the space I've left next to each item, that would be great."

His hand still held the pen in mid-air.

"If you have any questions about any of that, just ask. When you're done, we'll get out of your hair."

Buck smiled and extended his pen hand further.

As he talked, Buck was speaking loudly the way some people do when they think their listener may not quite understand the language. Angie had a slight accent, but she appeared to understand English perfectly well. As he spoke, I could have sworn I heard a door close somewhere.

Angie looked up almost with a start and finally took the pen. She returned to reading Buck's list, without writing. Buck and I proceeded to sip our tea. We kept sipping, and eventually Angie placed the paper on the coffee table and commenced short little scribbles. She paused at length between each scribble. We finished our tea.

Angie stood up. "I need to look up one of these names, if you'll excuse me," she said.

"Of course," I said.

"I'll get you some more tea." She picked up each glass and placed them on the tray.

"That's okay, we're good, Angie," Buck said, but she'd already turned and headed for the kitchen. Buck sat back on the couch and I picked up the *Town & Country*. The magazine layouts reminded me of furniture. I showed Buck one of the pages and pointed.

"Do you suppose I could pick up a chair like that this afternoon?" I was whispering again.

"There probably won't be time at the rate this day is going," Buck whispered.

"Yes there will. We'll nip over to Z Gallerie and Pottery Barn. I know exactly what want."

From outside I heard a car start up and from the kitchen Angie dropped something metal.

"Can we help you?" Buck called out.

In two seconds Angie walked back into the living room.

"I just dropped the tray," she said, and returned to the kitchen.

"I heard a car outside," I said.

"Probably just neighbors," Buck said, but he got up and went to look out the window.

Angie returned with the tray and fresh iced teas. She placed them on the coffee table, never taking her eyes off Buck at the window. He was wearing a black windbreaker over a Hawaiian shirt with pink and red flowers on a black background, black jeans and well-shined brown loafers without socks, but I doubted his sartorial splendor and manly charms were what engaged Angie. She clearly still appeared nervous.

Buck headed back to the couch.

"We're getting rain again," he frowned.

Angie addressed the paper again, reading but not writing. This house was also given to procrastination. Buck chug-a-lugged his tea, completely finishing it in a few gulps as if to signal Angie that *tempus fugit*. She began writing at last and looked back and forth at the window as if the view provided inspiration. I never saw any indication of where and how she retrieved the information she said she had to look up, but I was feeling too restless to quibble.

Suddenly she lay down the pen and handed the paper to Buck.

"It's done."

Angie stood. "It's over now. You can go."

She spoke forcefully as if the words carried great weight. We weren't going to be without drama in Nan's absence after all.

"It's okay to leave now," she repeated.

Buck looked puzzled and I'm sure I did too.

"You seem upset, Angie," I said.

"I'm not upset. I'm okay now. I was upset but now I'm not." She folded and hugged her arms again.

"He's gone now," she said. "Scott Kelly was just here. But he's gone now."

CHAPTER 51

"WHAT?!" BUCK STOOD UP ABRUPTLY with a fierce look, bordering on outright anger.

With that, Angie Rios sat down abruptly, with a sad look bordering on outright tears.

I went to the kitchen in search of Kleenex and booze. What I found was some cans of Miller Light in the fridge and paper towels. Good enough. I placed my supplies on a plastic tray I spied near the sink and returned to the living room.

Buck was regurgitating a stream of the inevitable why-what-where questions. Angie wasn't speaking but had switched from lamenting to sibilating—rocking back and forth, emitting a hissing sound. I handed her a section of paper towel and one of the Millers. She ignored the beer but reached for the towel and blew her nose.

"Let's all sit down," I said, sitting down.

Buck sat, chugged the beer.

"Okay, Angie, Scott Kelly was here in this house," I said. "Just please tell us what he said and did." I paused for effect. "Start from the beginning."

A banal instruction, but it's what they always say on TV cop shows.

"Can I get you something to drink other than the beer?" I said.

Angie picked up the can of Miller and tipped it back and forth, as she took about five healthy swallows in a row.

Guess the answer is no.

She returned the can to the table in a slow, prim little motion and clasped her hands tightly in her lap.

"I let myself in the house same time I always get here, about nine." Angie looked not at us, but in the direction of the window as she spoke. "I hear man's voice coming from upstairs the minute I got inside. He cursing loud, and I got scared. I thought maybe a robber. I start to go call 911, and then I hear the voice better. I hear him say…well…he used the Lord's name in vain and then he say *damn*. That time I can tell it Mr. Kelly's voice. I go upstairs and ask him what's wrong. He have one of those…he have duffle bag and he stuffing clothes in it. When he see me, he say, 'Where the hell is my laptop?' I say I no know."

"Had Nan Kelly told you where it was?" Buck said.

"No, no, she no tell," Angie said. "Mr. Kelly, he say over and over, 'You must know, you must know.' That the way he is. I see him be that way many, many days. He always thinks people are lying if they no say right answer. But the only place I ever see it is in his office, so I say I don't know. I told him Mrs. Kelly must have it, and that just made him madder."

"When you guys rang the bell, Mr. Kelly say, 'Who the hell can that be?'" Angie continued. "I lie. I say probably a decorator Mrs. Kelly told to come. I say he supposed to be here today. He say take whoever at door to the living room and keep talking to him. He say he no feel like seeing anyone. He made me promise not to say he here. He say he fire me if I did."

"Just so you know," Buck said. "I have the laptop. If Scott Kelly should contact you again before I talk to him, you may tell him I have it. You may explain his wife hired me to find him, and I took possession of it in conjunction with my search." Buck took a sip of beer. "Actually you don't have to explain anything. Just remember to tell him I have it so he's not ragging on you."

Angie nodded.

"What else did he have to say?" Buck said. "Did he talk about where he'd been or where he was going?"

"No, no, he no say. And I no ask."

It was clear there was no point to interrogating Angie further. Scott Kelly did not have to answer to his housekeeper regarding his whereabouts nor justify his purpose in being in his own home. Buck retrieved his question sheet from the coffee table, folded it into a pocket in his windbreaker and took a final swig of beer. We offered Angie a ride home, but she insisted she'd feel better if she finished her remaining chores plus she had plans to meet friends and take a later bus home with them, so we left.

Mellowed by the before-noon beer, Buck agreed to take me furniture shopping. We chewed on the subject of Scott Kelly's appearance as we headed for Santa Monica's Third Street Promenade area. There wasn't much to discuss because we still didn't know a lot. Kelly doubtless chose this day to pick up some clothes and his laptop because he knew it was Nan's spa day, and he'd avoid a confrontation. Buck thought the whole continuing scenario reeked of something more substantial than one of his little marital sabbaticals. I wasn't so sure.

We found a parking spot in the garage near Macy's. The sun had come out again, and the area was unusually full of people for a weekday. The air had warmed, but Buck kept his jacket on to conceal the holster and gun he wore at all times these days. He'd been further mollified regarding a shopping expedition when I'd mentioned I planned to finance the expedition from my savings. I think he'd harbored the possibility that I would hit him up for a loan, given the relatively limited funds I'd collected from modeling so far.

Despite the crowds, the Promenade itself was low key. It was too early for the street performers and too chilly for the forty-something lady who frequently graces the streets in high heels, short dress with spaghetti straps, abundant décolletage and a sunburst of platinum blonde hair.

I thought I spied another regular—a sixtyish woman always garbed in black pumps, black tights and a black suit jacket who advised me once she was the Promenade's resident nurse. She too sported a large halo of hair, gray in her case. Hair clearly is the first bastion of eccentricity. A homeless man, getting a late start on his day, was just rolling up his thin collection of bedding in front of a Tommy Hilfinger's store. A man with a little boy waiting in line at the Cineplex Odeon theater looked a lot like Dennis Quaid, but I couldn't be sure.

We popped into Pottery Barn, and I bought some glasses and two vases, which only began to replace the smashed glassware courtesy of my would-be burglar. He'd destroyed much of the contents of my condo, but some of Gram's lovely pieces were intact. He hadn't bothered to smash the Italian gilt wood mirror, and the Louis XVI loveseat would just need reupholstering. Therefore I was going to purchase new things that would blend in.

"I don't want anything too pristine," I told Buck. "I want things that look like they have the wear and tear of centuries of use." He groaned.

We backtracked to Z Gallerie where I selected two chairs upholstered in bright yellow and trimmed in distressed white wood and two black wicker chairs, mainly because their cushions boasted a print in the red and yellow color combination that would match. Each store had promised to make delivery on a Saturday. Next we wove our way through the Santa Monica Place Mall, crossed Colorado to Sears and therein purchased a queen bed for my room and two twins for my guest bedroom, all with super firm mattresses. I opted not to get their matching headboards. Somewhere else on another day I knew I could find antique iron bedsteads.

Pottery Barn and Z Gallerie committed to deliveries in four weeks, but Sears promised the beds this Saturday. All these happy acquisitions would further slenderize my already shrinking savings account but what's a girl to do?

"I'm set," I announced to Buck. "Let's go eat. How's a nice stroll down the boardwalk to the Sidewalk Café for their great burgers and some Corona beer sound and then to the antique stores in Venice?"

"Sounds like sheer folly, kid. I'm playing hooky as it is from the High Top tail. Let's grab some Chinese."

We headed north toward Wilshire Boulevard, moving through a light crowd of a few locals and tourists, three panhandlers and a very large woman handing out Jews for Jesus pamphlets.

"I thought Holly King was directing her zeal toward exonerating hubby in the Avarson place shooting instead of the infidelity thing," I said. "Besides when we got Luke exonerated from a trespassing charge didn't we blow our cover?"

"Thought I told you. When your friend Whitehorse filled me in on the scene at the stationhouse, he said that when King learned Luke was doing a tail for me and I'd been hired by wifey he not only declined to press charges he said he didn't want any of this to get to Holly King."

"So he doesn't want his wife to know he knows she's had a private eye nipping at his heels?"

"That's the deal. King said he'd explain to Mrs. King that it was all a case of mistaken identity, that Luke was visiting in the neighborhood, just picked the wrong house."

"Strange. You'd think he'd be one pissed hubby. So Luke's been made as far as she knows, but you're clear to do the tail and she's still hot to catch High Top in unacceptable social intercourse."

"She flip flops," Buck said as he held the glass door of the restaurant for me. "Every day she calls the service and gives me different marching orders. I get these messages where she's half yelling and half coughing. Woman smokes like a fiend."

After a quick lunch at P. F. Chang's, I made Buck haul me to Pavilions on Montana Avenue so we could pick up some provisions and avoid the dining-on-pizza rut. I got what I needed to rustle up simple salad-steak-baked-potato dinner and eggs, cream cheese, Tabasco pepper sauce and milk for a special breakfast concoction Gram taught me to make that would replace the Crispy Cremes tomorrow morning.

That accomplished, we headed back to Buck's. He parked the car in front and helped me carry the groceries. As we walked up the path to the house, I entertained the lovely idea of a long, hot bubble bath and a tall, cold diet Pepsi. Buck turned the key in the door, set his grocery bag on the floor and said, "Adios."

As I started toward the kitchen, I heard the phone ringing and made a beeline for it.

"Hello."

I said I was feeling much better in answer to the caller's first question. And I was feeling better still when I answered *yes* to the second question. It was one Detective Guy Whitehorse asking me to dinner tomorrow night.

CHAPTER 52

"This clown is apparently hated by his co-workers," Buck was saying as he stirred his coffee. "So why not his neighbors? It's worth a shot."

We'd finished breakfast and were sitting at the dining room table planning our day. Luke had surprised us five minutes ago by arriving at the door, ready to escort Jeanette to work in his roommate's new Jeep Cherokee.

"Breakin' it in for him," Luke had said.

Holly King had advised that High was under wraps and at home until the afternoon when he had an interview scheduled at Chateau Marmont with *Vanity Fair* magazine. Buck would catch up with him there. Thus our morning was free, and he was plotting the possibility of more research on Sid Avarson.

"Workalcoholics like Sid don't usually *know* their neighbors let alone have time for issues with them," I offered.

"Point taken. But didn't you say he works from home a lot? So I go and grill the neighbors. Can't hurt. Plus last night Jeannette said she'd had phone conversations with him where the background noise sounded like people splashing in a pool and a couple where he was calling in from his kid's little league game. Sounds like ole Sid finds some time for social interaction when not placing nose to grindstone."

"And think of the Hernandez boys," Luke had commented. "What the hell were they doing at High Top's house?"

"Don't know. But they're all musicians," I said.

"Yeah right," Buck said. "At opposite sides of the financial spectrum I'd say. When two polar opposite segments of society get together, it's been my experience something fishy is going down."

"Okay. Could be worth it for us to check all of them out," I said.

"Where do you get this *us* concept, Tonto?" Buck said. He laughingly held up his hands in front of his face as if to dodge a slap from yours truly. "And that's a Lone Ranger pun, not a Chief Whitehorse dig."

I couldn't think of a snappy comeback, so I settled for getting up and leaving the room to pour myself another cup of coffee. I returned and sat down.

"To show you there's no hard feelings I'm not only going to let you take me along to meet Sid's homies I'm going to accompany you to the *Vanity Fair* interview and let you schlep me to Banana Republic for office duds afterward."

"In you, my little friend," Buck said as he rose from the table, "I have someone who clocks less office time than any other assistant on the planet." He frowned and drank the last of his coffee.

"Are you saying, you dick, my time would be better spent filing and answering the phone? And *dick* is a private detective pun, not a comment on your personality."

"I'm saying you've earned the right to go with me today, Fred."

He stood, leaned over and kissed me on the forehead. My breath caught, and I felt a warm ripple inside. Only not in the forehead area. Such a reaction didn't jibe with my preoccupation with Guy. *What was wrong with me?*

We both left the dining room to take showers. In *separate* bathrooms. *Separate* showers. We dressed and hooked up in the living room. We were on the same wavelength wardrobe-wise: Buck wore a Hawaiian shirt in just two colors, black and gray, under a black wool blazer with khaki pants. I wore khaki pants, a black leather jacket over a gray turtleneck and white Reeboks. Buck couldn't resist one bow to color in the form of orange Nikes, but for the most part I thought we looked like we could fit in with the suburban Beverly Hills rich and famous.

The early morning rush hour had passed, and traffic was

comparatively light so we took Wilshire into Beverly Hills, then turned left on Beverly Drive. We located Sid Avarson's house and pulled into his driveway. We didn't plan on talking to anyone in the Avarson household, just using the driveway as a parking spot. Buck had in fact called ahead and been advised by the housekeeper that Sid was out of town and Sid's fourth wife, Erika, who was a buyer for Neiman Marcus, was as usual at work.

Sid's was the northernmost corner house on the block, a sprawling one-story affair in a pale rose color with a red clay-tile roof. The air was fragrant with the musky scent of eucalyptus. Palm trees of varying heights had been planted in an attractive scattered approach in the front yard and sides As we got out of the car and walked down the street, we glimpsed a partial view of a backyard pool and a tiny guesthouse in the same architectural mode as the main house.

"Let's go to across the street and work our way back to Sid's," Buck said.

"Fine with me."

Our first stop was a large English country-style mansion. Tapered cypress trees bracketed each side of the house. A short, stocky woman in a traditional maid's uniform—gray dress, white apron—answered the door. She advised the master of the house was an attorney and was away on business. The lady of the house was also—as she phrased it—"a professional woman", also out and at work. Madame's profession was also law.

Our next visit was to a Mediterranean house, more sprawling than Sid's. Off to one side stood a quartet of stately magnolias. Again, a maid answered our knock, this one clad in jeans and a pink tank top. In this case, the owner was a widow—her profession, pediatrician. The maid volunteered that the late mister had been a heart surgeon.

"Do you notice the dearth of residents who are private eyes or models in this neighborhood?" I asked Buck.

"Life is strange," he said.

No one answered at the third house, a two-story cream-colored edifice covered with bougainvillea. Either they had no household help or the servants were taking a coffee break, which didn't include door answering.

That left the house immediately next to Sid's. It would have resembled a cold, gray fortress but a lush collection of trees and shrubs of every description had a softening effect. Wisteria twisted around a side patio. Buck rang the bell and a male answered. He was about my height with pale skin and thick black hair pulled back in a ponytail. He wore a long-sleeved brown tee shirt and blue jeans. On his feet were well-worn yellowish work boots, and he appeared to be around thirty to thirty-five.

Buck flashed his P.I. card yet again.

"We'd like to talk to the owners of the house," he said.

Black Ponytail leaned forward, squinted at the card, then answered, "You're lookin' at him."

"No offense," Buck said. "We've been up and down the block and the person answering the door has been hired help so far."

"No offense taken. How can I help you?"

"Could we come in for a minute?" I asked.

"Oh, yeah, sure, sorry," he said, stood back and waved us through.

Ponytail proceeded through a large living room, a dining room, then crossed the kitchen into what appeared to be a family room. He never said "follow me" but we did. There was one couch and chairs of various styles and sizes scattered about the room and two floor lamps. There were no tables, and a small fichus tree in a corner was the only plant life. The floor was marble tile punctuated by a faded oriental rug fronting the couch.

"I was about to have a beer. Join me?"

It was ten thirty in the morning. Between this invitation and the beers at Nan Kelly's we'd soon be doing twelve-step. Of course the beers at Nan's had been my idea.

"Or don't you guys drink on duty, mister…" Ponytail stole a glance at the business card he'd been handed, "…Lemoyne."

"We're not cops so on-duty rules don't apply. A beer would be great. Call me Buck. This is Freddy Bonnaire, my associate."

"Right," Ponytail said. "I'm Andy Sherman. Maybe you've heard of my wife? Charlotte Rossiter? She kept her maiden name. EVP at Universal?"

"Yes, I've heard of her," Buck smiled.

"Lemme get the beers," Andy said and left. His movements matched his verbal communications—casual and slow with a hint of indifference.

He never said "please have a seat" but we did. Me on the black leather couch and Buck on one of two captain's chairs facing the couch. Andy returned with three bottles of Corona. He pulled the other captain's chair closer to the couch, sat down, took a healthy swallow of beer and said, "Shoot."

I proceeded to describe the shooting incident at Sid Avarson's. Andy had read about it. I mentioned the day and time and discussed the possibility the shot had been intended for Avarson. I further elaborated on the police investigation and the avenues they were pursuing, primarily that someone wanted Doris dead.

Andy took a long, slow drag on his bottle, cocked his head to one side, allowed himself a small grin and said, "Excuse me, Miss, is there a question here on the horizon?"

I then asked Andy where he'd been on that day and time. What he happened to know about the Avarsons. If he'd seen any unusual events on the day in question or unfamiliar visitors or vendors.

Andy then commenced a rambling soliloquy of his own. He talked about how his wife was the main socializer in their family and went on about her career and time commitments, how she was rarely home, how he cooked for himself frequently and even how the maid and gardener treated him.

"Excuse me, captain," I said, "Is there an answer here somewhere on the horizon."

Andy threw back his head and laughed.

"Touché," he said, and offered some answers.

Andy didn't remember where he'd been that day. Couldn't say for sure that he was home, couldn't say for sure he wasn't.

"What's the level of your relationship with the Avarsons?" I asked. "Do you socialize with them? Just greet them now and then? Run into them at social events?"

"The level?" Andy shook his head and chuckled softly.

I love it when I'm witty.

"Their level, little lady, and my level are two entirely different things."

He paused and looked away from me, gazing ahead at nothing in particular. There was a slight smile on his face as he just sat quietly for several beats.

"My wife's at work, by the way," he finally said.

This interview promised to be the equivalent of getting information out of Nan Kelly. If I was going to help Buck with this case, I would have to learn to endure this sort of thing with far more patience than I'd demonstrated so far. On the other hand, Buck, a former cop and a private detective of several years, never seemed to fare much better.

"Sid Avarson," Buck began, "has a lot of entertainment clients. Do you think your wife may know him professionally?"

Andy lifted his beer, started to take a swallow, thought better of it and shook his head again.

"God knows who my wife knows professionally, Lemoyne...that your name? Lemoyne?"

Buck nodded.

"Surely she would have mentioned it to you if she knew your next-door neighbor Mr. Sherman," I said.

Andy put his bottle down on the floor, crossed his arms on his chest. He ignored my comment and referred back to the prior exchange with Buck.

"Sorry, man. Always been lousy at names. Listen, you'll have to ask Charlotte. I go to industry gigs with her sometimes. She introduces me. I meet people. I forget their names the minute I get home."

"I'm sure you got these same questions from a police detective," Buck said. "Just tell us what you told them. But we're hoping, since some more time has passed, maybe you'll remember something extra."

"Told them what I've told you."

"Do you recall what your wife said when they questioned her?" I asked.

"They questioned Char at her office. I wasn't there."

"May I ask what you do, Andy? Your profession I mean."

I don't give up easily.

"What I do?" Andy said. Now he grinned. "This is it," he said, spreading his arms as if to take in the whole room, or the whole house, or perhaps the universe for that matter. "This is what I do."

Buck placed his beer on a small table next to his chair and stood. He retrieved another business card from the inside pocket of his blazer and handed it to Andy.

"Tell your wife we stopped by. If she can tell us anything, please call us. I'll be calling to make an appointment to see her anyway, if that's okay."

Andy shrugged. "Good luck to you if you catch her being home."

"I'll give her a ring at her office then," Buck said.

Andy favored us with a soft chuckle again. "Fine by me, man. Let me see you to the door."

Etiquette at last.

At the front door, we all shook hands. Andy was the most animated he'd been since our arrival, clearly delighted to see us leave.

As we made our way down the path to the street, I said to Buck, "Our friend Andrew's low on communication skills, isn't he?"

"And high on something."

CHAPTER 53

It wasn't quite time to link up with High Top de King at Chateau Marmont, but Buck and I were both ravenous for an early lunch after the protracted interview with Andy Sherman. Besides, if we hurried and sat down to eat quickly we could always say the beers we'd just consumed had simply accompanied our mid-day meal.

"Let's just head out Sunset and find a coffee shop or something near the hotel," Buck said.

"Dining at the Chateau is not an option?" I asked.

"Not unless you've come into an inheritance I don't know about."

As we drove east on Sunset Boulevard I enjoyed what I was able to view of more large, pricey homes. For the most part, they were obscured by walls or trees or shrubs or combinations thereof. When we reached Doheny Drive, the commercial area began and private residences were limited to smaller homes dotting the hills on our left that rose behind the various stores, restaurants and occasional small hotels. On our right, the horizon consisted of one billboard after another. Just beyond La Cienega Boulevard we spied the majestic Chateau Marmont high upon a hill to our left. What we didn't spy was an inviting restaurant or diner appropriate to our budget, so we settled for a McDonalds in a small shopping area directly across the street. Actually I settled for quite a lot. To be precise, a Big Mac, two milks and an apple pie.

"Damn, Fred, no wonder you're not real skinny any more," Buck said.

"Shut up and eat your fries."

Buck grinned. "Did I mention I once dated a girl who's one of the cooks at the Chateau?"

"How nice for you."

He bit into his fish filet and chewed for a minute.

"Called her when Holly told me about this gig." He sipped his Coke. "She's still there."

"Humph," I said.

"Name's Yolanda. Don't let me forget to pop in and see her before we leave."

"Wait a minute, let me write that down," I said.

Buck grinned again. "Eat your Mac."

Fifteen minutes before High Top's interview was scheduled, we left the car in the shopping area parking lot and walked across the street to the hotel. Buck had said from the outside it lived up to its name if you were content with a Hollywood bastardization of a French castle. I told him I'd read that it had been modeled after a castle in the Loire Valley and that it had been standing on the hill in all its pale yellow stone glory since 1929. I'd heard that for some time now it's been a trendy place for the movie folk to go to for lunch, dinner, drinks or to secure a room and hide out indefinitely from scandal fallout.

On the inside, it reminded me of a medieval church. You entered through a heavy, dark wood door onto a tiny lobby. It contained a couch and two matching chairs covered in fabric in a muted gold design overlaid by wine colored stripes. A slender coffee table stood in front of the couch and beyond that a small cubicle and desk. An attractive black woman of thirty or so stood behind the counter top desk arranging small melon balls in a bowl. Three steps down and to our left was a large room that appeared to be the main lobby. Three open archways divided the two lobbies.

The windows on the left side of the larger lobby were also arched, and the sunlight that filtered in provided the only real cheer in a room consisting of carpeting, couches and chairs in musty shades of red, gold and green. Through the windows you could see an empty outdoor dining area covered by wicker tables and chairs and a bar beneath some trees with five stools. The tables were in groups of two's and four's and, all told, the arrangement would seat just fewer than thirty. Even in the large lobby there were only about five round tables. Clearly this was not a venue for the unwashed masses or even very many of the washed masses.

There was a grand piano to your immediate right as you entered the room and against the back wall stood a huge Christmas tree decorated solely in tiny lights that I'm sure were red up close but appeared orange. It was hard to imagine holiday caroling going on in this sedate, restrained atmosphere.

"See that guy alone in the back," Buck said, nodding toward a booth arrangement to the left of the Christmas tree. "He's gotta be the *Vanity Fair* writer waiting for High."

"Since the only other people in the place are those four women having lunch, that's a reasonable deduction, Detective Columbo."

"Okay wiseass, I'm going to go say hello to Yolanda. Take that table near the couch and order me a Martini," Buck said and disappeared down a flight of stairs to the left of the reception desk.

I sat down at the table as instructed and ordered Buck's Martini and a Perrier with lime for me, figuring I'd capped out my daily calorie count at McDonald's. Preceding the arrival of the drinks and the return of Buck was the arrival of one High Top de King. I'd been gazing out the window to my left and immediately recognized High. He was without his two bodyguards, although I was certain they were lurking somewhere. High had apparently gotten the memo on how conservative this joint was and was in non-hip hop attire of a well-tailored black blazer, pressed jeans and a gray crew-necked ribbed jersey. Black Gucci loafers replaced his signature high top sneakers. An expensive looking watch and narrow sunglasses completed the look. The *Vanity Fair* reporter was a stocky, red-headed guy of medium height, and he rose as High approached. They shook hands and sat down. A waiter immediately appeared at their table, took orders and left.

High and the reporter began chatting and laughing. Exchanging banalities no doubt until the real hard-core questions like what-do-you-eat-for-breakfast and where-do-you-buy-your-shoes commenced. Our drinks arrived and I looked around for Buck, but no luck. If High planned an assignation with a mistress, this hotel was a good venue for it, which was why I imagined Buck had decided we'd opt for indoor surveillance.

I sipped my Perrier and continued to check out High and the reporter via my peripheral vision. Their manner had turned serious with the reporter sitting back and talking and High not looking at him, but gazing straight ahead. Suddenly High Top got up and started walking in my direction. He was also smiling in my direction. I suppressed the urge to look behind me to ascertain the target of his smile and just sat still and looked down at my drink. Then I heard a voice.

"I know the face, I just don't know the name," High Top said and smiled.

He was talking to me. "Excuse me?" I said, queen of quick repartee.

"I know you've been following me for some time. Are you a reporter or just a very devoted fan?"

He was still grinning pleasantly, clearly more amused than annoyed. He had large brown eyes that mirrored the sincerity of his smile.

"Uh…I'm not…uh…sure what you mean," I said.

Thank God my quick wit doesn't desert me at times like this.

"Look," High said, "It looks like you've been stood up and I could use some friendly company to ward off this vulture I'm stuck with, so why don't you join us."

"I have a friend joining me any minute," I said.

"She can join us too."

"It's a he and…"

"All the better," High said. "Teach him a lesson for making such a fine woman wait."

He placed a hand gently under my elbow so the only thing to do was to stand up. However, I'd still stand firm.

"I really can't…"

"Listen this guy is starting to grill me big time. If you just look pretty and interrupt from time to time maybe I can deflect his nosiness."

"I don't think…"

"It's boring stuff but I don't want to slip and say the wrong thing or get sucked into talking too much. He's zoning in on this lawsuit I got going on and…"

"I'll be happy to join you," I said.

CHAPTER 54

"Mr. King!" a voice called out. "Randy Goldman, *National Enquirer.* How are you, sir? I wonder if I might have a few minutes of your time."

High Top and I had taken about four steps toward his table when a short, slightly chubby twenty-something guy sporting glasses, a ponytail streaked in various shades of brown and blonde and a large camera hanging from his neck came running from behind and then stepped in front of us.

"I'm in the middle of an interview right now," High said, ignoring Randy's outstretched hand. "If you call my assistant, maybe we can arrange something."

"Well…okay if I just hang around? Maybe when you're through I can walk you to your car, couple of questions, quick shot."

"Suit yourself," High said, making a step-aside wave with his free hand.

The *Vanity Fair* reporter stood as we arrived at the table. He was even cuter close up.

"This is Kevin Hall," High Top began, "And this is…"

"Freddy Bonnaire," I supplied.

"My very good friend, Freddy Bonnaire." High grinned. "We go everywhere together."

Randy Goldman pulled a chair close to the table where we'd gathered and sat down.

"Nice to meet you," Kevin said, as we all sat down. "Are you on Mr. King's staff?"

"She's my conscience you could say," High Top said. "Follows me around to make sure I don't do anything wrong."

"I see." Kevin looked puzzled but had more important issues to pursue. "Back to your lawsuit against Potter, Wood & Penn, Mr. King. Do you…"

"My new CD dropped on Tuesday," High interrupted. He looked at me when he spoke, offering a smile and a wink. "Got good advance reviews. One critic said it was emotionally charged and highly self-revelatory. Another said it was a kind of psychedelic poetry. I especially liked that last one because…"

"Excuse me, Mr. King." It was Kevin's turn to interrupt. "I'm not the magazine's music critic. Know zip about that. My piece deals with your life outside the recording studio, most specifically your legal issues and…"

The three of us were leaning forward, clasping our drinks, elbows on the table. Kevin and High Top because they were each resolute on the subject at hand, me because they both spoke softly and I had to strain to listen.

"Look," High said. "I can't…"

"I understand your claim is that Potter, Wood & Penn had conflicts of interest they didn't disclose to you. That this was in conjunction with monies of yours that they diverted and which…"

"The case is still pending, Kevin." High Top pronounced his name with special emphasis on each syllable, making *Keh-vin* sound like a threat. "You can understand that my lawyer forbids me from discussing this matter."

I felt I was expected to jump in anytime and somehow distract Kevin Goldman with my compelling looks, feminine wiles and biting wit or a combination thereof, but I was too interested in the answers myself to rise to the occasion.

"To an extent, yes, of course," Kevin said. "But many aspects have already been made public. I just need your comments on these. Some further elaboration, as it were. One of such aspects is…"

"Sugar, do you know they got actual cloth towels in the ladies room here?"

Another voice rose from behind us—this time a female one. High and I turned around simultaneously.

"But otherwise it's damn dreary in here."

It was Holly King. She was in full costume again; this time the theme was western. She waggled her right index finger at Kevin as two silver and diamond charm bracelets tinkled on her wrist.

"Are you pickin' on my husband?"

"No mam. Let me get you a chair," Kevin said and headed to a nearby table.

Madam King's ensemble consisted of a black cowboy hat, a lime-green suede jacket with fringe, black tights and brown and red cowboy boots. Large round silver earrings with a small turquoise stone in the center were on her ears, and a large turquoise stone on a silver chain together with a small orange and white cotton scarf provided the neck adornment.

I could have used this girl as a wardrobe resource in Santa Fe.

Kevin returned with a chair, which he placed next to his. High Top stood.

"Honey, this is Freddy Bonnaire and Kevin Hall."

Holly remained standing.

"Which is which?" she asked, pointing a shaky finger at Randy, then me.

"This is Kevin," High said, touching Kevin's shoulder. "He's a reporter with the magazine *Vanity Fair*. And this," he moved his hand, palm upward, toward me, "is Freddy Bonnaire. Freddy is..."

"I know who Freddy is."

Holly grimaced as if she'd just sucked on a lemon, then took a long drag on her cigarette and removed her cowboy hat. Obviously she knew I'd been made as hubby's stalker and just as obviously was offended by my lack of professionalism.

I'm with you on that Holly baby.

"Look, Potter, Wood has already spent almost a million fighting your case, Mr. King," Kevin said. "So they obviously take your claims seriously and so do I."

He plastered his best sincere expression across his face in an attempt to get this interview back of track.

"Ain't none of your business, boy," Holly said.

Madame King's aversion to reporters apparently equaled her contempt for wanna-be private eyes.

"Can we talk about their consultant who also represented Excon Records. He bilked $2.5 million from your funds and…"

"And he admitted it, bozo," Holly waved her cigarette around in the air to dramatize her point, then dropped it to her side, her arm trembling.

She was in full protective mode of High Top. *Why did she consider such defense necessary?*

High Top stood, put his left arm around Holly's shoulders and rested his right hand on her arm, gently raising her from her chair.

"Let's do this another time Mr. Hall," he said.

Kevin nodded, stood and made a slight bow toward Holly. "I'll call you," he said.

I watched as the Kings swept from the main lobby, up the stairs and through the door to the right of the reception desk, Holly's glossy black hair, diamonds and boot spurs sparkling in a slant of sunlight, Randy Goldman trotting after them.

I stood up as Buck suddenly appeared.

"Well, lone ranger," I said. "Where you been in all the excitement?"

"Sitting over in that corner. You're obviously busted. No need for High Top to make me also."

He grabbed Kevin's hand and shook it.

"I'm a friend of Freddy's. We'll be going now."

I remembered Hall's last question.

"Who's the consultant you mentioned who allegedly ripped off Mr. King?" I said.

"Lemme see," Kevin thumbed through the pages of a narrow spiral pad.

"Here it is. Scott Kelly."

CHAPTER 55

I'VE NEVER BEEN VERY GOOD at dating. Well, obviously I've been married and had relationships. But that invariably happened when dating was not the intent. When the atmosphere was environmental and not transactional. If I want to be typically American, I could blame my dear, departed mother for this deficit in my approach to *l'amour.* Francine Toussaint, before she met and married my father, Claude Laurens, was quite the belle as she would tell it. Invitations from smitten gentlemen in abundance, beaus too numerous to list, marriage proposals galore. She'd recount her romantic past with no hint of vanity, merely matter of factly. It is the way in France. The French have no word for *dating*, in the sense Americans use it. To them love is a game, in the best sense. But it is not a game stifled and bordered by the numerous rules, protocols and manipulations self-help books in the U.S. would have us abide by. *Mai no*, I cannot blame my delightfully natural mother for any romantic failures I may have experienced, nor for any faults I may have. *Ma mère* was my inspiration and my comfort, and she had the good sense to warn me against my marriage, but then to accept completely my country-western-singer husband when our bond was a *fait accompli.*

I met my ex, Sonny Bob, after I'd seen him, and he'd seen me, numerous times at a coffee shop frequented by models. We'd sit at those little tables for two, he with his companion—usually one of the models—and me with my companion, usually another one of the models, on several occasions. Once he sat alone very near my table when I was with Jeannette and once I sat alone when he was with a model I knew and some other guy. Finally, we each sat at one of the small tables, both alone. He nodded and sipped his coffee and I nodded back and chomped on a particularly hard poppy seed bagel. Then he struck up a conversation about the dietary attributes of a bran muffin versus bagels, and we were off and running.

After our divorce, I had a seven-month relationship with my divorce lawyer and when that went south I had a three-month fling with my divorce lawyer's favorite waiter at Café des Artiste.

So here I was all dressed up, sitting in Buck's guest bedroom awaiting the commencement of my first date since Santa Fe with Guy. I was alone. Buck, Yolanda, Luke and Jeannette had headed out earlier for the Staples Center in downtown L.A. to enjoy the Lakers versus the Utah Jazz game. I was feeling optimistic. Two days ago, from thirty points behind, and by scoring forty-four points in the fourth quarter, my boys had beaten the Dallas Mavericks, 105-103.

I was feeling less optimistic about tonight's date. There'd been such gaps in our get-togethers, such a feeling of indifference emanating from my detective friend. But Gram always used to say if you feel afraid, charge ahead and act as if you don't. So I had.

Earlier today, after the histrionics at Chateau Marmont, Buck and I had gone to his office so he could do some paperwork. He'd loaned me the Honda for some errands, and I'd picked up some brand new sheets, pillowcases and a comforter—in a leopard print yet. I'd also purchased some candles, wine and gardenia-scented room spray. That done, I went to my apartment to set the stage. The beds from my spare bedroom and headboard from my bed had been removed by Buck's maid as unsalvageable, but my queen-sized mattress remained on the floor of my room. It had been slashed and was earmarked for eventual delivery to good Will but had avoided most of the Clorox anointing by my attacker.

I made up the bed with two bottom sheets, the top sheet and comforter and placed three fat white candles on either side of the bed, leaving a little box of matches alongside one. I sprayed the room with gardenia scent. Then I took the bottle of wine to the kitchen. My new glasses had not arrived, and all I could find intact was one brandy snifter glass and a champagne flute. Would have to do.

Tired of sitting on the bed and staring at my reflection in the mirror, I got up, went to the dresser, sprayed a little more Carolina Herrera on my neck and stared at my reflection in the mirror. I'd first put on what was my New York uniform for years: skinny jeans, black suede boots with a big bag and usually my favorite Isabel Marant brown jacket and one of several five dollar neck scarves purchased from sidewalk vendors around midtown. But Jeannette had talked me into a form-fitting white nylon turtleneck, a black skirt with a slit up one side and stiletto heels, white suede with black trim. So Victoria's Secret. So seductive. So obvious.

"*So what!*" Jay had said.

The doorbell rang. I opened the door. There stood the object of my anxieties in a plain black sweater, gray cord pants, black socks, loafers the color of mahogany that looked just a little scuffed. I bet no staring-at-reflection-in-mirror went on behind that debut. Handsome though I must admit.

A *hi* from each of us, a quick kiss on mouth.

"I remember in Santa Fe you said you liked French cuisine, so I picked out a couple of good places. You take your pick. Either..."

I pressed one finger to his lips.

"Surprise me," I said.

Enough decision-making had already been spent on this event, I wasn't up to more.

We drove through the darkness, making light chitchat, mostly reminiscing about Santa Fe. In about fifteen minutes we pulled into the restaurant parking lot. I saw the familiar red awnings and was immediately skeptical. Guy got out, came around and opened my door. I got out. Slowly. We entered the restaurant. The place was nearly full, the bar especially busy and a waiter was serving as the maitre d'. He smiled when Guy said "two" and led us to a table near one end of the bar. We sat down and another waiter appeared to take our drink order. Guy ordered a club soda. I said I wanted to think about it. Then just as he turned to leave, I ordered the house red wine. He smiled again and said fine. Then I said no, the house *white* wine. A few feet away I felt someone's eyes on me. I suspected whose eyes they might be, but just to be sure I did a slight hair toss number to confirm this with a quick glance. I was right.

"Guy," I said, "this place seems lovely but, you know, I'm kind of in the mood for Italian tonight. I know this very nice place not far from here. Would you mind?"

"Of course not." Guy got up immediately and pulled my chair out. "Wherever you say. Let me go cancel the drink order."

Guy caught the eye of our waiter and lip-synched that we had to leave, pointing to the door.

As we exited Emile's, I could still feel Nick's eyes upon me.

The service at Il Fornaio was impeccable as always. It was dark and romantic, and I put away my first white wine spritzer quickly and started on a second. Getting a nice buzz started to ameliorate the vicissitudes of the evening thus far. We both ordered ravioli filled with Swiss chard, pine nuts, basil and Parmesan and topped with artichokes and red and yellow tomatoes. I sipped my wine slowly. Guy deigned to break his club-soda regimen and ordered a chardonnay. He proceeded to get as mellow on half of one chardonnay as I was with my more consumptive libations, at least it seemed that way.

Over coffee and desserts of chocolate mousse cake soaked in triple sec with raspberries and orange crème anglaise, I asked Guy about the vacation he'd taken not long after Santa Fe. He had gone back to his reservation for rest and healing. The latter, he said, was accomplished via a sweat lodge ceremony.

"What exactly is a sweat lodge. Physically, I mean. What does it look like?"

"Well, they often last for several years but on my last trip we built a new one. *We* being the participants in the ceremony. You dig a hole, eight to twelve feet in diameter, then create a covering three to four feet high of blankets, then tarps. These provide insulation and hold in the heat. In ancient times, they used animal skins."

"Sounds cramped."

"You do crawl in on your hands and knees. But before that a mound is created east of the door. People place on the mound objects that have special meaning to them. Inside a pit is dug. Rocks are placed in the pit, then logs, then rocks on top of this. Beforehand the rocks are blessed with herbs, tobacco, sweet grass. You light this pile of wood all around. The heat is very, very intense."

"Sounds punishing. Don't know if I could take it."

"Lodges are usually built near a creek so that people can take a break when they want to and cool off."

"What do you do once inside and how long does this ceremony last?"

"About two hours or so. You sing songs, make prayers. The significance is you've created a womb in the earth."

"How many people fit into these lodges?"

"Usually about twelve or fifteen, thirty in the big lodges."

"Hmmm," I said.

I sipped my third spritzer and gazed at the stunning Native American across from me. Good looking, smart and spiritual besides.

I ruminated on this last attribute. My religious inclinations were largely ecumenical, but I didn't know if that included chanting in sweat lodges. I'd gotten to know the wonderful Pastor at St. Monica's, Father Lincoln, when Buck provided security at a large fund-raising gala months ago and had taken me along as his date. Since then, I rarely miss Sunday Mass. His homilies are always down to earth, delivered with much warmth and wit. He makes it a point at every Mass to welcome non-Catholics, which impressed Buck when my detecting buddy deigned to attend with me at Easter. Buck. His name seemed to reverberate in my brain.

Realizing I'd become distracted, I took a huge gulp of wine and smiled at my companion.

"Think you'd like to go there one day?" Guy asked.

"Go where?"

"To a sweat lodge."

I smiled again. "Think I'd just like to go home right now."

We drove to my apartment mostly in silence. Guy had one hand on the wheel and held mine with the other.

I got out my key and let us in, turned on the restored floor lamp.

Guy was taken aback. "Not much furniture here."

"Sure there is," I said. Sly smile. "I'll show you."

I took his hand, led him to the kitchen and handed him the bottle of wine.

"With good wine, who needs furniture?" he said.

"We do."

Clutching the glasses in one hand, I put my arm around his waist and led him out of the kitchen. At the bedroom door, I said, "Wait there," crossed to where the some of the candles sat and lit them.

Guy placed the bottle of wine on the floor, crossed to the bed, bent down, drew some matches from his jacket pocket and lit the candles I'd placed on the other side of the bed.

I felt an odd sense of unease. I deliberately and with great care created this scenario for seduction. In a way, I envisioned it as a surprise, even as a gift. Surrendering myself to the man I believed I was falling in love with.

Such a silly, old-fashioned notion.

And here was Guy, seemingly fully on board with the story line, as it were. Moving comfortably within the confines of my bedroom as if he'd been there many times before. My God, this room in its current condition seemed strange to *me*. The candles, the sheets—all of it new and unfamiliar.

I observed this tall, mysterious man as if I were watching a movie and wondering what would happen next. I don't know what I expected of this night, but something didn't feel right.

Guy walked around to the other side of the bed, knelt and lit the other three candles. He picked up the wine bottle, pulling out the cork with his teeth.

My face felt flush, and I could feel a bead of perspiration on my forehead. I was clutching the glasses in what amounted to a death grip. I turned and walked back to the kitchen. Guy followed, seemingly unaware by what, to me, was my obvious distress.

He smiled slightly. "Shall I pour?"

"I…I don't seem to feel well all of a sudden, Guy."

"Can I get you anything?" he said.

I pulled a bottle of water from the fridge and began taking intermittent gulps from it, while staring at the opposite wall. Not wanting to look at Guy, not knowing what to say.

"Maybe you should sit down," Guy said.

"No, but I probably need to rest."

I turned my body so as to face the front door.

"I guess I feel sleepy all of a sudden," I said, still gazing at the door.

"I see."

He visibly stiffened, paused for a few beats and then inserted the cork into the bottle. He held the bottle for what seemed like interminable minutes, but which was mostly likely mere seconds, then quietly placed the bottle on the counter.

Guy placed his hand gently on my cheek, cocked his head and seemed to study my face—again—for what felt like an eternity.

"I'll see myself out," he said softly.

CHAPTER 56

I opened my eyes and saw the wall and three extinguished candles. I rolled over, expecting to see a tussle of dark hair, closed eyes on a tan face, a formidable shoulder to reach out and caress. Then I remembered the romantic assignation I'd envisioned the day before never occurred. It might have in my dreams, but in real life I myself had sabotaged any such erotic encounter.

Frédérique Bonnaire, you've obviously got a problem.

I pulled the covers up and mused further on my romantic predilections or, more accurately, the lack of same. I could see a shrink, but I don't believe in shrinks. I certainly couldn't discuss the subject with Father Lincoln. I could talk to Jeannette about it, but her response was entirely predictable…and not here printable. Buck was out of the question, as was Luke. I sat up, crawled to the end of the bed and picked up the warm ball of fur nestled asleep there.

"What do you make of my date last night and the way I handled it?"

Pierre lifted his little head in my direction and gave me a this-is-what-you-woke-me-up-for? look. He then stretched, jumped off the bed and headed for the kitchen.

I lay back down, feeling dejected and rejected, thought about getting up, putting the coffee on, and going for a run. Then I thought about the fact that I was in my apartment, not Buck's house. My coffee pot had been smashed; I had not yet replaced it. My running shoes were over at Buck's. Then a more startling thought penetrated my early-morning cathexis: this was Thursday. I was supposed to report to work at Potter, Wood!

I sat up and groped around for my watch. Found it next to one of my shoes. It was ten minutes to nine; I was due at eight thirty. There was nothing to do but shower, put on last night's clothes and call a cab. All of which I did in fast-forward motion.

The cabbie let me off at the corner of Avenue of the Stars and Constellation in Century City, and I walked the half block to the sixteen-story building housing Potter, Wood & Penn, among other corporate monads. Potter, Wood occupied two floors, nine and ten. The elevator had mirrored walls, and I examined my reflection with unnecessary concern. It's not as if my appearance somehow betrayed a night spent in the throes of passion. I looked a little over the top for a business-casual dress code, but I'd pass.

I got off on nine. A woman was standing next to an unoccupied receptionist desk, apparently bawling out a young man standing in front of her. He rested his elbows on the handle of a metal cart that looked like the ones you use in grocery stores, except it contained stacks of mail, magazines, some Federal Express boxes. The woman and the youth were both about five foot three. The apparent transgressor appeared to be about eighteen, although he was probably older. His face looked so sad, maybe that made him look younger. He wore glasses and had ash blonde hair combed back behind his ears. His attacker appeared to be around forty, maybe late thirties. She had light brown hair caught back in a ponytail, a chunky build and very muscular legs. Probably a partner who'd failed to receive mail delivery in a timely fashion. She wore a fierce-looking scowl and her tone was one decibel short of screaming. I overheard her say, "Well, why didn't you?" but I couldn't catch the rest of the diatribe.

An older gentleman approached them. He had a head of thick gray hair, a thin moustache topping a small goatee, and wore a dark blue Brioni suit and an Oxford shirt with gold cufflinks. He said a few words to Miss Irate and her facial expression and voice immediately softened. Must be a senior partner. Brioni Suit then continued down the hall, and Irate whipped into a savage mode once more. I remained where I was standing which was just in front of the elevator, keeping my distance.

The nameplate on the receptionist desk said Lisa Connors. Where the heck was she? I did not know where I was supposed to be located. Jeannette would be in by now and at her desk, but I didn't know where that was either. I saw the young mail cart guy turn away toward the hallway bordering the reception area and say to Madame Irate, "Okay, Lisa, I will." Ah-ha. Our stormy crazy mama is *the* Lisa Connors. Love it. A receptionist who has power. Or one who thinks she does, at any rate.

The emission of what was probably just a portion her daily bile quota accomplished, Miss Connors sat down behind her desk. I approached and gave her my name, adding I was to temp for Sid Avarson.

"Fine. Let me call Abigal Nelson. She's head of Human Resources."

Lisa picked up the phone, dialed an extension, announced my name.

"Miss Nelson will be here in a minute," Lisa gave a brief smile, then waxed stern. "Have a seat."

I went over to one of the narrow gray armchairs and sat down. I really felt like standing but you don't want to mess with Lisa. I had to get up again almost immediately as Abigal Nelson arrived. She was slim, with very short dark brown hair, pink lipstick and a warm smile.

"Hi. I'm Abigal Nelson."

She extended her hand and I noticed she had light hazel eyes that looked kind. I hoped she'd never have to get in the ring and put on the gloves with Miss Connors. She would be outmatched by far. Abigal didn't comment on the fact that I was late.

"Nice to meet you. Freddy Bonnaire."

Abigal turned toward the reception desk.

"Lisa, I'm going to get Freddy situated. If Frank Berman calls, please tell him I'll call him right back."

Lisa nodded.

I followed Abigal down the hall, past several window offices and then to a small square room of cubicles divided by the hallway. In front of one desk stood Jeannette and two other women. They were comparing what looked like Xerox copies of some small illustration and laughing hilariously.

Abigal seemed not to react to the obvious goofing off.

"Hey ladies," she said. "Here's your new colleague. Freddy, this is Jeannette Sullivan, Linda Rogers and Maris Burns."

Abigal nodded toward me. "Freddy Bonnaire. Jeannette will be working with you, Freddy, in helping Sid. Linda works for another partner, Bernie Green, and Maris is our computer tech expert."

We all shook hands, even Jay.

"Jeannette," Abigal said, "Will you get Freddy started. I've got to run."

Jeannette said, "Sure."

Abigal thanked her and scurried down the hall.

"God, I'm glad you're here," Jeannette whispered.

Linda and Maris giggled. Linda was tall, skinny and very pretty. Maris was short, chubby and very pretty.

"Show Freddy what we were laughing at and then describe the boys," Linda said. "Give her a laugh to start her day."

They handed me the two sheets of paper that were Xerox copies of the driver's licenses of Sid Avarson and Bernie Green. I smiled; it was somewhat amusing. I didn't need a description. I remembered Bernie from the New York office. Both he and Sid were short men, barely five feet four. The height given on both licenses read five feet, nine inches.

"That *is* funny," I said.

Linda and Maris declared it was nice to have met me and left.

"This is your spot," Jeannette said, indicating a cubicle right next to hers separated by a Formica partition. The desks, paneling and carpeting were all in a washed-out, dispirited gray. The chairs were swivel, in secretarial size, and black. I sat down at my desk feeling "cabined, cribbed, confined" to quote Shakespeare. I could almost hear Elvis singing "Jailhouse Rock." Jay came over and perched on my desk.

"How's it going? Anything interesting?" I asked.

"This shit is soooo boring, " Jay whispered. "Every day I do twenty-four-hour schedules of airline flights. He'll know he has to leave for, say Dallas, on Friday morning for an eight o'clock, but I still have to type up every airline and every flight for that day up to midnight. How many planes can that little prick take?"

"Don't hold back, Jay. Say what you really think." It was my turn to laugh.

"I know, I know," she said. "You told me he was demanding. But when he calls in he's always so freaking nasty on top of it."

"I told you about that part of it too. Now you tell me what you've seen or heard that would tell us that someone around here hates Sid enough to take a potshot at him."

"Yeah, me."

"Seriously."

"Seriously, girl, and I've only been here two days. But, okay, I'll tell you this. He's apparently up for some kind of promotion or 'expanded role' as they're calling it. I'm supposed to check his emails when he's out of town and Sid baby's been sending notes to a couple of guys above him, feeling them out about this new role. When they've written him back...I can't be sure...but it sounds like he's got competition."

"Hmmm. Would one of his competitors be a Scott Kelly?"

"They never mention the competitors by name. Isn't Scott Kelly the guy you said was missing for a while?"

"Yeah. He's still missing."

"Well, he may be missing but he's alive and well somewhere."

"I gathered that," I said. "We just don't know where."

Jeannette shrugged. "Since I've been here, he's been sending ole Sid emails almost every day."

CHAPTER 57

"Lunch break, girlfriend. I'm gonna order in."

Jeannette was leaning on the divider panel between our cubicles as she handed me the one-page menu of a nearby deli.

"I'll call it in. Tell me what you want," she said.

I studied the choices.

"How's the Cobb salad?"

"Lousy. Get the Caesar or the chicken curry."

"Caesar," I said, "and a fruit cup on the side."

"You got it."

Jay went back to her desk to call the deli.

I'd spent the morning rounding up a hotel for Sid in Denver. It was tedious, but I was grateful I only had to work the phones as my wounded arm trembled somewhat whenever I typed. I still wore some bandages on my fingers from the cuts I'd suffered, but probably no one would really notice them. One week when working for Sid in New York I'd developed a rash on my hand from nerves and stress, scratched them with a vengeance and had been forced to worn bandages much the same way. If anyone asked, I could say *these* bandages constituted advance planning.

The hotel for Sid's trip had to be no more than a ten-minute drive from the client's office, bed must be king-size, room must be smoke-free, the mini-bar must include chocolate chip cookies and the hotel must have a health club facility. It was all coming back to me from my New York Potter, Wood & Penn stint. At least room price was not a consideration. Sid liked to live high on the hog, as Gram would say. I found an almost perfect hotel just as Jay called out that our lunch orders had arrived. It possessed all the amenities Sid required but was twenty minutes from the client. If I could persuade the limo driver to burn rubber, I'd be home free.

We took our lunch bags to the small company kitchen down the hall. There were two round tables with four chairs surrounding each of them, a machine dispensing sodas and one for candy, chips, cookies and the like. The small room also boasted a large coffee urn and a microwave. The only other diner in residence was the young mail guy I'd encountered earlier. He didn't look up when we arrived, just continued reading his newspaper.

I had change so I got a diet Coke for Jay and a Pepsi for myself. We ate in silence for the first few minutes. Various young associates, assistants, even partners drifted in, got a soda or coffee, then left. Neutral was the word of the day, fashion wise. There were a lot of blue dress shirts worn by the males with khaki or black pants. The women often wore a more feminine version of these combinations and sometimes a completely similar imitation. They wore flats rather than heels, rarely any jewelry. Only a young and pretty Filipino assistant and the glorious Lisa departed from the apparent subtle-solids dictum and wore an aqua suit and denim skirt respectively.

The mail guy left, and Jay spoke to me. "Abigal chew your ass for being late?"

"No. I was surprised, but she didn't."

"She's cool," Jay said. "Plus she knew Sid baby's not coming in until three today."

"Oh rats," I said. "My first day and he decides to come in."

"Guess you don't live right, babe."

"Did you set it up so I have access to Sid's emails?" I asked.

"Did that yesterday."

"Great. It's so darn quiet. I was hoping to see some of the troops come in from the field so I could chat them up and eavesdrop a little on conversations. Get a feel for the morale around here."

"The morale? Ha!" Jay snorted. "What do you think it is? Linda and Maris tell me he has people like us for lunch. Thinks he has to scare people shitless to get them to work. Maris says he thinks the louder the tantrums, the more motivated everyone will be."

"Glad to hear nothing's changed," I said. "The good news is he's only loud and vulgar on the phone. When he's around people in person, he's milder. Well, I mean he doesn't yell. In person, he's just sarcastic."

After lunch I set up the limo pickups in conjunction with the Denver trip and started flight schedules for a trip to Hawaii Sid was taking two months from now but needed this afternoon. At twenty of three two level four consultants arrived in advance of their three o'clock appointment with Sid. Jeannette chatted with them briefly and from this I learned that they were named Dave and Greg. The men took their laptops into Sid's office and set to work, Dave at the desk, Greg at a small round conference table. Jeannette brought them mugs of coffee.

Sid's office was relatively small, especially considering the mogul he pretended to be. The walls and carpeting were the same washed-out gray as the rest of those on this floor, the furniture a dark wood. His desk was an L-shape and behind it stood the usual office unit- -cabinet on top, a counter space, file drawers on the bottom. The counter surface, like the desk, was mostly bare: three or four books on corporate management and related topics, little knick-knacks with client names and logos on them, the usual accoutrements of pencil cup, notepaper holder, business card holder. On the desk, clustered near the phone, were a collection of framed photos—one of Sid and Erika on their wedding day...*I wonder what it's like to dress all in white to be someone's fourth bride*...a few of his three sons by the third marriage at different ages, several baby pictures of his daughter by Erika and one of the little girl at her current age which was about six. A very healthy fichus tree stood on the floor in a corner near the window in a gray ceramic pot. No drapes on the one wide window, just Venetian blinds.

At three forty-seven Sid arrived for the three o'clock appointment. He passed Jeannette without acknowledging her *good afternoon* and marched wordlessly into his office, head down. Dave quickly transferred his laptop and papers to the conference table and both he and Greg greeted Sid cheerfully, just as if he hadn't kept them cooling their heels for the better part of an hour.

Sid stood behind his desk, fished three sets of stapled papers out of his briefcase and handed a copy each to Dave and Greg who'd pulled two client chairs in front of Sid's desk and were sitting in them, at attention. They immediately became engrossed in the handouts.

"This is the org chart I was talking about," Sid said, still standing. "Plus the deployment plan."

Dave crossed his leg and said, "Looks good." Greg nodded and mumbled something that sounded in the affirmative.

"Is Reilly transferring to San Francisco?" Dave asked.

"What do you think?" Sid said, frowning.

Dave uncrossed his legs, slouched lower in his chair, ignoring the question. "I like the RFP lineup," he said.

Greg leaned forward and spoke so softly I couldn't hear what he said. Whatever it was, Sid replied, "I'm not the answer man here. You figure it out."

Greg coughed a little and said, "I'll run it by the RM."

Sid scribbled some notes on his copy. He apparently was not going to sit down. Both Greg and Dave were about six feet; I guessed Sid wanted to maintain a physical advantage.

Jeannette went to the office door to advise Sid she had his wife on the line. Sid sat down and took the call from Erika. They talked for about three or four minutes; he assured her he was picking up their daughter from ballet class in fifteen minutes, said "okay, bye" and hung up.

"Okay, guys, that's it," Sid said. "I need to call Pat Duncan in Philadelphia, then I'm outta here."

Thus dismissed, Dave and Greg gathered up their laptops and papers, voiced a lot of baloney about how it was good to see Sid and left. Dave had driven in from Orange County for this ten-minute meeting and Greg had flown in from Tucson. They left, ostensibly pleased as punch just to have been granted the audience.

At Sid's instruction, Jeannette called the Philly office to reach Duncan. It was after seven in the evening there, so he'd left for the day the operator advised. Jay promptly dialed Duncan's cell phone, he picked up and she put him through to Sid.

What followed was a classic Avarson tantrum. The focus of his venom in this instance seemed to be Duncan's supposed mishandling of an important East Coast client. Sid commenced by spelling out in detail exactly how Pat had conducted himself like a first-class moron.

He alternately snapped, snarled and fairly growled as he enunciated his points. He never cursed; I'll give him that.

Sid named various executives of the client company and outlined meetings and work plans Duncan should orchestrate. He concluded with a reiteration of precisely how Duncan had initially screwed up the project and exactly how he'd proved himself to be an idiot. Before hanging up, he let go with one final invective: "You should die!"

I jumped up and gave Jay the flight schedules Sid wanted so I could hopefully avoid an encounter with him when he left his office. She nodded, clipped it to some other papers and I slunk back to my cubicle.

Sid stood up, put a few loose papers back in his briefcase and exited his office. He paused at Jeannette's desk long enough to say, "You have something for me?"

She said, "Yes, I do," and handed over the clipped papers.

Sid said, "Thanks," and marched back down the hall, once again head down, an intense expression on his face.

I had started down the hall, heading for the supply room and Sid passed me without a word. As he crossed the reception area to the elevators, a large burly man who'd been sitting in one of the guest chairs rose and joined him. Interesting. A bodyguard?

Jay and I stayed and worked until six. Linda stopped by my desk as we were preparing to leave and offered a ride. She planned to do some shopping near Buck's place. We gratefully accepted, but I asked her to deposit us at my apartment and assured her we could walk to Buck's from there. We arrived at my condo at six thirty, got out and thanked her.

"Why we stopping here?" Jeannette asked, as we headed for the elevator. "My feet are killing me, and they're telling me no way can they walk to Venice."

"We'll call a cab. I need some more clothes and I want to check my messages."

"Ah ha, " Jay said. "Doesn't a certain Detective Whitehorse have your cell number?"

"Matter of fact, I don't think he does."

"Okay," Jay grinned. "Let's see what mushy message he's left."

"You don't know the good detective, my friend." I got out my key and opened the door. "Mush is not his specialty."

As Jeannette headed for the kitchen, I went to the bedroom to raid my closet for whatever clothes remained and would suit the Potter, Wood environment, suppressing an urge to check my answering machine first. I found two more black skirts and a pair of gray Capri pants. I hoped Jay would stay in the kitchen; the candle arrangement around the mattress looked embarrassing after the fact. Minutes later, she came to the bedroom but headed straight for my closet and a pile of shoes.

Under a camel jacket I found a blue cotton blouse I'd long forgotten. All of it had been behind a garment bag full of car coats and heavy sweaters and had escaped the ministrations of my recent assailant. I kept them on the hangers, folded them neatly over one arm and carried them out of the bedroom. Jeannette was happily immersed in trying on my shoes and making a new pile, presumably of pairs that would fit her.

I draped my clothes over a living room chair and headed for the kitchen and the answering machine. There was one message, and it was hardly mush from Guy Whitehorse. In fact, it was more reminiscent of a Sid Avarson epithet, but it didn't sound like Sid on the machine. It was the low gravelly voice I'd heard days earlier with a similar communication, this time declaring, "*You'll get yours, bitch*!"

CHAPTER 58

"WHAT THE HELL ARE YOU talking about?"

Buck brought the knife down with force. He was slicing the catfish I picked up for dinner after Jay and I'd completed our stop at my condo. Jeannette had no sooner showered and changed clothes when her dinner date—one of the Potter, Wood consultants, quick worker she—arrived at the door and whisked her away. Buck had arrived home when Jay and I were in the guest bedroom conferring on her attire for the great event. He showered, changed into Levis and a white tee and joined me in the kitchen where I had okra boiling in a saucepan and was slicing some red onions to go with the okra. I chopped part of the onions to go with rice. The okra was canned and the rice was instant but, hey, this wasn't New Orleans. We chatted just long enough for me to reveal A, I'd been receiving some threats and B, I'd spent last night at my place.

"Just some threats. Probably nothing. Probably not related to the break-in. Probably a model I offended a few weeks ago, probably her booker. Probably related to my business in some way like that."

I spoke calmly and added the sliced onions to a bowl I'd filled with paprika, white pepper, onion powder, garlic powder, dry mustard, red pepper, thyme leaves and basil leaves. We Louisianans are big on seasoning.

"One more *probably*, Fred, and I'll slice off a lock of that blonde hair. What kind of threats? Phone calls? Emails? Letters under your door or in your mailbox?"

"I'm going to do some investigating of my own, Buck. Ask around. Maybe just wait and see if it happens again."

"So you won't tell me what precisely happened. Great." Buck fairly snarled as he spoke. "Well, *probably*, Frédérique, our would-be killer is out there, and we don't know the goddamn who he is and you freaking spend the night alone in the same place he invaded. And with all your goddamn furniture shopping I haven't heard word one that you've gotten the lock changed."

Buck waved the knife in the air, using it to punctuate key words. He went back to catfish cutting and shook his head.

"I don't know what the hell to do," he said.

"You know what you can do?" I said angrily.

He turned to look at me.

"You can chop up the celery and that green pepper for the rice." I grinned.

"Yeah, yeah," Buck said wearily.

He retrieved from the cabinet some pre-packaged batter called Seasoned Fish Fry and proceeded to empty it into a large chrome bowl.

I went to the sink and drained the okra into a colander.

"I wasn't alone."

I added the okra to the seasonings bowl, realizing I'd mumbled that last comment.

"What?"

"I wasn't alone."

"The hell you weren't. Jeannette was here all night."

Buck took his knife and commenced an assault on the green pepper.

"Guy was with me."

I barely heard myself speak.

Why in the world was I mumbling?

Buck apparently shared my curiosity.

"Why the hell are you mumbling?" he said.

I started chopping the celery with Buck-like vehemence.

"Detective Guy Whitehorse was with me that night. Ergo, I was well protected. But I appreciate your concern."

I realized my comment made it sound as if Guy had *slept* at my place. *C'est la vie.*

I abandoned the celery chopping and switched to adding oil, vinegar and salt and pepper to the okra bowl, then proceeded to mix it well. Buck began to chop the remaining celery with vehemence.

"Okay, fine then," he said. "Why didn't you say so?"

I didn't think the question really required an answer, so I started the rice cooking and put some oil in a skillet to heat up and use for frying the okra.

Buck completed his celery attack, leaned against the kitchen counter, regarded me for several seconds, then returned to chopping.

We finished our dinner preparations in silence. Pierre trotted in and meowed as we worked. We took turns offering him little snippets of catfish and okra. He chewed a little and spat out a little. Then he lapped at his water dish some and left. Possibly the silence got to him.

We took plates of food and two bottles of Samuel Adams Light to the dining room table and dined. Gram always made catfish with a spicy hot red gravy that she made with tomatoes she'd canned Cajun style with lots of cayenne peppers and garlic. This was a poor imitation but, as I say, we were not in Noo Orlawns.

I'd started coffee percolating earlier. "We have some key lime pie for dessert."

"From where?" Buck asked. "The grocery store."

He didn't exactly snicker when he spoke, but it was in his tone.

"No. From Polly's Pies on Wilshire."

"Sounds good."

We drank the coffee and ate the pie, and I think we both felt better from the simple fact of having full stomachs.

"Do you still think you can't identify this mystery caller?" Buck's voice was pleasant when he spoke and he puffed on his cigar.

When he'd finished his pie, he'd gone to get the cigar and an ashtray, sat back down and lit up. I just sipped my coffee, deciding this was not the time to make an issue of second-hand smoke. Big of me; it was, after all, his house.

"It doesn't sound like anyone I know. And I still can't understand the *hypocritical* crack with the first message."

"Crackpots don't have to make sense."

"I know. It can't be related to this Avarson case. Whom have I offended about that? True, High Top made me as his tail but he seemed unconcerned and amused about it. So, who?"

"Don't know. Have you spurned any would-be lovers lately?" Buck scowled, vigorously crushed his cigar in the ashtray even though it was still fresh and got up with his mug to get more coffee.

I don't know why but I had a feeling he somehow regretted the question as soon as it escaped his lips. I also felt it was another question that didn't really require that I answer, so I adopted silence.

I sat facing a window and could see rain droplets beginning to form on the pane and wind-battered palm trees bending in the darkness. I decided to get up and get myself some fresh coffee as soon as Buck returned. He came back to the table with his coffee mug and a second piece of pie. I stood.

"I'm going to get some coffee," I said.

"I'll alert the media," Buck said, then smiled slightly.

I returned with my coffee and a second piece of pie.

"I guess High Top has a motive to shoot Sid what with the lawsuit and all," I said.

It wasn't a brilliant statement, but I was eager to get a real conversation rolling.

"In theory, yes. He might be that kind of wigged-out crackpot."

"Why would he have to be so crazy? He's reportedly furious about the money he feels Potter, Wood & Penn lost; he possibly wants a revenge greater than any rewards the lawsuit would produce."

"True. So he kills Sid. So what. He still has to go through with the suit to try and recoup his losses and now he's a murder suspect."

"Okay then, why doesn't he have an alibi for the timeframe of the shooting? Don't his bodyguards go everywhere with him?" I asked.

"Most places yes, from what I've seen. But even celebs must get tired of those goons breathing down their necks."

"Do the cops like Scott Kelly for it?" I said.

"Him or someone like him. Both he and High Top are the number one persons of interest. Scott went missing since before the murder. Doesn't look good."

"And now Nan's gone missing. What do the police make of that?"

"Puts her in the spotlight no question," Buck said.

"Speaking of Scott, I learned today that he's been in touch with Sid the entire time he's gone missing."

"Okay, that's interesting. I'll check in with Holly tomorrow morning. Tell her I'm going off the tail long enough to question Avarson. She oughta see the value of that. Is he in town?"

"Yes. He'll be in town tomorrow and all weekend. Leaves for Denver Monday morning."

"Cool. I'll go interrogate the bastard first thing tomorrow. Nicely, of course," Buck said.

"And what about the Hernandez boys and their connection to High Top? Why in the world were they at his house the day Luke got shot?"

"Another mystery, Fred."

Buck got up to fetch another cigar.

"I'm hoping to catch them hanging with him again while I'm following him," he spoke loud enough for me to hear as he rummaged around the living room. "That's the main reason I'm going along with Holly on continuing this damn infidelity tail. God knows the man doesn't seem to have any action on the side. I'll question those kids when I catch them with High Top; otherwise, not gonna get a thing out of them."

"Are the cops still considering that Doris may have been the intended victim?"

"Don't get the impression they've dismissed it entirely; but it's definitely on the back burner."

I took several quick sips of my java. Here I was asking Buck what the cops thought, assuming he knew what they were up to and he did. And his source for all this knowledge would have to be Guy. *Smart, Freddy. This was taking the conversation down the wrong road again somehow.* Buck seemed to read my mind.

"Another detective is assisting Whitehorse on this caper," he said. "Beverly Hills PD told her to cooperate with me."

Her?

"Do I know him?"

"Her. Detective Rosie Benson. Nice woman. Smart."

"Oh."

I got up to throw out my remaining piece of pie.

"That's great," I said.

CHAPTER 59

AT SIX THIRTY THE NEXT morning Jay shook me awake, announcing we were going for a before-work jog. I didn't feel up to it, but she was sweetly persuasive.

"Get your fat butt outta that sack, heifer," I believe was her exact sweet, persuasive entreaty.

We threw on sweat pants and layers of tee shirts and sweatshirts and took off toward the Santa Monica Pier, turning left at the one-hundred-plus year old Merry-Go-Round onto the boardwalk, then back in the direction of Venice. The weather prediction had been for warmer temperatures, and it was already almost sixty degrees. Behind us the Santa Monica mountains were rose-colored, the sky a clear, cloudless blue. Across the sea, on the horizon you could see Catalina clearly. The strand was quiet and serene, largely unoccupied. A herd of jogging young marines, all in white tees and navy shorts, passed us. Then we were alone for over a mile until two middle-aged ladies, arms pumping as they power-walked, passed us. Jeannette exhaled all of a sudden and stopped running.

"Tired?" I asked.

"Tired my ass," she was panting. "Just occurred to me I should be scared. *You* should be scared."

"It's perfectly safe around here."

"For those marines maybe. They ain't been getting threatening phone calls. Just occurred to me we're out here alone. Perfect targets. Sitting ducks."

Late one night, even before I confessed to Buck, I'd finally divulged to Jeannette the fact of my weird phone messages, but sworn her to secrecy.

"As I told you, I think it's just some crackpot. Maybe my burglar, but the messages are so dumb. So unoriginal."

"Oh now that's a relief. Everyone knows you can't get killed by a crackpot who's got no imagination. Now if his sorry ass could rhyme, then we'd be in trouble."

"Buck find out where this last call came from?" she asked.

"I told him *I'd* look into it, and I will…soon."

"*Soon* is not soon enough," Jeannette said. "God, I don't like this. I don't like this at all."

"Let's go back," I said. "I don't want you scared."

"Good. You don't want me scared; I don't want you dead. We got us a mutual admiration society."

We jogged back with greater speed than our outbound pace, were back at Buck's in plenty of time to shower, dress, and catch the bus to Century City. As we arrived at our building, the wait for the lobby elevator made us about five minutes late.

"Good *afternoon*, ladies," Lisa said.

Ah, another wonderful day at Potter, Wood & Penn, the tone already set. We went to the kitchen, got Starbucks coffee in paper cups and sat down at our respective desks.

I checked my voicemail; there were seven or eight messages from Sid. In the first one he actually expressed his appreciation regarding my choice of a hotel in Denver, the second expressed anger over an email I was to forward to him and didn't (I did), and in another he was angry over a phone message I was to leave on his voicemail and supposedly had not (I had). The remaining messages were instructions for new flight schedules and local dinner meeting reservations. I re-sent the email Sid had claimed I'd forgotten, being careful to forward my original missive to illustrate his misconception. I used his password and went into his voicemails, retrieved the message he insisted did not exist and again attached it to a new voicemail to emphasize his mistake. I rather enjoyed these little exercises but knew they'd make no impression whatsoever on Master Avarson. Tomorrow he'd be back in the blame game, combative as ever. Business was not just serious to Sid; business was war.

At noon, I stepped over to Jeannette's cube. "Want to order in? My treat."

"Hate to pass that up girlfriend but gotta lunch date," she said.

"You hussy. Last night's dinner date, huh?"

"Nope. He's outta town today. Different dude."

"I repeat: hussy." I grinned.

I returned to my desk and dialed the deli. Foreswore my usual salad for something more like comfort food: hot Chicken Teriyaki. I got up to get a Pepsi from the kitchen and ran into two of the twenty-something male associates, both slim and good looking. I knew the tall blonde's name was Steve but hadn't put a name to the medium height dark-haired Asian guy.

Tall blond smiled at me and said, "Freddy, isn't it?"

"That's me," I smiled.

"I'm Steve Cohen, this is Philip Lee." Philip offered his hand and we shook.

"We're just eating downstairs. Why don't you join us," Steve said.

"I'd love to. Can you wait a minute while I cancel my deli order?"

"Sure thing," Steve said. "We'll meet you by the elevator."

I went back to my desk, cancelled the Chicken Teriyaki and quickly freshened my lipstick. The boys were standing in front of the elevators near the reception area, laughing and talking. They wore the standard Potter, Wood garb: Steve, khakis with a blue cotton shirt; Phillip, khakis with a black cotton shirt. Lovely receptionist Lisa wore the standard Lisa grimace: stern and disapproving.

We went to a medium-sized restaurant housed in the lobby level of the building called The Pit. There was a long bar to your right as you entered and numerous round tables spread in helter-skelter style over the rest of the area. The bar and tables were a walnut design; the barstools and table chairs were covered in slightly worn red imitation leather. There were wall lamps shaped like lanterns here and there but the overall atmosphere was pleasingly dark.

The maitre d' showed us to a table in a corner and left menus. A waitress appeared immediately. I ordered an iced tea and Phillip and Steve both ordered Cokes. I'd rather hoped they'd trump my iced tea with beers or scotch or something, and then I could change my order to a white wine spritzer, but no luck.

We studied the menus and the waitress returned. I ordered the trout and the guys went for burgers with fries.

"So you're Sid's latest victim," Steve grinned.

"I think that's an apt term," I smiled.

I couldn't decide if I should reveal my past New York stint with Sid. It was not an immoral act and, if anything, fortified my viability as a temp secretary but ever since Santa Fe I'd acted as if the words assistant-to-private-investigator were emblazoned across my forehead and I must conceal as much of my past, as well as my present, as possible.

The drinks arrived and Philip said, "He's a real piece of work."

"How long have you guys known him?" I asked.

"Hell, who knows him," Steve said. "He's rarely in the office. When he does come in, he streaks by, heads to his own lair, barks commands, belittles the staff, and leaves."

"He's not exactly a small-talk guy," Phillip said. "No one seems to know if he likes movies, if he reads books, if he watches football. No clue. Nada. Zip."

"At the few company parties we have, the guy doesn't eat," Steve added. "You'll have this first-class buffet spread; everyone else is chowing down like gangbusters. Ole Sid just nurses a drink, doesn't touch the food."

"Smart guy though," Phillip said. "No one doubts that."

Our food arrived. The guys were happy with their burgers; my fish was a little dry, so I waved the waitress down and ordered more lemons.

"Oh bullshit, Phil," Steve said. "Lotta people dispute he's so damn smart. Guy's got the right curriculum vitae yeah, but he's got no vision."

Philip munched on a fry. "He sure as hell thinks he does. Thinks he's the company's great white hope."

"Do you think he's resented by his peers, the other partners?" I asked.

"Oh yeah, in spades," Phillip said. "I can't say by one hundred percent of them. But certainly by many."

"You ever hear Kelly sound off whenever he's in?" Steve directed the question to Phillip.

"No, you sit closer to his office than I do."

"Scott Kelly?" I asked. *This was getting interesting.*

"Yeah," Steve said. "Supposed to be best buds. Get together with their wives now and then, do couple stuff, go to the same country club. Never know it when Scott's running his mouth."

"He criticizes how Sid does business?" I asked.

Steve waggled a French fry at me as he spoke. "A lotta times, yeah. And to other people too. Makes wisecracks to the secretaries. Badmouths him about the way he runs up his expense account, how he's never in the office. Petty stuff."

"At the risk of sounding stuffy," Phillip said, "I think it's very unprofessional."

"Oh shit," Steve said, "when are those yahoos ever professional? When clients are around. The rest of the time they're guerillas."

Philip waved the waitress over and ordered a second Coke. He looked at me. "It doesn't help that Sid aced Scott out of a promotion a couple of years ago."

"Really?" I said. *All girlish curiosity.*

"Yeah," Philip continued. "The general consensus was that Scott had consultants on the beach too much."

On-the-beach I knew to be a Potter, Wood term for not working, not occupied.

"I've heard that," I said.

"Scott works hard himself," Steve offered. "Just lousy at managing the troops, so they gave the leadership role to Sid. Sure as hell can't say Sid under-works anyone."

"Thinks he's the great motivator, thinks he's spurs people on to do their best, " Phillip said. "Doesn't work that way."

"Just pisses 'em off," Steve added.

The two men lapsed into sharing anecdotes about Sid Avarson mishaps—primarily his poor treatment of his peers, then segued into sheer gossip—his four marriages, outlandish spending on trips and on and on.

"I've heard rumors about downsizing," I said. "Do you think that could happen to Sid?"

The check arrived. Steve insisted on getting it and gave the waitress his credit card.

"Nah," Steve said once she'd left. "They're afraid of him. Afraid he knows too much."

Phillip seemed to shoot him a dubious look, but said nothing. The waitress returned with the check and Steve signed. We all stood, walked to the elevators, entered a car with four other people and rode silently up to nine. In the reception area, both men thanked me for joining them, said we'd have to do it again soon, and we went our separate ways.

The rest of the afternoon passed with the usual hum of phones, hallway conversations, the tapping of keyboards. At around six fifteen, Jay came to collect me for the bus ride home. At the stop on Santa Monica Boulevard, we were lucky and an MTA number four arrived after just a five-minute wait. Jay told me all about her lunch date—they'd gone to Jade West in the ABC Center, had martinis—and I gave her a thumbnail sketch of my chat with Steve and Philip.

"They never made reference to the shooting at Sid's," I said.

"Whatta you want, " Jeannette said. "They're nerds. Geeks. Live in their own little world."

"Maybe. They really warmed to the subject of Sid, then seemed to clam up toward the end."

"Well, how many beers did they have?"

"None. Had cokes."

"I rest my case. You can't trust a man who doesn't drink at lunch."

We got off the bus and walked over to the mall to pick up Chinese take-out, enough for Buck and us, then grabbed one of the cabs parked next to the AMC Theater. When we got home, Buck was already there, sitting at the dining room table with a half-full bottle of Sam Adams and one empty bottle next to it. He looked pensive and frowned at me when we approached.

"Am I in trouble?" I smiled. "Jay was protecting me all day, I promise."

He got up and went to the fridge, brought two bottles of beer and handed one to Jeannette, one to me.

"Sit down," he said.

I sat.

"You got a phone call a few minutes ago. Doris Hernandez died."

CHAPTER 60

"How 'bout eating on the Third Street Promenade? I'll drive."

Buck had knocked on the door of the guest bedroom, then called in his question.

It was Saturday and Jeannette and I were already up and almost dressed. She went to the door, opened it a crack, peering out at Buck.

"Yeah, but will you treat?"

"Don't press your luck."

Jeannette turned her head to toward me. "Freddy, man here says he'll take us to breakfast but won't promise to pay."

"Tell him yes, " I said. "We can dazzle him with our feminine charms when the check comes."

Jeanette faced Buck. "Hear that?"

"Tell her to get a move on and then ask her what charms she thinks she's got."

Jeanette closed the door, then spoke loudly so Buck could hear.

"Says to haul ass and then added a lot of sweet talk."

I put my black leather jacket on and checked my hair in the mirror. "Nice to get some sweet talk," I mumbled. "It's not coming from any other quarters."

"I'd guess that means no date tonight with the hunky Indian detective," Jeannette said.

"Nope. Saturday night is perhaps no big deal in his culture." I sighed. The French have a saying for my dilemma..."

"Don't they always?" Jay said.

"*Il aime moi un peu, beaucoup, follement, pas du tout.*"

Jeannette offered a sigh of her own. "Translate, *s'il vous plaît.*"

"He loves me a little, a lot, passionately, madly, not at all."

Jeannette shook her head in apparent disgust and shrugged on a brown aviator jacket, adding a pink wool pashmina for warmth and dramatic effect. I myself had had enough drama with my condo break in and battering, the shooting of Luke and now, worst of all, the loss of lovely Doris. At two o'clock this morning, Rosa Torres called me. Between soft gasping sobs, she repeated the message she'd left earlier with Buck: that Doris had succumbed to her bullet wound.

"Our Doris...our sweet Doris...she gone." Rosa repeated variations of this statement about three times. I sobbed quietly with her.

"God bless, Rosa. God bless."

I didn't know what else to say.

We drove to Santa Monica Place. Buck parked the Explorer in the mall parking lot. As we walked over to the Broadway Deli, I returned to daily life and its mundane concerns, as we mortals are prone to do. I remembered that the delivery of my new beds had been promised sometime today between ten this morning and two, and reminded Buck we'd have to take care of this after breakfast.

We were ushered to a booth by the long row of windows with a view of the Broadway street traffic and the entrance to the mall. Jay and I ordered avocado and sour cream omelets, Buck, steak and two eggs over easy. The waitress brought coffees for Buck and me and a tea for Jeannette, then left.

"I should have ordered a Bloody Mary," I said.

"Doris?" Buck said.

"Yeah."

I sipped my coffee. Buck left the table. Jeannette emptied two sugar packets into her tea. We both stared out the window. Two homeless men were standing next to a scrawny, leafless tree, arguing. The traffic was light and the sun was already bright. Unusually warm temperatures were predicted for the next week. It would be nice to have hot, sunny weather. I was ready for a little *plage de temps*...beach time...and grateful to be alive to enjoy it.

"How's Luke these days?" Jay asked.

"Buck says he gave him a brief call the other night. Feeling fine, keeping busy. Didn't say doing what; guess he's mainly recuperating. He's okay, that's the main thing," I said.

Buck returned and drank his coffee with gusto. A waitress appeared with a Bloody Mary for me and a pot of coffee for refills. I whispered a "thank you" to Buck as our meal orders arrived. We finished eating and drinking twenty minutes later, Buck paid, we located the car and took off.

"Jeannette, if you don't mind," Buck said, "I'm going to drop you at Fred's to wait for the beds to arrive," Buck said. "So you and I, babe," he turned to me, "can go interrogating."

"Cool with me," Jeannette said, "Freddy's got plenty of books around I can read."

The yellow glow from the sunlight and Buck's Hawaiian shirt of bright red with a floral design in golds and greens seemed all too exuberant for my current mood. Then a jumble of words, a quote from George Bernard Shaw, drifted into my consciousness: *Life is no brief candle…it is a splendid torch, which I have got a hold of for the moment, and I want to make it burn as brightly as possible…*

I couldn't remember the rest, but it was enough to quell my mourning and energize me.

"Who are we interrogating you might ask," Buck said. He could tell I was lost in thought, so he answered his own question. "The houses we missed on Avarson's street."

"Don't the cops do that?" Jeannette asked.

"They do indeed but our client doesn't trust the cops. Therefore our mission, should we choose to accept it…"

"Jay, are you sure you don't mind waiting for the delivery?" I said.

"Hey you could receive another threatening phone call or, better still, another burglar visit. I can use all that excitement for reference in my acting career."

"Happy to be instrumental in your first Oscar," Buck said.

We dropped Jeannette off, and headed for Beverly Hills.

Sid was quite possibly at home, so we parked the Explorer a block away from his street and proceeded on foot. The whole time I kept casting covert glances toward his house. *Still fearful after all these years*, to paraphrase Paul Simon.

Our first stop was the English country manor where the residents were the husband and wife attorneys. The maid we'd met during our prior visit was standing in the front yard conferring with a stocky man holding gardener's tools. The gardener headed for the back of the house as we approached as the maid simply looked annoyed. In answer to Buck's question, she advised that both barristers were again absent. She didn't actually use the term *barristers*, but she did sound convincing. Buck gave her his card.

Next, we tried the home of the widow, a pediatrician. It was the largest house on the block, a Mediterranean wonder with a huge weeping willow on one side. Again, the maid came to the door. She was dark-haired, dark-eyed and voluptuous—she matched the Mediterranean motif. We re-introduced ourselves and learned that her name was Dama. She told us the widow, Dr. Adams, was home, but "indisposed" and could we come another time. Buck handed over two business cards, one for the maid he said and one for Dr. Adams. He asked that the doctor be so kind as to call him to suggest a convenient time and that Dama also please call him if anything concerning the day of the shooting occurred to her.

"We should have suggested the lawyers' maid contact us also, don't you think?" I asked.

"You're right. Dama somehow made more of an impression on me." Buck squeezed my arm and winked.

CHAPTER 61

WE CROSSED THE STREET TO the cream-colored house, a two-story rectangular home with a protruding entry and English bay windows set into half-towers in the front. There were awnings and railings that gave it more visual dimension than the other houses on the street. The front door was completely open, revealing a cluster of floor plants of various heights and a large oriental umbrella stand. We knocked anyway.

"Come right on in and go up the stairs," a female voice called from some distant room. We stepped inside and stood in the foyer.

"Buck Lemoyne," he called out. "Private investigator."

A tall, sturdy woman with frizzy strawberry-blonde hair that seemed to float as she walked came toward us, wiping her hands on a blue dishtowel.

"Oh, I'm Jibby Smith," she said. "I'm sorry. I thought you were the tile man."

"I'm Buck Lemoyne," Buck repeated. "This is my associate Freddy Bonnaire."

Jibby smiled and extended her hand, which we both shook in turn.

Buck asked if she was aware of the shooting recently at the Avarson house. Jibby responded she'd read about it in the paper and that it was awful, just awful. She was so shocked, she said, that she still could still recite the day and time of the shooting. Buck said we had a few questions for her if she was agreeable to this and if this was a convenient time.

"That would be just fine," Jibby said. "Why don't you join me in the kitchen. I've just made some tea."

We followed Jibby through a comfortable looking living room filled with lots of fresh flowers, plants and pillows. A huge chandelier hung from the center of the room and some kind of fountain surrounded by gray stones gurgled from a corner. Through an archway, I could see a dining room with a dark orange cloth covering one entire wall. In the middle was a long, rectangular white table with chrome legs. An enameled green bowl full of lemons sat on the table and white upholstered chairs surrounded it. Both Jibby and her home had a decidedly bohemian feel.

We entered the kitchen.

Jibby said, "Let's just sit here if you don't mind. It's cozier."

Buck and I sat down on straight-back chairs next to a round table covered with a cloth in a paisley design. It *was* a cozy room. There was a large bowl of fruit on the table and lots of earthenware pots on top of the kitchen cabinets. Two ceiling beams were wrapped in a bright orange gauzy material and a cluster of green plants stood on top of the refrigerator.

"Like I said, I made green tea," Jibby said. "But maybe you'd like something else. I do keep sodas around for some guests."

"Tea would be fine," I said.

She brought oversized white mugs to the table, filled them and sat down to join us.

"I'm sorry about mistaking you for the tile man. It's way early for him to be here anyway. But he's like that, sometimes comes late, sometimes comes early."

"That's quite all right, we just..."

"It took me so long to find the right black and white tile. The bathroom really needs it, to ground the energy you know."

"Ground the energy?" Buck said.

"Are you familiar with Feng Shui?" Jibby asked.

"No, but..."

"Oh, I *am* surprised. I thought everyone was these days. It stems from the Chinese. Feng is the force of wind and Shui is the flow of water. If you place objects in the correct places and decorate your home properly the energy from these natural forces can be made to flow in a way that's beneficial to everyone in the home." Jibby beamed, proud of her knowledge.

"That's very interesting..." Buck began.

"If you're a private investigator, you must have an office do you not?"

"Yes, I do," Buck said. "But..."

"Well, when you go back to it today, you might want to check your file cabinets. Or your wall cabinets if you have them. Storage that is too high can be oppressive, especially if it's over a desk."

Buck frowned and tentatively sipped his tea.

"And you need to have some nice, soft pillows to add Yin energy. An office is mostly Yang space, so that's important," Jibby continued. "And electrical things like computers and fax machines and so forth are very Yang so a Yin plant helps diffuse that energy."

A chocolate Labrador was dozing in a corner. He or she never awoke or looked up the whole time we were there. Zoned out on the good Feng Shui no doubt.

"I'll make a note of that, Mrs. Smith, and..."

"Oh, it's Ms. Smith," Jibby corrected. "I've taken back my maiden name." She paused long enough to take a quick gulp of tea. "Do you have a laptop? They're very good Feng Shui as they can be placed out of sight."

I worked on emptying my own mug. *Where were Andy Sherman and his morning beers when you needed them?*

"The Avarsons. How well do you know them?" Buck quickly made his point to avert another interruption.

"Oh, not well at all," Jibby said. "We don't travel in the same circles. They're both professional people and I'm an artist, sculpture mostly although I've done a few ocean and mountain scenes in acrylics."

"Then you're at home all day?" Buck asked. "Were you home the day of the shooting?"

"Oh, heavens yes, sure I was. My studio is that little guest house out back. I would have kept it as a guest house, but I don't really entertain that much and I need it much more as a..."

"Did you hear the shots or hear or see anything unusual?" Buck said.

Jibby pursed her lips. She could dish out interruptions, but she appeared not to receive them well.

"You know the police asked me just such questions already," she said tersely.

"I know that," Buck said gently. "But my client has interests in this matter and insists I personally follow up."

"What happened to the poor lady who got shot?" Jibby asked. "I heard she was in a coma."

"She passed away," I said.

"Oh, now that's so sad. Why did they shoot her? I read she worked for Mr. Avarson."

"Yes, she did. But we suspect the shooter meant to aim at Avarson. That's the point of our investigation for the most part," Buck said.

"And the police are pretty much following the same line, Mrs. Smith," I added. "That's what we're trying to find out. Who hates Sid Avarson enough to try and kill him."

Might as well call a spade a spade.

"Well certainly not me," Jibby pressed her hand against her chest. "I told the police and I'm telling you: I hardly knew the man. I knew him by sight, but that's all."

"And we believe you," Buck said softly. "Just tell us if you saw or heard anything unusual."

Jibby stood up.

"As I told the police, I was in my studio at the time. I was working very hard on a sculpture of my niece's head. It wasn't going well and it had my full attention. Normally I have no trouble capturing the essence of my subject but she has unusual features and..."

Buck and I stood almost simultaneously.

"I understand," Buck said. "It's an unsettling thing to have happen in your own neighborhood. You're a creative person; you were absorbed in your work. We'll get out of your hair. Thanks for your time."

Jibby begun to smile and visibly relax after the *creative person* part of Buck's comment. She followed us out of the kitchen and through the living room, saying she was sorry she could not have been more helpful. We stopped at the foyer, smiled and thanked her again. We left through the still open door, making our way down the slate walkway.

"Mr. Lemoyne!" Jibby called out when we were halfway to the street; she was still standing at the open door. She motioned with her hand for us to come toward her, and we returned down the path to the door.

"There is one thing."

"Yes?" Buck said.

"Now I remember. At one point, I left my studio to go to the kitchen. When I walked out, I noticed some shrubs in the yard that needed trimming. I went on walking to the front of the house to see what else in the garden might need work. I was surprised about the shrubs because the gardener had been here the day before, but he's new and...well, never mind about that. The thing is I started meandering around the front yard and I looked down the street. I saw a woman in a maid's uniform...something like what Caroline wears...roaming around near the Avarson house. I've met their maid. She walks past my house to catch her bus in the evenings. We've chatted. It wasn't Caroline running. It was a different person."

"Thanks a lot, Ms. Smith," Buck said.

He took my arm and we turned and headed once more for the street.

"About that maid thing, think she's got a clue?" I said.

"I think Miss Jibby's pretty clue-*less*,"

CHAPTER 62

"THIS LOVELY LADY IS MY current lady friend, Frédérique. Don't you think we make a charming couple?"

My friend Mr. Nazitto was referring to a new nurse who was filling in for the redoubtable Hannah and obviously doing a good job of it in his eyes. He introduced me to Viola Matthews, an African-American woman around five feet seven in height and around two hundred pounds in weight. She was indeed lovely with big brown eyes framed by long lashes and large, but graceful, hands that sported a professional-looking manicure in a vivid coral.

It was Sunday and I'd walked over to Morningside for a long-overdue visit with my elderly friend. He seemed unaffected by my protracted absence and sweetly understanding when I recited all the reasons for this. I was sitting in a straight-back chair on one side of his lounge chair sipping coffee Viola had provided shortly after I arrived. She was sitting in a similar chair on the other side, also sipping coffee. If she had other duties, she wasn't concerned about them and demonstrated every intention of staying and joining in on our visit.

"I hope Hannah isn't ill," I said.

"Oh, no," Viola answered, smiling broadly. "She has relatives in town all this week, but she didn't have any vacation days coming so I'm filling in for her as a favor. She's a good friend of mine, and I worked in a nursing home years ago so it was fine with Mr. Finley, the director, that I help out."

"Viola has her own business, Frédérique," Mr. Nazitto said. "She's quite successful."

"That's great. What's the nature of your business?"

"Got my own domestic help agency." Viola stood offered another of her dazzling smiles. "Excuse me while I get some more coffee. Anybody else want some?"

Nazitto and I both shook our heads in the negative.

"Viola mostly visits with the patients," Mr. Nazitto said, as if he could read my mind. "We have a lot of laughs."

"This is a coincidence of sorts," I said. "I've spent a lot of time recently talking to domestic help in Beverly Hills."

"Really? I would wager Viola knows the very ladies you talked to, my dear. She told me her clients are not your regular *hoi polloi*. Her customers are the best people in Beverly Hills, Bel Air and oh, what's that beach area near here where a lot of actors live?"

"Malibu?"

"That's it. Well, Frédérique, when I say the *best* people I mean those with considerable financial resources. How actually virtuous they may be is a matter of conjecture."

As I nodded my head in agreement, Viola returned and sat down, both hands resting her fresh mug of coffee on her ample lap.

"I understand you have high-end clientele," I said. "I wonder if one of your Beverly Hills clients is Sid Avarson."

"The Avarsons." Viola beamed. "Now they're one of my best customers. You know them?"

"Well, I used to work for him in New York, and actually I'm doing temp work in his office now. Difficult man."

Viola laughed heartily.

"Difficult don't begin to describe it, honey, but he sure makes *me* a lot of money. They go through maids like that box of tissue over there. And I charge him a fee for each new one. It was a pain in the neck in some ways, but it made me a chunk of change for a long time, like I say."

"He *was* a pain in the neck? You don't work with him any more?" I asked.

"Oh, it's not like that. He finally found someone who'd put up with him. Yeah, Caroline has been working for them well over a year now. Can't stand him but she hangs in there."

The next obvious question occurred to me.

"I trust you read about the shooting at the Avarson house. So Caroline was there the day of the shooting?"

"Oh, no, I…I'm pretty sure not…least ways I don't think so," Viola said, frowning slightly as she plumbed her memory. "Yeah, that's right, I remember now. She wasn't there because she needed the day off. But a friend of hers filled in for her." Viola smiled. "Just like I'm filling in. Good to have friends who'll pitch in on a moment's notice, you could say."

"Yes it is. A neighbor told us she saw someone who appeared to be a maid near the Avarson home that day, but she didn't recognize this person as being the Avarson's regular maid. This neighbor is a bit on the ditzy side. She almost inferred it was an interloper or burglar or something, but the substitute would explain it."

"Sure it would," Viola agreed. "Nothing strange about Caroline. She wouldn't have lasted this long with the Avarsons if she weren't efficient and hard working. And I gotta believe any friend of hers is the same way."

"I'm sure that's true. My partner and I should probably talk to her. Would it be possible for you to give me her name and number?"

"Frédérique's so-called partner, Viola, dear, I should explain is her private investigator friend. And, Frédérique, what's this about your working in an office?"

"If I may, Mr. N, I'll explain another time." I smiled, patted his hand and turned to Viola. "My friend represents a client who has hired us to look into the shooting. Her husband is a suspect and she wants his name cleared."

Viola sipped her coffee and looked thoughtful. I waited, hoping she did not think I was asking her to breach professional ethics.

"I can always ask Mr. Avarson if you feel uncomfortable telling…"

"No, no, it's not that," Viola said. "Trying to think of her name. Never actually met the woman. Told Caroline any friend of hers was all right with me. I remember she had a name like some old song my grand nana used to sing."

Viola shook her head, as if to dislodge some cobwebs, and focused her gaze on the contents of her coffee mug. I turned my attention to Mr. Nazitto. He was wearing a slight smile, seemingly pleased to be privy to top-level detective work in process despite his disdain for the profession. He nodded toward a table behind me.

"Those gardenias are courtesy of Viola." His smile broadened.

"They're beautiful," I said.

I'd been dimly aware of a wonderful aroma in the room but hadn't thought about the source. *Some investigator*. I also realized his happy mood was undoubtedly due to Viola's jolly presence, rather than my scintillating conversation.

"Nellie," Viola said at last. "That was her name."

"Last name?" I asked.

"Blye."

CHAPTER 63

"No, this is *Jeannette*. Who are you?"

I could hear Jay's irate tone as I trailed Buck, both of us heading for the kitchen. He had just wandered out of his bedroom and was in search of coffee. Buck was wearing a white tank-top undershirt and the pants to his one good black suit. I think it came from Sears, but on him it was every bit as chic as any designer duds Jay or I possessed.

I'd happened to leave the guest bedroom seconds later with the same destination in mind but my beverage of choice was some nice, ice-cold water. I followed him, also dressed in black but at a more progressive stage. I had on a Ralph Lauren pants suit, unadorned white jersey shirt underneath and the most conservative black shoes I owned: Manalo Blahnik sling backs. Jeannette was uncharacteristically understated in a Donna Karan number—a long black jersey dress, low-heel black boots, pearls at her neck. The purpose of the formal attire was not to make a fashion statement but, sadly, to be dressed respectfully for Doris Hernandez' funeral—a Mass at St. Monica's. Rosa had intended it be held at their neighborhood church, but Sid Avarson was reportedly footing the bill for the burial and all other expenses and the church in Santa Monica was his choice.

Jeannette was still grilling someone on the other end of the phone as we entered the kitchen.

"I just told you who I am. Who the hell are *you*? No, for the fifth time, this isn't Frédérique. Do you wanna to speak to her?" Jay looked at me, as she made a less than complimentary hand gesture intended for the caller. "No? Buck? Yeah, he's here." She handed the receiver to Buck.

"Lemoyne here. Hey…oh you are?…oh, sure…well, he would have…yeah, that's the right address. It's south of Sunset, just below Montana. Of course, they'll appreciate it…that's very nice. We'll see you there and afterward we can…" Buck held the receiver out for a moment. "She hung up."

Jeannette filled a mug of coffee. "Who *she*? No, I'll tell you. She one rude bitch."

"Just a diva client, Jay. Goes with the territory."

Buck gingerly sipped the hot, black coffee.

"Amanda?" I asked, taking a half-empty bottle of Pellegrino from the fridge.

Outside of the kitchen window, all was gray. Temperatures had dropped once more and rain was forecast for the afternoon. Pierre wandered in and rubbed against my leg.

"No," Buck squatted down to stroke Pierre, an unusual gesture for him. "It was Holly King. Wanted to verify location of the church."

"She and High Top are coming to the funeral?" I asked.

"That they are," Buck said. "Seems when he and Sid were still doing business on a friendly basis High Top and his assistant both got to know Doris well and were very fond of her. Ole H.T. wants to pay his respects. He, Holly and his male assistant—Greg somebody—all gonna be there. Tried to tell her we'd meet them for a drink afterward."

"That's lovely that they're coming. I keep saying High's a nice guy. And judging by our relentless surveillance, not a cheating hubby," I said.

"Wouldn't blame him," Jeannette said. "Wifey's a piece of work."

"Nah," Buck countered. "Just the jittery type. Little paranoid maybe, but sweet."

I opened a can of cat food for Pierre and emptied it into his dish. A reception at Il Fornaio restaurant near the ocean was scheduled after the Mass. It would be a long, unhappy day.

CHAPTER 64

FATHER HOWARD STOOD OUTSIDE AT the entrance. We hurried inside Saint Monica's as he began to sprinkle the coffin with holy water, then placed a white cloth on the casket. As we moved toward the front down a side aisle, the funeral procession entered and commenced slowly down the center.

The incense had the aroma of sage. Christmas decorations were already in evidence; garlands of pine with tiny white lights interwoven were draped around the thick ivory columns. Two large but simple green wreaths adorned either side of the all-white sculpture of Jesus on the pale-blue wall behind the altar with double rows of garlands coiling from each side in long, graceful loops. More tiny white lights sparkled amidst the wreaths and altar garlands.

To the left of the altar, the same lights adorned two short, sparse pine trees perched next to the manger scene, the figures all copper colored. Clusters of pine and Poinsettia stood at the base of the manger grouping.

The long, black ceiling chandeliers were lit in deference to the darkening afternoon sky outside. A slight mist had begun as people filed into the church, the low, ashen clouds seemed to threaten a downpour.

Most of the mourners I'd anticipated were seated when we arrived. As we made our way to our seats, I could see Rosa and several other women I recognized huddled together in the front. One elderly woman wore a cream-colored lace mantilla on her head, a practice abandoned many years ago in most American Catholic churches. On either side of the line of women sat several Hispanic middle-aged men, undoubtedly husbands and brothers.

The organ had been playing and a soloist commenced *Grant Them Eternal Rest.* As the opening prayer was given, I was surprised to see Carlos, the taller of the two Hernandez boys, rise and give a reading:

"No eye has seen nor ear heard, nor the heart of man conceived, what God has prepared for those who love Him..."

A brief responsorial psalm was sung

"The Lord is my shepherd; there is nothing I shall want."

We ended up sitting toward the back, affording me a view of most of those in attendance. There were several of the Potter, Wood partners present and even more of the younger associates. Rosa walked to the front to give a reading: She looked pale and decidedly thinner than the last time I'd seen her.

"At the evening of life, we shall be judged on our love..." Her voice, belying her appearance, was strong and clear.

Al-le-lu-ia! Al-le-lu-ia! Al-le-lu-ia!

A familiar figure moved to the front to give a reading. It was the Potter, Wood receptionist, Lisa Connors. She wore a navy-blue caftan-like dress and a small black bowler hat.

"All the dead will rise; those who have done good, to the resurrection of life, and those who have done evil, to the resurrection of judgment."

Lisa read in a low, but distinct voice, her features suddenly sweet and benign. I felt a softening of my own heart toward my recent office nemesis. I watched as Lisa returned to her seat. Then I saw a familiar figure that had been sitting on the other side of Lisa, previously blocked from my view: *Nan Kelly.*

I nudged Buck and nodded in Nan's direction. He saw her, looked at me and, with his hands still in his lap, gave a thumbs up. Whatever she'd been up to, we now knew she'd returned and was safe.

The Priest, Father Howard, was of medium height, with a slight tan. Under his traditional black vestment his white robe swayed as he moved to the left of the altar, almost touching the well-shined black shoes he wore. As he arrived at the lectern, a clap of thunder boomed from outside. He chuckled, a small moment of comic relief. Father Howard commenced his homily.

"Neither scripture nor modern-day theology presents to us an adequate vision for a picture of life after death..."

I couldn't avert my gaze from Nan Kelly. Nan had moved to Lisa's aisle seat, and Lisa returned to sit on the opposite aisle after giving her reading, providing me with an unobstructed view. Nan was twisting some object in her hands, Kleenex or a handkerchief. She looked down and then up several times and at one point looked backward as if she were expecting someone to arrive. Her nervousness was puzzling. I'm sure she was sympathetic over the passing of Doris, but they had hardly been close and Nan's demonstration of grief seemed excessive for the circumstances. I looked away.

"...Christians must vigorously cling to the two following essential truths: on the one hand, they must believe in the fundamental continuity..."

In front of me, to my left, I could see Holly and High Top King. Between them sat a slender young black male around twenty. He must be High's male assistant. All three sat erect and calm, seemingly lost in the ceremony.

"...by the grace of the Holy Spirit, between our current life in Christ and the future life..."

Holly suddenly bowed her head and turned slowly in order to glance behind her. She stared in our direction, then averted her eyes and seemed to scan the adjacent areas to our right and to our left. Undoubtedly searching for High Top's paramour, even now.

"...on the other hand, they must be clearly knowledgeable concerning the stark division between this present life and the future one because the storehouse of faith will be replaced by the storehouse of the fullness of life..."

Among the young Potter, Wood & Penn staff, several of the female members were dabbing their eyes. To a woman, they were dressed in black suits with v-necked cotton blouses in white or blue, not very different than their daily office garb.

Sid Avarson sat hunched between his wife, Erika, and a muscular male who I guessed to be his new bodyguard. Next to Erika sat their daughter. She was tall, like Erika, and nearly as restless as Nan. In a dramatic gesture, Erika Avarson was wearing a large black picture hat, complete with veil.

"...we shall be with Christ and we shall see God, and it is in such promises that our hope essentially lies..."

I looked back at Nan. I'd noticed from my peripheral vision that she'd turned slightly around, looking backward now and then, making little pretense of listening to the homily. The Hernandez boys—Pedro and Carlos—sat directly behind her but did not seem to be the objects of her attention. At least she appeared to be deliberately gazing beyond them. Pedro shifted and looked uncomfortable each time her eyes darted backward.

"...Our imagination may not be literally capable of assailing these heights but our hearts do so with God-endowed instinct."

I hoped Doris was among us. I hoped she could see these faces, even hear Father Howard's words. I found myself looking backward, as if I expected to see her spirit. Instead, as I quickly glanced backward, I saw a very alive figure standing by the last row of pews at the edge of the door. *Scott Kelly.*

CHAPTER 65

The Priest stood at the entrance to the church. I watched as he began to sprinkle the coffin with water, then placed a white cloth on the casket. Finally the funeral procession moved inside the church.

The aroma of incense was stifling. Christmas decorations were all over the place; bunches of pine encircled every standing column in the church. Two huge wreaths hand been slapped on the wall on either side of the cross and the angels with more pine hanging around them, scores of little white Christmas tree lights were blazing from all the pine, looking as hedonistic as could be. Did they imagine there were lots of those tiny light bulbs providing glare two thousand years ago?

To the left of the altar, there were two flimsy pine trees with more of the same damn lights next to the usual manger scene. The replicas of Mary and Joseph and the three Wise Men, the baby, the hay, the whole bit done in some kind of brownish finish. At the bottom looking like some kind of department store display some genius had stuck more pine and pots of Poinsettias. Tacky. And I'm supposed to be the agnostic here.

At least most of the ceiling lights are on. It's getting dark as hell outside and with my luck there'll be a downpour the minute we get out of here. I didn't want to come but it seemed like a good idea. That old broad meant nothing to me. I doubt she meant anything to most of the people sitting here, all dressed in black, looking sad for appearance's sake.

At least everybody I expected to show up did. No surprises there. Her sister and the other Latino women look ridiculous. All of them are sobbing and carrying on. Haven't they heard of keeping a stiff upper lip? And that old woman with the scarf on her head. She looks ready to keel over herself and yet she's clasping her hands and praying like crazy. Does she think they'll be giving out Oscars for acting performances? And the men. What a pussy-whipped looking bunch of jerks. They're blubbering and dabbing their eyes as much as their old ladies.

That organ is giving me a headache. Now the tall Hispanic kid is going to give a talk, or read. He looks angelic up there, but he'll be out boosting hubcaps two hours from now. Grant Them Eternal Rest? I know exactly who I'd like to give some permanent rest to. And will. Soon.

"No eye has seen nor ear heard, nor the heart of man conceived, what God has prepared for those who love Him…"

No, and they won't be prepared for what I've got in mind next either, padre.

"The Lord is my shepherd; there is nothing I shall want."

God, is there going to be a lot of singing before this thing is over?

Potter, Woods is well represented. Some of the young associates brought their kids, of all things, with most of them sitting near Rosa Torres, fawning like they give a damn. God, now she's getting up to speak. She looks like hell. Couldn't she shine it on for this one day?

"At the evening of life, we shall be judged on our love…"

Her voice is loud as hell at least.

Al-le-lu-ia! Al-le-lu-ia! Al-le-lu-ia!

I see Buck Lemoyne got duded up for this event. Musta killed him to put on that white shirt and tie instead of one of those corny Hawaiian shirts. Man must have hundreds of them. People move out here; right away they go Hollywood. Is there something in the drinking water that makes everyone fantasize they're a movie star?

"All the dead will rise; those who have done good, to the resurrection of life, and those who have done evil, to the resurrection of judgment."

God, more speeches. That porky receptionist yet. In that hat she looks like an obese Charlie Chaplin.

At last the priest is going to talk. That means we're getting this show on the road. Those black shoes look pricey. Hey, what about that vow of poverty, father? Get to the podium. Don't take all day. Shit, was that thunder? This suit will be ruined the minute I set foot out of this place.

"Neither scripture nor modern-day theology presents to us an adequate vision for a picture of life after death..."

There's Freddy. Typical blond WASP ever there was one. Where's it written years of being some hotshot model make you a private eye all of a sudden? What was Buck thinking when he hired her? Why am I even wondering? She's boinking him. No other possible answer. And what's up with her girlfriend, the redhead? God, they must be both six feet tall in heels. Buck probably does them together. When they're not leading him around by the nose. All he needs is a third chick and he can call his agency Charlie's Angels.

"...Christians must vigorously cling to the two following essential truths: on the one hand, they must believe in the fundamental continuity..."

Freddy's looking around. She's probably as bored as I am. I wonder if she and Lemoyne drop those southern accents when no one's looking. Christ, her snooping has finally gotten on my nerves. But we'll fix that soon, won't we?

"...by the grace of the Holy Spirit, between our current life in Christ and the future life. . .

What about my current life and future life? Is anyone in this room worried about that? They're not worried about my life. And I sure as hell am not worried about their lives. I snuffed out one life. I can do it again.

"...on the other hand, they must be clearly knowledgeable concerning the stark division between this present life and the future one because the storehouse of faith will be replaced by the storehouse of the fullness of life..."

There's Avarson with Erika baby. Their kid is a clone of her mother. Could the three of them look any more arrogant if they tried? And Erika's hat. It screams look-at-me. Sid's suit is custom made, so's his shirt. The bastard gets paid three times what he's worth and he has the audacity to flaunt it.

"...we shall be with Christ and we shall see God, and it is in such promises that our hope essentially lies..."

We shall see God? Not me. But one person here is going to have that opportunity any day now. Any day now.

"...Our imagination may not be literally capable of assailing these heights but our hearts..."

What imagination? Too much imagination going on around here if you ask me. Buck, the cops. They pretty much stick to procedure. Freddy baby is the loose cannon. She's got no procedure to stick to. She's been one fucking threat to my plans all along.

"...do so with..."

Thank God. It sounds like the good father is finally winding down.

"...God-endowed instinct..."

I'm going to follow my instincts. My instincts about one Amazon bitch named Frédérique Bonnaire. A real live wire. She's not going to be live much longer.

CHAPTER 66

"I don't know what you're smoking over there."

Sid had been bellowing over the phone. The smoking jab was his charming way of expressing that he believed I was in error concerning a supposedly omitted item on his expense report. Of course, I had to do more than just state I was certain of my facts. So forty-five minutes-of-research and eleven-copies-of-previous-reports-and-related-bills-faxed-to-Sid's-home-office later, I had proved my case and breathed a sigh of relief.

Other than the Avarson temper tantrum being a little more excessive than usual, it was an uneventful day at the office. I knew it was going to be a quiet day and had considered playing hooky again and joining Buck on his rounds. I was curious to talk to the maids on Sid's street, particularly the substitute, supposedly named Nellie Blye. I was even more curious to meet with Nan Kelly in person and confirm that I'd seen Scott at the funeral and that they were back together again. Were I married, I could not imagine tolerating the sporadic vacations that Scott enjoyed. Of course, I'd been cultivating of late a sanguine attitude regarding the absence of a certain American Indian police detective so perhaps I should reserve judgment. On the other hand, this latest disappearance of Scott's seemed like something more and I suspected Nan felt the same way.

Buck nixed my sleuthing rather than secretary-ing, saying it was more important that I keep my eyes open at the office. He trusted Jeannette but since I had worked for Potter, Wood & Penn before and knew more of the players I was a more valuable resource in his view. I wasn't so sure of that, particularly since Jay had yet another luncheon rendezvous with yet another of the younger consultants or, as she characterized it, "dating one nerd after another."

Buck had called Holly and begged off the usual High Top/mistress surveillance in favor of the maid interviews and a meeting with Nan Kelly who, judging from her presence at the funeral, had emerged from her own missing-in-action scenario. Holly had approved with the proviso that he tail her husband until three o'clock at which time High Top was scheduled to return home, and Buck could then attend to the other matters.

I finalized Sid's expense report and commenced the tedious chore of scotch taping the numerous receipts he provided to paper for presentation to the guy in Accounting who processed all ER's. Sid often incurred unauthorized charges and was known to live high on the hog, as Gram would say, when traveling. Last week he'd ordered roses sent to Erika Avarson and the charge appeared two days later on his expense report as a client gift. What a great guy. Maybe it was someone in the expense department who'd tried to shoot him.

My own Potter, Wood buddies, Philip and Steve, stopped my by with a lunch invitation. I agreed so we three trooped over to the Jade West in the ABC Entertainment Center. Philip had just completed a project for a major client. He advised they were able to "charge them up the wahzoo." He was feeling expansive, hence our restaurant upgrade from the lobby's The Pit to the more high-end Jade West. During luncheon chitchat, his expansiveness didn't translate into more juicy tidbits regarding our mutual friend Monsieur Avarson, but I decided not to press the matter.

Around two thirty my curiosity about Nan Kelly got the better of me so I decided to give her a call. I would hear all about Buck's meeting with her tonight at home, but I guess I craved some girl talk versus the facts Buck would cull. At my first call I let the phone ring three times and then hung up. I really did not want to talk at this time to her maid, Angie, nor did I want the answering machine to pick up. But after four or so three-ring attempts at fifteen-minute intervals I decided to go for broke and just let the phone ring until Angie or the machine picked up or, better yet, Nan herself.

I did the multiple-ring procedure several more times, timing them again around fifteen minutes apart. I continued this right up until it was time to leave for the day at six o'clock. Nan could be shopping or out for an early drink with a girlfriend, but she told me once she hated being out after dark and I could always reach her at home by late afternoon.

As it turned out, I didn't have to worry about chitchat with Angie or announcing myself on the Kelly answering machine. Each time I let the phone ring endlessly. I tapped a pencil impatiently. Through the blinds in a nearby window I could see the sky was dark and lights from the adjacent office buildings were the only discernable view. No one—not Angie, not the machine, not Nan—answered. It occurred to me that Buck may have taken her out some place for their interview. At least, I hoped that was the explanation.

CHAPTER 67

Paul Sunderland and Stu Lantz were providing the color, and doing a great job, but I still missed the late, great Chick Hearn. They announced there was a crowd of 19,000 in Phoenix to cheer the Suns on against my beloved Los Angeles Lakers. At the rate we'd been losing lately, Phoenix wouldn't have to kill themselves with cheering in order to achieve the victory they prized.

Jeannette and I left work promptly at six. With our one-day use of the Honda, we drove to Ocean Avenue Seafood restaurant in Santa Monica. Buck had called earlier to designate this as our rendezvous for dinner tonight, adding he'd treat. I was glad I'd brought my small transistor radio to work as I now—*rudely*—sat with it plugged into my ear, listening to the Laker game. Buck had yet to arrive so, feeling expansive, we ordered a seventy-five dollar bottle of white wine from Burgundy, France, circa 2006. It was our treat for Buck, and I think we both believed we were drawing our previous New York modeling salaries. We sipped our wine, me listening to my radio, Jeannette people watching. Twice Jay asked about the game; she'd never been a big basketball fan, but she'd developed a serious crush on Derek Fisher, which was enough to engage her interest.

I removed the plug from my ear for a moment. "I've been meaning to ask you—on these luncheon sojourns of yours—do you pump your dates about Sid?"

"Don't have to pump; they spill their guts. Well, I mention that you worked for Sid in New York and that sets the ball rolling. Herbie, my today's luncheon special, said they might downsize Sid's ass outta there."

"My sources don't think that's possible. They believe enough of the big guns think well of him."

Jeannette rose slightly from her chair before commenting.

"I think that's Sandra Bullock and her husband over there. Look, behind you and to the left."

"It does look like her," I said. "How do you know that's her hubby, could be a date."

"Don't be ridiculous. She's married. Husband's name is Jesse James."

"Now who's being ridiculous?"

"Seriously. Haven't you learned *anything* since you've been out here? Jesse's got a television show, builds motorcycles."

"Whatever you say. Now what's your take on Sid's rep?"

"Oh yeah, Herbie mentioned the top dogs don't complain about Sid. Well, leastways they don't *know* what the big guys think. More discreet bunch maybe."

We were nearing the end of the first quarter. Kobe Bryant sunk the ball to bring the score to 17-16, Lakers. Maybe there was hope.

"Probably so. Although Scott Kelly's one of the big guys, but he's not discreet around the office I hear."

"Not discreet about cheating on Nan baby either," Jeannette said.

"Yes, it's occurred to me that his absences mean there's a girlfriend on the side. But what explains Nan taking off?"

"Simple," Jay said. "What's good for the goose is good for the gander."

"I don't mean to be naïve, but that doesn't sound like Nan."

"Frédérique, girlfriend, you hear about broads like Nan taking up with the pool man, their personal trainer, their tennis coach, whatever, all the time."

"True enough. Still can't see it for Nan."

Jeannette shot me a dubious frown, returning her attention to Sandra and the resurrected outlaw who was apparently her dinner companion.

Halfway through the second quarter the Suns were ahead 32-25.

Laker coach Phil Jackson called a time out, and I went to the kitchen for a second Heineken for sorrow drowning.

Jeannette's stargazing was so resolute, I couldn't resist a second peek of my own. As I looked, I saw Sandra and mate heading toward the door just as Buck was arriving. He shot them a glance, nodded and smiled. For all I knew, maybe they were among his clients. As he neared our table, he wore an expression that appeared to be a mixture of fatigue and irritation. I poured some wine for him.

"Tough day, dear?" I grinned.

He sat down. "Tough, long and not according to schedule."

Luke Walton made a basket, bringing the score to 38-27, still in favor of the Suns.

"How did the talks with the maids go?" I asked.

"Didn't happen." Buck sipped his wine and seemed to be contemplating the wire in my ear. I looked around for our waiter, deciding to let the poor man catch his breath before pelting him with any more questions.

Pau Gasol, Kobe Bryant and Lamar Odom had scored but by the end of the second quarter the Suns still led, 49-40.

"Is Luke joining us?" Jeannette asked. "How is he?"

"Luke's fine," Buck snapped.

The Lakers were not in the best of spirits either. We were eleven points behind and the Suns' hot hand, Shawn Marion, made two free throws. The score was Suns 88, Lakers, 75.

"How was Nan when you met with her?" I said.

"That didn't happen either." Buck poured himself a second glass. "Never got to the maids or Nan Kelly. When High Top was done at the studio, he and his cronies headed out to Malibu instead of home. Holly called me on my cell and let me know that was the new last-minute plan. She said to stick with him of course. They had to shoot part of a video on the beach. I hung out there, followed him home and here I am."

Our waiter appeared, scribbled furiously as Buck ordered lobster tail and filet mignon. Jay and I both selected the Louisiana , blackened catfish, with sautéed spinach, sweet corn and remoulade sauce.

Unconsciously I stared at Buck, searching for a clue to his feelings, although I could guess he was simply frustrated over the usual daylong

High Top tail and the fruitless project of catching him *flagrante delicto.*

Buck caught sight of my gaze out of the corner of his eye and returned the look.

"The autopsy showed the bullet in Doris Hernandez was 22 calibers."

"But the cops haven't found a gun?" I asked.

"No."

The Laker-Suns game was in the third quarter. The game announcers chatted away.

"The announcer just said, 'kill the clock'," I said to Buck. "What's that mean?"

"It's usually done to protect a lead," he answered. "You run out the remaining time on the clock by dribbling and passing and maintaining possession rather than attempting a shot."

"So they hang onto the ball, just mark time," Jay said absently.

"Right." He bowed his head, sighed and rubbed his eyes.

"Feel like that's all *you're* doing these days?" I commiserated.

"Damn right, Fred. Spinning my wheels."

"Think of it as lying in wait," I offered.

"No, that's what your threatening phone caller is doing."

He was right, of course. Now it was my turn to pause and reflect.

Buck joined me in the contemplating-one's-naval exercise, staring at the opposite wall, oblivious to us and the din of voices in the restaurant. Not a very productive day for either of us.

Not productive for my Lakers either. They lost, 109-97.

CHAPTER 68

Before me were more guns than I'd ever seen before or ever hoped to see. I was about to learn that what I was looking at was a six-inch Colt Python revolver, a two-inch Colt Magnum Carry, a Ruger .357 New Model Blackhawk, a Smith & Wesson .357 Magnum Model 65, a Glock 36 and a Smith & Wesson Model 66.

Buck had this collection of deadly force spread out over the dining room table along with boxes of bullets. He was in the process of cleaning one of the S&W's. Jeannette had left for work extra early for—what else?—a breakfast date. She usually got up before I did anyway and headed out for a morning jog toward the Santa Monica Pier and then back along the beach boardwalk south, returning to Venice. Sometimes I joined her; more frequently I slept in. This particular morning I was determined to take the bull by the horns, as Gram would say, and go for a run even without company or encouragement—get back in shape.

Buck, it seemed, had other plans for me. He looked at me over the rim of his coffee mug as I passed through the dining room resplendent in my running attire of black nylon sweats, gold and purple Laker sweatshirt and white Nikes.

"Sit down, Fred. We've got work to do."

"What? You want me to help you clean and load those babies? Lil' ole me? I don't think so, my friend. I'm going to run my buns off until five pounds drops from my hips in sheer surrender."

"You don't have five pounds of excess on your hips or anywhere else, kid. Sit down. I'm about to teach you self defense."

"Flattery would normally get you, or anyone, everywhere," I said as I headed for the kitchen. The aroma of coffee was tantalizing. Wouldn't hurt to delay my sprint until after a good shot of caffeine, so I poured myself a cup. I returned to the dining room and stood watching Buck while my coffee cooled to what was, for me, an acceptable lukewarm level.

"I'm going for a run. Then I have to report for my undercover sleuthing at Potter, Wood & Penn, in case you've forgotten. Why aren't you nipping at the heels of our rapper friend? He could be enjoying an early-morning assignation even as we speak."

"Ole High is on the beach with a bunch of bikini babes shooting a video even as we speak."

"Even more motivation for you."

"True enough. But something else is motivating me this morning. Sit."

I put my coffee mug on the table, pulled out one of the chairs and sat down. "I'll humor you for a minute."

Being super intuitive, I knew this talk would have something to do with guns. More to the point, my carrying one. I'd survived in New York City for years without a weapon, and I was not about to start now. I smiled at Buck, took a big swallow of coffee, looked into his eyes for three beats and began in a more serious tone.

"I'm grateful you're letting me help you find the monster who murdered my Doris, but I'm not a candidate to become a licensed P.I.; and I feel safe here until we find my crazed caller so please, Joseph Buckley, no more about guns."

Buck looked into my eyes for about five beats, matched my serious tone and raised me one in intensity.

"I know the novelty of working for...with...me is wearing thin, Fred. More importantly, I know you're still mourning Doris. I get that. But your crazed caller friend is no small matter. Sure, you're safe in my house. But you're not always *in* my house."

He took a gulp of his coffee and favored me with three beats of glare.

Through the dining room window I could see lots of blue sky. A white blur of full moon still hung in the sky, and I knew that outside on the streets leading to the beach there'd still be the intoxicating perfume of the night-blooming jasmine. A perfect morning to be outdoors. Such a brilliant perception deserved to be shared, and was certain to distract Buck with my powers of observation.

"It's a perfect morning to be outdoors," I said.

"You're going to be outdoors, babe. It's called target practice."

Still in a stern, no-nonsense voice, he began naming the various guns on the table.

"So I take it we're both going to play hooky from toiling and tailing and take aim at tin cans somewhere?"

"You got it."

Buck had gotten up, cup in hand, and shouted back to me as he headed toward the kitchen.

I followed him and called in sick to Potter, Wood from the kitchen phone. Lisa Connors took my message with undisguised skepticism, and I felt like adding a shot of whisky to my mug of java. I said goodbye to her, coughing as I did so for dramatic effect, then joined Buck back at gun stash central.

"Has anything, besides crazy, mad telephone guy, prompted this emergency course in shooting?"

Buck had gotten up and was walking toward the television.

"Knew you'd ask that. Just watch."

From the dining room we had a clear view of the T.V set, and I turned my chair to face in the proper direction.

"What am I supposed to see? Is the morning news going to tell me my horoscope for today says by all means carry firearms?"

"In a sense, yes. You didn't catch the eleven o'clock news last night did you?"

"I didn't need to hear a review of the Laker loss."

"Thought so. I did. Watch the news, that is. There'll be a repeat this morning. Just watch."

"Why don't you just tell me? Now you've got me frightened and worried."

"Good. That's the way I want you. Just watch. First I want to go over with you some common sense things to bear in mind after you've used one of these on someone."

"We're already to the *after* part?"

"We're at the before-I-forget part. Other stuff we'll go into at the range."

On Channel 7 a female anchor, all fresh and perky with neat, short brown hair and obsequious cheerfulness, was turning us over to the weather guy who, all thinning gray hair and obsequious cheerfulness, was predicting a possible slight drizzle.

"First off," Buck began, "Remember that you'll be in an emotional state after you've wounded or killed someone…"

"Gosh, I'm glad you cleared that up."

"Just listen, Frédérique." Buck lifted a meowing Pierre from the floor and began to stroke him. "You'll call the cops after a shooting. They'll arrive and have questions. Anything you say you can amend later but that won't make your original remarks disappear. If you blurt out something stupid it can come back and bite you in the ass later…"

"A painful sounding hypothesis all by itself."

"Yeah, well, just remember you'll have the right to remain silent—don't interrupt me—and you have the Fifth Amendment right against self-incrimination. I know you wouldn't do anything like placing a weapon on the victim. With today's forensic science you *will* get caught at dumb acts like that."

I started to open my mouth but thought better of it. On Channel 7 a reporter in a helicopter was yakking about the traffic, and I fantasized again about an easy jog to the boardwalk and sun dots twinkling on the sea's surface. At least it distracted me momentarily from what supposed threat lurked as part of the hard news segment.

"There's a legal principle called the *reasonableness doctrine.* And if you yawn or even look like you're gonna interrupt me again I'll pour this coffee over you."

I sat up straighter and saluted. Buck had moved to a spot across the table from me so that both he and the television were in my line of vision.

"The deal is any action you take with your gun must be based on the circumstances. If you—the good guy—continue to use force after you've stopped the attack of the bad guy, then you're looking at some major legal hassles."

"If I'd been home and had a gun when that jerk came to rip apart my apartment and attack me I could have shot him as he stood in the hallway," I said, only half-kidding.

"No way. It's like when a guy sees somebody trespassing in his yard. He thinks he can shoot the bastard, then drag him into his house. Do that and you'll be prosecuted. And you oughta be, because that's not the proper use of deadly force. And it's that kind of thing that gives the anti-gun clowns ammunition to disarm all citizens."

"So how do I know when to shoot?"

Philip Palmer, who I think is so cute and looks a lot like Buck actually, was reporting on some drive-by shooting in south central L.A. I pointed to Palmer as I gave Buck a questioning look. Buck shook his head in the negative. Apparently I was not being armed for gang warfare.

Buck eased Pierre to the floor, picked up both our cups and headed out for refills.

"First," he called out over his shoulder, "you ask yourself if the bad guy has the ability to cause you serious physical harm or death."

He returned with two steaming mugs. I smiled because he'd added copious amounts of cream to mine just the way I like it.

"Second," he continued, "You ask yourself if the bad guy has said or done anything to make you believe you're in danger of said death or serious bodily injury. If he's holding a gun and says *I'm going to shoot you*, that would mean you're in jeopardy."

"I'd pick up on that right away. Nothing gets past *moi*."

"The other factor, wiseass, is opportunity. This usually involves distance. If the bad guy has a knife he's not much of a threat if he's about one hundred yards away from you. If he's ten feet away from you, that's a different story."

A commercial came on touting a medicine with a catchy name that treats acid redux disease. It concluded with the proviso that there may be side effects of headache, sexual dysfunction or possible stroke. It made me decide a little reduxing of my acid wouldn't be all that bad by comparison.

I turned my attention back to Buck who was rapidly finishing the last of his coffee. He stopped abruptly.

"Here it comes. Watch!"

Suddenly the image of Nan Kelly appeared on the screen. She had forsaken her usual neat ponytail and her hair was coiffed in a sort of fifties flip. She had on more makeup than usual, and she was wearing a black suit over a beige blouse with a demure high-necked collar. The camera moved back for a long shot revealing an infantry-like formation of reporters gathered in front of her. She was standing next to the beachfront side of her house, and you could hear the muted sound of tide splashing upon sand in the distance.

"...and I assumed my husband, Scott Kelly, was on a work-related sabbatical," Nan was saying.

She touched a well-manicured, wine-colored fingernail to the area just below one eye although I didn't see any tears there.

"However," she continued. "I observed my husband, Scott Kelly..." Nan was speaking with the precision and articulation of a person on a witness stand in a courtroom, not to mention enunciating Scott's name with every other breath.

"...in attendance at the funeral of the victim of a recent homicide victim who..."

A short bald man in a charcoal suit, blindingly white shirt and red and black striped tie moved to Nan's side. He'd apparently been out of camera range or had just arrived on the scene. A lawyer?

Nan went on to describe the funeral in unnecessary and unrelated detail and continued on to extol the virtues of Doris Hernandez whom she barely knew. The bald-possible-attorney guy whispered in her ear and she nodded.

"Since said observation of Mr. Kelly..." Nan returned to the main subject at hand—Scott. "I have not seen him, heard from him or been able to make any kind of contact with Mr. Kelly..."

Mr. Short and Bald moved out of camera range.

"I therefore..." Nan drew herself up to an even straighter posture. "...believe that my husband Scott...Scott Kelly...is...for all intents and purposes...in hiding."

Apparently Scott's appearance at the Hernandez funeral escaped her notice, despite the fact she'd been rubber necking during the Mass just as I had. If she'd seen her husband but preferred to characterize him as missing, the question was *why*?

CHAPTER 69

It had been pitch-black dark, and the assailant and I had had little actual bodily contact. In the weeks since the attack, wisps of memory would float into my consciousness now and then. They were unbidden because I'd consciously tried to forget the experience. It seemed so largely blank and unknowable that I felt nothing productive would come of dwelling on that night, of plumbing my brain for snippets of facts. But I'd had some sense of the general physicality of the intruder. He was shorter than I, as was Scott Kelly. From the floor, I'd grabbed his calf at one point. It was trim, muscled. Scott Kelly worked out religiously and was very slim but obviously firm and strong. Buck seemed to feel Kelly who, according to his wife was now in desperado mode, posed a definite and newly amplified threat to my safety and well-being.

Thus it was that Buck and I were cruising along in his Honda and I was to be spared a day of the Potter, Wood & Penn tedium that made one's soul feel dead so I could learn to properly use a steely little weapon for the purpose of rendering some soul truly dead. I rolled down the window on the passenger side, rested my arm on the ledge and cocked my head slightly outward to drink in as much of the day's beautiful sunshine as possible. I was not to enjoy the outdoor target practice in the hills of Malibu Buck originally promised. He'd remembered a pistol permit course offered by a community college in West Los Angeles and enrolling me there was the new plan. The course was administered by a friend of Buck's, one Frank DeCarlo. They'd known each other back in the day each were New York cops at the same precinct. Buck had made a quick call to Frank after our morning coffee *cum* firearms session, and Frank had responded there was an opening in his class and even had there not been for Buck he'd kick someone out and make room. No blood runs thicker than law-enforcement blue.

We pulled into the parking lot in back of Bell Community College, a collection of about five three-story yellow brick buildings, and headed for a side door of the nearest building. We went down a short hallway, opened a heavy door with a paper taped to it bearing *Firing Range* in large block letters. Inside the room was chilly. Coincidentally the only hint of color was the same institutional gray found at Potter, Wood. The air seemed to smell like a gym locker room, but perhaps what I was sniffing was gunpowder.

There were four other future sharpshooters—three women and one man. The latter looked to be around seventeen with lots of curly hair and acne. I shuddered to think of deadly force in his hands in the midst of a hormonal rage. The three women looked to be very close to my age, somewhere between twenty-eight and thirty. They provided a somewhat comforting familiarity: just us girls learning to kill and maim. The four shooters wore stiff leather holsters on wide belts and oversized earphones. They were feeding their revolvers with bullets stored in narrow carpenters' aprons made of a thick material and sporting some kind of advertising.

On the sidelines stood a stocky man, about five foot seven with well-developed and tattooed biceps and an ample gut. Buck waved to him; he waved back and removed his earphones. As he turned to walk toward us, I could see he had a handsome face and a head full of gorgeous gray hair. He and Buck shook hands, then hugged, grinned and called each other profane names.

"Frank, this is my associate Freddy Bonnaire. Freddy, Frank DeCarlo."

I extended my hand to Frank and, surprisingly, he raised it to his lips and kissed it.

"Buck, you sonovabitch." Frank grinned. "I'm going to start up a practice myself if this is the kind of associate private investigators have these days. Why aren't you posing for Playboy, honey?"

"Actually she's a model and...," Buck began.

"Actually Frank," I interrupted, "I'm taking this course precisely so I can shoot the next guy who asks that very question."

Frank laughed as if that were an extremely witty remark.

"Beautiful and feisty. Buckley, you know how to pick 'em. Don't take me seriously, sugar. I don't."

Mercifully, we then got down to business. Frank escorted us to an empty stall and outfitted me with earphones, holster and bullet apron. It all felt heavy and strange. Buck was going to give me his Glock as my personal weapon but, for purposes of this class, I was to use a Smith & Wesson .38 revolver. Frank began instructions, slowly showing me how to load, holster, grip, unholster, aim, fire, reholster. He left me to practice these movements and headed for another stall. Buck watched me for a few minutes, then announced he had to get back to the High Top surveillance.

"Luke is in town this afternoon," Buck said. "He doesn't have a run until tomorrow so I've arranged for him to pick you up in an hour and take you to work."

"That's fine. It'll be nice to see Luke."

Since getting shot at High Top's house, Luke had been uncharacteristically anti-social. He didn't seem to blame Buck for his misfortune but you never know. I'd hoped his absence didn't signal the end of our friendships.

I could hear Frank DeCarlo barking instructions.

"Holster your weapon. Is the line clear? The line is clear. Clear to the right. Clear to the left. This is five rounds, hip-level, one shot. When I say fire, upholster and fire your weapons."

"Fire!"

Frank returned to my stall for more instructions. After a while, I commenced actual shooting. The first report sent what felt like waves of electric currents through my innards. After another twenty minutes, practice ceased and class was dismissed. DeCarlo unlocked the heavy metal door and we trooped out into the warm and sunny normalcy of the parking lot. Luke was waiting for me in a dark blue rented Chevy. He smiled and gave me a thumbs up. At that moment I couldn't remember a more welcome sight. I asked about his wound. He assured me he felt fine. I chatted away, but Luke was not in a talkative mood. He seemed wary and preoccupied. I took the hint and shut up. When he deposited me at the Potter, Wood building in Century City, I felt almost happy to be there. The clean lines of the office buildings, the green trees and shrubs—for me they appeared to have all the verve of a scenic backdrop for a Broadway musical. I even smiled at Lisa Connors as I passed her reception desk. She glared at me. It was good to be anywhere but the Bell Community College firing range.

We'd signed me up for three mornings of shooting practice. I'd persuaded Buck that to maintain my viability as an honest-to-god secretarial temp I could not take off three full days. So I'd called in to Human Resources and amended my initial sick-day report to advise that I was feeling better but a series of tests was warranted to determine the exact cause of my malady so I'd be working half days for the remainder of the week. I chatted with Jeannette briefly when I arrived at my cubicle, then went down to the lobby's drugstore to get the yogurt and potato chips that would sustain me for the rest of the workday.

At six Jay and I drove home to Buck's. I whipped up some spaghetti for dinner from supplies we had in the freezer, pantry and vegetable bin while Jeannette headed for the couch and her daily dose of Channel 4's *Access Hollywood*.

Pierre padded into the kitchen, sat upright, watched me and sniffed the air. I added some frozen shrimp I'd thawed the night before, along with garlic, chopped celery, onions, green pepper and a half-teaspoon of black pepper to the tomato sauce, let it simmer and checked my answering machine back at my apartment. I'd finally memorized the code for remote access, rather than driving over there to check my messages.

Holy mother of miscreants, as Gram would say, there was a message from none other than Detective Guy Whitehorse actually inviting me to dinner Sunday night.

"I sure as hell am not going to call him right back," I announced to Pierre.

Pierre refused to comment.

"I'll wait a day. Maybe two days," I added.

Pierre lay down, resting his head on his front paws. Clearly, my lovelorn pronouncements bored him.

The other call was equally surprising; it was from Caroline, Sid Avarson's housekeeper.

She began by saying, "Freddy? This is Freddy?" in a voice that at first blush sounded hurried and anxious. This was followed by a long pause, after which she seemed to collect herself. She must have run for the phone or been doing something physical and then caught her breath. She continued on in a more cheerful, chatty style, asking me to call her, "Oh, just whenever it was convenient."

"Just to chat," she said. "Catch up," she added. She concluded by saying, "See you later" as if we'd been girlfriends forever.

It had been a totally strange day. I was exhausted. I added some more chopped garlic and some canned crabmeat to the simmering tomato sauce. In my fatigue, I decided both Guy and Caroline could, like my spaghetti, stew in their own juices before chatting up one Frédérique Bonnaire.

CHAPTER 70

THE FIRST SIGN THAT SOMETHING was amiss was the two black suitcases sitting inside the door of Buck's house. Jay and I had just returned home from work. We dropped our purses on the coffee table and headed for the kitchen for some healing libation to take the edge off a Potter, Wood day. On our way I called out Buck's name. No answer. Jeannette grabbed a Heineken from the fridge, and I poured myself some white wine.

After a nerve-wracking day of wielding a pistol at Bell's—I could still hear Frank DeCarlo's voice booming on about ejector rods and single-action shots—and an only slightly less nerve-wracking day at Potter, Wood, the elegance of good *vino* as opposed to more pedestrian beer was warranted.

Jeannette carried her brew into our guest bedroom, calling out "hello, hello" several times. I took my wine and peered into the half-open door of Buck's bedroom, called his name once more and then went to join Jay in our bedroom. She'd moved to the adjoining guest bathroom and was now fairly yelling, "Yo, somebody?"

"Swear to God, Freddy, there's just two twin beds in here, and I sure as hell ain't sharing mine."

I sat down on the bed, momentarily musing over Jeannette's love of derivatives like *ain't* despite the fact that she'd had some college and her parents were educated. Must be a Bronx thing. Jay joined me in the bedroom.

"Well, whatta yah think? Who'd that bozo invite to camp here?"

I sighed. Then yawned.

"Don't know, Jay. Right now I'm thinking that I'm tired and hungry and that the more pressing question is whether to order in Chinese or something from that Greek place."

I took a sip of wine.

"I'm also thinking it *is* Buck's place and he can jolly well invite whomever he wishes," I said.

"Well, if he looks like George Clooney I'll share my pillow. Otherwise, fugedabout it. But, you're right, it *is* the man's place."

Jay tipped her bottle of Heineken at me and moved to the hallway.

"I'll go call the Greek place; there's a menu in the silverware drawer. I'll even order mucho amount so our mysterious guest is covered. You want musaka again?"

I lay back on the bed, carefully holding my wineglass at my side, and barely had the strength to murmur *yes*. I closed my eyes and thought of nothing but the sound of Jay's chatter from the kitchen phone as she ticked off musakas, fayito, makaronia, briami and baklavas. My simple reverie was broken by the sound of the front door opening and slamming shut. A male voice yelled, "Yo, babes?" and a door slammed again. I got up and headed for the living room. On my way, I found Jay. She was standing at the kitchen door, the phone still in her hand, her mouth open, her brow a perplexed wrinkle.

"Who was that?" Didn't sound like Buck. "Who's here?" I asked.

"Yeah, that's my whole order. Yeah, yeah. Thanks." Jeannette hung up the phone.

"The *who* was Luke," she said. "And no one's *here*. He blew in the door, yelled, and left. Well, guess that answers who's moving in."

We looked at the site of the two suitcases. A large red duffle bag had been added to the luggage assemblage.

"Looks like he's moving in piece by piece," Jay said. "Couldn't he have hauled everything over in one trip?"

"Luke doesn't seem to be himself these days," I said.

It was all too much excitement at the end of a day for both of us. We looked at each other blankly and took our drinks into the living room.

Jeannette plopped on the couch as I turned on the telly, then joined her. *Extra, Extra* was promising the latest Hollywood couples tidbits. Brooke Shields was expecting a baby. Now this was good news. This was solid, hard fact. A child was on the way. Mother Nature at work. Positive, irrefutable fact. I could peacefully wrap my mind around that. It didn't require I wrack my brain about matters inscrutable.

Things like strange suitcases, sporadic calls from one Detective Whitehorse, Beverly Hills maids and their erratic responses, why Nan and Scott Kelly kept popping on and off life's radar, why High Top de King did not have an alibi for the time of the shooting of Doris Hernandez given that he was always surrounded by hangers-on, and, by the way, who the heck did send me those card-less red roses at the hospital?

Extra's hostess, Dayna Devon, had let her hair grow since I'd last caught the show. She looked great, but I liked the shorter bob. Dayna was letting us in on the scintillating details of the latest vacation resort favored by Tom Hanks and his missus. It was too much. I was not *this* brain dead. Some kind of productive activity was called for.

I went to the bedroom, got my cell phone and dialed Detective Guy Whitehead's home number. He'd typically be at the station even though it was evening but that was fine. I only wanted to deal with voicemail. I left a message sweetly advising most of Sunday was booked, but I was free for a quick lunch. *Let him chew on that.*

Next on my calls-to-be-returned list was that of the chirpy, gleeful Caroline. I had Sid Avarson's number in my purse, which was still on the living room coffee table. The temptation was great to lie back down on the bed and nap until our Greek feast arrived. But I resisted. Beneath the brittle cheerfulness, there was an undercurrent of something oddly unsettling about Caroline's calls that deserved to be addressed. I dragged myself back into the living room and retrieved my purse. The indefatigable Miss Devon was sharing that Brad and Angelina were seemingly on the outs and Jay was seemingly entranced. *Why do people obsess about such trivia?* I sat down on the couch just for a moment to hear just why Brad and Angelina were tiffing. *Not that I really cared.*

The rumor of a Pitt-Jolie spat turned out to be from an un-named source who heard it from another un-named source. Thus relieved over their marital state, I headed back to the peace and quiet of the guest bedroom. I dialed the Avarson's and Sid's wife, Erika, answered. I was so flummoxed by the sound of Erika's voice rather than Caroline's that

I immediately punched the off button. I lay down on the bed after all. Caroline was a live-in housekeeper five days a week. She should have been there. Maybe just taking a break. I decided to call again in twenty minutes or so. I willed myself upright once again and went to join Jay in the living room. Dayna might have some more imperative news.

Extra had signed off and *Access Hollywood* had commenced. This was good. Jay and I would now be so *au courant*, so savvy regarding world events, at least within the Tinseltown perimeters. In five minutes the *Access* dramas were to be interrupted by dramatic arrivals at *chez* Buck.

The first scratching at our front door was—thankfully—the delivery boy from Zorba's, loaded down the piping hot Greek fare. We paid him plus tip and carried the food into the kitchen. Jay and I were spooning our portions onto our individual plates, then carefully rewrapping each dish, when the front door flew open and Luke appeared, bearing a six-pack of Samuel Adams.

"Food! Great!" Luke exclaimed, sounding like his vibrant self for once.

He put the six-pack in the fridge, fetched one of the other cold bottles already there, got a plate and did some serious portion allocation of his own.

"Are you moving in on us, bro?" Jeannette asked.

"You got it, roomie. How lucky can you babes get?" He grinned, and it was good to see.

"For how long?" Jay asked. "I mean just how long is three bags worth?"

Luke opened the silverware drawer and got a fork. "That duffle do hold a lot, don't it? Gotta maintain my rep as a well dressed man."

"Then what's in the other two fancy suitcases?" Jay asked. "I thought truckers traveled light."

"Those not mine, babe. Buck's."

Luke carried his plate and beer to the living room coffee table. He returned for napkins.

From the kitchen he called out, "Brought a ten pound watermelon with me."

Luke returned to the living room. "You folks be good and I'll fix you my special spiked watermelon."

"I'll bite," I said. "What's a spiked watermelon?"

Luke swallowed hard and answered, "You take three cups citrus-flavored vodka, cut a hole in the top of the melon, pour in almost one cup of vodka, replace the plug and let it sit for four hours. Keep doin' that till all the vodka's soaked in. Stick it in the fridge, have it later."

Jeannette looked at Luke, a small smile pursing her lips.

"Anyone make one crack," Luke said, "'bout watermelon and my ethnic roots and they're a dead woman!"

We all laughed.

Neil Simon couldn't have written a more compact Act One as three minutes later, the front door opened and Buck entered. He looked tired and just waved *hello* without speaking. Buck did the get-a-bottle-of-Sam-Adams-and-ladle-food-onto-a-plate drill and joined Luke on one couch. He put his drink and dinner on the coffee table, picked up the remote and changed to a news channel. Jay looked at me, shook her head in exasperation and joined them in the living room. She got two oak-colored TV tables from their stand and put one in front of each of the chairs surrounding the now-crowded couch. As I carried my wine and musaka out, I heard her say, "So?" To no avail it seemed, as I heard no response. I put my meal down on the little table and went to fetch my cell phone. It seemed my best bet if I wanted someone to talk to.

Buck ate with great gusto and focused intently on the television screen. He was obviously hungry and looked so frazzled it would have been heartless not to delay our curiosity about his travel plans. The beer and musaka felt good to me too and in my own weary state even the weather report was engaging. It was completely dark outside now, and Jay got up to turn on a few lamps. Our cozy dining scenario was not to last.

My cell phone rang. It was Sid Avarson's housekeeper, Caroline. This time there was no professional posturing nor determined mirth.

"I must talk to you, Miss Frédérique. It's a matter of life or death." She then immediately hung up.

CHAPTER 71

"I'LL NEED A SINGLE. YEAH. Starting tomorrow night, got one? Great. Don't know for how long."

We'd finished our meals and were relaxing. Buck was on his cell phone to the New York Hilton. He gave them his credit card number, scribbled his confirmation number on a copy of the L.A. Times resting on the coffee table and hung up. He'd explained to us that one of Lemoyne Investigation's favorite high-end clients, Martha Naples, was off to Manhattan and had issued a royal command that Buck accompany her. Martha was a youthful actress of eighty-two whose career in film and stage was still going strong.

"Since when," I asked, "Does Martha stay at the Hilton? I thought she usually sequestered her entourage at the Michelangelo."

"Usually does." Buck chugged on his beer. "Her assistant says Michelangelo's full. More likely, she owes them money. Amazing attitude these Hollywood types have toward debt."

"Does she pay up to you?" Jay asked.

"Oh yeah. They know who they can screw with, and who they can't."

"At her age, she probably just checks out and forgets to pay," Luke said.

"That would be more her style. She's actually a great lady," Buck said.

Buck looked my way, his eyes narrow slits of fatigue.

"By the way, Fred, I told Holly you'd do the Beverly Hills maid interviews while I'm gone. She said she preferred you tail High, then thought about it some and agreed with me. She's so sure he's got a little chippie on the side, but I convinced her it was more important to exonerate her husband from suspect status in the Hernandez murder."

"How your clients feel about all this amateur help they paying for?" Luke asked.

Buck grinned, and like Luke's earlier smile, it was good to see. Hated to see the men in my life sullen, which reminded me of the real man in my life, Guy, and I smiled to myself when I imagined his reaction to my quick-lunch-only phone message.

"It's my little bit of harmless hyperbole," Buck said. "As far as Holly King knows, you're my associates and you're fellow licensed P.I.'s."

"Like the sound of that," Luke smiled. "Tired of truckin' anyhoo."

"Speaking of which, you haven't been on the road in a while," I said. "Is everything okay?"

"Everything fine," Luke said and resumed the tense expression he'd adopted of late.

Buck picked up the remote and muted the sound. An episode of *Law & Order* was playing, Elliott Stabler giving off the same tense vibes as my current companions. Jay and Luke watched as the dialogue played across the screen in white lettering.

"Did you say that was Avarson's maid you spoke to a minute ago?" Buck asked.

I sighed. "Yes, we're playing phone tag. Just now, she declared it was a matter of life or death. She's as melodramatic as Amanda Roberts, speaking of divas. One minute she's Chatty Cathy on the phone. The next she's in professional maid mode and cool. Makes it hard to take her seriously."

Buck leaned back on the couch and rubbed his chin. The TV sound remained muted.

"Avarson's maid doesn't fall into the diva category. More likely she's just having trouble articulating whatever she's got in her craw."

"I realize that," I said. "Plus my guess is she has a problem with being on the house phone and having privacy to talk. Maybe she has no phone in her room there and no cell. I'm not dismissing it; I'll keep calling her."

"Good," Buck said and got up to get another beer.

When he returned, I had a question for him. "Buck, I have a proposition for you..."

"'bout time you propositioned me." he grinned.

Jay had turned the sound back on. Buck muted it once more.

"Instead of my interviewing the maids why don't I first go see Nan Kelly?"

"Damn. Not the proposition I was hoping for. Okay. Good idea. I was going to call her before my flight and..."

"When is that?" Luke interrupted.

"Tomorrow, eight a.m. Was going to call Nan Kelly and find out if she wants me to locate Scott after all, now that she's made her hubby *in hiding* statement. But you sounding her out in person is better. She likes you plus I'd like her business."

"How long you be in the Big Apple, boss?" Luke asked.

"Indefinitely. Martha's boyfriend just got word he starts rehearsals in a play there so she's traipsing after him. She's also gonna try and set up some personal appearances while in New York, get out to see-and-be-seen, usual show biz drill."

I went to the kitchen for more white wine and grabbed two more bottles of beer for Jay and Luke while I was there. As I was handing them out, the cell phone on my chair rang. I dove for it, nearly spilling my drink, anticipating a luncheon confirmation call from Guy. It was Caroline; she of the breathless, hurried phonespeak.

"Freddy? It's Caroline."

"Yes, Caroline. Talk to me."

"Can't talk. Can you meet me Sunday? Five o'clock. I don't usually work Sundays but the Avarsons are throwing a big brunch. I'll be through cleaning up and everything in the afternoon. I'll get a ride with a friend to Wilshire. We can meet at El Cholo's. You know where that is?"

"Yes, at eleventh."

"That's right. My friend will pick me up after. We can talk, you and me."

"Okay. It's a date. Give me a hint. What are we going to talk about?"

"Gotta go. Picture. In newspaper. Last week. You know, that *Calendar* section."

"What day? What picture…?"

She hung up.

"Well that was enlightening." I sipped my wine.

"What's Caroline's story?" Buck asked.

"No story," I said. "A picture, according to her. In the *Times* I guess. She said *Calendar* section. Last week. Wouldn't say which day. This is exasperating. Methinks she likes playing detective."

"Not to worry," Buck said. He yawned. "In my bedroom there's a bunch of papers. Last two weeks or so I think."

"Great," I said.

I sipped some more wine. The channel had been changed to some sitcom taking place in a hospital. Buck turned the sound up, and joined Luke and Jay in giggling over some dialogue from the officious chief of staff.

Clearly if anyone was going to get up and retrieve the newspapers from Buck's bedroom it would have to be me so I got up to do just that.

I'd never seen his room before and couldn't resist standing stock still and surveying my surroundings for a couple of minutes even though I immediately spied the papers on the floor by his night table. It was surprisingly neat and well organized. The sliding door to his closet was halfway open affording a glimpse of his signature Hawaiian shirts, all in a row pressed and crisp. On the floor of the closet was a lineup of highly polished loafers, some of which I'd never seen. Two large healthy philodendron plans bloomed on top of a black armoire and a copy of James Lee Burke's *White doves at Morning* rested on his dresser. I don't know what I'd expected. Collegiate filth and clutter I guess. I gathered up the papers and carried them out to the living room.

The couch potatoes thankfully had forsaken the medical comedy and switched back to *Law & Order.* I sat on the floor and spread the papers out in front of me, sifting for just the *Calendar* sections of each. After glancing at four days' worth, the fifth seemed to yield Caroline's probable reference.

On the front page of the section was a large photo taken at Chateau Marmont of High Top de King and his wife.

What did this indicate to Caroline? Had she seen High Top on the premises the day Doris was shot? This I did not want to hear, but I *would* sound her out on this—probably by phone rather than a time-consuming, furtive meeting at El Cholo.

CHAPTER 72

"HE'S OUT WITH THE FLU. There'll be no class today."

"I'm sorry to hear that," I said. "Will there be a class Monday?"

"Probably," the female voice said. "Frank bounces back fast."

"Glad to hear it," I said. I added a "thank you" and a "goodbye" and hung up.

"All *right*!" I shouted. "No gun class today!"

I was exalting in the kitchen, mostly to myself. Jeannette had left for work, and Luke was still dozing in the living room. My intention had been to call in sick, to both shooting practice and Potter, Wood & Penn. Although I was sorry to hear that Frank DeCarlo was sick, it saved me from the agony of voicing my first planned lie of the day.

I poured myself a second cup of coffee and dialed Potter, Wood, steeling myself for a confrontation with America's favorite receptionist, the lovely Lisa Connors. She answered on the first ring. I affected a hoarse voice and declared I seemed to have the flu that was going around. Lisa said she was so sorry to hear that and hoped I would feel better very soon. I thanked her and said I would probably be in tomorrow. She sweetly advised me that I'd be missed but to be sure and not come back until I felt my usual energetic, efficient self. *My usual energetic, efficient self*? And I'd be *missed*? Someone important must have been standing near her desk I thanked her again, coughed and said *bye.*

I said, "Yehhh!", again aloud and to no one in particular. Pierre pussyfooted in, remedying my lack of companionship, eyed the bowl of Fancy Cat I'd prepared earlier, and proceeded to eat his breakfast. I felt strangely and wonderfully free today. Not because of the double blessing of getting off easily with both the target practice and work but because, I realized, Buck was out of town, and for a protracted period of time at that. I felt in charge, strong. I had a plan and it was to first swing by Nan Kelly's and convince her of her need for the services of Lemoyne Investigations. Then I'd head for Beverly Hills and chat up the maids we'd met there. Have a just-us-girls talk with them, which, I was certain, would yield much more than our meetings with them where Buck was present, all intimidating muscles, firm jaw line, loud Hawaiian shirt and testosterone. I would then have a coherent conversation on the phone with Caroline if it took fifty calls to do so. I was very curious about her allusion to the photo of High Top in the *Times* and what implications that suggested to her. I remained convinced he was good and decent and not the killer of Doris Hernandez.

Then this evening when Buck called to check in I'd inform him of this wildly productive day, and he would be so proud and impressed I knew I would feel the positive vibrations through the telephone wires.

"You're taking the Glock, right?"

Luke's question cut thru my reverie. He'd padded barefoot into the kitchen, freshly showered and wearing black jeans and an olive green tee shirt.

"Would a professional like me go anywhere without her gun?" I grinned.

Luke poured himself a cup of coffee and didn't smile.

"I want to see you put it in your purse."

His tone was heavy with no-nonsense inference. I didn't want a blemish on my thus far non-confrontational morning so I went to the bedroom, got my oversized brown alligator purse and the Glock and carried them back to the kitchen. I placed my purse on the counter, unzipped it, gave Luke a serious look, inserted the gun inside and re-zipped.

"Where you off to today?" I smiled up at him.

"Errands."

"Ah," I said. "No runs to The Windy, The Dirty Side or the Corn Patch?"

"Nary a one."

Luke got some cream cheese out of the fridge, then opened a bag of bagels.

Luke had just confirmed he had no deliveries to Chicago, New York or Iowa. Business must be lousy for him lately and would account for his moodiness. He'd already gulped down his coffee so I poured some more into his mug.

"You taking off now?" Luke asked.

I slung my purse strap over my shoulder and headed toward the front door. "This very minute," I called back to him.

"Well, hit the bull's-eye every time."

I said, "No class today," and closed the door behind me.

As I headed toward the driveway, I heard Luke yell "What?"

He had opened the front door and was stuffing his feet into white Nikes.

"Instructor's sick. Class cancelled," I said.

Luke turned to go inside. "Okay, well enjoy typing and stuff."

"Not doing that either."

I climbed in the Honda, took a couple of minutes to check my makeup in the car mirror and keyed the ignition.

Luke came breathlessly bounding out the front door, carrying a black briefcase and a blue denim shirt.

I gave his briefcase a quizzical look. He came over to the Honda, placed the briefcase on the hood, bent down as he shrugged into the shirt, and said, "Got things to do, people to see."

A short, blonde woman of around fifty came strolling down the sidewalk. She was thin but busty and wore a low cut pink jersey shirt revealing a lot of cleavage. She also wore tight beige spandex shorts and little silver running shoes. She looked ready for some kind of action but not necessarily the sight of a tall, intense looking black man. She stopped, bent to tie a shoelace, pursed her lips and blinked her wide eyes erratically.

Luke seemed to divine the effect he'd had upon her. He smiled slightly and softened his tone. "Where are you off to, Freddy?"

"Nan Kelly's." For some reason, I whispered.

"Nan Kelly's," Luke repeated. "Good enough." He headed toward the pickup parked on the street, smiled again and gave me a little salute. "Have a lovely day."

His gaze took in the blonde as well as me as he spoke.

"I'm Penny Jenson," the blonde said in my direction, as I slowly pulled out of the driveway.

"Freddy," I called out.

"I'm in that blue house across the street," Penny added. She beamed.

"She's Holmes, I'm Watson," Luke said.

I'd never seen her before but she was one of Buck's neighbors and seemingly felt prompted to be friendly and announce herself. That, or she wanted Luke's name, the real one.

I made a mental note: maybe the little blonde would be just the diversion he needed. She gave Luke an aren't-I-charming smile, adjusted her cleavage, and said, "Nice to meet you Watson."

Then again, maybe not.

The usually enjoyable drive along Pacific Coast Highway to Nan's was less than inspiring. Southern California weather had reverted to its typical winter mode and the sky was gray with early-morning smog, the air chilly, the sea flat and colorless. I tried to recapture my earlier cheer by reminding myself of the stellar day of detective work I had ahead of me.

I pulled the Honda into the small lot adjacent to Nan's home, walked over and rang the bell. Angie, the Kelly's maid, opened the door, then grinned.

"I'm so glad to see you." She beamed.

"It's nice to see you too." I squeezed her hand. "Is Nan in?"

Probably Angie thought of Nan as *Mrs. Kelly* but I had a problem being so elitist at this early hour.

"She's on the back patio," Angie said. "I'll go tell her you're here."

"No need, Angie. I know where it is."

"Well, she's…" Angie stopped short.

"She's what?"

"Just-in-a-mood," Angie ran the words together, then more brightly said, "Can I get you some hot tea?"

"That would be great."

I had somehow sensed a mood, that's why I'd not allowed Angie to announce my arrival. I stepped outside to the patio and found Nan sitting on a cushioned white lounge chair, bundled in a heavy black and navy plaid car coat. Her arms were tightly folded in front of her, hands tucked in the opposite sleeves of the coat. I quietly sat down in a small director's chair facing her and noticed her pants were actually striped flannel pajama bottoms and on her feet were black cotton socks and light blue terrycloth bedroom slippers. She wore no makeup.

Nan darted her eyes in my direction for only a fraction of a second, then returned her gaze to the sea. She looked more upset than I'd ever seen her. Small talk would have been insulting.

"Tell me what's wrong, Nan."

This time it made sense to whisper.

"Scott's gone. He's gone for good."

"Why do you think that?" My voice was calm, my cadence slow. "What has he done?"

"What do you think he's done?" Her face contorted into an exaggerated grimace, but remained pale. "What do you think?"

"I don't know," I said. "Please tell me."

I sensed her tolerance for my visit was limited so I posed another question immediately. "Do you want Buck to find him?"

"No I don't want Buck to find him." She said the words in a high-pitched, mimicking tone. "And I want you to leave," she shouted.

I got up slowly, placed my hand for a moment gently on her arm, went through the kitchen to the hallway and let myself out.

Angie was nowhere in sight and had never brought the hot tea.

CHAPTER 73

I EXITED THE KELLY'S FRONT DOOR and stood looking out at the ocean for a moment. A lone bicyclist pedaled down the boardwalk, his dog, a Golden Retriever, trotting behind. The rider stopped for a moment and just sat on his bike, seemingly to admire the ocean, then looked back, seemingly at me. He was slim and fit, but I couldn't make out his age. His dog wore a bright red collar and sat patiently during his master's reverie. The sky had added some blue to its predominantly gray palate, and the sea had a hint of green.

"Well, that went well," I said aloud.

I seemed to be doing a lot of talking to myself this morning. Didn't bode well for the highly proficient investigative day I'd planned.

I headed for the warmth of the Honda, got in and closed the door. Took out my cell phone and dialed Caroline. She answered on the third ring.

"Caroline, it's Freddy. Sorry to bother you but I just wondered it we could reschedule our meeting. Would you maybe be free this evening? Or are you alone there? Could I come over?"

"Mr. Avarson is here but he has company and can't be interrupted."

Her voice was almost tremulous with strain and at the thought of Sid Avarson I didn't feel all that jolly myself.

"I understand, Caroline. I'll call you again. If another time comes up before then you'll let me know?"

"That will be fine."

I switched off the phone, fired up the Honda and thought about what my next great move would be as I slid onto Pacific Coast Highway. I decided it would be food. I'd had only coffee for breakfast, having at the time no doubt decided that my agenda-fueled adrenaline rush was sufficient sustenance. Now I knew better. I drove south on PCH, up the California Incline and hung a right on Ocean Avenue headed for a McDonald's on Broadway.

I parked in the adjoining lot. They were no longer serving breakfast, so I ordered a small coke and a Big Mac. Elderly couples and the homeless took up most of the tables so I took my to-go bag out to the Honda and got in. I placed the coke in the car's cup holder and the Mac on the passenger seat and got out. The disappointing morning warranted additional comfort food I decided and went back inside for a large order of fries. Thus fortified, I sat in the car and alternately sipped coke and munched my food.

When the Mac and a fourth of the fries had been devoured I felt sufficiently healed to make a phone call so I dialed my home remote. The message I'd been anticipating began.

"Freddy, it's Guy. Listen, I'm sorry I've been incommunicado Lunch Sunday? Yeah, that works. Can we make it two o'clock? Should I pick you up at your place or meet you some place? Just call and tell me where. Can't wait to see you."

There was another beep but the remaining messages could wait. At least long enough for me to dial Guy, which I did. He was away and his recording came on. I smiled, savoring the masculine, sonorous richness of his voice. I savored so long I almost forgot to speak and heard myself blurt out, "Two o'clock, Emile's Café." Well, why not? It was my regular hangout. It's not as if the sight of us there together would elicit a frenzy of jealousy on the part of Nick Bernstein or any pulsations I inadvertently directed toward Nick would bring forth the green-eyed monster in Guy Whitehorse either, for that matter. Time to stop playing games, or rather even thinking in those terms.

I daydreamed momentarily about lunch with Guy, then put the remainder of the French fries along with the paper cup with half the coke in it in the brown bag, got out and deposited the bag in the outside trash receptacle. Guy's call had improved my day and obliterated the need for more carbohydrates. I got back in the driver's seat and dialed home for my remaining messages. Guy's message repeated. Then a second message came on.

"Busy, busy, busy little bitch, aren't you? Well, we'll see. Get it? We'll just see. We will see."

It was the same whiney, gravely voice of the other sick messages. Not a deep, full tone like Guy's, but low like a growl. Some words were emphasized more than others, for no apparent rhyme or reason. I hung up, dialed, erased Guy's message and listened to the second caller again.

Suddenly it seemed no longer so glorious and empowering to have Buck three thousand miles away. Luke was off somewhere doing his thing and I didn't know his cell number by heart, nor have it with me. With Buck away in New York, now did not seem the time to burden him with a report of the new anonymous phone call, nor did I want to involve Guy at this time. According to my phone company's records, the second *bitch* call, like the first, had come from my own home number. For the most part, I dismissed this as an in-house error on their part, but it remained unsettling. This home-number factor made it doubly hard to convey the situation to Buck or Guy. I'd procrastinated, telling myself I would tell the police about it if the calls continued. I was, of course, kidding myself. They *had* continued. If I had any brains I'd be worried and fearful, and I was. But nursing those fears felt wrong. Buck had begun paying me for my work, and I felt an obligation to be professional and not cave in over hostilities. This kind of thing was undoubtedly par for the course in the P.I. world.

On the other hand, the language the caller used was so weird, particularly on this latest call. It argued for the possibility that this was just some crackpot. Perhaps he did not even know who he was calling. As to my home invasion, I felt more and more convinced that the burglar at my apartment was just that—a crook that came to steal and felt frustrated over my lack of expensive jewelry and furs. That deduction would argue that he and this caller were two different people. Another way of looking at it was that the frenzied cutting up of my clothes was not typical burglar behavior. That would suggest that the crackpot destruction and the crackpot calls were the handiwork of one demented person.

I rubbed my scalp to forestall the beginnings of a headache and mused that if these threatening messages *were* connected to our involvement in the Hernandez shooting why were they not also directed toward Buck? Or solely toward Buck, for that matter. Perhaps Buck had received similar calls but didn't tell me for fear of worrying me. That would be like him. On the other hand, he *was* disturbed when he learned I'd received threats. Revealing he'd received similar abuse would buttress his case for caution.

I was sufficiently demoralized to the point that I didn't feel up to an afternoon of pumping the maids who worked on Sid's street for more information. It was always questionable as to whether they could supply any further hard-core facts; it had just seemed like one of those things Buck does when he admittedly does not know what to do next in a case.

But did we—or I in this instance—*not* know what to do next? Nan Kelly, clearly depressed and distraught, had emotionally stated to me that Scott had *done something*. I hadn't fully processed this, being so enamored of the total agenda I'd committed to for my day of productive sleuthing. I freshened my lipstick using the car mirror, popped a mint in my mouth and drove to the office.

Lisa was alone in the reception area when I arrived, and her earlier concern for my health and well being had diminished appreciatively.

"Thought you were sick." Her voice was listless.

"Started to feel better and thought I really should come in," I smiled.

She frowned, shook her head and went back to reading one of the many spirituality-oriented inspirational books she stocked at her desk. I'm going to go out on a limb here and say they weren't working.

I walked down the hall past the cubicles and noticed something here for the first time I'd long ago observed in the Potter, Wood New York office: the staff had little or no personal accessories adorning their stalls. In other offices where I'd temped in Manhattan secretaries and mid-level managers invariably decorated their space with combinations of plants, photographs of family, friends and pets, sports banners, postcards, toys and other minutiae to make what was largely an antiseptic environment more reminiscent of home. There was no rule against such décor at PW&P—I'd checked once—and yet, save for the odd photograph here and there, no one felt moved to put an individual stamp on their surroundings. I was reminded of my deduction about this in New York—no one really planned to stay. Most of the staffers mentally had one foot out the door.

Jeannette looked up in surprise as I rounded the corner to our row, got up and followed me to my desk.

"What up, girlfriend? You told me last night you planned to skip this house of horrors today."

I got to my desk but didn't sit down, put my purse in a side drawer and gave her a weak smile.

"It's a long story, tell you later. What's up with your day? I want to look at Sid's emails with you. Specifically any from Scott Kelly."

"Okay, come with me. You wanna get coffee first?"

"No, I'm fine."

"You don't *look* fine, honey, and…"

"I really am. Let's see what we've got."

I rolled my swivel chair over to Jay's desk and we both sat down. She cancelled out of the email she'd been composing and switched to Sid's library of mail. There were several from Scott.

"There's lots from Scott Kelly yesterday and today. Have you had a chance to read any of them?"

"Read all of 'em. Talky and boring. Acronym hell."

"Tell me about it."

I clicked on one of today's missives and opened it.

It was a memo from Scott to Sid. It talked about a project in San Jose in one paragraph, then came down two spaces for just one last comment: I pointed to it and Jay looked.

"He's mentioned that in a couple of other notes," Jay said. "And in the same way, never explaining."

"I'll contact you soon about that other matter."

I'd tell Buck about this when he called to check in. I'd leave out the news of the latest bitch call, of course. *Also omit my continuing sense that someone was following me.*

CHAPTER 74

Pizza, beer and wine. And more wine. That had been my Friday evening. Luke's too. Jeannette had sailed out for a dinner date. In this case an encounter for the third time with the same Potter, Wood associate, leaving Luke and I home alone. Feeling expansive, we ordered in a large pizza, which we washed down with lots of Heineken. Our thirst still not sated, it occurred to both of us to switch to wine, a transition Luke handled smoothly and I less so.

The Lakers were playing the Phoenix Suns, but I couldn't bring myself to watch. The morning paper had been full of gloom and doom in terms of my team even making the playoffs entitling an article *Reign of Error* and tossing about comments to the effect that resurrecting a team in poor condition was beyond the ken of Coach Jackson. It was all too depressing. Luke had rented a Jackie Chan movie and popped it into the living room VCR.

I retired to my bedroom, very woozy from wine, and attempted to read a paperback mystery I'd started months ago. My latest *bitch* phone message and ruminations about Scott Kelly kept interfering with my concentration. That and wine after affects. I finally gave up sitting upright after a while, switched on the small TV on the dresser and lay down, vowing to cut down on my new and excessive habit of alcohol consumption. A made-for-TV war movie came on, but I dozed off.

I woke up some time later as the news was in progress. A male anchor was reporting on a near-fatal car accident this evening just off Sunset Boulevard. A Toyota had been forced off the road and into a cement wall by another car, its sole occupant a woman who was badly injured but alive. The driver of the other car had fled the scene before help arrived, but had ultimately been captured. They flashed a photo of the victim briefly in a box in the upper right hand corner of the screen, then the hit-and-run driver, also a woman.

A headache was now playing behind my eyes. I raised my head and looked at the screen through barely open slits long enough to decide the driver pictured looked vaguely familiar. I lowered my aching head back down on the pillow and mused over who she could be. Then I mused over the fact that I badly needed some Excedrin. I got up, swallowed two, washed them down with water from the bathroom faucet and fell back into bed and deep, dreamless slumber.

The next morning, Saturday, I threw on my white terrycloth bathrobe and padded out to the kitchen, eager for copious amounts of caffeine. Only remnants of my hangover seemed to dance around my neurons but a little preventative medicine couldn't hurt. The twin bed next to mine was empty and still made up, indicating that last night's date had drifted into lollygagging, as Gram termed it, and Jeannette was enjoying room and board elsewhere, at least for today. Luke was already lounging on a living room couch, reading the paper.

"Lakers won, babe," he called out.

Rats, and I'd missed it. I'm a miserable fan.

"Score?"

I poured coffee into a mug, leaving it black, and joined Luke in the living room.

"Beat them Suns 99-90."

As if yesterday had not been unproductive enough I'd failed to support my beloved Lakers.

"Did Buck call last night?"

"Yep. You were out cold. He said don't disturb you. Asked me what you might have to report. I said far as I knew, nothing."

"You were right," I mumbled.

"What?"

"I said that's correct."

Clearly I needed to do something positive today to redeem my soul. I decided the first step was to whip up a breakfast for Luke and me of scrambled eggs with salmon, fresh sliced tomatoes and toasted bagels with cream cheese. That small act of contrition accomplished, I decided I'd call Rosa Torres and not just inquire as to her well being as I usually did but offer to pick her up and treat her to a day on Catalina Island or Disneyland or The Getty Museum, whatever was her pleasure. She'd suffered the loss of a mother and a sister. That her period of mourning might benefit from a touch of light-hearted relief seemed reasonable.

"Rosa, it's Freddy Bonnaire."

"Freddy, it so good to hear your voice. How are *you*?" Her voice sounded admirably cheerful.

"I'm missing Doris, as I know you are. How are you and how is your family holding up?"

"Oh, we fine, Freddy. You know we are a religious family. We know Doris and *mi Madre* are with Jesus. All goes well with them."

"I'm sure it does."

I paused to sip some coffee, hoping my suggestion would be welcome and not seem an intrusion.

"Rosa, I would love to spend today with you if you're free. We could go for a drive or to a museum or to the beach, anywhere you'd like."

Luke had come back to the kitchen and stood leaning against the counter sipping coffee. He lip-synched to me that he and I could drive out and pick Rosa up. I related this to her.

"Oh, Freddy, we're already going to the beach today. The whole family. We're going to let the kids go on the rides on the Santa Monica Pier, and then we're all going to have lunch at Maria Sol's. Don't you live near there? Why don't you join us?"

I protested that I couldn't impose upon a family gathering, Rosa insisted I *was* family and we agreed to meet for lunch around noon.

I hung up and smiled at Luke.

"Well, my day is set. Lunch with the Hernandez clan. Thanks for the offer of the ride for Rosa."

"No problem. Their whole family on board for that gig? Give me a chance to bust the chops of those teenage hoods again. See where they're at."

"You mean you're going to lunch with us? That's great, but don't feel you have to."

"Excuse me? Are you saying those Latinos don't want to have lunch with a brother? This racial bias I hear?"

I knew Luke wasn't serious so I just grinned at him.

"Nope, not racial. More a seething aversion toward anyone in the trucking business."

"Who says I'm in the trucking business?" Luke said and took his coffee mug out to the living room and a college basketball game on Channel 2, leaving me to ponder what he'd meant by that last remark.

My head was still a bit too sore for heavy-duty pondering, and I didn't feel like giving him the satisfaction of an inquiry so I drank another mug of coffee and made a plan to fill the time before leaving for the Pier with a long, hot shower, dressing and mystery reading. Maybe the latter would inspire my brain cells to make some shrewd deductions about the origin of my *bitch* calls, the dilemma of Scott Kelly and *who in bloody hell,* as Kraig's Tulabelle would say, was that female hit-and-run artist in the accident near Sunset. As it turned out, no brilliant conclusions spun forth but by eleven forty-five I *was* clean, outfitted in beige cords, white turtleneck, white Reeboks and ready to go. I did have one insight about the *bitch* call and that was to put the Glock in my purse.

* * *

Maria Sol was a Mexican restaurant at the end of the Santa Monica Pier. We'd taken the Honda and parked on the beach lot. Luke's shirt supply must have run low, as he'd borrowed one of Buck's Hawaiian numbers. It strained slightly over his heavier frame, but his crisp white jeans and new Converse sneakers made up for the wardrobe malfunction. We walked up the beach stairs and onto the wood-planked pier. The sun was white-gold, the temperature had again soared to an atypical eighty degrees and music from the amusement rides blasted in our ears.

Outside tables under umbrellas fronted the restaurant. We walked up a slight ramp to go inside. Hanging plants adorned most of the walls. The aroma of enchiladas, beans and hot chili peppers was intoxicating. We spotted the Hernandez family occupying three round oak tables on the left side of Maria Sol's in an area radiant with sun glare. Their lunch orders hadn't arrived, but there were beer bottles all over the tables and much laughter. Nobody seemed to mind or notice the piercing light. Luke shielded his eyes, then nodded toward the far left.

"I see Lil' Ice and Dangerous J. Wanna join them?"

I put my sunglasses back on for a look. The boys were relaxing, their bentwood chairs tipped backward, their instruments beside them, leaning against the wall. A group of older and taller young men made up the rest of their table.

"You go," I said. "Rosa's at that table over there. I'll sit with her."

The afternoon passed pleasantly. Rosa and her family were not unmindful of their recent losses but, as Rosa had indicated earlier, they were philosophical and at peace. Pedro (Lil' Ice) and Carlos (Dangerous J) played their guitars over at their table. The entire family ate with enthusiasm and laughed with abandonment. I ate almost as much as they did, but limited my libations to half a beer.

It was early evening, the sky pink and gold, when we left them. Luke and I walked to the car in a mutual, satisfied glow.

"You look happy," I said. "From giving the Hernandez boys the third degree?"

"That I did."

"And you learned something about their connection with High Top?"

Luke stopped as we reached the stairs and gazed out at the setting sun. Two chubby little kids, around eight, came bounding up the steps giggling and shivering in wet bathing suits.

"They're okay kids, Freddy. And High, not a bad dude."

"How's that?"

"Their connection? High Top lets 'em hang with him once in a while. Also lets 'em use his recording studio to rehearse, free of charge."

CHAPTER 75

"We used to call it Sunday psychosis, remember?"

Jeannette was referring to our Sundays back in New York, especially in summer. It would be a weekend when we'd made no definite plans, when we both were between relationships and at rather loose ends socially. The emotional landscape of the city on those Sundays didn't help matters. Sidewalks in Manhattan, usually pulsating with humanity, were dry and barren. People with ample money sought liberation from the torpid humidity of the city for the sea-breezed humidity of Long Island's seaside resorts of East Hampton or Southampton. Those with lesser resources found refuge in deep plastic pools set up in their backyards in Queens or the Bronx. Many Brooklynites escaped to air-conditioned movies.

Jay and I would usually hang out in the The Village—Greenwich Village, to be precise, if you've never been to that unique venue. The Village is on the west side of lower Manhattan, bounded by Broadway on the East, the Hudson River on the West, 14th Street on the North, and Houston Street on the South. It you're a real New Yorker, you know that Houston is pronounced not like the Texas city, but rather as *House-ton*. During the late 19th to mid-20th centuries it was known as a hotbed of bohemians and much of that vibe remains today. A major landmark is Washington Square. Jeannette and I spent many a lazy afternoon on its park benches. The residential areas consist largely of mid-rise apartments, 19th-century row houses, the occasional one-family walk up. A number of actors reside there—Julianne Moore, Liv Tyler, Uma Thurman, Philip Seymour Hoffman.

What was always most significant to me was the fact that Anna Wintour, the editor-in-chief of *Vogue*, calls it home. Jay's favorite piece of Village history is that Sullivan St. was home to Genovese crime family boss, Vincent, "The Chin," Gigante. The Village was his birthplace. He'd spent most of his adult life there during the day. According to F.B.I. surveillance reports, after midnight, he would be driven to a townhouse at East 77th Street near Park Avenue where he actually lived. His other moniker was the "Oddfather." Gigante allegedly feigned senility by walking around the streets in his bathrobe—a ploy adopted in the hope of eventually entering an insanity plea. The Village boasts an energetic art and music scene, but despite its colorful past and present, the Village on Sundays was devoid of its rest-of-the-week sound and fury. Still, it was dependably livelier than most of Manhattan. We'd have a late breakfast at a little place that offered jazz with brunch and then just roam around until it was time to eat again, browsing in all the little shops. We each have numerous silver rings of varying designs, all costing under fifteen dollars, that it seemed imperative to purchase from sidewalk entrepreneurs on those days. We never made a big deal out of lunch, just a quick coke and a salad to stave off mid-day hunger and then it was back to strolling around. That early on a Sunday the city's famous energy still lay dormant and we needed to move around, feel like we were stirring things up. Finally as evening approached we'd head for some cozy café like Titou's on 4th. Have wine and enjoy their roast chicken and herbed-goat-cheese tart, feeling relieved because the day was nearly over.

"That's the way I feel today," Jay added.

Clearly my rambling mental review of life in New York indicated I really missed the place. Was the universe telling me to move back? I couldn't leave before we found Doris' killer. I couldn't leave Buck. Buck? My brain cells were definitely in the doldrums. For, clearly, they meant I couldn't leave *Guy*.

We were lounging on the couches, reading the Sunday *New York Times*, courtesy of Buck's subscription. Luke was stretched out on the rug, engrossed in my paperback mystery.

"I almost feel that way," I said, "but it won't last. Meeting Guy for lunch at two. Supposed to meet Caroline at five, but left her a message and begged off."

"Well, aren't we the busy bee?" Jeannette said. "Not *moi.* Haven't got a thing planned today." She slid a subtle glance at Luke, who looked up briefly without comment.

"Well, what the hell are *you* doing today, big man?" Jay never stops at subtle.

Without looking up, Luke said, "Hanging out. Got stuff to do."

Lucas Jefferson, man of mystery.

I stood up. "Help me decide what to wear, Jay."

Energized by the portent of a defined project, Jeannette stood up and grinned. "Let's go sexy up your ass."

I slipped into a little black wool dress for Jay's approval. "By the way, did you get Sid on a new flight the other day? I know when I left for lunch, he'd as usual procrastinated and missed the scheduled one. I'll need to know which flight he actually took. He always blames someone when this happens."

"Too New York, Freddy. Try that navy print number," Jeannette said. In response to my concern, she added, "Never told him he'd missed the original flight, just got him on the one leaving two hours later."

"He was cool with that?"

"Sure. I told him he was taking the flight we'd originally planned but it was held up because of a bomb threat. Ergo, no harm, no foul, no one to chew out."

"Jay, you're a genius. I'll wear the navy."

CHAPTER 76

I SAT AT A TABLE FOR two in a cozy corner of Emile's Café. Jeannette had ultimately nixed my conservative navy dress and decked me out in a tiny black sweater set over a silky beige slip skirt and black satin Isaac Mizrahi slides. Could I look any more like walking date bait? I decided to arrive at Emile's a little before the appointed time, have a drink and thus be cool as an icy vodka gimlet when friend Guy arrived.

"By the by, like the roses?" Nick himself had come over to take my order.

Before I could ask a dumb question my brain's neurons and synapses collaborated.

"The beautiful red roses were from *you*. They were lovely. The darn hospital misplaced the card on them, or I would have thanked you long ago." I placed my hand on his arm.

"Thanks so much, Nick. That was so sweet of you."

Whatever emotion Nick was feeling, he gave no sign. "Drink?"

"I'll have a vodka gimlet."

"You never drink vodka gimlets."

"You're right. It was just a metaphor anyway. I'll have a white wine spritzer."

I sat back basking in the knowledge that Nick had thought to send flowers. What did it portend? Nothing. A friend being thoughtful. What did I want it to portend was the next question. No, the next question was why I was asking a next question as I sit here waiting to meet who I've come to regard as the current love of my life. The latter showed up.

"Hey." He bent down and kissed my cheek. "It's good to see you." Guy grinned broadly as he sat down.

"Wasn't sure you'd recognize me," I said.

Guy looked down at the table, softly chuckled and shook his head.

"I deserve that."

Nick arrived, order pad in hand and eyeballed Guy.

"How about you? You having a drink or a metaphor?"

Guy looked up abruptly.

"Uh, I'll have a club soda."

"Gotcha. Neither." Nick left.

Guy took my hand in his as we just looked at each other for several minutes. A waitress arrived for our food order. In the mood for shrimp I ordered the Coquilles St. Jacques, Guy, the Beef Bourguignon. By the clock, we had a long, leisurely lunch. By heart time, the hours flew.

Afterward we drove down the coast, parked and went for a barefoot walk on the beach. Over lunch, Guy had explained he'd been incommunicado because his uncle was ill and he'd flown back and forth to Idaho while juggling a heavy caseload, the Hernandez shooting, of course, among them.

That he could have made time for a phone call occurred to me but I was beginning to understand or believe that Guy's silences were a cultural peculiarity.

Coming from anyone else the sick-uncle alibi would come across as an abysmal pretext; from Guy, it presented with unerring certainty. I had a third white wine spritzer just to make sure I'd continue to feel certain.

We got our feet wet in the tide's foam, held hands as we walked and talked about everything. We talked about our families, laughed about childhood fears, discovered we were both thinking of taking up golf. And we talked about *the case*. Guy didn't really want to, but naturally I badgered a little. He was still mystified. His investigation was currently pursuing possible shady dealings involving Sid Avarson. Questionable affiliations and from there possibly dangerous characters.

I hadn't thought of this avenue, focused as I was over the Scott Kelly versus High Top suspicions.

I always regarded Sid as a classic pain in the ass but an honorable businessman. This was based solely on intuition.

As I looked at my watch, Guy said, "There's a place I want to take you for dinner. Granita, up on Malibu Road. Great food, beautiful place. What do you say?"

"I say what any self-respecting girl who's had three wine spritzers would say." I smiled up at him. "I say yes."

We high-tailed it back to Guy's car so I could retrieve my cell, call Caroline and confirm she knew today's five o'clock meeting was cancelled. Mercifully she was still at the Avarsons, picked up on the second ring and agreed. I said I'd call her tomorrow to set up a day and time. She said, "We already have a pool man but thank you for calling." Her voice sounded a little tense but I took her response to mean *that's quite all right, Freddy.* One can rationalize anything on three white wine spritzers, from sick uncles to abrupt cancellations.

Guy and I took a thin blanket from the car and went back to the beach to watch the sunset. We were in a deserted section of beach, not a soul within view. We drew the blanket over our heads and, as I felt the gentle, warming thrill of being in his arms, I was convinced I would forever regard heaven as a view of sky through a green plaid blanket.

Our togetherness was confined to long kisses and tentative caresses. When my movements announced a reluctance to make love, Guy recoiled briefly but then seemed to relax and drew me to him, his long arms wrapped tightly around me. I longed for consummation of this strong attraction I felt, but a restraint I did not understand myself kept it at bay.

Later as we stood up and shook out the blanket I spotted what looked like the same golden retriever I'd seen outside the Kelly's. Were he and his owner witnesses to our intimacy? I shook off the possibility as I shook the blanket, refusing to feel embarrassed or concerned. I seemed to be imagining intrigue at every turn these days. Proof positive that this girl should stick to modeling, and not detecting.

I also shook off any guilt about my lack of professionalism in regard to constantly postponing an interview with Caroline. Her initial call smacked of implicating High Top, and even Guy seemed not to be going down that road.

CHAPTER 77

THE CALL CAME AT A little before five thirty in the morning. My cell phone rested on the night table between my bed and Jay's in the guest bedroom. I usually shut it off for the night but must have forgotten in the distracting swirl of the day with Guy. I grabbed it and, in my early morning delirium, hit the off button, by mistake. I picked up my watch, noted the time, groaned, turned the cell back on. I sat up straight, clutching the phone in both hands. The hour did not bode well for good news. Had something happened to Buck? Jay was sleeping undisturbed so she was okay. When I got home late Sunday night, I hadn't noticed whether the door to Buck's bedroom was open or closed. Closed would have meant Luke was home and asleep. Pierre had been sleeping on my bed, his head curled next to my ankle. At the sound of the phone he arose, stretched and padded over to regard my face. As I was debating whether to check on Luke, the phone beeped again.

I said, "Hello," then realized I'd shouted.

"Well, *hello*, Freddy."

Especially in contrast to my own, the voice was calm and cheerful.

I hate having to say *who is this?* So I didn't. I waited. "Hi."

"I'm so sorry to call so early, but I wanted to be sure and catch you in."

The voice was so gracious I couldn't help but respond in kind.

"I'm so glad you caught me. Is everything all right?"

Whoever you are.

"Oh, everything's just fine. High and the boys already left to drive to Santa Barbara to shoot some interiors some place there. I'm all alone."

High? Ah, Holly King. "Holly, I didn't know. Do you want us to follow? You know Buck's out of town? If you'll give me the directions… you say you don't know the destination?"

Holly's voice was smooth as melted chocolate.

"Relax. I'm cool with it. You and Buck been doing a great job. You could use a day off. And I could use some company. I'm gonna just chill on the boat today. I want you to join me."

The last sentence had a definite imperious tone.

I weighed my options. Jeannette would be at Potter, Wood & Penn so that was covered as far as our corporate sleuthing was concerned. She'd be burdened with the task of doing her own work for Sid together with a project for him I'd planned to complete today. But the Kings were important clients to Buck, and this may be a prime opportunity for me to learn just why High had no concrete alibi for the time of the Hernandez shooting. There had to be a credible explanation. I always suspected they were not forthcoming due simply to a misguided position on celebrity privacy. If High were arrested, this would be revealed. But why wait until that occurred and nasty headlines ensued. All that cogitating convinced me I should visit Madame Holly, plus the fact that I wasn't making progress doing anything else anyway.

I sat up and looked out the window on the other side of Jay's bed. There was just enough sliver of a view between the drapes to afford a glimpse of sky. The sliver was gray and forbidding. The windowpane appeared dotted with raindrops.

"It doesn't look like much of a day for sailing, Holly. Are you sure you…"

"Oh, Frédérique, we'll just hang out on the boat and stay docked. I'll mix us up some daiquiris, we'll have us some girl talk, maybe go to lunch at Shanghai Red's."

"I'd love to join you Holly. Just tell me where."

Holly yawned and her tone became flat.

"Good. Gotta go back to sleep now. Call you back in a couple of hours."

"That'll be fine. It'll be great to..." I heard her click off.

I snuggled back under my comforter and ruminated about just how productive a shipboard afternoon with Holly King could be. On the one hand, she and High Top had stonewalled so long on their whereabouts during the Hernandez shooting that it was presumptuous of me to think I could make a dent in that resolve. On the other hand, this morning's Holly was more folksy and accessible than I'd ever experienced her. Maybe the promised daiquiris could assist in the further expansion of that state. I needed a third hand because there was a further consideration. Sooner or later Scott Kelly had to show up at the Potter, Wood office. I wanted to be there when he did. It would be just my luck that he'd make his grand entrance while I was drinking and dishing on a yacht in the Marina. Hard to justify to one Joseph Buckley Lemoyne.

It would be refreshing to escape the overbearing tedium of the PW&P office, but the visit with Holly might turn out be commonplace and dull. She didn't impress me as a woman with any interests save control of High Top, smoking and wardrobe choices. Had I developed sufficient interrogation skills to worm a shooting-day alibi from her? It was questionable at best.

Rein advancer, rein n'est acquis, as Gram would say.

Jeannette would probably say, "Forget that hopeless chick, get your ass to the office."

Luke would probably say, "Wait till Lemoyne get back from New York, babe, you meet with the missus together." I was inclined to go with Gram's "nothing ventured, nothing gained."

"Should I get up and go to work?" I whispered to Pierre. "Or do you think a day on deck with Mrs. King is the way to go?"

He yawned, turned around and resituated himself by my feet, which I took to indicate, "You've made the right decision, go back to sleep."

With Buck out of town, always nice to have another male viewpoint.

CHAPTER 78

MARINA DEL REY FANCIES ITSELF a high-end seaside resort community and, although the real estate rates would indeed suggest luxury, it more accurately resembles an office-building complex, but with boats. True, there's a smattering of apartment buildings and the obligatory restaurants, both seafood and otherwise, but the architecture is much like that of commercial Century City or downtown L.A. Call me an East Coast snob, but it's no Martha's Vineyard. On this day it was especially banal, thanks to the ashy clouds above, the rain that was just misting at that point and the dreary colorless hue of the water.

Holly had called back later in the morning and given me a precise verbal map of the area so it was no problem to drive south on Lincoln, swing to the right when I reached the marina, follow her directions to Dock 52 and park in the adjacent lot. From the lot I walked down a plank in search of slip number 463. To my left was a lineup of mostly yachts and some sailboats, their bows flush with the walkway. To my right I spotted the boat immediately. A sailboat, the King yacht and another yacht were docked sideways on the other side of the walkway so the name *My Sweet Holly* was visible. Holly smiled and waved from the upper deck, ducked down and reappeared on the lower deck. She was wearing a short black slicker, matching hat, green jersey sweat pants and white sneakers. A heavy gray cable knit sweater was under the slicker. She extended a hand to help me onboard.

"I'd say welcome aboard but then why?" she said, which I took to mean she was too cool for such a hackneyed opening line.

"It's good to be here," I said, then felt like adding my own riposte of *why?* It didn't qualify as the predicted all-day soaker yet, but the rain had graduated from mist to a light drizzle. The air was chilly, and the lightweight navy windbreaker I was wearing may have been nautically chic but it wasn't comfortably insulated. I told myself we'd have a quick social drink and then stroll over to the warmth of a nearby restaurant.

Holly led me up the stairs to the upper deck.

"This is a gorgeous boat," I said.

And it was, all white and shiny and bright even in the dismal weather.

"It's a yacht. Call it a yacht," Holly said as we arrived on the upper deck. "It's a Ferretti."

I don't know my boats, but the brand moniker was impressive. I myself had a closet full of designer stuff with similar names so it must be a good thing.

"A yacht, of course." I made the correction. "It's beautiful. You and Alex must have wonderful times here."

Holly sat down at a half-moon arrangement of bench and table and began stirring a pitcher of daiquiris.

"You know his first name is Alex."

It was a statement, rather than a question. I noticed for the first time that Holly's tone right now at noon was less chipper and friendly than it had been at the ungodly hour she'd first called me. Obviously a morning person.

Here, on this luxurious Italian-designed yacht, it seemed somehow inappropriate to refer to him by his rapper name. I smiled as warmly as I could and stated this thought as casually as I knew how to Holly.

Holly didn't join in the smiling, just handed me a glass of the booze and shook her head.

"This boat don't mean we're all of a sudden honky WASPs."

"No, of course not. I just assumed you call him Alex and so it seemed natural to…"

All of a sudden a slight smile.

"No big deal." Holly's smile widened. "I'm just playin' with you."

"No problem."

I returned the smile and then drank most of my daiquiri in a couple of gulps. Holly promptly refilled my glass.

I sat down on the opposite end of the small bench. Over to the right in front of the stairs I could see a small L-shaped bench that sported pale blue cushions. There were no cushions on the half-moon bench. I guess even wealthy Italian designers have to cut corners somewhere. Under this deck must be the kind of ornate living quarters I'd seen in *Yachting* magazine. I knew my rear end, which was feeling increasingly cold, would appreciate a tour. I was wearing a black Los Angeles Lakers baseball cap but it was about as effective against the current elements as my flimsy jacket. It would be pushy to suggest going below I decided until Holly was similarly inclined and besides I'd already committed the "Alex" *faux pas*. The weather seemed to have the same effect on Holly's disposition as it did on mine so best not to press my luck. I sipped some more daiquiri. There's more than one way to acquire warmth.

Holly mentioned the coincidence of our both owning Steve Madden boots, then launched into a discussion of shoes in general. She leaned over and refilled my glass. I looked at it dumbly, surprised that my sipping had rendered it empty so quickly. At this rate we'd both be high as kites in rapid order and sharing girl talk, recipes and shooting alibis in no time. I smiled to myself at this prospect. *Frédérique Bonnaire, crafty interrogator.*

Holly got up, walked to a point near the blue-cushioned bench and paused, looking out at some distant point on land. Whatever she was looking at—or for—she'd probably discover in a few seconds and then return to our icy bench. I'd give her another minute or two, then use her location as an excuse to move to the cushioned bench. I sipped my drink and hoped.

Holly's standing and gazing period passed the allotted timeslot. I got up and casually strolled to the bench beside her and lowered my grateful little butt onto the cushion. Actually I bounced down on the bench as the daiquiris had begun to take effect just a little and my strolling over had strongly resembled weaving over.

Holly glanced over at me, then resumed staring straight ahead.

"Did you know this marina was actually started by some Santa Fe Railroad guy?" she said.

"No I didn't," I said. "That's interesting."

It actually came out more like *thas int'resting* so I put my glass down on the deck floor. Enough refreshment for me. I'd only had one-fourth of a bran muffin and coffee for breakfast, which now seemed ions ago.

"Yeah, that's funny isn't it?" Holly said. "Back in 1887. Took forever. In 1916 a bunch of engineers told Congress it wouldn't work out. Then twenty years later they did another study and started planning it."

Holly noticed my glass on the deck and took a break in her recitation just long enough to carry it back to the pitcher on the table, refill it and hand it back to me. I took it and held it. Holly looked at me expectedly so I took a sip. She returned to her former post but turned around and faced me this time, leaning against a backboard.

"Then World War II comes along and screws up the planning," Holly continued.

I was impressed. She didn't seem the type to take an interest in marina history.

Holly moved to a little cubbyhole to the far left of the deck and sat down.

"Then in 1949 another bunch of engineers comes along and tells the big shots a marina could be built here for about twenty-three mil."

I wasn't finding this dry listing of facts all that compelling. I sipped my drink absentmindedly and gazed back out across the water. Understandably, there were virtually no boats in motion. About a hundred yards away a sailboat had taken off with three teenagers on board. There was a girl in a pink life jacket and two boys in green lifejackets, one wearing a baseball cap. The sails boasted wide red and white stripes and the name on the boat said Hunter 146. I waved to them and they waved back. Might as well make the best of this situation and get in the boat community spirit.

Holly was saying something about things really getting started in the fifties when I noticed another boat on the water—a fishing boat. It, too, was all white with the word *Albemarle* on the side, a marlin inserted in the middle of the lettering. I squinted and realized I was reading off the brand names on the sailboat and this fishing version rather than the christened names of the boats. Still squinting, I could see what appeared to be two men on board. The guy at the wheel looked tanned, had shoulder-length white hair and wore a yellow slicker that barely covered a large potbelly. I could just spot the baseball cap of the other man. He was crouched low, maybe ministering to the deck floor.

I waved. Yellow slicker appeared to see me but didn't return the wave. Neither did baseball cap. Marina fishermen are all business it would appear.

I returned my attention to Holly. She had continued talking as I'd been distracted and was saying something about President Eisenhower making the marina harbor a federal project. She was doing something else as well.

She was taking the boat out to sea.

CHAPTER 79

HUNGER WAS MAKING MY STOMACH feel like a clenched fist. If we were going out to sea, far from Shanghai Red's or any other source of food, I was by golly at least going to be warm. Holly King could stay on the upper deck playing Captain Bligh till the cows came home, I was going to investigate the inside of this vessel and forage for nourishment while I was at it.

I decided it wouldn't hurt to remember my manners and approached Holly. The cubby she'd moved to was the flying bridge station. She was standing at the steering wheel. A wind had kicked up, and I had to yell to be heard.

"I'd love to see the rest of the yacht. Mind if I go downstairs?" I smiled, ever the gracious guest.

Holly looked at me with a grimace that was either a response to the wind and the rain or an expression of irritability. I couldn't tell which and didn't care at that point, neither did my stomach nor my freezing extremities.

"Hold on," she said. "Lemme put this thing on automatic, and I'll go with you."

The way she said *this thing* made me wonder if she'd ever manned this boat before, but I didn't dwell on the concern. Cold and hunger trumped fear at the moment. I followed her down the stairs into a living room that indeed reminded me that I was on a luxury yacht. Holly spread her arms out and smiled.

"This is it," she said.

The opportunity to flaunt this particular perk of her husband's wealth immediately improved her mood.

"It was all designed by Marty Lowe," she added. "My boat is flyin'."

She smiled, closed her eyes and sighed deeply as if drinking in the yacht and all its splendor.

I'd never heard of Marty Lowe and, pre-boat purchase, I doubted Holly had either. She probably memorized certain names much like her rote-like accumulation of facts about the Marina's history. I was perhaps being unfair. I couldn't really explain my impression of her beyond intuition. During my few encounters with her, Holly seemed crass, self-absorbed and disagreeable. But that didn't mean she didn't know her interior designers. My physical discomfort was making me cranky.

"It's beautiful, Holly." I smiled.

The carpeting was a creamy beige as was the couch. There was a long coffee table in front of the couch and cabinets on the opposite wall, all in a high-gloss cherry wood. A chess set rested on the coffee table near a small white urn of artificial flowers. A huge circular mirror with a gold-leaf frame hung on the wall above one end of the couch.

A few minutes passed. Holly just stood still, her hands now on her hips, as if she felt all this splendor deserved about a half hour of concentrated appreciation.

"I have to tell you, you mentioned something about lunch and I'm just starving."

I smiled and chuckled a little as I said it. *So funny these bodily impulses.*

Holly looked perturbed again. Temperamental, these yacht owners.

"Hunger, hunger everywhere. I'll show you the bedroom first. Then the galley," she said.

The bedroom was the same combination of pale beige and cherry wood. A queen-sized bed was the centerpiece of the room with a beige quilted spread tucked into its sides and a collection of about seven pillows of various sizes in red paisley leaning against the backboard.

Brass wall lamps were mounted on either side above box-like end tables. The side walls each boasted an arrangement of small brown armchairs with an occasional table between them. Holly opened a closet door, and I pictured her tossing her wardrobe piece by piece on the bed for my admiration while I gradually grew faint from malnutrition, but she closed it after a quick glimpse. Through a window above one of the small tables I could see that the drizzle had escalated to a full-blown downpour.

"This is a wonderful room," I said. "Holly, the galley?" My voice was pleasant, but firm.

"First dining room, then galley," she said.

The dining room was predictably done in beige and cherry wood. I noted there was a very long table and lots of stemware in a glass cabinet but beyond that I was no longer capable of detailed observations. Naturally we stood for a while and just gazed. I knew protests or even further conversation would get me nowhere. I stared at the stemware as if each might just possibly be the Holy Grail and waited. It was a mistake because Holly apparently took my concentration for sincere fascination, and we stayed longer in the dining room than we had in either the living room or the bedroom.

"This way," Holly finally said. "Hunger, hunger."

Her voice became sing-songy. "Hunger like hate."

I apparently was not the only one feeling lightheaded and famished.

At least the galley was a departure from the beige and cherry wood, a combination that was beginning to grate on my rapidly fraying nerves. The floor was a shiny rust-colored linoleum, the walls and cabinets were white. The refrigerator and stove were quite large, even by normal home standards, and were black. Holly had hung her slicker and hat on a hook before we'd entered the living quarters, and now she paused to pull off her sweater. She had an orange tank top underneath, and I noticed how muscled her arms were. She noticed me staring at her and inexplicably grabbed her left arm and held it close to her body, a strange expression on her face.

"I love that the accessories are black," I said.

I wanted to say something to placate her apparent self-consciousness and that's all I came up with Any minute now she'd decide I'd somehow been lusting after her body and food would be denied me. I was hallucinating again.

"There's nothing in refrigerator right now," Holly said.

"Hunger, hunger, hunger," she whispered to herself.

She moved to a small chair, sat down and removed her sneakers.

That looked like a good idea so I took off my cap and windbreaker, hooked them onto a matching chair and took off my Reeboks. My tee shirt had gotten somewhat wet also but I only had a bra underneath so I thought it best to keep it on. Especially since Holly might be asking herself if I had certain sexual proclivities. She'd leap overboard for fear of being seduced.

"I need dry socks," she announced and picked up the sneakers, murmuring something to herself as she left the galley, which I couldn't make out.

Alone at last. I looked at the cabinets above the sink area. I opened the first one. Nothing but plates and bowls of various sizes and cups, all in black plastic. The next one did contain food. Barely. There was a bag of potato chips on one shelf and nothing else. I opened the third cabinet. More promising. There were a jar of peanut butter and a jar of mayonnaise, both apparently never opened. I went back to the potato chips since they were the most immediately accessible food. I almost jumped when I heard the rustle of Holly returning.

"Do you have any bread around?" I asked.

My hands were stiff and cold as I remained focused on struggling to rip open the pesky bag.

"No."

Holly's voice was so angry and harsh in tone I turned my head immediately to look at her. She had something in her hand but it wasn't bread.

It was a gun.

CHAPTER 80

"GOOD GOD, HOLLY, WHAT ARE you doing?"

Holly was not presenting the gun as in *this is part of the décor, a firearm we keep around, isn't it attractive?* She was pointing it at me. She was holding the gun with both hands, arms outstretched, as if she'd watched too many cop shows on TV.

"I'm gonna make you suffer like you've made me suffer, bitch."

Her voice dropped a register. It wasn't the voice of the chirpy, cheerful person who'd called me at an ungodly hour this morning. It wasn't even the voice of the person who'd become sullen once I'd arrived on the boat. But a wisp of recognition coursed through my brain as to which voice it could very well be. *The voice of my mystery caller.*

"In what way have I made you suffer, Holly?"

My own voice sounded strange to my ears—so calm, so controlled.

"Oh, you're not scared, huh? You wanna have some kinda intellectual discussion with me? Is that it?"

Her voice was gruff. It had gone up an octave in tone and several notches in rage. My seeming equanimity had surprised me and infuriated Holly.

"I've done nothing to you, Holly. You're my client. I've been working for you, trying to help you."

Strangely, I had to make an effort to sound frightened. It was because this scenario seemed so unreal I guessed. My image of Holly was entirely different. The insecure, clinging little wife who was jealous without cause. The tense, jittery person who smoked too much and had shot Luke impulsively, immediately taking a stranger for a burglar. Not this controlled woman who took command of this large boat and was now standing before me, pointing a gun, full of callous resolve.

"You didn't do shit for me."

The gun never wavered, still gripped firmly in both her hands. I thought of Holly's shakiness that I'd speculated was alcoholic tremor. My grandfather had smoked like a chimney. He'd been a distinguished Senator from Louisiana till his boozing caught up with him and he failed to win re-election. After that, he'd languished in Gram's backyard garden, one of the most beautiful in New Orleans. Granddaddy Toussaint had fouled the garden air as he wasted his last days sitting on an ornate white wrought iron bench, smoking and staring into space. Every now and then his left arm would vibrate of its own volition, and Gram had explained to the twelve-year-old me that this was alcoholic tremor.

Pain had begun coursing through one side of my brain. I recognized it as a hunger headache. The numerous daiquiris hadn't helped either, which made me realize that Holly didn't appear to have a buzz on and further that she hadn't been joining me in my libations.

"Holly, put the gun down and let's talk."

I sounded like a guidance counselor.

Have a seat, dear, and let's discuss the reason for your poor grades.

"You don't get it, do you, bitch?"

I decided to keep quiet. Anything I said would be wrong. Maybe if I just let her talk.

"I sent you to find his cunt on the side and you start balling him yourself."

"Holly, where did you get the idea that I..."

"Shut the fuck up! Am I blind? Did I see you together at that hotel? Did I see what was goin' down? Did I? And even before that, I figured it all out. I ain't dumb, bitch."

That day at the Chateaux Marmont. When Buck disappeared to greet some ex-girlfriend and High Top had come over to my table, and invited me to join his interview with the reporter.

"That was an accidental meeting, Holly."

I think the hunger was keeping me calm. I felt too weak to react. I hoped I would not feel too faint to argue my case.

"Accident my ass. You was seein' him all along. I followed you when you tailed him. Followed Buck too. Knew I couldn't really trust either one of you. You had lunch with him, bitch. I repeat, you think I'm blind?"

I searched my memory. I'd had lunch once at the same restaurant near his studio that High Top frequented with his bodyguards and the lady lawyer. But I was alone. What else could Holly have observed? And why had she hired us to follow her husband if she was doing it herself? If I had any suspicions the woman was whacko, they were confirmed now.

The sound took my breath away and my hands flew to my ears by automatic reflex.

Holly had fired a shot. And missed.

"That's just a warning you overgrown blonde. I'm just startin' with you."

I couldn't decide whether to feel relief that she'd deliberately missed or fear that her marksmanship was so good she could decide when to hit and when to miss. On the other hand, she was standing a mere four feet away from me. It would be impossible to miss if she chose not to. *Overgrown* blonde?

"I am not having an affair with your husband, Holly. You've seen innocent events and allowed your imagination to exaggerate them." I heard my guidance counselor voice again.

I have confidence in you, Holly. You can improve your test scores if you'd only apply yourself.

Holly heard it too. *She fired another shot.* I took a small step backward. I was hoping Holly's shooting skill would diminish if I put additional space between us. I couldn't see how she'd allow me to gain distance, but it was better than doing nothing at all.

"You kept telling me you never found no girlfriend on the side. I'm supposed to believe that? Whaddya do? Have a threesome?"

Holly was warming to her delusions now. She didn't notice my movement. I took another tiny step.

"What kinda name is Buckley anyway?"

She drew out the first syllable to *Buuuuuuck* and the second to *Leeeeeeee.* Now she had completely changed the subject. A good sign. Hopefully it meant she was distracted, by her own rage or whatever drugs might be contributing to her state of mind. I took another step. If I could get to the door I could run. To *where*? I could get a weapon of some sort from somewhere. Then hide, come up behind her and surprise her with a blow to the head Now who was delusional? That grandiose plan was dependent on Holly being so befuddled by my sudden bravado that she stood still and didn't run after me. Not likely. Of course if my Glock were in my purse, not at Buck's in a dresser drawer, there'd be that option. If I lived to tell about this, I would not tell about this.

"His full name is Joseph Buckley. Buckley was his mother's maiden name."

Of such trivia could life-saving delays be composed?

"He used to be a cop in New York…he was a very good one…won lots of awards…that's how we met…he was security at events where I worked…"

I ran for the door and made it to the dining room.

I looked back for a second, misjudged my position and my foot collided with a chair, just long enough to halt my flight for two seconds.

Another shot.

I dropped to the ground. Glass flew everywhere. Holly had apparently hit the stemware cabinet. I rose to a crawling position. The nearest promise of safety was another door. I rolled over and through it. I was in the bedroom. There was a closed door there. I ran to it, grabbed the handle and pulled it open. It was a clothes closet. Another shot. I dropped to the ground again, felt a sharp pain in my elbow. I examined my arm and saw I'd picked up shards of broken glass. I saw something else. Metal, shiny. A weapon? Some inner caution impelled me to touch it gingerly rather than grab. It wasn't a weapon, at least not a formidable one. It was the spurs to Holly's cowboy boots. I heard Holly yelling from the next room, but I had a second to think. What I thought was what would have happened if I'd touched the spurs carelessly. My hands would be slightly cut and bruised but not deeply as if I'd made intense contact with the glass shards. It would be just like the hand wounds I'd suffered after the burglary. Then I remembered grabbing the leg of my assailant, thought of Holly's well-toned arms and how she undoubtedly had calves to match.

I saw Holly's silhouette in the bedroom door. She was about five four, six inches shorter than I was, but that didn't matter when she was standing and I was prone. And she had a gun. *That too rather mitigated my height advantage.*

"You think I'd let your skinny ass get away from me? You dumber than you look."

Right now I couldn't argue with that characterization. I turned around and sat up. The drapes were parted on the narrow bedroom window. I could see rain outside, looking like a swift, violent stream.

"Holly, let's sit down and talk."

Good guidance counselors don't give up easily.

"I'm not going to sit down, slut. I ain't goin' nowhere. *You're* goin' somewhere.

"Where are you taking us, Holly?"

"There ain't no *us* going nowhere, you lying bitch. Just *you*."

"Me? Where am I going?"

If I weren't feeling so cold, hungry, frightened and in pain, I'd feel weary. This banter was getting boring.

Holly grinned. She removed her left hand from the gun grip momentarily and punched it back and forth in the direction of the window.

"Overboard," she said.

CHAPTER 81

Everything had been going so well. Guy was busy as ever but calling more often. Jeannette was rather enjoying her undercover post at Potter, Wood & Penn and had settled into dating just one of the consultants, a very nice guy who went to Mass with her on Sundays. I also had high hopes that, if nothing else, time was on our side and the probability had to be high that when Buck returned from New York, the collective efforts of he, Guy and the police in general would lead to significant progress toward resolution of the Hernandez murder case. And last, and least, the Lakers had rebounded from their early slump and had won seven games in a row, Kobe Bryant scoring a record 51 points in the last game. *Now this.*

Holly seemed to be in no great rush to get to the upper deck. It gave me a little time to think. I was now barefoot and without my jacket. I doubted Holly would let me bundle up pre-man-overboard event, so I was not looking forward to being on the upper deck due to the cold and rain in addition to the prospect of an unscheduled swim. On the other hand, my purse was on the upper desk, with my cell phone in it. If I could somehow get to that, long enough to call 911, there was hope. I was delusional again, my brain dulled by daiquiris. Holly was holding a gun and would not allow me access to my purse, she'd shoot me first. Maybe my optimism rested on the fact that she *was* clearly crazy and seemingly dedicated to letting me slowly drown as opposed to a more rapid demise by gunshot. I rubbed my aching head. *Think.* My real chance of survival lay in getting the gun away from her. It was that simple.

Holly was still grinning, enjoying my fear. I thought I saw her hands tremble momentarily but I wasn't sure, mesmerized as I was by her face and its fiendish glee and distracted as I was by my muddled thought processes.

"Stand up, bitch."

The fun of standing around looking menacing had run its course for Mrs. King.

I stood up. Holly motioned with the gun for me to get in front of her and I did. She directed me to the stairs by poking me sporadically in the back with the gun.

"Holly, stop. That could go off."

Shooting me when she actually intended to drown me would be poor planning. I was appealing to her sense of organization.

She didn't respond. We arrived on deck. The rain hadn't abated since my view from the bedroom window. Neither had the wind nor the cold.

"Keep going."

Holly nudged me toward the stairs to the upper deck. Apparently she considered it more dramatic for me to take a flying leap from a greater height than simply be pushed over into the drink from the lower deck. This was good news, of course, because my purse with its cell phone was on the upper deck. I took each step very slowly in order to think. Or try to. The gun. *Get the gun.*

As I took the final step, I saw the fishing boat. It was hard for me to judge its distance from *My Sweet Holly*, but it appeared to be going west whereas we were headed east. Had they heard the shots? And called for help? I could barely make out the portly gentleman in the yellow slicker. He was standing, gazing off in the distance but not in this direction. I saw him lift something to his mouth, a bottle of beer. He didn't look like a man who'd just heard shots and alerted the harbor patrol. If I ended up in the water, could I swim to his boat or at least yell and be heard? It seemed dubious.

Once on deck I turned around and faced Holly, then immediately slumped down to a sitting position.

"Get the hell up and turn around."

"I…feel…so…weak."

"You ain't weak. Stand up!"

Still sitting, I swiftly placed my left foot next to my right ankle, put my right foot on her right knee, then pushed with my left and shoved with my right. Holly fell backward, the gun flying from her hands. I heard it clunk on the deck at some spot in back of me. I turned to retrieve it. As I did I felt her hands squeezing my throat. Holly didn't have those muscles for nothing, she'd recovered and gotten upright quickly.

Her grip was fierce, and she was yelling. Once Buck had given me a lecture on self-defense. I remembered him saying that in this circumstance you should tense your neck muscles and grab your attacker's little fingers, rip them upward and back. I did this and Holly yowled some more, this time in pain. My neck was free. I stood up, and turned to face her in time to see her spinning away. She bent over slightly. I figured I'd really inflicted lasting pain. In seconds she bent her right leg, glanced over her shoulder and thrust her leg backward, her foot connecting with my stomach.

It was my turn to double up. The rain continued, and my feet felt cold and raw on the deck floor. Holly pivoted back and faced me. Her legs were spread widely apart, slightly bent at the knees. Her fists were clenched. Her left arm was bent at her side, her right arm extending straight out toward me. She stepped forward. Her arms were raised upward like a prizefighter's.

I can't fight you. I thought it, rather than said it aloud. *Gotta get gun.* I took a step backward. Holly moved forward, her right fist hit my jaw. An odd sound seemed to announce itself in my head and my vision blurred. Holly was bouncing around on her feet now, grinning again. Enjoying the moment.

The blow had knocked me off my feet. *Think.* I wasn't going to win any fight with Holly. I still felt dizzy. I didn't see Holly's gun anywhere. Any minute she'd lunge again and this time send me flying overboard. If I was going to go over, maybe I could choose the site of my dive. I'd noticed a ladder on one side of the boat. If I could go over near the ladder, I could immediately grab it and get back on board or at least not have far to swim from wherever I hit the water back to the ladder. I pretended to try to stand, then slumped forward and down on my knees. If my powers of observation were correct, the ladder was behind Holly and I had to get over there.

"Get up! Get up!"

"Trying...trying to."

I stayed crouched down, but moved forward slightly. I didn't know why Holly cared whether I was up or down but she obviously knew karate, and maybe I needed to be upright for her next move. Unfortunately I was right. I rose but only partially. It was enough. Holly stepped backward on tiptoe, bent slightly, then kicked me under the chin. My head snapped back. I felt her hands on me and my next sensations were the ringing in my ears, then hitting the drink. My eyes and nose immediately filled with water.

I flailed around, struggling to be more conscious and get my bearings. I could see the ladder. I don't remember how I got to it, a combination of dog paddling and lunging. I grabbed a hold and paused, gasping for breath, summoning strength. I took the steps. At the top I rolled myself over and on board. I looked up to see Holly standing at the opposite side of the deck, now appearing less evil than vulnerable somehow and in shock. She was also holding the gun once again with her two-fisted grip. *Okay, not totally vulnerable.* She once again had the advantage, but she didn't look as happy about it. Her hands were trembling, her face contorted.

"Hol...Holly..."

I figured at this point all I could do was plead again for mercy.

Mercy suddenly arrived in the form of large, commanding presence behind Holly.

"Drop the gun!"

It was Luke. In a flash he appeared from the side of the cabin, soaking wet and resolute. He had his right arm around Holly's neck. With his left he grabbed Holly's left arm. She'd dropped her arms when he first grabbed her and was holding the gun in her left hand only. Holly shifted the gun to her right hand. With her left she reached down and squeezed Luke's testicles. He yelled in pain, she broke free.

Luke doubled up for a couple of minutes. Holly did her stand-and-look routine, only this time she was shivering and looked inexplicably scared. I saw my purse now. It had been on a bench but had somehow slipped off and was a mere two feet away from me. I crouched and stretched, grabbing it. I was taking a dangerous chance, but I was lucky.

Luke had straightened and had raised his arms in the standard surrender position. He'd also been speaking as I'd made my perilous reach, thus distracting Holly.

"We've called the Harbor Patrol," Luke was saying. "Put the gun down."

Holly stared at Luke. She was trembling more than ever and her expression was wide-eyed but also uncomprehending.

I found my cell phone and turned it on. The battery had run down. Rats! I stood up so Holly could see me with it and pretended to be speaking into it. When she saw me, she shifted the direction of the gun from Luke to me. I saw Holly begin to raise her gun. I then saw Luke step in front of me. *She'd shoot him!* I yelled.

I think I yelled *no* or *don't*. I couldn't see Holly; Luke was blocking my view. I looked out on the water for help. *Hurry.*

I heard the shot before I turned my gaze back to the action on the deck. When I looked, what I immediately saw was the body, prone on the deck. Blood already pooling. Seconds later Luke told me how it had happened.

Holly had placed the gun in her mouth, and fired.

CHAPTER 82

"HOLLY HAD BEEN DIAGNOSED AS paranoid schizophrenic...as if that wasn't enough..."

Alex King spoke haltingly. He'd gained fame and a luxurious lifestyle from his career as the rapper High Top de King. Now he sat, bent forward, his elbows on his knees, his head cradled in his hands. He was sobbing. His words came out in anguished high-pitched spurts, punctuated by labored breathing.

We were sitting in a long, black limo in the parking lot fronting the Marina del Rey Sheriff's station. Through the tinted windows I could see the long white pole facing the brick walkway leading to the station, it's flags smacking the air from the furious wind. Two tall palms stood side by side to the right of the path, planted curiously close together. High had come without his entourage. Only a driver was here, a burly Japanese gentleman who now stood outside the car in the cold night air, arms folded over his massive midsection, seemingly standing guard. Luke and I sat opposite High Top, both of us soaking wet, but wrapped in blankets the police had provided.

Minutes after Holly had placed the 9 mm Beretta inside her mouth, the harbor police had arrived. They made an incongruously colorful and cheerful sight in a slender, bright orange patrol boat. The two boat operators wore olive-green combat pants, their badges embroidered on polo shirts of the same color. In a rolling coil of activity the operators had *My Sweet Holly* hooked to their boat for towing, called in the longitude and latitude of our location along with other terminology unfamiliar to me, helped Luke and I onboard their boat and instructed the fisherman, who'd called them, to follow us back to the station. Luke was in almost as much shock as I was but he'd managed to explain that he'd been tailing me daily for some time. Buck had hired him to do so and made it financially well worth his while to give up several lucrative runs.

"I'd done it for free," he assured me as we sat in the patrol boat, both of us looking intensely down at the deck floor, anywhere but at the beautiful yacht bobbing behind us with its sad cargo.

When we reached the pier, the fire department paramedics were waiting, ready to pronounce Holly. Once inside, Luke and I were fingerprinted and gave statements. The fisherman also gave a statement. His name was Tony Ferrigno and he was more fascinated with the details surrounding Luke's initial request at the dock to ride along on his boat and discovering he and I both emigrated from New York than with the shots he'd heard or any speculation concerning them.

The three of us sat in the tiny interrogation room as Tony, in a voice like a roar, advised, "Officer Carvallo, you can trust a New Yorker. This little lady says the broad shot herself, the broad shot herself."

Now Luke and I sat with Alex in the velvety warmth of the six-passenger limo, fortified by some scotch from the built-in bar but still feeling raw and in almost as much pain as the grieving widower before us. With a clap of thunder we heard the intermittent rain return once again and a door slammed as the Japanese man ducked back into the driver's seat. No one suggested we move or drive somewhere; we waited for this to occur to Alex. I pressed some Kleenex into his hand Id retrieved from my otherwise soggy purse.

He sat up straight and dabbed his entire face with it. Alex had been in the car, returning from Santa Barbara, and a mile from his home when we'd reached him on his cell. He'd arrived at the dock seconds after the paramedics left and stood in the rain questioning the patrol boat operators, and me and Luke and Tony, over and over. Suddenly, as he leaned back against the car seat, he seemed enveloped by the composure that numbness mercifully brings. Luke handed him a jigger of scotch. He took two small sips and held the glass, resting it on the narrow table between us.

"That's where I was when she tried to shoot Avarson." He looked at Luke and I intently before our puzzled expressions registered.

"I was meeting with a top psychiatrist, an expert in schizophrenia. His office was in San Francisco, and I flew up there. Ironically he held out more hope than anyone else I'd consulted. He felt with the right medication and extensive counseling Holly could function normally."

He took another sip of the scotch and looked absently out the window.

"She'd be happy," he added.

His face contorted and I thought more tears were to come, but he pressed a fist to his mouth briefly and sat up straighter, willing quiescence.

"This guy, this doctor," Alex began, "he felt we now know the causes of schizophrenia. He claims it starts with an emotionally hurtful childhood."

He turned toward the window again.

"Man, I could vouch for that. I know something about Holly's childhood. She had an older sister, taller than Holly, a little prettier, had great pipes. Parents focused on a singing career for the sister, forgot about Hol most of the time. Sister rubbed it in too. Figured Holly was her inferior, treated her like a maid. That's how we met. Her sister sang backup with my group for a while. Real diva. After awhile fired her butt but kept the good stuff. Kept sweet Holly."

Alex held his glass out toward Luke for a refill. It wasn't an imperious gesture, although he was used to being waited on. His eyes looked too wounded to convey arrogance; he merely knew we were there to help.

"Did Holly know you were seeking help for her?" I asked.

"She didn't know about the San Francisco trip but, yeah, she knew generally. When we first noticed her…her problem, I got her to a doc. Local guy, a Dr. Tyler. Did a whole workup—blood tests, full physical exam, x-rays. And more tests. The whole nine yards. That was when she was diagnosed and that was the last time I got her to a head doctor."

Alex returned to looking out at the intense rain.

"Holly told me she started hearing voices in her twenties," he said. "She didn't tell me that right away; in fact she just told me a couple of weeks ago it had been going on for so long. We married after knowing each other about two months. About a month after that I got home from an out of town gig and she was different. Talked kinda crazy;

sometimes strung words together that made no sense. Or she'd smile and laugh when there was nothing funny. I thought she was just having some kind of nervous breakdown, figured she couldn't stand being alone and away from me so I started taking her everywhere I went. Seemed to work for a while, then she got tired of the travel and the crowds. It made her worse."

He sipped his drink.

"She started saying thoughts were being inserted in her head. After the Dr. Tyler episode and the diagnosis of paranoid schizophrenia, she refused treatment, insisted the voices had disappeared. I wanted to believe her. Then when things got spooky again, I made a new appointment with Tyler, made several in fact. I was insistent and said I'd go with her. I'd make the appointment and make time to go with her and a day or an hour, sometimes minutes, before we were supposed to leave for the doctor's office she'd throw a fit and refuse to go. I dropped the subject for a while, let it lie. She seemed to get better, or pretended to be.

Then the day after we'd thrown a party at the house she was agitated again. Said she knew other people could hear her thoughts, was completely weirded out. I looked for another psychiatrist. Thought a different name would entice her. Told her she could go to the appointment by herself, figured she might have felt self-conscious with me there. Didn't work. Same routine. Joey, one of my bodyguards, always drove her to the appointment. Once they got as far as the reception room of the office but Holly bolted. Got up, saying she was going to the ladies room, then ran outside. Got over a mile away before Joey caught up with her. The other times they'd be halfway to the place and Hol would make him turn around and go home. That or drive her to some crazy destination, like The Hollywood Bowl or Grauman's Chinese Theater."

Alex looked back at Luke and I, his lips twisted in a half smile.

"She could be inventive, my girl could."

"Freddy said she seemed to know karate," Luke said. "Was good at it."

"Yeah," Alex answered. "Oh, yeah, she did. Had a brown belt."

'That's pretty darn good," I said.

Luke refilled Alex's glass and he nodded a *thanks.*

"There's a kind of well-known saying in karate," Alex said. "It's that a brown belt is the world's most dangerous animal."

He paused to look at us as if to gauge whether Luke and I appreciated the profundity of the statement.

"How so?" Luke offered.

"Because a person who reaches the brown belt level knows almost everything you need for know for a first degree black belt but that person doesn't know how to control power like a black belt does. They have the ability to defend themselves. They have the technique. They have the strength. May not have the refinement, the restraint."

"And Holly lacked restraint in the first place," I said.

"Exactly," Alex said. "But she was proud of her skills, her strength. It was the one thing that seemed to make her feel good about herself."

He bowed his head, looking downward at nothing in particular.

"That just made it all the worse."

"Mental condition naturally make her life worse?" Luke said.

"No." Alex shook his still-bowed head. "She'd picked up karate in her teens. It meant so much to her…and then the threat of losing it. She couldn't bear it."

"Forgive me," I began. "But…"

I paused, unsure if I should pursue my query.

Luke finished my thought for me.

"Out there on the boat, man, didn't look like she lost it."

"But she was destined to," Alex said.

He raised his head and looked at us.

"She'd just been diagnosed with Parkinson's Disease."

CHAPTER 83

I don't remember when I was aware the car was moving. Alex had never ordered the driver to go anywhere; he'd made the decision of his own volition. Just as he'd decided to go to a restaurant, stop, get a take-out order of hamburgers and coffee and serve them to us. I think Luke had noticed the car had stopped at one point; he'd briefly glanced out the window but made no comment and joined me in remaining fully absorbed by Alex's recitation of Holly's history.

I never bothered to look out and identify the restaurant, but the burgers were definitely several Zagat notches above fast-food quality. Alex looked up in surprise as the driver placed the food on the small table, then nodded in gratitude. He didn't ignore his burger, but he didn't eat with enthusiasm either. When the meal arrived, Alex had been in the middle of describing Holly's Parkinson symptoms, among them the arm tremor I'd once attributed to an alcohol problem.

"Holly once mentioned seeing a doctor on her own," Alex continued. "She was deliberately vague about it, as she always was, but he apparently prescribed some medication. And there were some clues that...well, despite the fact she balked at going for treatment when it was my idea...that she was maybe going for treatment on her own. Unexplained brief absences, stuff like that."

"So she found out about the Parkinson thing on her own?" Luke asked.

"No. It was during the one other time I got her to a doctor—a regular M.D. this time. Told her we both needed to go for physicals, said it was for insurance. The doctor examined me, then Hol. I'd already described the symptoms to him that turned out to be PD. At first he thought we were looking at side effects from some medication she'd gotten on her own for the schizophrenia. He said the meds for that are generally something classified as neuroleptic drugs."

Alex took a gulp of his now-cooled coffee. He placed the paper cup carefully down on the table and studied it for a moment.

"I'm probably boring you."

"No, not at all," I said.

"Talk, man. Do you good," Luke added.

"A side effect of those drugs is sometimes a sort of pseudo-Parkinsonism reaction. But, to make a long story short, we eventually ruled that out. It was definitely PD."

The driver had restarted the car right after delivering the food to us, and we were moving through the night. Whatever our route, it was largely devoid of traffic noise but the rain continued.

"Holly seemed to take the diagnosis of Parkinson's calmly. I should have known better. After the M.D. visit, there were a series of tests to confirm PD and then medicine was prescribed. From then on, she wasn't very communicative but, like I say, she was calmer, serene even. I guess I welcomed it and didn't want to question it. I told myself maybe she was almost relieved to have a physical problem. Maybe it distracted her even from voices and that craziness, gave her something else to cope with, focus on. Sounds silly now that I say it."

I'd cut my hamburger in two and given half to Luke and he was now gratefully chomping away. His sneakers were still soaking wet and my attention slid from Alex's conversation for a moment, as I thought of how lucky it had been that he'd been following me and how grateful I was that Buck had insisted he do so.

"I assume you told Holly about the San Francisco doctor, about his optimism for the schizophrenia?" I said.

"I did. I got back in town and was looking forward to it. I told myself that, despite the fact she had a medical history that read like a soap opera, we could lick both these things."

Alex paused, pressed his palms against his face, seemed momentarily distraught but then recovered.

"The San Francisco doc said he could guide her toward really becoming aware of her hurts and her defenses and the things that go with all that—the depression and denial. His theory is the patient gradually learns self-analysis, starts to follow the thinking of the doctor. Gets strength from this. Doesn't become totally cured but functions better."

"Your wife buy that when you told her?" Luke asked.

"Hol went ballistic. She said…God, she said so many things. Basically she said it wouldn't work. She cussed me out, she rambled. Most of what she said made no sense. Finally I just shut up and waited for the yelling to stop. We were in our bedroom when we were having this conversation. After a while she got in bed of her own accord, curled up in the fetal position and went to sleep."

Outside lightening creased the blackened sky. The car had stopped.

"Look," Alex said, his tone more deliberate. "This is the bottom line. After Hol's histrionics I went downstairs, fixed myself a drink and thought. I sat and tried to piece together all the things she'd been raving about. What I came up with is that she'd very likely been the one who tried to shoot Sid Avarson and hit that poor woman instead."

Alex leaned over, got the bottle of scotch and poured some in his now empty coffee cup.

"From that deduction it was all down hill," he said.

He had been glancing back and forth at Luke and me as he spoke; now he gazed intently at me.

"And, yes, I heard about the so-called burglary at your place and I've got reason to believe it was Holly who attacked you."

Alex abruptly got out of the car and held the door open. He spoke in a terse, clipped manner.

"We're at my house. I've got lots of guest rooms. I'd like you to stay the night. You've been through a lot."

Luke and I got out. Alex had turned around without waiting for agreement from us and was headed for his front door. He turned back after unlocking it.

"And, yes, I'll make a statement about all this to the cops tomorrow."

CHAPTER 84

Holly King had drawn some lousy cards in life. Blessed with a loving husband who provided a luxurious lifestyle and possessed of a certain strength and agility making her capable of expertise in the martial arts, her mind and body ultimately failed her. In her own way, she struggled to persevere despite an abusive childhood and mental disease, but the body blow of a future with the debilitating scourge of Parkinson's disease undid her. Treatment was available for both disabilities which could have affo30-rded her many satisfying years of life, but her troubled mind could not embrace such possibilities, and she struck out angrily against a world she perceived to be hostile and evil.

I've been privileged to have a loving family, years of a glamorous New York modeling career, excellent health and good friends. Now I had an opportunity to crash the modeling world of Los Angeles, be an asset to Joseph Buckley Lemoyne Investigations and hopefully help some people along the way. I hadn't done a banner job of either of these goals thus far. Hadn't seen the Holly King connection. Maybe it was obscure for the most part but if I'd concentrated on the maid interviews... Holly had been the substitute maid at the Avarson residence the day Doris Hernandez was shot. Through women she knew at a domestic agency, she'd scored the assignment, convincing them she wanted to play a practical joke on her friends the Avarsons by dressing up as a maid. Her cohorts never made the connection between the bullet to

Doris' brain and their charming friend. Holly's own husband was instead a suspect. He chose to keep his whereabouts at the time of the shooting—consulting with a San Francisco psychiatrist on behalf of his wife—secret for as long as he could.

Our mistrust and distaste for big business and its practitioners—a not wholly misplaced prejudice—led both Buck and I to perceive corporate greed and chicanery as the motivating factors for an attempt on the life of Sid Avarson. Scott Kelly's mysterious disappearance had been, in part, exactly what Nan Kelly purported it to be—one of his vacations from his marriage. Only this time it contained an added element. Scott had fallen in love with another woman. And planned to divorce Nan. He was cowardly about it, lurking in some undisclosed love nest, avoiding a confrontation with his wife but all the while conducting his business affairs from afar.

I'd hidden something also—my own gut feelings. When I replayed my thought processes over the last several weeks, I'd had some strong hunches about Holly King. I'd lived with feminine wiles and jealousies and pettiness to an extent in the modeling world. I dismissed much of Holly's behavior as recognizably similar. But all the while there'd been snippets of revelation lurking on the edges of my rationale suggesting that her eccentricities were something more. What did I have to contribute to helping Buck if not my female intuition? Fancying myself a viable asset, I'd pranced along to his drum and focused on Scott Kelly and reveled in the idea of undercover work at Potter, Wood & Penn, my old corporate nemesis from my New York days.

I couldn't beat myself up entirely I had divined from the start that High Top de King was not a viable suspect. There I'd used my gut. Since Alex was a handsome, glamorous figure, Jeannette had insisted a body area other than my gut had been involved. When Id suggested my heart, Jay had a response but it's unprintable.

Even the threatening bitch messages eventually yielded an explanation. In talking to the police after Holly's death, I'd described the calls plus the fact that phone records revealed the source had been my own home number. The detectives I spoke to investigated the matter and later advised me of an unusual device.

"You get an access number that allows you to make a phone call to anyone and choose the number that appears on their phone when you call," the detective said.

"It's legal," he added, "but it can be used illegally of course. It's called a SpoofCard and costs five bucks. The guy doing this bypasses voicemail passwords and can also access your personal phone messages or delete your messages."

Their investigation revealed, as I'd suspected that day on the boat, the person using this device was Holly King herself.

I was indulging in all this cogitating while flying 30,000 miles above the earth en route from Los Angeles to New Orleans. A lot had happened and not happened in my life of late. I decided I needed a break from California. Besides, I couldn't bear to tell Gram over the phone or by email or letter that so many of her precious antiques and long-held possessions had been destroyed courtesy of Holly's rampage.

At LAX I'd sat nursing a diet Pepsi and reading a paperback while waiting for my flight to board. My cell had rung and I'd heard Jeannette tell me Gram had called and wanted me to call her before I left for the airport. It was obviously too late for that. As I began to dial Gram's number, they announced we were boarding. It gave me an excuse to delay the call. I feared her message was to bring with me her prized antique bowl or Waterford stemware—things she'd given me but now missed. Things that were now shattered and gone.

Now I was on the plane and, of course, the use of cell phones was not allowed. Two stewardesses came down the aisle, their carts rattling with lunch and beverages. I was sanguine about the prospect of the usual airline food—struggling as I'd been of late to get back to my New York weight—but the usual beverage would not do. I asked for wine, the better to take the edge off if Gram brought up the subject of precious glasses or bottles or any other *objet d'art* now a memory.

I made swift work of the bland chicken and veggies. A small brownie sat at the corner of my tray, taunting, tempting. My seatmate, a tall, slim and very chic woman of about sixty, read my mind. She smiled, picked up her brownie and held it aloft, like a champagne glass she was ready to clink with mine. I tapped my brownie against hers. We gobbled up. If she looked like that and indulged in the occasional brownie, by God, I could too. Our trays were removed, and my seatmate left to stretch her legs. I sipped my wine.

I'd missed the real window of opportunity to call Gram. When I got to New Orleans, I'd just grab a cab to her home. I pictured her now, waiting for me. She'd be watching out the window for my arrival, then meet me at the door with an enthusiastic hug.

She'd sigh, "Oh-h-h-h-h, Frédérique."

Her gentle southern accent would be, as usual, soothing in its familiarity. She had a low, husky voice family lore claimed was abetted by a youthful whisky habit. I saw no real evidence of it in these later years. *Well, not excessive evidence.*

All would once again be right with my world.

ABOUT THE AUTHOR

Sunny Kreis Collins, unlike Freddy, was not born in Paris but is a passionate Francophile and lover of all things reminiscent of New Orleans. A member of Mystery Writers of America and Sisters in Crime, she lives in California, where she is at work on her next Frédérique Bonnaire adventure. Email the author at desertscribe6@msn.com.